EVERY WISH WAY

EVERY WISH WAY

A Novel

SHANNON BRIGHT

First published in Great Britain in 2023 by

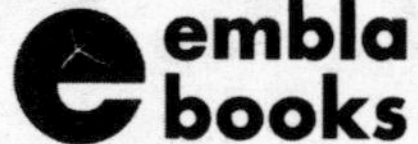

Bonnier Books UK Limited
4th Floor, Victoria House, Bloomsbury Square, London, WC1B 4DA
Owned by Bonnier Books
Sveavägen 56, Stockholm, Sweden

A CIP catalogue record for this book is available from the British Library.

ISBN: 9781471415845

This book is typeset using Atomik ePublisher

Embla Books is an imprint of Bonnier Books UK
www.bonnierbooks.co.uk

For Shawn,
who is a wish come true

CHAPTER ONE

It is a truth universally acknowledged, that a single woman in possession of profound independence and a successful occupation must *not* be in want of a husband.

Except being lonely sucks.

It's Friday night, and I'm sitting in a restaurant alone. Mingling smells of pancetta and parmesan permeate the air, and my stomach churns, not with hunger, but with nausea.

I won't be alone much longer. That fact should be comforting. But since it's my mother who will be joining me and not a Mr. Darcy-esque soulmate, the whole situation rises to a brand-new level of pathetic. As it turns out, caring for an asthmatic cat and a demanding career as an architect leave little room for romance.

I know I don't *need* a romantic partner, but I do wish for one. What's the use of good fortune when you have no one to say things to you, like *"You must allow me to tell you how ardently I admire and love you"*?

Surely there's a way to balance it all. If Jane Austen were alive today, writing romance novels about career women, she wouldn't make them sacrifice anything for their relationships. It must be possible to have independence, an occupation, and love.

I check my texts for at least the tenth time. There's nothing new.

Me: Dinner tonight? Have something I want to talk to you about.

Mom: Reservation for 7:00 @ Olive Garden.

The texts mock me. *"Look at Iza, the grown woman who has to seek approval from her mother before making decisions."*

"Shut up," I say under my breath, glaring at the phone.

"You shut up!" A little kid, a table away, shrieks with laughter and points at me.

His mother shoots me a scathing glare.

Yikes. Setting the phone aside, I give myself a pep talk. I'm not seeking approval. I'm simply telling Mom about the plan so she'll be forewarned she's about to dine on crow.

I choke on my own saliva and nearly die as Mom enters the restaurant, whipping her oversized sunglasses onto her highlighted hair. The door swings shut behind her, and her leopard-print cardigan billows in the draft from the air-conditioning like a Disney villain's cape.

Her voice booms strong and crisp, audible even from my seat on the other side of the buzzing dining room. "I'm meeting my daughter, Ms. Kiches."

The hostess points her in my direction, and Mom plows forward like a tank.

Grimacing, I start mentally filling out a witness report, waiting for her to bulldoze over some frail old guy or perhaps the small child still happily chanting, "Shut up, shut up."

Thankfully, she reaches me without causing anyone bodily harm.

I stand, wiping sweaty palms on my slacks. "Mom." I resist the urge to bow.

She looks me up and down, blue eyeshadow glinting. "You didn't freshen up and change after work? Honestly, Eliza, when you wear black outside the office, it looks like you're trying to relive your angsty teenage years."

I chew my lip, which is already sore from being gnawed on all day. I wear black in order to be taken seriously at work, and not changing was supposed to keep me confident. It was *supposed* to show her I'm the person she wants me to be—someone to respect.

Heels clicking as she rounds the table, Mom plucks a hair from my blouse. "Not to mention black is an unforgiving color when one sheds like a golden retriever."

Her heavy amber perfume infiltrates my nostrils, resurrecting memories of stiff hugs and tense car rides.

I sit back down. "Thanks, Mom."

"Shut up!" the kid a table away yells.

Hanging her coat on the back of the chair, Mom turns to the kid's parents and says, "You ought to learn how to control your child better." Mom then takes the couple's stunned stares as an invitation to launch into a parenting seminar with herself as the primary speaker. Okay, the only speaker.

Bouncing my leg, I watch Mom's hair as she spews quotes from parenting books. It's crispy from too much hairspray, and as she talks, it barely moves. Where her blonde hair comes from bleach, my frizzy mass of coiling hair the color of "I Can't Believe It's Not Butter!" comes from a sperm donor.

By the time I was old enough to express interest in meeting said sperm donor, the "useless bastard" (Mom's words, not mine) had already gotten himself run over by an Amish buggy while he was out riding his bike. According to police reports, it was the slowest collision in the history of the world, but dear old Dad managed to die anyway. Learning the information provided me with mild disappointment, but it devastated Mom.

And not because the guy died.

She berated herself for choosing him at the sperm bank, questioning my destiny as a result of his seed, fearful of a hereditary correlation between parents who get run over by buggies and their offspring suffering the same fate. The whole ordeal sent her into a six-month obsession where she conducted an investigation into the man's past to put the FBI to shame.

The results of her toils?

I'm doomed.

Mom finishes her verbal flogging of the innocent family.

The innocent family in question promptly asks for a different table, away from us.

Shaking her head, Mom settles into her seat, reaching for the wine I ordered in preparation for her arrival.

My tongue sticks to the roof of my mouth, and I swallow hard. *Tell her. Tell her. Tell her.* Adrenaline surges through my veins, and my vision swims.

Mom gives me a long look over her wineglass. When she sets it down, lipstick clings to the rim. "What? You look like you did the time you tried to swallow a peanut butter sandwich whole."

"I'm thinking of joining a dating website," I say, like I'm confessing to murder. Cold sweat breaks out under my armpits.

The lines around Mom's mouth deepen. Her acrylics click against the wineglass. "I thought you came to your senses after that last breakup, when you told me men are the lemmings of human society—hideous rodents rushing toward destruction." When I say nothing, she purses her lips. After a moment, she sucks in a breath and asks, "Are we talking Tinder or Match?"

"Not Tinder."

She scowls. Wrong answer.

"I'm not looking for a casual hookup," I say, my words coming faster. I pull at the fabric of my shirt, peeling it away from my clammy skin. "I want something real."

Crossing her legs, Mom leans back, clutching her wine to her chest. "Your career, Iza," she says, voice sharp and clipped.

"Oh, because no woman who ever worked also managed to keep a husband?"

Mom snaps upright. Wine splashes onto the table. "Husband?"

"It's not a dirty word, Mom."

Leaning forward, Mom grips the stem of her wineglass so hard, I expect it to snap off. "You work fifty-hour weeks just to earn respect. How will making time for a man in your life benefit you long term?"

"You raised me and advanced in your career," I say, struggling to keep my voice level.

Mom's a senior director for a big, independent cosmetics company. She started at the bottom, and now she has a plethora of minions working under her. This means not only does she profit from her own sales, but she also gets to skim off a portion of her underlings' too. It sounds like a pyramid scheme to me, but Mom gets heated if I bring that up.

"It's not the same," Mom says. "A man will hold you back, and spending time trying to find one who won't will only hold you back more. And why *marriage*? What's the rush?"

The truth is too pathetic to share. It's not that simply being in a steady relationship isn't enough for me. It's that it isn't enough for Mom. I've had committed relationships before, and she still didn't trust they'd last.

If I find someone who loves me unconditionally, and that someone promises to marry me, that would show her in terms she can't deny: a contract. Mom wouldn't stare a contract down across a dinner table and say, *"I give you six months,"* not when that contract explicitly says, "Till death do us part."

Wanting to prove her wrong is somehow born both of rebellion and the need to please her. While it will be satisfying, I don't want her to resent me for it. I want her to see I'm right and finally respect me and my choices.

I clear my throat. "I have a plan." This announcement comes out with far less assertion than it did in my head. "Using dating sites, I can weed out undesirable matches before I even have to meet them, creating an efficient and pain-free screening process."

Something in her hard expressions softens just a little. "And how will this work?"

Hope surges in my chest. I sit taller. "As you know, I've had a lot of relationships."

She sips her wine and shrugs like she's saying, *"Obviously."*

"After extensively dating so many men, I can tell, based on a first impression, what kind of person someone is. I can see early warning signs that will manifest into big issues later on. It's like a superpower. All I have to do is listen to my gut."

Mom blinks very, very slowly. It's the look only she can give. *The* look. The look that says, *"Iza, you're a disgrace."*

"Are you calling your propensity for sniffing out particularly unsuitable men a superpower?"

I squirm. "Yes, but I can use my powers for good. Instead of dating those men, I'll avoid them. I'm pretty accurate, and I can tell you about a few field studies I've done, and—"

"Shut up! Shut up! Shut up!" It takes me a minute to realize it's the shut-up kid at his new seat a few tables away, not my own thoughts.

The kid's parents try to hush him, but he only yells louder, pointing a finger at their server. The server's smile never wavers, not even when shut-up kid bounces a crayon off his forehead. The parents take away the crayons and offer the server apologetic looks.

Smile growing stiff, the server fidgets with his ticket book as he asks the family, "Can I start you off with some appetizers?"

I scooch my chair in and lean across the table, lowering my voice so only Mom can hear. "Take that guy, for example." I size up the server. My brain ticks away, noting his untucked shirt, his nearly empty cheese grater, his strained smile.

Shut-up kid starts talking animatedly about dinosaurs, going into a whole lecture over their feeding behaviors, complete with sound effects.

"Or perhaps starter salads?" the server asks loudly over the pint-sized paleontologist.

I turn to Mom. "He's a pushover," I say triumphantly.

"The child?" she asks, picking at her cuticles.

"The server."

"What's wrong with that?" Mom takes him in. "It's preferable when men don't have spines."

I almost ask if she means literally or figuratively. With Mom, it could go either way.

As the server finishes with the other table and approaches ours, I sink into my seat.

"Can I help you ladies with something?" he asks, that smile still plastered to his face like he's the poster boy for customer service.

I try to look natural. "I think we're good, thank you."

"My daughter says you're a pushover," Mom says.

The server's smile fades.

I jolt to my feet, my chair screeching. I have to salvage this. "No, no. I didn't say that. Well, I did say that, but not in her tone." Okay, maybe *pushover* was a bad word choice. It sounded so harmless in my head.

Mom taps her finger on the table, waiting.

My hands shake. I'm torn between trying to preserve the server's feelings and convincing Mom I'm right. "Being a pushover isn't a bad thing. It means you're nice."

The server's lips turn upward.

Encouraged, I plow on. "It just means you cater to everyone else and never stand up for yourself." As soon as the words leave my mouth, I regret them.

His smile is gone. I'm digging myself deeper with every word, so I bite my tongue before I can say anything else.

"So he's timid," Mom says. "How does this help?"

The server blinks like he can't quite believe what he's hearing. I will be leaving the world's largest tip to this poor man.

I give the server a look that I hope conveys an apology as deep as the Grand Canyon before forcing the rest out. "It's metaphorical." I pause, then finish in a rush: "If I know a guy is the type to let you—I mean *people*—walk all over him, I know we'd never last."

A long silence ensues.

I want to sink into the floor. My stomach churns with renewed vigor. As much as I try not to be, I'm just as abrasive and insensitive as Mom. Even if my assessment of the server is accurate, all I've managed to prove is that I'm a jerk.

"So I'll give you ladies a few minutes, then?" the server says in a high, chipper voice that fools no one. With a sharp nod, he tucks his ticket book into his apron and whisks away. I'll have to find him later and apologize.

Mom shakes her head, her blank face radiating how unimpressed she is. "You shouldn't judge men."

Shame heats my face. "I know. You're right. Who am I to judge—"

"Because judging men is a waste of time when I can tell you right now they're all shit." From anyone else, this might be the punchline of a joke. Mom is oblivious and dead serious.

A few minutes later, a new server arrives to take our order, and I lose her attention completely. For the rest of the meal, Mom acts like we never discussed dating. I want to explain myself, but it's useless.

When Grandma was alive, she had my back, and I'm starting to fear she's the only one who ever will. With her, the three of us were almost a family. Grandma served as a lens of love. Through her, I saw Mom in a softer light, and I think, in turn, Mom saw me the same way. I was able to see the value in Mom's less-endearing traits. Being a workaholic meant she had a strong work ethic. Being stubborn meant she never backed down from the PTA. Being cold and unaffectionate meant—

Well. I still don't know what that means.

If I find someone perfect who can meet Mom's lofty standards, maybe I can establish a new kind of trio. If Mom respects someone who respects me, she could see me through their eyes. When I'm thriving in a harmonious life, enjoying a successful career and marital bliss, she'll have no choice but to settle herself into the picture.

Soon enough, dinner is over, and Mom's headed out the door. I hang back and leave an apology note and a sizable tip for the server before following after her.

As I step outside, heat wafts into my face. Overhead, the sun sinks low, splashing gold across the blacktop. I cross the parking lot to where Mom stands by her Lincoln SUV.

She pops the trunk, eclipsing the sky. Shoving a cardboard box into my hands, she says, "I was cleaning out your room, and I came across some of your old things."

"I thought my room was your guest room?" And maybe, someday, where grandchildren could sleep when they spend the night.

"I'm going to use it for inventory storage," says Mom. "My clientele is growing, and the basement isn't big enough anymore."

"Oh." My eyes sting. Taking the box, I open the back door of my Honda and shove it inside.

"Whatever happened to that Tyler man you were dating?" Mom asks suddenly. "Wasn't he a doctor? Never saw much of him. I liked that."

I scuff my shoe against the asphalt. "I never saw much of him either."

Mom beams. "Perfect."

I swallow hard. "During all the time we weren't seeing each other, he was seeing nurses at work. He saw a lot of those nurses." *Fuck Tyler.*

"Oh." Her face softens. "I'm sorry." A short pause, then she smiles brightly. "If even a doctor is no good, maybe you should give up!"

My shoulders slump. "Mom, I'm just—" My throat clenches. "I have my work, roommate, and cat, but I lack something more."

The skin around her eyes tightens, and her shoulders go rigid. She slams the trunk of the Lincoln. "What you lack is nerve, Eliza. Pure, hard nerve."

CHAPTER TWO

I shower until the water turns lukewarm. Only then do I pull back the green floral curtain and step out. The cool air sends goose bumps prickling across my skin, and my toes numb against the gray tile.

Mom will never understand. A relationship could add to my life, not take away from it.

Or maybe I'm delusional. Maybe I require too much, and my dream man doesn't exist.

Not that loyalty feels like a big ask. True, my dream guy would also have to have good mother-in-law management skills. Plus, Mom would want him to be financially stable. Mom would like a mature man, a serious man, a steady man. Mom might be impressed if he owned a house, but she'd only be wowed if the man spoke, at minimum, four different languages. She'd probably also ask for a background check and his family's health history and—

Okay. Maybe I ask for a lot.

Sighing, I tie my bathrobe closed, pile my hair into a messy bun, and walk out of the bathroom in a cloud of steam. With my roommate Lola out of town until Sunday night, Waffles (the asthmatic cat) is my only companion.

Our apartment is small but cozy, decorated in a vintage style, all dark wood, creams, and olive greens. Oversized art portraying wildlife hangs from the walls, thanks to Lola; and potted plants cover every available surface and hang from the ceilings, thanks to me.

I move from the hall into the living area—an open floor plan with a kitchen on one side and a living room with a fake fireplace on the other. When I flip the light switch, strings of yellow fairy lights sparkle to life overhead.

A copy of *Pride and Prejudice* sits on the couch. I put it back in its place on the bookshelf among all the other well-worn Jane Austen novels. I run my finger over the spines. There are the copies I've read so many times, the covers cracked, the pages loose. There are the collector's editions I've barely touched but bought, as though I thought buying more copies of books about love would mean I owned more love.

Crossing the room, I pluck the cardboard box Mom gave me off the armchair where I tossed it. Sinking to the couch, I slide the flaps of the box open and dump out the contents.

There are a stack of old birthday cards, my high school boyfriend's class ring, some old sweatshirts, and an ancient bottle of nail polish. In short, junk. Surprised Mom didn't throw it all away, I pick up the ring and twirl it around my thumb.

When I was a teenager, I'd incessantly listened to that one-hit wonder by Carly Rae Jepson, "Call Me Maybe." In the song, Carly mentions how, before she met the guy, she missed him. Mom said that was ridiculous. You can't miss something you've never known.

But I do. I've never experienced the kind of love that makes you want to trade your soul for a wish, but I still feel loss, longing, loneliness. If I ever do have that kind of love and lose it, this ache inside me will be unbearable.

I drop the ring and pull out the bottle of nail polish, holding it up to the twinkling fairy lights. It's a churning sludge of sparkling deep purple, blue, and black, like a chunk of the galaxy is contained inside the glass.

The urge to shake the bottle consumes me until I give in. The metal ball inside clatters against the glass in my palm. Refracted rainbows bounce over the walls like there's a disco ball spinning in my hands. It's magical, like the light particles have taken on a life of their own, dancing and spinning over each angle of the room.

A deafening crack splinters the air, somewhere between a thunderclap and a resonating gong.

I jump, then duck as the bulbs overhead flicker and buzz. The lights start to swing from the ceiling, as though manipulated by the force of an earthquake, but the rest of the room remains still. I whip my head, frantically searching for the source of the chaos.

Smoke fills the room. My heart jolts. *Oh, god, the building's burning down.*

My gaze locks onto my hands, and I gasp. Smoke coils around my fingers like the bottle's burning my skin. But there's no pain, and the smoke is purple.

Oh my god, oh my god! Maybe it's some sort of bomb. I yelp and drop the bottle. It hits the carpet with a dull thump and rolls under the couch. Waffles yowls and rockets across the floor, abandoning me.

I'm out of time. Smoke billows out from under the couch. I squeal and curl into a ball, bracing for the explosion.

A deep cough sounds to my right. Unwinding my limbs, I spin around. In the armchair—which had definitely been vacant a moment before—a dark figure sits. My stomach dips, a deeply unsettling feeling festering in my gut.

The silhouette coughs again, a distinctively masculine cough. He waves a hand in front of his face, eddies of purple haze swirling around his fingers.

As the smoke dissipates, he comes into view.

He's about my age, medium build, with dark shaggy hair. Apparently, Mom's conviction that I will meet my end via a slow-moving nonmotorized vehicle is false. Judging by this guy's salmon shorts, fanny pack, Hawaiian shirt, multicolored lei, and gigantic sunglasses, I'm evidently going to be murdered by a frat guy on spring break.

My murderer has gone silent and still, and those unnerving sunglasses are pointed directly at me. A slow smile spreads across his face, sporting a set of mischievous dimples that would make Shirley Temple jealous.

Running a hand through his mess of dark, shaggy hair, he lifts his chin. "'Sup, girl?"

CHAPTER THREE

I take a moment to analyze the past few minutes. The smoke, the flickering lights—the guy must have thrown a grenade to break into my home, and now he's going to stab me in the neck or something. Probably repeatedly.

But if there were a grenade, I should be dead. Unless it was one of those stun grenades—what are they called? Flashbangs? No. That sounds vaguely dirty. That can't be right.

The guy kicks his feet onto the coffee table and crosses his ankles. The casual occupation of my apartment by a complete stranger makes my skin crawl. Side-eyeing me, the guy unzips his fanny pack and withdraws a hard seltzer. He pops the top, wrinkling his nose as fizzy specs of liquid spew into his face. Droplets cling to the lenses of his sunglasses, glinting in the dim light.

As he takes a long drink, static electricity bounces from his hair to the cushioned back of the chair in tiny, purple sparks. "That's better." His words slur, and his voice is gravelly, like he's just woken up but is still delirious from sleep. "I feel like I haven't been this sober since, like, birth."

Who the hell is this person? I told Mom I was an excellent judge of character. To look at this guy, I'd expect his worst crime involved golf cart shenanigans, not serial killing. But still. He did break into my apartment.

I narrow my eyes, resolve strengthened. Past his head, I catch a glimpse of the entryway table. My purse sits on top. I have pepper spray inside. And a cell phone.

Drawing in a deep, steadying breath, I launch off the couch, hurtling for the door. As I charge by the armchair, his head swivels, following my trajectory.

I try the door, but the knob refuses to turn. Locked. Higher up, the chain hangs securely. Somehow, he grenaded my apartment and had time to relock the door after. Tears sting my eyes as I fumble with the chain. Waffles will think I abandoned him once I'm gone. Panic destroys my hands' dexterity until I feel like I'm trying to do open-heart surgery wearing mittens. Sounds of movement rustle behind me, and pure terror forces me to spin around.

He stands a few feet away.

Instinctively, I grab my purse and plunge my hand inside. My fist closes around the pepper spray.

His head tilts to one side, those giant glasses making him look otherworldly, like an alien studying a particularly interesting earthian insect.

Too bad this insect stings.

"No probing action today, asshole," I bellow. Fear has given me the battle cry of a buffoon. I shoot my arm out in front of my body so hard I nearly hyperextend my elbow. "For Waffles!" Squeezing my eyes shut, I start to press down on the cylinder.

The can flies out of my hand, ripped from my fingers by an invisible force. I clench my fist too late around thin air. Cracking an eye open, I find the guy, still standing out of arm's reach, somehow holding the pepper spray. I stumble back against the door, struggling to find breath.

He twirls the can, tossing it in the air and catching it again. "Wow. Rude. This stuff hurts, you know. Not as bad as my feelings right now, but still, pretty bad."

"Well," I sputter, "*you're* rude." Maybe it's not the most incredible comeback, but I'm not sure what etiquette dictates the correct response is after hurting the feelings of your home invader by trying to pepper spray them.

Taking off his sunglasses, he rubs his eyes. "God, this gets old." Letting his arm drop, he fixes me with a weary look. His eyes are a shade darker than honey and framed by thick, dark lashes. They're half lidded like he's tired, bored, or perhaps stoned out of his mind.

I'm struck by how beautiful they are, then immediately irritated with myself for thinking positive thoughts about the guy who broke into my apartment. "Get out."

"Easy, broski." He holds up his hands in the universal sign for surrender.

That gives me pause. I haven't heard anyone use the word *broski* in eons. "Did you just call me your *bro*?"

His gaze flits to my chest for half a second. "Yeah, that's my bad."

Gross. I pull my robe tighter and cross my arms. At least he's distracted. If I can keep him talking, get him rolling into a villain monologue or whatever, maybe I can get out of this.

"What are you doing in my house? What do you want?" Maintaining eye contact, I reach for my purse, hoping he won't notice the movement.

He rolls his eyes. "Our meeting was destined by the stars. To be honest, all I want is to leave, but here we are. Guess it's been a tough day for both of us."

I try to make my voice light and interested so I don't raise suspicion. "What do you mean 'we were destined to meet'?" My fingers close around the familiar shape of my phone. I begin to dial.

"I'm here to give you three wishes, Eliza." His voice falls to a serious tone.

My fingers freeze over the screen, and my purse hits the floor. "Iza." I correct the serial killer because I am the world's biggest idiot.

"Iza," he says softly.

"I'm sorry. What?" I drop the friendly act. "How do you know my name? Who are you?"

"Your name is all over the birthday cards on your couch," he says dryly. "As for me, my name is Beckett. Some of my previous charges took to calling me Beck. I'd be happy if you don't do that."

"You've lost your damn mind," I say, forgetting all about the police and that running from the room screaming is the proper course of action in this scenario. "You're not a genie."

"I never said I was a genie. I don't have my own powers. Someone else grants my wishes. You ever wonder what happens to people who wish for unlimited wishes?"

"No, because nothing happens to anyone who wishes for anything," I snap.

He spreads his arms. "False. You're looking at what happens. I guess wishing for unlimited wishes is considered selfish." He makes a face. "Who knew? Anyway, the star I wished on granted my request, to teach me a lesson. As punishment, she traps me in vessels and sends me to people who I'm forced to *help*." His expression of distaste deepens. "That lands us here, with me offering to make three wishes on your behalf. Only three because, apparently, that's the number that can drastically improve people's lives without turning them into power-hungry maniacs."

Realizing my jaw has gone slack, I shut my mouth. Then open it again to say, "You're saying some kind of sentient star woman makes anything you wish for come true, but you're stuck in a container where you can't make wishes until someone summons you out?"

"Correct. I literally live to serve. I can use my powers for myself but only for as long as I'm also helping someone else. Once you use your wishes, I get sucked into a new vessel until I'm summoned again. Think of me as a spiritual guide. I have to share my powers, among other things, to help you turn your life around. Congratulations, you."

"I wouldn't trust you to guide me across the street," I deadpan. "You can't grant wishes. The only thing you grant is distress. You grenaded my apartment."

"Grenaded your apartment?"

I wave my hand through the air. "Yeah, one of those . . . stun grenades."

He smirks. "You mean a flashbang?" And somehow he makes it sound downright filthy. "I didn't flashbang you. If I did, you'd know it."

"Please leave." I dial 911.

"No can do." He sighs. "I gotta give you the wish spiel."

"What if I wish for you to leave?"

"Then I'd leave, but your words wound me. Don't you know that sticks-and-stones stuff is crap?"

"There's something that hurts worse than words." I inch around him toward the kitchen, pressing the call button. "A cast-iron skillet to the temple."

He folds his hands over his chest, still clutching his seltzer. "Oof. Like a bullet to my heart." But he grins like he doesn't have a care in the world as he leans against the back of the chair.

He watches my progression toward my stash of makeshift weaponry (aka my pots and pans), making no move to stop me.

"Listen closely," he says. "I only want to go through this once." He holds up a finger. "You get three wishes, but even I have limits to what I can do." He holds up a second finger. "Don't try the wishing-for-more-wishes bullshit. Trust me." He holds up three fingers. "I can't make people fall in love or take anyone's free will." Four fingers. "No killing. It's a major downer. Shatters the whole chi of a place real quick, let me tell you." Five fingers. "No raising the dead. Even if my power could do it, that's literally how zombie apocalypses start. For real, don't be *that* guy, Iza. Nobody likes that guy."

"Nine-one-one, what's your emergency?" a muffled voice sounds through my speaker.

My killer rolls his eyes and takes a drink.

Scuttling backward, I raise the phone to my ear. "Hey—hi—yes. There's a man in my apartment, and he won't leave. I think he's on narcotics or something, because he's definitely delusional."

He gives me an indignant look and mouths the word *Ow*.

The dispatcher asks if I'm in danger. I eye the weirdo. I've already forgotten his name. Brock? Brent? Beck? No, not Beck. He specifically said not Beck. Whatever. "Probably. I'm pretty sure he's a serial killer."

I give the dispatcher my address, and she says someone is headed my way, before asking, "Is he in the room?"

"Yes."

"Does he have a weapon?"

He must still be able to hear, though the phone is pressed to my ear, because he grins and says, "Just my good looks."

I tell the dispatcher, "No."

"Has he been drinking?" she asks.

He nods and lifts his drink. "Most definitely."

The dispatcher stays on the line, asking questions and giving advice on how not to get killed. Meanwhile, my home intruder lets out a long sigh and perches on the arm of the chair. "This isn't going to do you any good, you know."

I cover the phone speaker. "Seeing you in handcuffs will do me a lot of good."

He lets out a low whistle. "Kinky."

The dispatcher advises me not to provoke him.

"I can't believe you actually called the cops." He scratches his ear. "Do you always overthink things this much? Make a wish, and I'll show you I'm real."

The dispatcher asks me what's going on. I ignore her. "Maybe I do have an overthinking problem, but at least I'm not the one who believes he's some kind of cosmic-powered deity."

"I'm not a deity."

"Just a cosmic-powered nuisance, then?"

He smiles and, for a second, looks like he might genuinely laugh. "Only for you."

I scowl.

"The denial stage is so boring." He yawns.

"Whatever, Benjamin."

"Beckett, but wow, what a burn."

A knock pounds on the door. "Police. Open up."

"This is annoying," Beckett says in a monotone.

Hanging up the phone, I scurry around the perimeter of the room to unlock and open the door. Two cops enter, their hands resting on their holsters as they eyeball Beckett, who's now fully sprawled in the armchair.

"Sir, you need to leave," one says gruffly.

Beckett stands and sticks out a hand. "Beckett." When the cops ignore the hand, he turns to me and whispers, "Watch this. I call it the Obi-Wan."

The second cop steps forward. "Okay, Obi-Wan, let's go."

Beckett waves a hand in front of the cop's face. "I'm not the man you're looking for."

The cop works his jaw. "Oh, we've got a funny guy."

My teeth clench in a triumphant smile. "So much for cosmic powers, huh?"

Ignoring me, Beckett addresses the cop again. "I live down the hall. Iza is my friend." His grin twitches. "My lover, in fact. We were engaging in some rather . . . explicit activities. I apologize for her state of undress and overall scruffy appearance."

My teeth clench harder, this time not in a smile.

"Come on, buddy," says one of the cops. "Don't push your luck."

Unperturbed, Beckett waves his hand again. "You want to leave now."

I start to scoff, then choke.

The cops are gone. Totally gone. Vanished.

Absolute silence envelops the apartment. Prickles run across my neck. I whip around to find Beckett barely containing a snicker as he crosses his arms across the back of the chair.

I scamper to the door. Heart beating in my throat, I stick my head into the hall and look both ways, but there are no signs of the cops. Horror floods into my veins. Turning in the doorway, I stare at Beckett. This shouldn't be possible. Magic isn't real. There has to be a scientific explanation.

"You're a hypnotist." I decide. "You're messing with my brain."

Beckett watches me with amusement. "Relax. I only sent them to the nearest cornfield."

I should run from here. I'll find another police officer to arrest him, and I can return to life as normal.

My normal life.

Where I'm alone, and Mom is right, and my only hope is a flimsy plan riding on dating sites and vibes.

But if this is real, the impossible could become possible. And maybe the only thing that can break me out of this endless cycle of my life—hope, disappointment, despair, rinse, repeat—is magic.

CHAPTER FOUR

Although being alone with a stranger doesn't seem like the best idea, I drift back into the living room. "If you're real, I need proof."

"If the multiple appearing and disappearing acts weren't enough, make a wish, and I'll show you I'm real." Beckett looks at me expectantly. "What is it you want?"

"No." I cross my arms. "Proof first."

He pinches the bridge of his nose. "The wish is the proof."

"I'm not stupid. I'm not going to wish for something worthless on the off chance you're real."

"There's that overthinking again." He finishes off his seltzer and crushes the can. "Fine." With a snap of his fingers, the crushed can vanishes, and another appears as though it's been there the whole time.

He waves a hand, and something crashes behind me. I whirl to find a giant canoe teetering on the crumpled remains of the coffee table.

"What—"

But there's another crash and a reverberating thrum. I spin again to find a massive gong standing in front of the door, trembling with vibrations.

A whooshing noise to my left turns out to be a miniature hot air balloon in the kitchen, a propane flame creating heat waves under a red and yellow bubble.

I turn in circles, my heart pounding in my ears louder than everything else. "What are you doing?"

"You wanted proof." Beckett has to shout over the noise, but his voice is somehow still a lazy drawl.

I freeze as a wooden treasure chest falls from the ceiling, slamming to the ground inches from my feet, falling open to reveal stacks of hundred-dollar bills.

A low growl to my right makes me stagger back. A black bear sits on my living room floor, licking its huge paw.

"Stop! Stop it!" I cry. "Make it go away."

Beckett steps closer, and I recoil, but he only bends down to pick up a few stacks of money, slipping them into his pockets. With another wave of his hand, everything vanishes. The only evidence left is the splintered remnants of the coffee table. He snaps his fingers. The rubbish disappears, replaced by a new table.

My breaths come shallow and quick. This is really happening. It's real. Every thought I've ever had is tainted. False. From my earliest memory to right now, everything I learned about the world is untrue. I'm a newborn again, blinking in a new reality outside my safe womb.

My brain still scrambles from the events of the past few minutes, and my hands are shaking, but something inside me is strangely . . . excited. Sure, I'm questioning reality and my state of mind, but if this is true . . .

I could have it all. With magic, I could find that elusive balance between home and career that Mom is convinced is impossible. I'd start my own architectural firm, be a confident and successful woman like Margaret Heafield or Marie Curie (well, before she died from self-inflicted radiation exposure). I could have a house in the country, surrounded by nature. I could wish for something to make a relationship possible.

Or I could maybe not be selfish.

"What about world peace?" I ask slowly.

Beckett mutters under his breath, "Great. She's one of those."

"Hey!" Despite my better judgment, I march forward. "What's that supposed to mean?"

"A do-gooder, a brown-noser." His head snaps up, his eyes locking onto mine. "A square."

Heat rushes to my face. "I'm not a square."

"Sure. To answer your question, for a world-altering wish like that, you have to be shipped off to a parallel universe where world peace exists."

Teetering, I stumble to the couch and sit down. "Parallel universe?" I squeak.

"Yup. Seriously, though, let's not talk about it. My head hurts if I get into it without a joint first—feel me?"

Of everything he's told me, somehow the existence of parallel universes is the easiest to accept. "I don't want to be shipped to another universe," I say, swallowing hard. "Not when nothing in *this* one would improve from a wish like world peace. I like this world, this life, the people here."

"You wouldn't even be able to tell," he says, rounding the chair to stand in front of me. "Everything except what you wished for would be exactly the same. Or if you want to stay here, wish for something smaller that actually exists in this reality."

I shake my head, the movement growing faster and faster until a dull ache surrounds my brain, and I have to stop. "No. No alternate universe. If I ask you if my wish will send me away before I make it, will you tell me?"

"I have to tell you if you ask," he says, sitting beside me.

Too numb to be distracted by the close proximity of someone I'd been convinced five minutes ago was going to stab me in the throat, I ask, "Why?"

"Rules." Beckett pops open his fresh can of seltzer. "You're my charge—or whatever. I'm supposed to help you, so I'm physically forced to answer all your questions, and I'm unable to lie to you." He takes a hefty drink. "Kind of a bummer for me, to be honest, but great for you."

If he's unable to lie, then when he said I hurt his feelings earlier . . . I really did. Maybe his sarcasm isn't as sarcastic as it seems.

A pang shoots through me, and I'm reminded of the server's expression after I insulted him. But this guy is no innocent server, so I push the feeling away. I have no proof Beckett can't lie, beyond his word, and my instincts tell me to be wary.

I take a few long, steadying breaths. I'm not the type to go barreling into a situation, so I give myself a moment to digest the past several minutes.

When I launched my mission to find the perfect partner, I decided to start trusting what I see with my own two eyes. I can't deny I saw magic. I also can't deny the dangers associated with it.

My gut tells me making a wish would be a bad idea.

Firstly, I don't want to transport myself into another world filled with other versions of everyone I know. Even if they're just like the people I love, it wouldn't be the same. I'd know they were different. Secondly, Beckett doesn't seem like someone I should trust with the responsibility of my future.

I stand and pace. "In every story about wishes, things always go wrong, usually because whoever grants the wish is a trickster." I drill him with a glare.

"Is insulting people a hobby of yours? Because I'm wounded, deeply wounded that you would suggest—nay, *accuse* me of—"

I stop pacing. "Cut it out. Are you going to be a jerk and manipulate my wishes to either render them useless—"

He squints. "Did you just say 'render'?"

"—or cause misery, chaos, and ruin?"

"I feel attacked right now," he says gravely, pressing a palm to his heart.

I can't believe I entertained the notion that his sarcasm is some sort of front to hide real feelings. "It's a yes-or-no question."

Squirming, he averts his eyes. All at once, he grows interested in the potted fiddle-leaf fig beside the couch. He rubs his fingers over one of the shiny green leaves.

My attention locks on his fingers. "Hey, be careful with that."

Beckett's already moved on, picking up yet another battered copy of *Pride and Prejudice* off the end table and thumbing through it. My heart constricts, as though he's holding it, instead of the book, in his hands.

Mom once said *Pride and Prejudice* used to be her favorite story, so it immediately became mine too. If I liked a book she liked, it would give us a shared trait, and there would be something about me she could approve of. But no matter how many copies I bought to display my love, she never displayed hers.

A meow behind me causes me to turn. Waffles's head sticks out from around the pantry door, his eyes wide, pupils huge.

Immediately, Beckett sets the book aside and scrambles off the couch onto the carpet, making little "pss, pss" noises, hand outstretched. It's a strange sight—this douchey party guy, kneeling on my floor, beckoning my chubby cat over.

Amazingly, Waffles—usually a reclusive hermit—trots across the floor to rub against Beckett's knee. Scooping Waffles into his arms, Beckett plops him into his lap and scratches the cat's haunch. "Historically, yes, I may have enjoyed screwing around with some poorly worded wishes. It depends on my mood and if I think what you wish for is asinine."

I groan and rest my head in my hands. "I'm not sure why the universe decided I should be the one 'blessed' with your help, especially when I can't even wish for love or anything else that matters."

His hand pauses over Waffles's head. "Love? You'd waste a wish on love? That's sad."

"It's not sad to want something real," I fire back.

Beckett's jaw tightens, and he stands, Waffles tumbling off him. "I gave up on real a long time ago." He moves toward the front door.

I scamper after him. Beckett's whole demeanor has changed in seconds—from flippant frat guy to broody rain cloud. It makes me question my first impression of him. "If I ask you something, you claim you'll have to answer, right?"

Beckett freezes, and I bump into him. As I make contact, the smell of sweet, woody cedar mixed with French toast wafts off him. It reminds me of the cigars my coworkers puff on self-importantly sometimes, but without the nastiness of the smoke and nicotine.

When I look up, he's facing me, eyes searching my face. A dark lock of shaggy hair falls over his brow, and I clench my fist to fight the irrational urge to brush it back.

He rests a hand on the doorknob. "Yes, but if you don't want me to manipulate your wishes, you shouldn't abuse the truth-telling thing." His expression grows calculating as his gaze flits over my face. "Maybe it's your turn to answer a question. Tell me, Iza, what would you do for love?"

"Anything," I answer immediately.

"Hmm." He opens the door and steps into the hallway.

"Where are you going?" Wrapping my bathrobe tighter around my body, I follow him out.

"Are all the apartments in this building full?" he asks.

"The one across the hall has been vacant for a while. Why?"

"It looks like your wishes are going to turn into a huge saga instead of a quickie, so I'm going to move in. I'll be around if you ever decide what you want." He eyes me. "I'm guessing that might take a while."

"You can't squat in an empty apartment."

Waving his hand over his shoulder, he walks away. "Please. You're hilarious."

Something twinges behind my ribs. That settles it. Beckett must be able to lie to me after all because I've never been accused of being hilarious in my life.

Beckett crosses the hall, and with a flourish, a key appears in his hand. Opening the door to the apartment, he pokes his head inside. "Yep. This will do nicely. Gonna throw some bitchin' parties here."

He snaps his fingers.

Music booms to life. The voice of Britney Spears blares down the hallway, all breathy, singing, ". . . Baby One More Time." Seconds later, multicolored flashes of light stream from the doorway to accompany the music.

Beckett leans back smugly, bobbing his head to the beat. "It's a Britney kind of day, isn't it?" he asks before dancing his way inside the apartment—very badly, and in a way that reminds me of my middle school history teacher at the Sadie Hawkins dance. In another circumstance, I'd almost find it endearing.

The door slams and the music grows muffled. Marginally.

That twinge behind my ribs tightens into yearning. If I were a different person, I might march down the hall and join him. I'd fire off three wishes and have the adventure of my life.

But I'm not that person. I'm me, and I don't have adventures. I have Excel spreadsheets and ten-year plans.

Numb, I go back inside and fall against my front door as I push it shut. My fingers and toes tingle as adrenaline subsides from my limbs.

Even when she's not here, I sense my mother watching over my shoulder, ready to highlight my every mistake. She would say to never rely on anyone or anything to create happiness for me. She'd say I have to make my own future. Using a wish to show her I can create the life I want is cheating. It won't mean as much unless I do it on my own.

I was wrong before. I don't need magic; I need nerve. Pure, hard nerve.

I should ignore Beckett and continue on with life as planned.

Music vibrates the artwork on the walls.

Then again, ignoring Beckett might be difficult.

CHAPTER FIVE

Ignoring Beckett is very difficult.

He must've used his powers to spread the word about his party because, when I peek out my door a few hours later, I find a long line of people wearing dark, slinky clothes lined up in front of Beckett's door like it's the entrance to a nightclub.

The music continues all night. By the time the noise finally stops, the grayish light of early morning glows through my window. Finally, I drift off.

It's after noon on Saturday when I roll out of bed. My subconscious kept my anger marinating during sleep. Now, my only thought is to march over and give the magical dick across the hall a severe tongue-lashing.

Wait.

That came out wrong.

He doesn't have a magical dick, and I certainly don't want my tongue anywhere near it. He *is* a dick. His level of dick has reached magical proportions.

That's not right either. That sounds vaguely complimentary.

Why am I thinking about this?

I'm just tired.

The point is, I had a plan to get myself everything I've ever wanted, and I don't need a mystical dudebro to do it. He's just a blip. And I need to tell that blip to keep it down so I can ignore him properly.

As quickly as I can, I change into a Tim McGraw T-shirt and jeans. The clothing, worn thin with age, is paradise compared to the uncomfortable work clothes I spend most of my life in.

I slam my front door and stalk across the hall. Pounding my fist against Beckett's door, I yell, "Hey, Brad, open up!" I knock louder, hoping he's nursing a hangover and that all the racket is irritating him at least half as much as his party irritated me.

My knocking is so loud I almost miss his voice from within yelling, "Come in."

When I try the doorknob, it turns easily. Beckett is nowhere in sight. His apartment is clean, the air cool and fresh, no evidence from the night before in sight.

"Hello?"

"Back here." His muffled voice comes from somewhere in the back of the apartment.

Carefully, I close the door behind me and tiptoe farther inside. His apartment is laid out similarly to mine, but the walls are all painted in rich, deep tones and lit by dim uplighting.

I turn the corner at the end of the hall to find Beckett standing in his bedroom, buttoning the top button of his polo as he examines himself in his dresser mirror. Though he also wears khaki shorts and brown sandals, the fanny pack and sun visor are thankfully absent from today's ensemble.

A giant four-poster bed dominates the center of the room, and heavy furniture looms against the walls, but the room's imposing vibes are ruined by a massively oversized bean bag chair slouching in the corner.

Turning from the mirror, Beckett looks me up and down. He smiles, those dimples splitting his cheeks. When he speaks, his tone holds the same sleepy, lazy tone it had last night. "Hey, you."

"What is this, your sex chamber?" I wrinkle my nose.

"It could be." Slowly, he winks. "It is my job to fulfill desires."

"Ugh." I walk up and jab a finger into his chest. A surprisingly solid chest that nearly breaks my finger in two. I fight back a wince and plow ahead. "You're a Kappa-Delta-Rho-yal pain in my ass, you know that? I only came here to ask you to keep it down. I barely caught any sleep last night."

Beckett's eyes have the audacity to twinkle at me. "I'm a royal pain in your ass, huh? I'm astonished and impressed that you yelled that pun at me with a straight face." When he grows serious, it's my turn to be astonished and impressed. "For real though, dude, the music is my bad. I didn't realize the soundproofing in this place was so terrible. I'll fix it. Won't happen again, promise."

"Oh." I shift my weight, unsure where to go from here. I'd been expecting pushback, a huge argument. "Okay, then . . . carry on."

He catches my arm before I can leave. "Aren't you going to stay? Maybe make a wish or two over breakfast?"

I should pull away, but something keeps me rooted to the spot. Curiosity maybe—the same curiosity that kills cats and people in horror movies.

Beckett's hand is warm. I blink up at him. His eyes are warm too.

Nope, nope, nope.

I stomp down every mushy feeling his unexpected kindness conjured. I'm supposed to be trusting my gut, and my first impression of him condemned him as a possibility. His type are the fuckbois who consider Flip Cup to be an Olympic sport. He'd make a good beer pong partner, not a good life partner. I shudder, imagining Mom looking him over.

I tug my arm away. "You just want to ruin my life over breakfast. No thanks."

Beckett lifts a finger. "Wait, hold on. Did we just have a moment there?"

"No."

Grinning, he leans against the bedpost, tucking his hands into the pockets of his shorts. "We had a moment. Don't deny it, Iza. You're running from your feelings for me."

I smile tightly. "You give me the same sort of feeling you get when you go to bed and start to drift off, only to remember you never switched your laundry from the washer to the dryer, and if you don't get up and do it, you'll have nothing to wear the next day."

"I make you contemplate becoming a nudist?" he asks with interest.

"You make me frustrated," I fire back. "Look, I'm not going to be making any wishes, so you might as well pack up. I've wasted enough time with this. I have a meeting with a big, new client on Monday, and I need to prepare."

Beckett whistles low. "It's worse than I thought. Even though you're unhappy, you're really not going to make a wish. You're too stubborn."

"Magic isn't real. Even though it's *real*, it isn't real." I huff. "I need to achieve things on my own."

"But I could make it easier." His tone turns enticing, inviting. "Wish for a few billion dollars and forget about work."

For half a second, a deep, aching longing swells within me. It's been forever since I've entertained the idea of letting anyone help me, but there's something fishy about his sudden compassion. I get the distinct feeling he's baiting me, like he thinks I'm a donkey ready to trot after a carrot on a stick.

I refuse to be an ass, so I ignore the damn carrot and his damn face and his pretty goddamn eyes. "You want me to make a hasty wish, but it's not going to happen." I cross my arms. "I'm going to watch everything I say so I don't slip up and say I wi—anything about wishes in general conversation." Panic clenches my chest from my near slipup. "I mean, I could offhandedly wish for it to be Friday, and my life would become a sequence of endless Fridays like *Groundhog Day*. To make it to the end of the week, but never quite the weekend . . ." I shudder.

"The horror." His lips twitch.

"I don't want to wish for money. I'm an architect, so I do well enough in that department, though I can't say it's added much fulfillment to my life." I continue to ramble. It's probably not wise to bare my fears to him, but it's too late now. "It's the work itself that fulfills my life, so why would I wish it away, replacing it with the one aspect of it I don't care about?"

"Hey." Beckett steps forward. "Chill. I shouldn't have done that last night with the magic. I know how trippy it can be. Magic can make normal life feel meaningless. Is that what's wrong?"

Maybe partly. I remember my thoughts from the night before about how my achievements don't count unless I attain them by myself. I shudder. "You don't know how I feel."

Beckett takes another step forward and touches my elbow, ducking his head, trying to catch my eye, but I won't meet his gaze. "I might."

"What, did you get a welcome packet with the SparkNotes to my life when I summoned you?"

He laughs like I'm actually funny, and even though I'm on the verge of a breakdown, a strange warmth goes through me. When he laughs, his features are unguarded, and I catch a glimpse of something behind the walls of his outward appearance. It's beautiful and intriguing, and I want nothing more than to free it.

"No. I don't know anything about you," he says. "But I'm cursed with the ability to have anything I want, and in the end, it still means nothing."

Now here is something real. I study his face intently, trying to pull out more, more, more. "What do you mean?"

Beckett's fingers fall from my elbow. He scratches his jaw, fingers rasping against the stubble shadowing his face. My eyes glue themselves to the movement, but I quickly tear them away.

Why am I distracted by a well-formed cheekbone? What's wrong with me? Beckett checks none of Mom's boxes. If I want to prove her wrong, I need a no-nonsense man, a guy I can see a real future with.

Beckett is a nonsense man. Total nonsense.

At last, Beckett answers my question. "That's the real punishment, Iza. It's not about balancing power by forcing me to share it. It's about giving me everything I want and ripping it away over and over again." His words come slowly, as though he's deliberating each one before letting them fall from his lips. "When I'm in a vessel, it's like I'm dead. As soon as someone makes their last wish, I blink, and suddenly I've been summoned by someone else to a new place years later. Whatever life I managed to build for myself the last time I was free is gone. Any physical item I wished for myself is meaningless in the end. The only signs I lived at all can be found in the ripple effects that come from helping someone else."

"So you're saying you've learned your lesson?" I ask skeptically. "You don't exactly seem like a euphoric George Bailey who's just realized how influential his life is."

Beckett's smile turns bitter. "Learning the lesson is pointless because being selfless won't get me out of the curse. I'm doomed to hear the same lesson over and over and over. Not even my magic can change the terms of my punishment. I might as well live selfishly because I barely live at all. Hell, maybe I'm still self-ish after all, because once, just once, I'd like to make my own waves."

Gone is the Beckett from last night. The man in front of me with the tortured eyes is a different man entirely, and I don't know what to make of him.

Squinting, I lean forward, trying to see through him. "Who are you, Beckett? What's your deal?"

"I'm me. What are you talking about?" A crease forms between his brows.

"It's like you're trying to be obnoxious with the douchey frat guy thing you've got going on, but then you're nice, and now you're . . . this. I don't know which one's real."

In an instant, his cheeky grin is back, dimples on full display. "Most chicks dig my nice side."

I flinch away. I've dated a version of him before: the guy who acts like he's opening up to you because you're special and differ-ent. You feel a false sense of intimacy, and you trust him with your secrets in return. Only to learn he shared the same story with eight different nurses at his place of employment.

Fuck Tyler.

And fuck Beckett. I *knew* he was gross and untrustworthy. I scowl at him. "So that's what you're up to. You act all mysteri-ous and tortured so your charge falls for you." I bet he thinks he's clever, getting people he's supposed to be helping to sleep with him.

Beckett's eyes shift away. "You've got me all figured out."

He didn't deny it. In fact, if he can't lie to me, then he confirmed my suspicion.

"Well, it won't work on me," I say, even though it already almost worked on me. "And I'm never making a wish. You're going to be stuck here forever." With that, I turn on my heel and stalk for the door.

Two soft words follow me out. "I wish."

* * *

Back in my own apartment, I open my laptop and pull up a dating site at random.

Quickly, I close it.

Nope. Not that one.

I do another search and pull up a site that doesn't contain the words *sexy, foxy,* or *hookup.*

All I have to do is find the perfect, balanced man to fit in my perfect, balanced life. He'll be a sublime mix of devoted to duty and devoted to me. I smile, pleased with myself.

As I scroll down the list of faces, the mouse wheel hums under my middle finger.

Screw you, Beckett. I fulfill my own desires.

Wait. That sounded wrong.

The perfect face appears on my screen. He's attractive, with a wide, open face. His name is Isaac. Maybe we'll keep the "I" theme when we name our children.

His profile says he's a prince of a small country, which must mean he has a sense of humor. It's satire, probably, making fun of how everyone lies on dating sites. Under his "About" section, it reads: *I enjoy pampering my dog, myself, and my future princess. I also enjoy long walks on the beach and spending with family.*

I assume that last one is a typo, and he means spending *time* with family. I'm not so uptight I can't forgive a typo. Mentally, I give myself a pat on the back for my graciousness. I scan the rest of his profile but don't find his real occupation.

So, I send him a message.

Me: What do you do for a living?
Isaac: I am a prince.

What a fresh and pure sense of humor.

In his photo, he's wearing a suit that costs at least three thousand dollars. Whatever he actually does, he's done well for himself. Mom will like that.

He's probably too humble to brag, and that's why he won't tell me what his job is. Maybe he longs for a real connection and is trying to filter out gold diggers. Whatever the reason, I'm charmed.

We schedule a date for tonight.

* * *

I slip out of my apartment that evening, expecting to get stuck in another line of party guests, but the hall is empty . . . for about two seconds until Beckett pokes his head out of his door, eyes hazy like he's been drinking.

He cocks an eyebrow at my black dress. "Oh my god. Are you cheating on me?"

Sticking with the plan, I ignore him and keep walking. I ignore the hurt expression on his face. I ignore how similar it looks to the server's at Olive Garden. As the daughter of the world's most notorious Karen, I'm often horrified to find myself following in her destructive footsteps, but in this instance, I think my coldness is warranted. Beckett did try to emotionally manipulate me into pitying him, after all.

"Tell me, Iza," Beckett calls behind me, "what kind of vessel did you summon me from?"

That catches me off guard, and I turn. There's an uncertainty in his expression I've never seen before. "Why does it matter?"

"Each new vessel I'm transported to is emotionally significant to the person I'm supposed to help to ensure they'll eventually pick it up and summon me out. I've learned I can tell a lot about a person by their vessel."

Despite my best efforts, my memories surface. Thinking about the nail polish bottle reminds me of another time, a time when I'd paint my nails with glitter, before Mom told me I was too old—before she told me I'd never be taken seriously with sparkly fingers. For a while, I kept painting them secretly when I stayed at Grandma's, wiping them clean before Mom came to pick me up. Now, I've cut frivolity from my life, trying to fit into the mold Mom made for me. And yet, I'm still too much and not enough all at once.

"Please tell me."

There's such desperation in Beckett's question, that I answer. "A bottle of sparkly nail polish," I say quietly.

"You don't seem like the sparkly nail polish type."

I look down the hall, talking *not* to him because it's easier than talking *to* him. "I used to be. Not anymore." When Beckett meets my eye, there's a glint in his expression like he's learned something. My chest tightens. "I'd better go. I'll be late."

"Good luck," Beckett calls after me.

Again, I tune him out. This time because I can't talk past the lump in my throat.

* * *

The restaurant smells of fifty-year-old wine and entitlement. It's offensively fancy.

Isaac is fancier yet.

Because he actually is a prince.

"Lamborghinis," Isaac finishes. He's been droning on for a while, and I've been zoned out, staring at his . . . crown.

Yes, he wears an actual crown.

"I'm sorry." I gulp my water. "Lamborghinis? Plural?"

He blinks. "Oh yes."

I adjust my dress on my shoulders and lean across the table, meeting Isaac's eye. "So, in your profile, where you said you liked spending with family, you meant—"

"Money." He waves a hand, though I'm not sure how. There must be a literal ton of gold rings weighing it down. "Now, I'm looking for a new special someone to spend my money with." He leans forward and takes my hand. "How do you feel now that your prince has come at last?" His suave smile says he thinks he's smooth.

Mom's words from long ago echo in my head. *"You shouldn't live in anyone's shadow."*

Shaking my head, I rip my hand away and stand so fast the glossy chair flips over.

The room falls silent. Countless disapproving eyes drill into me, like my mother possessed every person in the restaurant to witness this, to leer and say, *"Give up, Iza. You know Mommy's right."*

I can't prove to Mom that I can find the right man to build a relationship with if there's something wrong with even a real, honest-to-god prince. Maybe my Mr. Right doesn't exist.

Maybe magic is the only way.

I start inching away. "I have to go," I mumble before I finally turn my back on him, hunching my shoulders as I weave around tables and shuffle out of the restaurant.

My heels click over the smooth asphalt as I dig for my keys. I unlock my car, slip inside, and rest my forehead against the steering wheel.

Why am I wallowing in self-pity because Beckett might be mean about my magical, legit, honest-to-god *three fucking wishes*? What kind of ungrateful bitch complains about wishes? I can't chicken out because there might be consequences.

I'll seize the day, be my own woman.

Except *my own woman* is scared shitless and has no idea how to start wording an airtight wish.

I fiddle with my phone. Wise women seek counsel. Maybe I should call Mom. Her lawyer could write me up an impenetrable wish. There's no way I could explain this to her, though.

Instead, I text my roommate, Lola.

Me: Lola. I'm dead serious. I know it sounds crazy, but I accidentally summoned a supernatural frat guy from a bottle of nail polish, and he gave me three wishes. Come home now.

A string of laughing emojis comes back a second later.

Lola: Lol! I'll have what you're having. I'll be back tomorrow night. Until then, make good choices. Have fun. 😉

CHAPTER SIX

Ever since I asked Beckett to keep it down, the apartment complex has been so quiet I can practically hear the crickets in the basement three floors below.

I lie awake, remembering Beckett's face when he laughed and how I thought for sure there was something more there. When I sleep, I'm haunted by the server from Olive Garden. In my dreams, my voice turns into Mom's as I talk myself down a rabbit hole over and over again.

It's mid-morning Sunday by the time I finally roll out of bed.

Once Lola gets home tonight, we can have a nice, calm discussion. We'll plan out the wishes carefully, weigh the odds, and scheme the perfect plan to get my life on track.

I kill time by researching the new client I'm meeting with at work tomorrow.

I didn't tell Mom my boss put me on a multimillion-dollar project, designing a home for a VIP client. Even though she would've been overjoyed with the news, she would have used it as evidence that trying to balance a relationship with work right now is a bad idea.

But if I wait for work to slow down, I'll die alone. Maybe that's what she wants.

I push the thought aside and scroll through the search results. The client's name is Julia Felmont. She comes from money—the daughter of a late politician—but there's little else about her online.

By the time darkness falls, I'm drumming my fingers on my leg, staring blankly at the TV.

A light rap sounds on my door, breaking the radio silence from the hall. With a jolt, I turn the TV off and answer, expecting to find Lola. Maybe she forgot her key.

Instead, Beckett stands there, wearing a blazer with shorts, his floppy hair combed back. It's almost like—it's almost like he dressed up in his own weird sort of way.

The rich smell of spices meets my nose, and my attention falls to the take-out bags he carries. "Why are you here, Bernard?" I ask, suspicion turning my voice harsher than I intended, reminding me of my dream where my voice turned into Mom's.

"Beckett," he corrects. "But I'm pretty sure you know that by now. About last night—"

I grimace, remembering the awful date. I don't need Beckett rubbing it in. "I honestly don't want to talk about it. It was embarrassing and awkward."

He blinks. "Okay. Let's forget it happened."

I'm surprised he let it go so easily. "Great." I grip the edge of the door and look down the hall. "No party tonight?"

"Nah. In fact, consider this an apology for keeping you awake Friday. And for everything yesterday too." He lifts a bag. "I smelled gyros from that street vendor when I was out on a run, and my stomach was like, 'Brah, go get you some of that.' So I did. Then, my brain was like, 'Brah, maybe Iza's hungry too.'"

My stomach growls even as I protest. "I'm not helpless, you know. I don't need you to bring me food."

Beckett chuckles. "That's good. If you were going to starve unless I fed you, I should've come sooner." He pushes his way past me.

"Please, come in," I say dryly.

Tossing the takeout onto the coffee table, Beckett makes himself at home on the armchair he materialized on two nights ago. "What's this?" He leans over the laptop sitting open on the coffee table, with the dating site still pulled up. "Desperate4love.com? That's a bit on the nose, don't you think?"

I hurry over and snap the laptop closed.

Eyes dancing, he watches me. When I don't back down from his stare, he lets out a soft snort and unpacks the food. Before sitting, I go and grab two root beers from the fridge.

Beckett takes his without complaining about the lack of alcohol content, which is a bit of a shocker. Actually, every other move he makes is shocking. Just when I think I have him pinned down, stereotyped into a box that makes sense, he jumps out of it.

"Why don't you give up?" he asks abruptly. "On love, I mean." He waves at the laptop.

I hesitate.

There's no reason to think this hard about an answer. It's not like he really cares. "Because I can do everything else," I say finally.

"You're afraid of failure?"

I swallow. "It feels important to succeed at this."

The clock in the kitchen ticks in the silence. Beckett's expression is different. Serious.

Something shifts in his eyes, like he's decided something. "I really am sorry if I made you uncomfortable yesterday. Obviously,

I don't expect—I don't expect anything to happen between us." He looks away.

There's a tenderness to his voice that gives me pause. "Thanks," I say, unsure what caused this change in him.

"A girl like you, who cares about world peace and still has hope and still tries"—he finally meets my gaze—"please, don't ever look twice at someone like me."

Again I catch a glimpse of that something I saw when he laughed yesterday. He's a puzzle. I don't like not knowing things, and that makes me want to pry at the gates to his soul until they fly open.

"Why?" At his frown, I clarify. "You say you don't want me to look twice at you, but isn't seducing your charges your whole game?"

Letting out a long breath, he fiddles with the edge of the paper take-out bag. "Not usually. Actually, my whole game is to get people to write me off."

I snap my mouth shut. My gaze lingers on him as he unwraps his gyro. There really is someone with feelings beyond the obnoxious smirks and annoyingly flippant attitude. "Is the douchey frat guy thing armor?" The question tears from my throat, even though I'm not sure I'm ready for the answer.

Beckett's gaze locks onto mine, a vulnerability there I haven't seen yet. "Yeah." His throat lurches like he's physically forcing words out. "It's harder to be afraid of a guy wearing a fanny pack. I appear in the middle of people's lives, sometimes in their homes, and I never know how they'll react. It only takes one night wrapping broken ribs in a gas station bathroom to realize you have to be prepared for anything. Especially baseball bats."

I think of how I tried to pepper spray him the first time we met. It was a natural reaction that a lot of his charges probably have. *"That stuff hurts, you know,"* he'd said. He was probably speaking from experience. I imagine Beckett alone, lost, and disoriented in a new place, trying to scrub Mace from his eyes, and my own eyes sting in sympathy.

"Why are you telling me this?"

"I owe you an explanation."

"Why?"

"Because you're different. I did flirt with you, and I shouldn't have." Beckett sits back, picking at his paper sandwich wrapper. "If you think I have some kind of alluring tortured and mysterious thing going on, I want to ruin it by telling you about my past."

I roll my eyes, trying to lighten the mood. "Yeah, gotta watch out. You wouldn't want to accidentally seduce me."

"No. I wouldn't." His jaw knots for a moment before he continues, voice hard and emotionless. "Bear with me. Most people make their wishes wham-bam-thank-you-ma'am style. I've never had a reason to tell my origin story before. This is kind of new."

Beckett takes a long breath. "Before I got cursed, my best friend's dad had gotten sick and was unable to work. They were about to lose their house. With my own family struggling to make ends meet, I had no extra money, and there was nothing I could do.

"I'd had a particularly bad day after something small had gone wrong at my family's shop. Feeling helpless, I walked outside and looked up at the stars. I saw one fall and thought to myself, 'If only wishes were real, then maybe I could be of some use.' To my surprise, that falling star kept falling and falling, growing brighter as it descended, until a woman, glowing with starlight, stood before me. She said she saw my potential and rewarded me with a wish. Being young and hasty, and thinking I was clever, I asked for unlimited wishes. The star was disappointed in me but couldn't take back a wish she'd already gifted, so she had to grant it and every one I've made since.

"All I had to do was *think* a wish, and it was mine. Instead of helping my friend or even my own family, I began making wishes for myself. One thing after another." Beckett runs a hand down his face, heavy with regret. "The star grew even angrier. She'd given me an opportunity to make a difference, and when I abused her gift, she decided to force me to make a difference as a punishment. After laying out the terms of my curse, she trapped me in my first vessel and rose back into the sky, where she controls me like a pawn, deciding where I'll go and who I'll help. So, Iza, if I am tortured, it's only because I deserve it."

Utter silence consumes the room. For the first time in my life, being right about someone does not make me triumphant.

The crack of Beckett popping his soda open makes me jump. The next thing I know, he's reached over and opened mine for me too.

I start to protest.

"Calm down. I know you can open it yourself. I didn't have to." His eyes meet mine, and he shrugs. "I wanted to."

Oh.

The front door flies open, and I jump. My roommate, Lola, stands in the entryway, a bottle of wine clutched in each hand. I hold back a groan. So much for her and me having a calm, one-on-one discussion about wishes.

"How was the seminar?" I ask. Lola works as a vet for the St. Louis Zoo and has been away learning about turtle care all weekend.

Lola blows her bangs from her lashes and gives Beckett the stink eye. "Don't tell me this is the same guy you shared your oh-so-magical night with Saturday."

"Magical night?" Beckett says, slowly turning to face me, a grin crawling from one side of his face to the other. The weighty tension in the room dissolves. "Oh really?"

My face heats. "Spending time with him isn't magical. *He's* magical." Oh god. That sounds so much worse. "He has magic *powers.*"

Beckett's eyebrows shoot up. If possible, his smile grows wider

Kicking the door closed, Lola hurries forward, depositing the bottles before us. "Is that what the kids are calling it these days?"

I hug a couch pillow to my chest. "Beckett, do the thing with the canoe and the hot air balloon, so we can move on."

"I don't normally like dragging a bunch of people into this. It tends to get messy." Beckett lowers his voice. "But since we're friends now—"

"Are we, though?"

"—I'll make an exception." With a flick of his wrist, three crystal wineglasses appear, dangling by their stems from his fingers.

"He's into magic?" Lola pinches her razor-sharp eyebrows together, placing her hands on her slender hips. "Come on, Iza. That's sort of cringy."

"No, he's real," I say. "Showed up in smoke, gave me three wishes, the whole nine yards. I need your help coming up with airtight wishes."

Lola's eyes sparkle. "All right, all right. I'll play." Sitting beside me, she opens the first bottle. "Say all that's true. He seems nice enough. Just make a wish."

Even though Beckett and I may have had a moment earlier, I still don't trust him. If anything, all my reasons for why I shouldn't trust him have been confirmed. "Haven't you ever read stories about wishes? Things always go wrong. Plus"—I drop my voice to a whisper—"Beckett is the unscrupulous type. It has to be worded right."

Beckett shoots me a sidelong look. Damn. He totally heard me.

"Okay." Lola pours three generous glasses and passes them around. "Not saying I'm convinced, but for shits and grins, what do you want?"

Beckett snorts. "Iza doesn't know what she wants."

"There's a difference between not knowing and being cautious." I take a healthy (or not so healthy, depending on how you look at it) swallow of the sweet red wine. "Maybe I'm content with how things are."

"Thus the dating website," Beckett says under his breath, so low I barely hear.

"Well," Lola says, refilling my glass, "liquid encouragement has a way of pulling the truth out of everyone."

* * *

Only an inch or two remains in the last bottle, glowing crimson from the strings of lights overhead. Beckett has switched over to his magic hard seltzers, and Waffles purrs on his lap.

I sniff loudly, snot rattling around in my sinus passages. "It's not that I *need* love, not when I have you, Lola, and Waffles and my career, but—"

"Find a hookup on Tinder and get it out of your system," Lola suggests.

"Not sex, Lola," I say, sloshing wine onto my shirt. "I mean, sure, sex would be nice. But if that's all I wanted, it wouldn't be this difficult." I take another long drink, letting the tangy wine roll around over my tongue before swallowing. "He can't be just any man. He has to be better than any other I've dated. One who can keep up, who Mom will approve of."

Lola's hand drifts aimlessly through the air. "Keep your mom out of your love life."

"Is it so bad to want my mom to get along with the guy I date?"

Beckett leans forward, clearly squishing Waffles, but the cat doesn't seem to mind. "It's clear there's one personal aspect of your life you're unhappy with. You should start there."

"Exactly," Lola says. "Amen. Why don't you wish for your dream man? It's obviously what you want to do."

Sitting back, Beckett says, "I was going to say fix your relationship with your mother, but that works too."

I ignore Beckett and turn to Lola, setting my glass on the table. She's right. Though I can't wish for love, I can wish for my perfect match. "You're onto something, but *dream man* is way too vague. I want him to be his own person, fully fleshed out. I don't want him to exist just to be my boyfriend. I have to specify the guy down to the number of hairs on his head so Beckett over there won't ruin it for me."

Beckett offers a noncommittal shrug.

"Couldn't you wish for a character in a book or a movie?" Lola asks. "That would be pretty specific, as the character has already been described at length by someone better with words than you—no offense. It would leave little room for error and deviation." Lola stands and stumbles over to the bookshelf filled with books and DVDs. "You need someone who's his own man, unapologetically."

"Yes. Smart," I say, then add, "and *he* has to be smart too."

"And so hot, right?" Beckett rolls his eyes, rubbing Waffles's ears.

"For sure," I say, pretending to miss his sarcasm.

"Christian Grey?" Lola asks. "He's supposed to be all hot and good in bed and stuff, right?"

"You're on the right track," I say. "Mom would like that he's successful, but he's too high maintenance."

"How do you know that?" Beckett asks. "Based on a movie? Without meeting him yourself?"

Lola sighs. "It's Iza's thing. She thinks it's a superpower, like she can take one look at a man and identify their flaws, all the reasons they're wrong for her."

"That's kind of judgmental, isn't it?" Beckett asks. He looks at me, his eyes bright. "What about me, then? Why was I wrong for you?"

I shake my head. "You're laughing at me."

He bites his lip to stop his curving mouth. "I'm not. Come on. What did you think when you first met me?"

"I didn't think anything," I stammer, face burning. "There wasn't anything wrong with you."

Lola snorts with laughter.

Beckett's smile is challenging as he says, "Then why didn't you ask me out?"

My stomach dips like I've swooshed around a loop-the-loop roller coaster. For one wild second, my buzzing brain thinks, *Yeah, why didn't I just date Beckett?* It starts to imagine all sorts of strange things, like Beckett's hand gently holding mine, that cocky smile finally sobered because his mouth's too busy pressing kisses to my skin—

"I thought you were a serial killer," I say a bit too loudly, to silence my thoughts. "Then I thought you were a player."

"A player?" Beckett's smile fades, and not in the fun way that involves kissing. "Ouch."

I shove aside any lingering daydreams and focus on the facts. "Yeah. I thought all you cared about was having a good time. I thought you were only looking out for yourself. I thought you were the type who'd play games and never commit."

"Right. I'm unscrupulous." He nods and looks away. "How could I forget?"

A stab of something hits me behind my ribs. Guilt? Regret? Shame? Whatever it is, it's the same feeling I had after assessing the server.

I almost say, *I don't think that about you now.* But I do think that about him now because earlier tonight Beckett told me a story that affirmed my first impression. Maybe he was decent enough to warn me to stay away from him, but it's because he knows the same flaws about himself that I do. His selfishness is what landed him here. Why should I feel guilty for being honest? Is it judgmental if it's true? My mind is a fuzzy mess.

Lola's eyes shift between us.

"Sorry. You asked."

Beckett shrugs and smiles, but it falls flat. The skin around his eyes lies dead, motionless, instead of crinkling up in the corners like it normally does.

Wait a second. Sometime between summoning him out of a bottle, being completely put off by him, and yelling at him to keep it down across the hall, I've noticed how Beckett's eyes normally look when he *smiles*? This is dangerous territory.

"Everyone has baggage," Beckett says finally. "Explains why you need to bring a fictional man into the world to be your soulmate. Poor bastard. Will you dump him at the first sign of distress?"

The feelings inside me harden to stone, and I glower at him. I can't believe my imagination was strong enough to create pleasant daydreams about someone so infuriating.

Lola whirls around, almost falling over. "Let's be supportive here." She leans against the shelf to steady herself, squinting at the row of books inches from her nose. She runs a finger down the spines. "Edward Cullen?"

"He doesn't have a job," I grumble. "Mom would hate him."

"The fact you have to resort to a fictional man concerns me a bit," Beckett muses, leaning back and crossing his ankle over his knee. "Do you even want a real person—or a sex robot?"

God, he can't let it go. I blink back anger and bite my tongue, fearful whatever I snap back with will summon that nasty guilty feeling from a second ago.

Lola narrows her eyes. "What's your problem?"

"Nothing," Beckett says. "But this has to be one of the more hare-brained wishes I've experienced, second only to the two-foot penis."

That catches both Lola's and my attention. She squints upward, shuddering. "Good god. Like a tripod. Not an image I ever wanted."

"I can't actually alter anyone's body," Beckett clarifies. "I gave the guy a two-foot sculpture of a penis, and he was upset about it for days. I'd like to say this isn't a common occurrence, but I've handed out more oversized dildos in my lifetime than I'd care to admit. Give a man a wish, and what's the first thing he thinks of?"

"His schlong," Lola says, like she's receiving a revelation from on high. "Incredible."

Wobbling, I stand. "You're comparing the desire for true love to some idiot who wished for a two-foot penis? What's wrong with you?"

Beckett blinks. "What's wrong with *you* that you have to wish for a perfect fictional man to get a relationship to work?"

I teeter around to exchange a look of solidarity with Lola. At least she sympathizes.

Waffles lets out a huff and jumps off Beckett. He pants heavily before waddling out of the living room, clearly bored with our human nonsense. As I watch him go, my eyes catch on the shelf behind Lola, specifically on one book in particular: *Pride and Prejudice* by Jane Austen.

"Fitzwilliam Darcy," I say, rocking forward. "It's so obvious."

"Who is Fitzwilliam Darcy?" Beckett asks. "Sounds boring."

Flicking the book off the shelf with one finger, Lola asks, "You don't know who Mr. Darcy is? He's considered the most swoon-worthy leading man in literary history."

Mom said *Pride and Prejudice* was her favorite book. The declaration had surprised me, but everything about that evening had surprised me. I'd been in my early teens. Mom was supposed to have a bunch of clients over for a product demonstration that night, but even Mom wasn't impervious to the common cold. She'd had to cancel, and so I decided to watch my movie in the living room, where it was more comfortable.

I'd just started the DVD when Mom shuffled by on her way to bed. She paused, seemingly enraptured by the image of Elizabeth Bennet wandering through a field. "Is this *Pride and Prejudice*?" she asked. When I nodded, she said, "This used to be my favorite book."

A few minutes later, we were both on the couch under a mountain of blankets, me buzzing from a soda-induced sugar rush, her drunk on DayQuil. At first, I was stiff, unsure how to watch a movie with my mother, but then Mr. Collins appeared on-screen. Mom muttered under her breath, "I'd nearly forgotten about that little bastard," and the tension broke. Soon, we were rolling our eyes at Mrs. Bennet, giggling over the sisters' antics, and sighing over Mr. Darcy.

The next morning, I thought things would have changed, that suddenly we'd have an unbreakable mother–daughter bond, but it wasn't to be. I went to school, she went to work, and life went on. When I bought a copy of *Pride and Prejudice*, she picked it up and gave me an ironic smile, as if to say, *"Weren't we so silly that night we giggled over a romance movie?"* Then she asked me to please put it away because it was cluttering up the kitchen island. But I'd seen the truth. Under everything, Mom was someone who'd uttered the phrase, "I used to think Mr. Darcy was so dreamy."

It was so unusual to hear Mom compliment any man, real or fictional, that it stuck with me.

To create the life of harmony I want, I need to bring Mr. Darcy back into our lives in a way Mom can't put on a shelf.

Either that or I need to keep my mother drugged on DayQuil.

The former seems more ethical.

Mr. Darcy helped my mom and me get along before. He's already received her seal of approval, and I have no doubt I could eventually fall in love with him. He'd fit right in. Surely the gentlemanly, duty-oriented Darcy would be able to understand an overbearing mother-in-law and a few nights home late from work. We could be a family.

I take a steadying (or not so steadying) drink. "I'm ready. I'm going to make my first wish. Mr. Darcy is es-est-established"—it takes me three tries to get out the word—"in his life and with who he is. He's got impeccable morals, a heart of gold, and he's stoic—not one to crave constant attention. Mom wouldn't be able to question Mr. Darcy's commitment or say he's holding me back."

Lola places a hand on my shoulder. "Are you sure? You're talking about wishing a nineteenth-century man into modern-day society. The poor guy will be petrified. Not to mention, walking him through life when he's used to carriages and chamber pots exhausts me just thinking about it."

Her face swims before my eyes. "Relax," I say, plucking the book from her hand. "I've got this. It's going to be . . . epic."

"Hey." Beckett smirks. "That's what two-foot-penis guy said too."

Lola chews her lip. "Maybe we should wait until tomorrow."

I sway, and Beckett stands, steadying me with a hand on my arm. "I think you should listen to Lola. Remember when I told you to stick to wishing for things that actually exist? This wish might—"

I spin on him, the world tilting. I blink hard. "You be quiet, Becky."

He lets his hand drop. "Fine. You know what you want, yeah? Go for it."

Lola bites her lip. "Iza . . ."

I tune out Lola's fretting.

I will have love, despite Mom's misgivings. There's nothing wrong with a woman wanting love and going out to get it. A confident woman wouldn't hesitate. Marie Curie would've made her very own Frankenstein companion if she were so inclined and hadn't been happily married.

"I want my Frankenstein sex robot." My words mash together but are unfortunately still decipherable to my companions, judging by their gaping mouths and wide, horrified eyes.

"That's a new one, I must say," Beckett says.

"That's not my wish." I huff in frustration.

"Good," he says. "Because that would be terrifying. No one's ready for that."

Lola chews her lip. "Maybe you should sleep off the wine . . ."

"No, Lola." I fling out my arms, nearly smacking Beckett in the face with *Pride and Prejudice.* "It's *my* wish. I'm sick of everyone telling me what I should want." I backpedal to the opposite side of the room before they can stop me. "I want—I *wish* for a twenty-first-century version of Mr. Darcy, complete with his own family, career, and house, in this time period."

"Why do I feel like you left that way too open to interpretation?" Lola mutters, her voice sounding very far away.

I clutch *Pride and Prejudice* to my chest.

Beckett's brow furrows. He swallows hard, then snaps his fingers.

CHAPTER SEVEN

A splitting headache wakes me more effectively than any alarm clock ever has. Rolling over, I pull my blankets over my head. Hangovers in college never felt like this. My eyes twinge and burn from the sunlight filtering through my sheer green curtains.

Groaning, I push off my white quilt, squinting my eyes open and inhaling the scent of living greenery and rich dirt.

Although the rest of the apartment sports plenty of plant life, my bedroom is more jungle than living space. Tall plants line the walls while shorter ones scatter before them on the floor. More pots are staggard across the dresser, nightstand, and windowsill. Vines trail across the ceiling. A pair of ponytail palms share the loveseat at the base of my bed, tufts of stringy leaves peeking above the white, peeling footboard. They look like a duo of wild-haired gossiping old biddies sitting there, and if it weren't for the hangover, the thought might make me smile.

Hangovers.

Last night.

I shoot upright, my temples throbbing with renewed vigor from the sudden change in altitude.

I used my first wish.

And absolutely nothing happened.

Beckett's words swim around my brain, floating in a sea of stale wine and anxiety. *"Did you expect a man, who you wished to have his own house and life, to come into being in your living room?"*

"Where is he, then?" I'd asked.

"You'll meet him soon" was his response.

Something on my nightstand tucked between a money tree and an African violet catches my eye—a blue Gatorade, a bottle of aspirin, and a note. The Gatorade could be an oasis in the desert, the way I lunge for it. Cracking it open and taking a long, blissful drink, I read the note. It isn't Lola's familiar scrawl, but thin, looping cursive.

> *Figured after you fell asleep in a puddle of your own tears, you might want these. —Beckett.*

I take another drink, my muscles melting into relaxation as my electrolytes rejuvenate with every cool swallow.

I read the note again. Fell asleep in a puddle of my own tears? My attention catches on the black mascara smears on my pillow. Then on something else half hidden under the sheets: Beckett's blazer.

Oh, god. I slam back two aspirins.

I look down. I'm still fully dressed. Relief washes over me.

A blurry snippet of a memory swims into focus.

"Darcy's going to arrive with his wife, Elizabeth Bennet, and six children in tow, thanks to that little line you added about family," Lola had said.

"I thought he'd miss his sister!" was my tear-filled response.

"He didn't even exist until a second ago!"

The memory fractures into fuzzy, disjointed snippets.

Me, bawling my eyes out because I was still alone, even after magically wishing my dream man into existence. How he might never meet me because freaking Beckett probably conjured him into reality in China or some crap. How, if Darcy didn't arrive with an inconvenient wife alongside him, Marie Curie would come back to life, and *she'd* be his Elizabeth, not me. How I should've just wished for the Frankenstein sex robot after all.

Beckett, covering my mouth with his hand before I could actually make the Frankenstein wish.

Lola, telling me my wailing reminded her of a birthing elephant.

Beckett, leading me to my room, tucking me in. How soft his shirt was against my skin, the way the tendons moved in his forearms when he took off his blazer and covered me with it because I couldn't stop trembling, the warm cinnamon and cedar smell cocooning me, the—

Groaning, I lean forward and press my palms to my eyebrows, willing the pounding away. I'm burning with mortification but try to comfort myself. Beckett tucked me in. That was all. Drunk-me didn't do anything stupid.

Well, unless wishing Mr. Darcy into the world is considered stupid.

I can't remember the last time I've been that drunk. Of course, the one time I am, I have three wishes from a disconcertingly good-looking man at my disposal.

Good-looking? Where did that come from? Beckett was nice to me a few times, and I'm swooning over him? I make myself sick. Well, the alcohol made me physically sick, but I sicken myself on a mental level.

Get a grip, Iza. Don't forget, he wished your true love to China.

Except Beckett had said, "You'll see him soon," and he supposedly can't lie to me.

My alarm blares to life, sending fresh pain searing through my skull with each piercing screech. Damn it. It's Monday. I'll have to look for Darcy right after work. I decided to wish for him, so I'll see it through, even if that decision seems less wise in the light of day.

Unbidden, Beckett's voice echoes in my head again. *I'm guessing deciding what you want might take a while.*

I used to know what I wanted. When you're six, life is simple. Then, one day, your clear goals grow muddled and complex.

I'd been at Grandma's house that day. It had been springtime, and all the windows were open. Grandma's red curtains—the ones with the chickens on them—blew in the crisp breeze. A batch of cookies was in the oven, filling the air with vanilla and chocolate.

I was watching one of those princess movies, one of the old ones before everyone realized stories about waif-thin girls being rescued by princes instills children with unrealistic body expectations and obliterates female independence.

Mom came into the living room as the credits started to roll. "I wish you wouldn't watch those movies," she said. "You don't need a prince."

I met her eyes with a challenging glare. "Of course, I don't need a prince. There are no ogres or dragons in the real world."

Her jaw tightened. "You don't need to be the princess to someone else's prince. You shouldn't live in anyone's shadow."

"So I'll be the prince."

She smiled tiredly. "Men don't like being the princess."

"I'll find one who doesn't care."

"Those types of men are as real as the ogres and the dragons."

Then Grandma walked in with a cookie tray and said, "A partnership can be part of her goal, can't it?" When Mom started to protest, Grandma gave her a look and said, "Her future isn't your past"—whatever that meant. Then, she'd shoved the cookie tray under my nose and told me to take *a few*, which meant at least eight.

After that moment in Grandma's living room, I vowed to show Mom my life could continue after the happily ever after; it wouldn't come to a halt because I found a man. I could have love too, as long as I could find the right prince.

And now, I have.

I just need to close the deal.

Even a real prince wasn't good enough, but this fictional man, straight out of a storybook, he has to be right. If he's not—

He will be.

Ignoring my head and churning stomach, I do my makeup with more care than usual, adding foundation and bronzer to my usual mascara, blush, and lip gloss. First impressions matter, after all. I even whip my hair into a French twist, leaving a few curly tendrils loose around my face. After throwing on a silky black camisole and my best black pantsuit, I head out, grabbing Beckett's blazer at the last moment.

Lola stands in the kitchen, cracking a raw egg into a glass. She holds up a hand before I can say anything. "Don't talk. You cannot comprehend the depth of my suffering."

I hesitate before I say, "Last night, did Beckett and I do anything—"

Her look could flatten a monster truck. "Shh." She makes *settle-down* motions with her palms, then continues on in a whisper. "You think I'd leave him alone with you when you were that drunk? I was listening outside your door to make sure you were okay. You're welcome, by the way. You guys talked forever. Well, you talked. He did a lot of listening."

I don't have time to ponder that because she lifts the glass to her lips, and I can't watch that yolk slip into her mouth.

In the hall, Beckett's waiting for me. He sits in front of his door, ankles crossed, a bag of fast food in his lap. Fresh morning dew and grass stains smear the sides of his sneakers, and his hoodie sports a dark "V" of sweat below his neck, like he was out running. "Morning," he says.

The greasy smell of fried cheese and seared meat wafting from the paper bag in his lap makes my stomach churn. "I'm sorry about last night." I bite the inside of my cheek before adding, "Hopefully, I didn't say anything too weird. I'm usually not—"

He stands, eyes trailing up my body as he rises. "Damn, girl. Sweet threads. You drawing buildings today or drawing attention?"

My face flushes. I shift my weight and clear my throat. "I—I'm going to be late." What's wrong with me, blushing over a stupid line?

"Right, sorry." He steps away, rubbing the back of his neck. "That was a—how'd you put it? A 'douchey frat guy' thing to say?"

At a loss for words, I do some sort of laugh/shrug combination that probably looks like a convulsion. "Thank you for the apology. It can't be easy shedding an act you've put on for so long."

His whole face softens, the corner of his mouth twitching into a smile. "Yeah. At least that line probably made you even less attracted to me."

"Totally," I say, my insides growing gooier by the second.

Trying to shed the feelings, I shake my head, redoubling the throbbing in my temples. I wished Mr. Darcy into existence. I can't grow distracted now by the guy I used to get him here. The guy who admits to being self-serving and who's never said for sure that he won't ruin my life, which likely means he *will* ruin my life.

Plus, who knows how long he's been cursed? He could be, like, two thousand years old or some shit, which . . . gross.

Beckett eyes me. "Also, don't sweat last night. You were pretty blitzed, but you didn't say anything too weird. Other than telling me that being the result of IVF means you were born of immaculate conception and are therefore basically Jesus's sister."

"Oh my god," I mumble. My face is sweating at this point. "I'd better get going." I thrust his jacket into his hands. "Here. You left this last night."

"Thanks. Knock 'em dead today, eh, killer?"

I give him an indifferent nod—as though I hadn't spent a fair amount of time blubbering in his arms about a fictional man last night—and walk away.

It pisses me off how hard it is to dislike the guy who probably wished my true love to China.

* * *

I'm stuck in a hungover haze, reliving the fuzzy memory of Beckett tucking me in over and over. I can almost smell him, feel his warmth, hear his low, bemused voice in my ear—

I stab a letter opener into a stack of sticky notes so hard the picture frames and flowerpots on my desk rattle together. I need to focus.

A few coworkers glance my way, hopeful for something to break up the monotony of the day. When they see it's just me on the verge of a meltdown, they turn back to their computer screens.

I take a careful sip of coffee from my paper cup. The bitter liquid hits my stomach, giving the bile something to hold onto, and my world steadies slightly.

The office of Knight Skyline Drafting and Design sits in downtown St. Louis. Inside, beams and ductwork crisscross the ceilings while exposed brick lines the walls. Our interior designers claim the style is industrial. From what I can see, *industrial* basically means they haven't done any decorating at all.

Our desks span one-half of the open second floor, and glass offices occupy the other half. There's a spiral steel staircase in the middle of the room, leading to a catwalk and the offices of the higher-ups, which are situated to overlook our desks.

Lofty windows line the building's walls, displaying a view of a railroad station on one side and a picturesque scene with the Gateway Arch in the distance on the other.

I look down at the stack of sticky notes. The top one reads: *Get back at Kalyan.* My grip on the letter opener tightens. I vaguely remember writing the note last Friday after my coworker Kalyan filled my drawer with Jell-o. That punk needs to learn he can't get away with his shenanigans.

Shenanigans. One of Grandma's favorite words.

I release the letter opener. Her laughter echoes in my head as though she sits beside me.

A memory of a cool spring breeze tickles my skin, and I can almost hear tree leaves rustling overhead. I smell green tomato plants and marigolds and taste tangy lemonade on my tongue.

Helping her in her garden when I was little gave me my love for plants. Mom sold the house in the country after Grandma died, leaving me with memories and the fiddle-leaf fig I keep in the living room. Mom says I'm only drawn to the country because of Grandma's memory; I'm projecting, and it's not really *my* dream at all. She says if I ever pursue it, I'll end up full of regrets.

My career means sacrificing the open, rural living I'm drawn to, since the commute to work would make living outside the city impossible. So I compromise by bringing the outside inside.

A sudden tightness in my chest makes me blink back tears.

Easy, Iza. Now's not the time to spiral. My coworkers won't take me seriously if I start bawling at my desk. Thanks to Kalyan's pranks, they hardly take me seriously now. It's hard to be professional with Jell-o in your desk. For a while, I tried not to stoop to his level, but he's relentless.

The pressure in my head intensifies my migraine. I turn back to the sticky note. Below *Get back at Kalyan,* I add another line. *Febreeze grenade?* Nothing says, *Screw you and your bullshit, Kalyan,* better than a toxic cloud of limited-edition clove and evergreen air freshener from Christmas six months ago.

Kalyan's fascination with harassing me is a mystery, especially considering my other (mostly male) coworkers avoid me as much as possible. An outsider might think the natural conclusion is Kalyan likes me.

He doesn't.

He's unromantic in his ceaseless torment, carrying out every prank with feigned innocence so no one can call it out for the warfare it is.

That's a bit harsh, isn't it? No. It's a fact. Kalyan has an ulterior motive. I'm just not sure what it is yet.

He acts like we're old friends, like I'm in on the game too. After each prank, he stares at me with a giant, expectant grin while he waits for me to crack. I hate that. Kalyan knows nothing will break me faster than him pretending like a very serious office rivalry is fun. It's not fun, damn it. It's work, and if he wants to get ahead of me, he should spend more effort on his actual job rather than childish games.

Letting out a deep breath, I lean back and rub my temples.

"Eliza!"

"Iza," I correct automatically. Then, I see who addressed me, and I plaster on a pleasant smile. "What's up, Chester?"

During my interview, I mistook Chester Bailey for an intern instead of my future supervisor. Between his wild red hair, which he contains in the forever-crowd-favorite man bun, and his boy-band physique, he looks better suited to a life as a barista than a senior manager.

He blinks about a thousand times, his pale, freckled face spasming with each movement. "Meeting in thirty. Don't forget."

"You've got it." It's cute when he tries to act like a boss. From the moment we first met, I knew he was a people pleaser.

Chester turns to go but then pauses, his slender fingers drumming across my desk. "One more thing, Iza. The new client, Julia Felmont, she's a bit . . . eccentric. When you meet her, be cool, 'kay?" With one final slap of his fingers across my desk, he shoots me a smile vibrating with caffeine-induced tremors before zipping off.

Eccentric? After everything that happened this weekend, I can handle a few eccentricities.

Boisterous laughter sounds from the lounge area in the middle of the room. I swivel my chair around. Kalyan and a few of his buddies stand around the espresso machine like they're the leads on *Friends* instead of actual working people with things to do.

Kalyan catches my eye and offers a blindingly cheerful smile. That innocent-looking smile is a declaration of war if I've ever seen one. It sets me on high alert.

I slash a line through *Febreeze grenade* and write *Actual grenade?* underneath. Then, I drill Kalyan with a glare. "Don't you have things to do?" I call.

The guys roll their eyes and exchange looks.

"Notice anything different about your desk, Kiches?" Kalyan calls back.

Gaze snapping to my desk, I look for anything out of the ordinary. Nestled among the plants and crystals on my desk are photographs. Usually, they contain pictures of my friends and family. Today, they all contain very up-close photos of Kalyan's smiling face.

"Very funny." I roll my eyes heavenward, draining my coffee.

The empty cup falls from my hands, and I nearly choke as my swiveling eyes catch on something overhead. It's a subtle thing, like the differences in one of those games where you have to spot the changes between two nearly identical pictures.

Along the catwalk overhead, there's an extra office.

CHAPTER EIGHT

My breath catches somewhere between my roiling stomach and my gaping mouth. Gaze darting from one door to the next, I count the offices again. When I come up with one extra, I swallow hard. I scan the glass rooms until an unfamiliar desk inside one catches my eye—the dark silhouette of a man behind it.

I spin my chair, throw open a drawer, and pull out a pair of binoculars I have in there from a complex prank I pulled on Kalyan last year. I press the lenses to my eyes and dial them in until they focus on the gold plaque tacked to the door:

"Senior Architect—F. Darcy."

"Yo, Peeping Tom, isn't littering bad for plants?"

I spin to face Kalyan, the binoculars still pressed to my eyes. His face is about a mile wide in the lens. Quickly, I lower the binoculars.

Kalyan leans over my desk, an eyebrow raised pointedly at the cup on the ground. Hurriedly, I pick it up and throw it into the wastebasket under my desk.

Kalyan's other eyebrow shoots up to join its brother as I straighten. "Is that alcohol I smell on you, Kiches?"

"Probably your own breath" is the sad excuse for a snappy retort I manage to dig up. Apparently, showering and brushing my teeth three times didn't disguise the evidence as I hoped.

And then a fuzzy memory skips through my head. I'd gone to the kitchen last night for some crackers to go with the wine. *"Need help?"* Beckett had asked from behind me. I turned too fast, bumping into him, making him spill a bit of his drink onto my pantsuit jacket, which had been slung over the back of the chair next to him. *"Party foul,"* he'd said, gaze lingering as he looked down at me, inches from his chest.

I'd taken the jacket to my room with the intention to clean it later. Instead, I'd put it on this morning.

Now, I take the jacket off, even though it makes my outfit look less professional. Smelling of alcohol is worse.

"I'm on a juice cleanse," Kalyan is saying, lips turning down in a rather snooty way. "Haven't touched alcohol in weeks. Do you know what that stuff does to your body?"

"You were talking about getting beers after work *last Friday*," I say, turning to check out the mysterious new office again. "Hey, what do you know about . . . Fitzwilliam?" Mentioning the name in a serious tone in the context of a conversation with my coworker in the middle of a workday feels ridiculous.

"Darcy? The new senior architect?"

I guess I shouldn't be surprised that Darcy goes by his last name even in the twenty-first century. The man probably emerged from the womb as Mr. Darcy.

Kalyan leans even closer, the spicy, pungent odor of Axe body spray leeching off of him. "Why are you curious? You checking him out?"

I shove the binoculars behind my back. "No."

He rolls his eyes. "I know as much as anyone, I guess. He's some long-lost friend of Chester's. Chester must trust the guy's sticking around if he built him his own office after only three months. Like, where's my office, Chester?"

Three months. Everyone thinks Darcy's been here for three months. That's a little weird, but okay. I can work with it. "And what do you think of him?"

Kalyan shrugs. "Can't say. Haven't worked with him much, ya know? He's sort of hard to read too, but you've probably noticed. You guys are going to get all cozy, considering you'll be working under him on the Julia project."

I gulp. "I will?"

"Unless he likes being on the bottom." Kalyan snickers.

I stare ahead, mute.

Kalyan squints. "You really did have a wild weekend, didn't you?"

"You have no idea."

As soon as Kalyan leaves, I put the binoculars away, inconspicuously snap a picture of the new office, and send it to Lola.

Me: It's real. You're looking at the new office of Mr. Darcy.

Lola: OMFG I thought you and some guy you were hooking up with were trying to get one over on me. Excuse me while I go have an existential crisis in the penguin enclosure.

"You know office romances require a certain amount of paperwork to comply with protocol?"

I jump, my feet jolting against the floor and sending me and my chair careening. The back of the chair smacks against my desk. On impact, picture frames and succulents rattle together. A long shadow falls across my face. Gulping, I look up.

A man towers over me, his hands clasped behind his back. He wears a solid black three-piece suit and a grim expression. His nose is long, his lips thin, and his hair dark, streaked prematurely with gray. Though his skin has the pasty, office pallor many of the rest of us share, he's somehow still handsome . . . in sort of a severe, disappointed-professor kind of way.

"Well, did you and Kalyan fill out the official 223 form?"

Dumbly, I follow his dark eyes to the grinning photographs of Kalyan scattered around my desk. All identical. All embarrassing.

"Oh, we aren't dating." My voice comes out about an octave higher than usual, thanks to the shrine to Kalyan behind me. I glance at Darcy's ring finger. It's bare. I remember I'm supposed to be conveying that I'm very much single and very much ready to mingle. "It's sort of a prank war we have going on. That Kalyan initiated. I only reciprocated in the name of self-defense."

His frown deepens. My skin burns and tingles all at the same time as I look him up and down. I sense no red flags. He's Classic. Romantic. Timeless. "Meeting in fifteen, Iza," he says, and the words could be the grandest of love sonnets the way my stomach flips. Or maybe that's still the alcohol.

How did Elizabeth keep her cool around him? Maybe I should invest in smelling salts or something. Then again, she hadn't been aware she was in the presence of the guy who would become every woman's fantasy. That, and she wasn't real.

Wait. Darcy and I have both been silent a long time. Am I currently under the scrutiny of one of his signature smoldering stares?

I take a peek.

No. He looks a little pissed. Maybe I should say something.

"Okay," I say, ever the wordsmith.

I wait for him to bow or brush a kiss across my knuckles, but he fails me when, after a final contemptuous look down his straight nose, he turns on his heel and heads toward the meeting room.

So much for first impressions. Freaking Kalyan ruined everything.

I find my stack of sticky notes.

Inspiration leaves me.

Short of physical violence, I have no retaliation suitable enough for the embarrassment Kalyan inflicted on me. Even I know violence is an intense revenge tactic in an office prank war. Taking a calming breath, I suppress my inner Karen before she can sharpen her sunglasses into a shiv.

I write, *You will pay for this, Kalyan,* and leave the note on his desk on my way to join the others in the meeting room.

* * *

I sit next to Darcy himself. Beyond him sits Chester. On the other side are an engineer, someone from the design team, and a woman from HR. I side-eye her, unsure why she's here.

Julia Felmont sits at the head, flanked by two burly bodyguards as if she's the president instead of the youngest daughter of a dead senator.

Between stealing looks at Darcy and coming to grips with this whole, crazy situation, I've tuned out quite a bit of the meeting. This is happening. It's really happening. Darcy is here, and he's perfect. We even work together, which opens all kinds of wonderful opportunities, like carpooling, lunch dates, and janitor closet sex. Okay, no. Not closet sex. Even if I didn't draw the line there, Darcy surely would.

"So you're saying you want all progress expedited?" Chester pinches the bridge of his nose, elbow resting on the long conference table.

Julia wears her thin, blonde hair pulled back into a tight bun and has oversized, cat-eye glasses, which she pushes up her pointy nose. "If me saying I want my bomb shelter done by next spring means production must be expedited, then yes. Expedite production."

Chester's Adam's apple bobs. "Eight months is a tight deadline for a project of this magnitude."

"You can't handle a project of this grandeur, this . . . expense?"

Chester's head snaps up. "Let's not make presumptions. We can multitask, have our architects start on schematics while we focus on permits and contractor selection."

Darcy deigns to add his input. "We can set up a time to view the site as soon as possible." In contrast to Chester's excited tones, his deep voice is flat, bored.

Julia looks over her glasses like a disapproving librarian. "It's a ten-acre field where I need you to build an underground bomb shelter. What's there to see?"

Darcy flips through the stack of inspiration photos Julia gave him. I lean over his elbow, and he flinches away like I carry the plague. Each photo shows an elaborate room of a mansion, with dripping chandeliers, curving staircases, and even a ballroom.

"To clarify," says Darcy, "there are no upper floors? You want everything belowground?"

Julia smacks her hand across the table, and Chester jumps. "When the world ends, I don't want the upper half of my house destroyed."

"What if the less necessary things, such as the ballroom, spare bedrooms, and billiard room were above ground, and the essential rooms were below?" Chester asks.

Julia shudders, her hands trembling violently. "They're all essential." Her voice wavers somewhere between rage and hysteria.

Wordlessly, one of her bodyguards hands her a tissue. She dabs at her eyes, pursing her lips together and looking away.

Darcy furrows his brow. "You mentioned earlier you live alone." He leans back, interlacing his fingers before him on the table. "Should the world end, who will you be inviting to your ball? Or do you expect your guests to travel across a radioactive wasteland for the privilege of basking in your esteemed presence?"

Now, I understand why the woman from HR is here. Darcy must have a reputation for being blunt in client meetings.

Chester winces, looking close to tears himself as he rapidly blinks his glassy eyes. Julia's face turns as red as the Mars-like expanse Darcy described. In short, things are going poorly.

Before I can second-guess myself, I stand. "If the world does end, I think it's smart to think long term." Every eye drills into me. "Sure, first and foremost, we must consider survival, but after that, if we're unable to leave our shelters, we must consider quality of life. How is living in three 'essential,' cement-walled rooms better than perishing? I think an underground mansion, where one might feel at home, comfortable, and happy, as well as secure, is a brilliant idea."

Julia looks up at me as if I lead the way to eternal salvation. "Yes, exactly," she says. "Chester, I'd like to have her design it."

Darcy makes a discontented noise in his throat. "I'm designing the structure. Ms. Kiches works under me and will certainly have input."

Julia sniffs and stands. "Well, we'll see how you do, I suppose." A bodyguard drapes a fur coat over her shoulders. (Why? It's June, for Christ's sake.) "I'll check back in a week or two," she says before turning to me. "I expect you to keep him on track. I don't want a metal cot, cinder block wall, or can of spam in sight."

I nod. "I'm sure we can meet your expectations."

"What do you think of a pool?" She fiddles with her glasses.

"Underground?" Darcy nearly chokes.

At the same time, Chester says, "Anything's possible."

Julia pushes her chair out of the way and walks up to me. "You know HGTV—the Home and Garden channel?"

"Sure," I say. I can't stand HGTV. Shiplap is never the answer.

"Think HGTV while you design my palace."

Her palace? It's a palace now? An HGTV palace? "Okay—"

"That is, if you threw twenty million dollars at HGTV."

"So, not HGTV?"

She sighs. "I thought you were the one who understood. Yes, HGTV, but with Persian rugs."

"That's more of an interior designer's—"

"Make it happen," she snaps right before her voice breaks again. "Just, please?" She conjures the tissue back out of her pocket, waving it through the air like Scarlett O'Hara. "I'm counting on you." With one last sniff, she beckons to her entourage, and the trio sweeps from the room.

As soon as she's out of sight, Chester lets his head fall into his hands. The head engineer and design manager make a hasty exit. Sighing, I begin collecting the photos.

"Phenomenal work, Iza," Darcy growls, "I love how you've promised the impossible."

I open my mouth. A strangled noise escapes. I saved our asses. We would've lost the client if it weren't for me. I force my mouth closed, reminding myself that I know the real Darcy behind his cold exterior. It's a good thing I have *Pride and Prejudice*; otherwise, I might be a little worried about my seemingly foolproof plan.

Darcy swipes one of the photos off the table before I can grab it. It shows a rendering of a lofty, three-story library made of solid mahogany. "Fuck me," Darcy says under his breath.

His crassness makes me jump, but I brush it off. I know he'll get better the longer I get to know him. Besides, he did just tell me to fuck him, so I guess you could say things in the romance department are progressing as planned.

* * *

After a brief order for me to "Work on one of your other projects for now," Darcy sequesters himself in his office. Behind the glass walls, he pores over sheets of paper as though he's drafting sketches for the Empire State Building instead of some paranoid person's underground bomb shelter. If "disheveled artist" were a look, he has it going on. His jacket is discarded on a chair back, his shirt sleeves are rolled up, and his tie is pulled loose. It's working for him.

The day passes in a blur. I'm barely able to concentrate. When it comes down to it, getting Darcy to agree to date me is a more daunting task than I'd originally expected. Considering he hardly leaves his office, I don't have a chance to talk to him again, much less ask him out.

In the last hours of the day, I manage to lose myself in transferring a sketch of a back-burner project to the 3-D modeling software on my computer. I hardly notice when everyone begins collecting their things and filtering out of the office to go home.

Only when the murmurs of voices by the water cooler catch my attention do I look up.

Chester and Darcy stand there, talking low. Chester leans over the cooler, letting water trickle into a cone-shaped cup. "Kalyan told me about your little incident with Iza earlier."

Slumping in my chair, I hide my face behind my computer but continue listening intently.

"I'm not sure what you're referring to," comes Darcy's classically clipped response.

"Come on, Darce. I know you accused her of dating Kalyan. Do I sense jealousy?"

I smile. Seems a bit early for jealousy, but I'll take it. Maybe he's fallen for me hard and quick. He did the same with Elizabeth, so perhaps it's a character trait.

The scoff issuing from Darcy is more scornful than it really *ought* to be. "Please. She's tolerable, but the only thing holding my attention in this office is your Julia project."

"Come on," Chester teases him. "You can admit Iza's pretty enough to be distracting."

Chester's not a bad wingman. I should either report him to HR or send him a thank-you card.

"I'd rather jerk off with sandpaper," Darcy says.

My pen clatters to the floor. *What the hell?* Where's the classy gentleman from the story? This isn't right. This isn't right at all. This can't be Darcy. If it's Darcy, I can never love him, and if I can never love *Mr. Darcy*, how can I love anyone?

From under the bottom edge of my screen, I can see the legs of both men as they turn my way. *Crap*.

Scrambling, I collect my things and speed-walk for the elevator. When it doesn't show up in half a millisecond, I do the unthinkable and take the stairs.

Mr. Darcy is supposed to be an adorable, socially awkward, misunderstood teddy bear. Instead, he's a disgusting prick. Beckett must've given me a defective version. When I find him, I'll strangle him until he amends his mistake.

I imagine Beckett smiling with my hands around his neck.

My skin flushes hot all over.

Okay. So I'll *yell* at him until he amends his mistake.

CHAPTER NINE

I park my Honda in front of my apartment building, next to a flashy, classic car I've never seen before. Cherry-black and low to the ground, it looks like it's straight out of an old gangster movie. The paint gleams in the setting sun, glossy and slick.

I round the corner of the apartment building. Another long line of partygoers stretches out the front door and winds down the sidewalk. Lola stands outside, still in her khaki uniform, arms crossed.

"Why hasn't anyone complained?" I ask when I'm close enough.

Her brown eyes narrow to slits. "I tried. The landlady said Beckett is a model tenant and an angel, and shame on me for suggesting otherwise. He must've wished himself up a lease to make his occupation of the apartment legal."

I'm impressed with how Lola's taking the existence of magic. She seems to have totally accepted it.

"Plus"—Lola gestures at the line—"it's not like they're being noisy."

She's right. The line of people is quiet. Creepily quiet. They stand there like a row of robots, their mouths clamped shut.

I walk up to one, a guy in a punk rock T-shirt, and ask, "Is everything okay? Why isn't anyone talking?"

The guy frowns, looking me up and down. He whips out his cell phone and types something on it. When he's done, he holds it up for me to read: New rule. No talking or no entry. Sucks.

Beckett's certainly making good on his promise to keep it down. If only he made good on his wishes too. We push past the congestion of people at the entrance and fight for a path up the stairs.

"So, Darcy is a jerk," I say. "Maybe Mom's right and all men are shit."

"Are you sure?" Lola asks, elbowing a group of underage teenagers out of the way. "He's famous for terrible first impressions. Being arrogant and unkind is his trademark. Actually, he's pretty awful for a good chunk of the story."

"What he said goes beyond saying I'm tolerable, but not handsome enough to tempt him. But don't worry. I'm going to make sure Beckett fixes this." We approach his door.

"Warthogs eat anything." Lola's eyes gleam behind her wispy bangs. "Just thought you should know in case there's a body involved."

A bouncer stands in front of the apartment. I tell him my name, and he lets me past. He doesn't, however, let Lola by. She waves me on ahead.

Thundering music swells as I step through the doorway. I'm plunged into a world where the only light comes from a DJ's epileptic-seizure-inducing light show.

This time the party is in full swing. Furniture is pushed against the walls, transforming the living room into a dance floor. Bodies writhe together in a drunken haze, jostling me to and fro as I battle my way through.

The further I go, the more tightly packed the dancers are. Perfume, heavy, hot breath, and humming conversations assault my senses, disorienting me. A woman's pointy elbow slams into my arm, sending me sideways into a burly guy, who curses me colorfully. A hand flies against my temple. My hair snags in someone's sequined top. Someone touches my butt.

And then, the people around me go still. The crowd parts, and I look up through my hair. Beckett stands in the middle of the newly created circle. When he notices me, a smile splits his face, one of the real ones, crinkles and all, and his dimples crease his cheeks. "Didn't expect to see you here." He has to shout over the music. "Did you see my car? Neato, right?"

"I'm not here for your party, Bartholomew." I plow forward, catching his sleeve and dragging him to the back of the apartment. "Is there a place we can talk?"

The smile vanishes, and he nods, pulling me sideways into a bathroom. As he shuts the door, the music becomes bearable. Beckett looks me up and down. "You're a mess."

I straighten my wrinkled pantsuit. "It's been a day. One tends to get sort of rumpled when one's dream man turns out to be an insufferable jerk."

Beckett's already half-lidded eyes narrow even more. "In English, please. What are you talking about?"

"Don't act like you don't know you sent me the wrong guy. Or maybe you manipulated Mr. Darcy from a quiet man with a heart of gold into a vulgar, egotistical pig."

He frowns. "I gave you what you wanted."

I open my mouth.

"I can't lie to you."

"So you keep saying," I snap. "I'm not sure I believe it. Saying you can't lie is probably a lie in and of itself."

"Why do you try to start a fight with me every time we talk?"

"Because you're ruining everything."

He straightens, his tone rising a half step above his usual disinterest. "I'm helping you."

"Helping me?" I ask in disbelief. "Helping me by bursting into my life and causing all this chaos? Helping me by throwing your ragers all night? Helping me by ruining what might be my only chance at love because no real man is enough?" The fear rises inside me before I can quench it. "Or maybe I'm the problem. Maybe I'm trying too hard. Mom says I care too much about silly, unimportant things like relationships and plants and nail polish."

Beckett's eyes flick over my face. "Nothing you want, however small, is unimportant. I am trying to help you, even if you don't believe it." He lifts a hand and moves aside a lock of wild hair hanging over my cheek, the movement cautious, like I'm a stray animal who may run away in fright or bite his finger off. His knuckle grazes my temple as he clumsily tucks the hair behind my ear. His Adam's apple bobs. "Sorry. It was . . . distracting."

All I can do is stare.

He moves his hand away, leaving behind traces of cinnamon and firewood. "You're not too much, Iza."

"But I'm the common factor in all this failure." I bite my lip.

There's a moment of silence before he says abruptly, "I take it he wasn't everything you hoped for?"

At once, my mind is blank. "Who?"

"Darcy."

"Well, he said he'd rather . . . do something sort of intimate with sandpaper rather than with me, if that tells you anything."

Beckett steps back, making the gap between us seem insurmountable. "But you wished for him, knowing being a prick is one of his character traits? I thought you didn't like unscrupulous men."

The bathroom door crashes open, and I have to dodge to avoid getting clobbered. Lola stands outside, breathing hard. "I had to tell your bouncer I'd sic the tigers on him if he wouldn't let me in." She pants. "Anyway, I was listening in on your conversation, and I'm pleased to report it sounds like your romance is right on track, Iza."

"It is?" I ask.

"Is it?" Beckett leans against the sink.

Lola wedges her way between Beckett and me, to close the bathroom door. "Yep. I've watched the movie. I know how this goes. Darcy has no filter, which makes him seem cruel. Like, the first thing Darcy does is he insults Elizabeth by not dancing with her before commenting on her appearance to his friend. Well, if you're Elizabeth in this scenario, the sandpaper thing is the twenty-first-century version of that insult."

I cross my arms. "I don't know. The twenty-first-century insult seems way harsher than the one in the book."

"If you compare Elizabeth's feelings to yours, she was probably as pissed as you are. To *be* insulting nowadays, this Darcy had to step it up a notch because of inflation."

"Inflation?"

"Sure. Insult inflation," Lola says, as though insult inflation is a real thing we should already know about. "Like, with the deflation of decorum and with the birth of *South Park*, insults don't hit the same as they used to. What used to be unimaginable back then is now a joke."

"That sort of makes sense." I nod. "In the book, Darcy is considered disagreeable. Being blunt isn't enough to be considered unlikable in today's society. Nowadays, he has to be crass to reach the same level of unpleasant and insulting. So there's still hope. I just have to keep harassing Darcy like Elizabeth did when she invited herself over to Bingley's house after Jane caught a mild cold."

"Right," Lola says. "Remember when Caroline and Elizabeth were walking around the room, and Darcy said it was so their figures could be admired? They were shocked by it. In the day, that was probably the equivalent of saying, 'Dat ass though.'"

"I'm trying really hard to follow all this." Beckett presses his fingers to the sides of his head. "I'm distracted about the ass thing, but if I'm understanding, Lola needs to catch a cold, and you need to barge into Darcy's house, and this will spark love?"

Lola and I exchange glances. I smile. "Pretty much, yeah."

Pride and Prejudice is basically the handbook to Darcy's heart. I'll create my own epic love story.

* * *

The next morning, I keep sneaking peeks at Darcy's office. Earlier, when I asked for his address from HR, under the guise that I needed to mail him something, they told me, "Absolutely not." If only I could get a hold of it, I could create a reasonable explanation for why I have to show up randomly on his doorstep. Which sounds a bit stalker-ish, yes, but I have to reenact the book if I want a love story like Elizabeth's.

There is something else to attend to, and that's the matter of a snarky comeback for Darcy's rude little remark. As the resident embodiment of Elizabeth Bennett, I need to live up to her reputation for always having a retort.

I text Lola.

Me: Do you think I could commission a florist to deliver a bouquet of roses made of sandpaper to Mr. Darcy's office?

After I spend a few minutes clicking away at my computer, her reply chimes in.

Lola: OMG please do that.

If there's such a thing as insult inflation, retaliation inflation must exist too. While Elizabeth's comments might've been carefully crafted and clever to avoid breaching social decorum, because of retaliation inflation, I figure I can get away with a much more blatant approach.

A few secretive calls on company time later tell me the skills of local florists pertain only to vegetation. Bouquets made from woodworking items are a no-go. I break the bad news to Lola and go back to work, when my phone chimes again. It's a text, but not from Lola or any other contact in my phone.

Unknown: Heard about your little florist problem. Know who could help with that? Hint: Me. 😉

Lola, you meddling sneak, I think. Then, another text comes in as I finish reading the first.

Unknown: It's me, Beckett, BTW. Sorry. Should've made that clear.

Unknown: Shit, now I've trashed the cool, sexy thing I was going for.

Me: I'm not going to use my second wish on a bouquet of sandpaper flowers.

Beckett: But it would be hilarious. ☹
Me: No.
Beckett: ☹ ☹ ☹

The rumble of plastic wheels over the hard floor causes me to look up. Sitting in his chair, Kalyan slides himself across the office, kicking off the floor and pushing off desks. Many eyes follow his journey before their owners realize it's Kalyan being Kalyan, and they don't actually care.

As he sidles up to my desk, he asks, a little out of breath, "Got lunch plans?"

What does this guy want from me? My gaze shifts to my computer screen. "I was thinking about having work for lunch. I have to finish reviewing the dimensions of these renderings for"—I choke—"Darcy." Plus, I haven't exactly been a dedicated and focused employee all morning.

"You can't let me go alone." Kalyan leans over my desk and lowers his voice conspiratorially. "Didn't you hear we're dating now?"

I forgot I need to fix those pictures he swapped out. "Didn't you get my note?" I counter.

He rolls his eyes. "Oh yes. 'You'll pay for this.' I'm trembling. Anyway, word around the office is you're searching for Darcy's address. Weird. However, I could enable your obsession. But not here." He looks over his shoulder. "Too many ears to overhear us."

If he has the address, he could just email it to me. But of course, he has to turn it into one of his conniving little games. I lean in, my nose filling with the sharp odor of his body spray. "You know his address?"

"Charmed it out of HR. I'm an excellent wooer."

"Wooer?"

"One who woos."

I darken my computer screen. "Fine. Lunch. But only if you tell me the address."

He winks. "See? I can be very persuasive."

"It's less to do with your terrible wooing abilities and more to do with necessity," I assure him.

* * *

We eat at a round table positioned on the sidewalk outside a diner. A cheerful red and white striped umbrella casts shade over us, shielding us from the sun, but not the humidity.

I shift my gaze this way and that, fervently hoping none of our coworkers will spot us. The last thing I need is for the rumor that Kalyan and I are dating to catch on.

We order—a Reuben for me and a fried chicken sandwich for him.

"What happened to your juice cleanse?" I ask.

He blinks. "What do you mean? I'm still on it."

"You do know a juice cleanse isn't just adding copious amounts of apple juice to your existing diet, right?"

His eyebrow twitches. "Um. Yeah. Of course."

I don't press the issue. Getting him all wound up by arguing won't help my cause. "So, how about that address?"

"Geez, let me eat my lunch before you use me, at least."

I open my mouth to respond, but an all-too-familiar voice interrupts. "Eliza, darling? Is that you?"

I whirl about in my seat. My mother stands there, a massive purse dangling from her elbow and her bedazzled sunglasses shooting refracted light into my eyeballs. I swallow and stand. "Hey, Mom."

She hurries forward, her heels giving her a stilted gait. Pulling me in, she plants a loud air-kiss near my ear. I wince as my eardrum rings in protest.

"And who might this be?" She stands there, head tilted, fidgeting with her French-tipped nails, somewhere between curiosity and suspicion.

"My coworker, Kalyan. Kalyan"—I gesture wearily at Mom—"this is my mother."

He stands as well. Something about her presence seems to demand that response from people. Whereas I always fight the urge to bow before her, Kalyan actually does it, dipping into a little bend that would make the most gracious of courtiers proud. I pinch the bridge of my nose, but Mom bursts into a glaring smile. Her nails click together with excitement, like she can barely contain herself.

"How nice to meet you." She sweeps a third chair from a very occupied table without asking and, with a flourish, positions it in front of ours. Sinking into it, she clasps her hands before her.

I offer Kalyan an apologetic look as we sit back down. He reciprocates with a look of his own that says, *"I'm giving you so much shit for this later."*

Mom beckons a server over with the air of an impatient empress and orders lemon water and a salad. Then she plants her sunglasses on her head and contemplates us both. Her olive eyeshadow brings out her eyes, and her green irises look like laser beams as they drill into us. "So, is this the first of your conquests, Iza?"

I hasten to reply. "Oh, we're not—"

Kalyan's foot connects with my shin. He raises one eyebrow and smirks. The smirk clearly reads, *"Let me handle this, or lose the address and your only chance at love forever. Contradict me, and you might as well start imagining dying alone."* Amazing how much those eyebrows can convey.

I scowl.

Kalyan's smirk transitions into what he probably thinks is a winning smile but closely resembles the Cheshire Cat's. "It's all very new, ma'am. We're still talking. Taking it slow."

My jaw clenches as Mom nods along, almost as if . . . as if she approves. "It's nice Iza found someone with similar career goals. And how convenient you work at the same office. Why, neither of you have to set apart time for each other when you already spend time together all day at work."

As if, even if Kalyan and I were together, staring at each other over building renderings would be enough to constitute quality relationship building. But Kalyan's nodding sagely as he fights back a smile. "Indeed. What an excellent observation, Ms. K."

"Please," Mom says, "call me Lauren."

Kalyan places a hand over his heart, and my teeth grind harder. "How kind," he says. "But I'm not sure I feel right about such informality toward a highly respectable woman such as yourself."

"And I just threw up in my mouth a little bit," I comment.

Kalyan's heel presses over my toe, and Mom shoots me a glare. "Be kind, Eliza. It's not often I come across well-mannered men. Goodness knows, you've never brought one home."

This declaration causes Kalyan to grin so widely I wonder if his face might crack open.

When our food comes, my appetite's uncharacteristically lacking. Mom stays with us for the whole lunch hour and even follows us all the way back to the office. As Kalyan goes inside, I linger by the door.

"What's gotten into you?" I ask as soon as he's out of sight.

"What do you mean?" She checks her nails.

"Why are you being . . . supportive?"

Sighing, she looks up. "I saw how upset you were the other night when I told you this plan of yours is unwise, so I thought I'd give it a chance."

My mouth falls open. Warmth blooms in my chest.

"I can help you with your screening process."

I snap my mouth shut. So that's why she's interested. She wants to be here to find the flaws in my relationships that will prove my plan won't work. The warmth in my chest turns to fire. "Absolutely not."

"This one doesn't seem so bad," she goes on. "What does your sixth sense say about him? Polite? Humble?"

Her pretending to buy into my gut instinct about people feels like a mockery, like she's throwing it in my face to show me how silly it is.

"He'll do for a little while, perhaps," she continues. "You could take him to a few events before you move on—weddings and the like."

"I'm not looking for a guy to parade around to make myself look good," I grit out. "Besides, Kalyan and I aren't even dating."

She smiles like she's five, and I told her she could have ice cream for dinner. "Oh thank god."

"Unbelievable." I throw open the front door and stalk inside.

The worst part about the whole meeting is Kalyan didn't have a chance to tell me the address. At least he was decent enough not to reveal my cringy stalker tendencies to my mother. She'd come unglued if she knew how far I'm willing to go to make things work with Darcy.

I plop into my desk chair with a huff. Every grinning portrait of Kalyan surrounding me intensifies my boiling insides. Each set of eyes watches me, and each smile twists into a sneer.

Something sitting on my keyboard catches my eye. I roll forward and examine it more closely. It's an origami rosebud, exquisitely crafted in delicate folds of gray and black paper. Underneath it, a corner of cream-colored stationery with writing on it sticks out. When I lift the rose, I realize it isn't made of normal paper, as I'd assumed, but fine, high-grit sandpaper. My breath hitches. I read the note, which is written in familiar, looping cursive.

This one's on me. XO —Beckett

I spin around and look up. Inside the glass walls of Darcy's office, I glimpse a massive bouquet of sandpaper roses sitting on his desk. Each flower is a different shade: browns, blacks, tans, and grays. I twirl the rosebud in my fingers, admiring each tiny detail.

A door slams and I snap my head back up. Darcy stands outside his office, looming over us all. The glass walls still thrum with the vibration of his slammed door. Placing his hands on his hips, he glowers downward, searching the room until his eyes land on me, and his frown deepens.

Holding his gaze, I smile, even though my heart pounds, and wave with a little flutter of fingers.

Face turning bright red, he whirls, flings open his door, and retreats inside.

A throat clears behind me, and I pivot. Kalyan's there. He hands me a sticky note. Taking it, I read the scrawled address. Maybe it's not such a bad day after all.

I pull out my phone and send a text.

Me: Thank you, Beckett.

Beckett: I knew you were only pretending not to know my name.

CHAPTER TEN

I'm unlocking my apartment door after work when I hear a sound behind me. Looking over my shoulder, I see Beckett leaning against his doorframe.

"What's up?" His dimples threaten to make an appearance around the smile he's trying (and failing) to hold back.

"Hi," I say, suddenly awkward. Guilt ravages my insides. The last time I saw him, I accused him of sending me the wrong Darcy. A classic Karen move. I toe the carpet. "Look, I'm sorry. For when I accused you of messing with the Darcy wish."

Beckett breaks into one of his crinkle smiles. "No worries. He's a real dick, though, huh?" He asks the question with relish. "Did you see I sent over lotion with the flowers? And a note that said, 'Have fun!' with a little winky face?"

Beckett looks so *happy* that an irrational urge to close the distance between us and fling my arms around him takes hold of me.

But I don't. That would be ridiculous. So I smile and say, "I appreciate it. And again, I really am sorry." I open my door.

"Wait."

I pause with my door half open.

He grimaces. "Are you aware your *zamioculcas zamiifolia* has root rot?"

"Excuse me?" I gasp because now he's the one accusing *me* of being a serial killer. "My ZZ plant does *not* have root rot."

"It absolutely does. I noticed it the night we met. I can't stop thinking about it. Knowing it's in there dying is eating me up inside. I'm actually begging you to help the poor thing."

I'm stunned into silence. Beckett paid attention to my collection. Not only that, but he's now accusing me of the most heinous of plant crimes. "You don't know what you're talking about."

"That's called denial. We both know what yellowing leaves, mushy stems, and soggy soil add up to." He shakes his head sadly. "For shame, Iza. For shame."

Clutching my metaphorical pearls, I race into my apartment. My stomach plummets as I skid to a stop before the plant in question. It is indeed dying. The plant usually requires so little care that I hadn't noticed. *"No,"* I whisper. "I'm too late."

I fall to my knees in anguish.

"We can resuscitate it. There's still time," Beckett calls from my doorway.

Shaking my head, I gaze at the gruesome scene before me. "This is all my fault."

Closing the front door, Beckett crosses to me. "It's overwatered. That just means you cared for it a little too hard, that's all."

I tried too hard, and everything fell apart. It's the story of my damn life. It's been a long day, and a single tired, frustrated tear slides down my cheek. Beckett totally notices but has the decency to pretend that he doesn't. From his perspective, I look like I'm crying over a plant. He must really think I'm pathetic.

Reaching over me, Beckett scoops up the plant. His face is set with the sort of determination I've only witnessed from hot doctors on *Grey's Anatomy* who are going through something deeply personal that's affecting their professional life and giving them an unhealthy savior complex. "There will be no lives lost today."

With the speed of an EMT, he whisks the plant to the kitchen table. Shoving aside the salt and pepper shaker, he lays the plant on its side.

I gape, my tear still damp on my cheek.

Beckett wiggles the plant free of its pot, soil spilling onto the table. "Scalpel." He holds his hand out, palm up, like he expects me to hand him a surgical instrument.

"I don't need you to rescue me."

"Needing help doesn't make you weak. It means you're human." He takes a step back. "I'm not here to rescue you. I'm here to help you if you ask for it."

I'm floored. For someone who's supposedly selfish, Beckett's been paying attention to someone outside of himself. He's gotten to know how I think and operate, and he's putting real effort into learning how to interact with me.

Asking for help has never been an option before. My whole life, there has been an expectation that I will succeed on my own. In the eyes of society, each time a woman asks for help, we go down a rung on the ladder to the top.

I hesitate, my feet stuck to the floor. This isn't a professional setting. This is my own home, and it should be okay to relinquish a bit of control. It's not like Beckett is going to write an email to my boss that says: *"News flash, Iza does not have her shit together."*

I don't need his help, but I think I want it. With a nod, I go and fetch the sterile scissors I reserve for pruning plants. Returning, I place the tool into his awaiting hand. With sure, adept fingers,

Beckett loosens the plant from the soil and begins snipping away the blackened roots. His movements are capable, passionate.

Unbidden, my mind wonders what else those deft fingers are capable of. My face goes hot.

"To be honest," says Beckett, "I've been dying to get my hands in your plants."

My brain, still firmly lodged in the gutter, takes the liberty of ignoring the "L" in the word *plants*, translating his harmless statement into a euphemism. Heat consumes my entire body now.

"I wanted to ask if you'd let me water your collection, but I didn't figure you'd let me come anywhere near it." He shoots me a gently teasing wink. "Looks like you keep your soil plenty wet without my help, though."

It must be the literal dirt everywhere that's making everything he says sound figuratively dirty. "Wha-huh?" is the brilliant word I come up with when I finally find my voice. "You like plants?"

"Oh yeah. I like the thought of being a little part of caring for something that will live on after I'm gone."

I sink into one of the kitchen chairs and watch him work. Surprisingly, I'm not itching to take over. I trust him with this one small thing. It feels like the beginning of something, like maybe, one day, I could trust him with more. It's nice. It's really nice to sit here and know that I could take care of the problem, but I don't have to.

"Why were you crying?" Beckett asks without looking up from the mushy root ball.

Quickly, I swipe at my face to find the tear already dry. For a moment, I debate telling him that it's none of his business, but he's here, and the concern he has for my plant almost feels like concern for . . . me.

"You know how people always say they don't want to turn into their mothers?" When Beckett nods, I continue. "Well, I *really* don't want to turn into mine. She's blunt and stubborn and doesn't care about anyone else's opinions and—well, sometimes I find myself doing the exact same things. Not that I'm trying to make excuses for myself, I just—" I let out a long breath. "All my compassion is stuffed inside me because my whole life I've been told to never let it out. I desperately want to have a different life than Mom has, so I overcompensate. I force my feelings out and try to build something from nothing."

"Creating something from nothing is impossible," Beckett says, still snipping away at the plant.

"I know." Seeing that he's nearly finished dissecting away the rotten roots, I walk to a cabinet and find a bag of fresh potting soil. I set it on the table next to him. "But I'll keep trying anyway because the alternative is turning into her."

Beckett sets the scissors aside and contemplates me. "Believe me, I get it. Patterns are hard to break." Placing the plant into the pot, he begins pouring fresh soil around its now meager root system. "But if you don't want to be like your mother, then why do you care what she thinks?" He waits for my response.

I don't have one.

Beckett hands me my plant. It looks feeble and sad now, but I know it's stronger than it was before. I sort of feel like that. Torn down, but like maybe I'll come out okay in the end. "Thank you," I say, but those two words hold more than gratitude for tending to my plant, because I think, in a way, my neglected heart has been tended to as well.

CHAPTER ELEVEN

We wait until Saturday to execute our plan. Beckett's question lingers in my head, but I push it aside. The whole point of any of this—the dating websites, the wish—it's all been about finding someone to build a life with.

For me.

Not just for Mom.

At work, Darcy started ignoring my existence entirely, aside from instances where projects demand our interaction. I tell myself this is due to his shy nature—he's embarrassed for being caught saying something he probably didn't even mean. Still, his coldness makes me nervous, especially because Lola and I are currently sitting in my Honda outside his house.

The weather conditions are perfect, the sky overcast and drizzling cool rain. The sun hangs low in the sky, pale light peeking through heavy clouds. The stars are aligned, and Darcy will have no choice but to fall for me.

Darcy's house is certainly expensive enough—an old Victorian mansion in the heart of St. Louis, on a large lot—but it's rather . . . yellow. Far from Pemberley, that's for sure. "Well, it's not quite what I expected." I read the Post-it Note Kalyan pilfered from HR, making sure we're at the right house. We are.

Lola eyes the tulips lining the cobblestone path to the porch. "You sure he's single? I bet we're going to knock, and Elizabeth herself will fling open the door, wiping her hands on a dish towel, with a snot-nosed kid clinging to her apron strings."

"Chester talked to him about me like he's available," I remind her. I push up my shirt sleeve and read the notes I scrawled onto my arm. There are a few key points this encounter must cover to move my love story forward.

1. Tell him you're fond of walking.
2. Tell him you like to read.
3. Get him to say his good opinion once lost is lost forever.

The first one's a lie. The last one is partially for my own wish fulfillment (no pun intended), and also because it seems like an important emotional connection for Darcy and me to make.

"This seems like a bad idea." Lola chews her lip.

"It'll be fine. Remember your story?"

She rolls her eyes. "Sure. My car broke down, and I caught life-threatening pneumonia while walking for help."

"Great, but skip the melodrama. You don't feel well, and your phone died. You just need to make a call. That's when you'll call me, and I'll show up, the ever-loyal and wonderful heroine, to save you."

Lola looks to the heavens. "Never thought I'd be playing wingman so my roommate could hook up with Mr. Darcy."

"Go get 'em, champ." I grin, unlocking the car doors.

"I'll have you know when I played the lion in *The Wizard of Oz* in middle school, my own father said his favorite part was the ending." When I don't say anything, she adds, "Not because of the happily ever after, Iza. He liked the ending because it was finally over."

"I cherish you and appreciate your effort?" I try.

With a heavy sigh, Lola swings herself out of the car and trudges up the path to Darcy's door. Slumping lower in my seat, I watch as she hunches her shoulders against the rain and shoves her hands in her jacket pockets. I owe her big time.

After knocking, she turns and gives me a dirty look, turning back as the door opens. Darcy fills the doorframe. He wears a green sweater vest and a small pair of reading glasses, further strengthening his hot professor aesthetic. From inside the car, I can't tell what Lola is saying, only that she's doing a lot of saying, whereas Darcy's doing very *little* saying. In fact, he's doing . . . none. He watches her impassively as her arm movements become more and more emphatic. At one point, she flings a dramatic hand over her brow, black-and-white-romance-movie style.

Darcy peers around her, looking both ways, as though suspicious something's up. Sucking in a sharp breath, I slip down farther into my seat. By the time I risk another peek out the window, Lola and Darcy have vanished, presumably inside. So far, so good.

As the minutes pass and still no call from Lola, I get nervous. I drum my fingers over my phone screen, the taps of my nails echoing the rain pattering against my windshield. When my phone finally buzzes on my leg, I jump, nearly clobbering my head on the roof of my car.

"Hello?" I answer.

"Hi!" Lola's voice holds a theatrical pitch that's borderline ridiculous. "My *car* broke down, and my *phone* died. Could you come *rescue* me? A *very* nice man let me use his cell. I'll send you the address."

I lower my voice so Darcy won't be able to hear through the speaker. "Does he suspect?"

"No, he *doesn't* have a phone charger," Lola says in the same exaggerated voice.

Okay. No more questions. It's best to keep the amount Lola has to talk to a minimum. "I'll be there in a few minutes," I say.

She thanks me, pouring on way more praise for my selfless heroism than is strictly necessary. She slathers it on thick, going so far as to say my bravery rivals Joan of Arc's because of my willingness to go out in such a downpour.

The clouds outside part, the setting sun streaming down in ethereal, heavenly rays to illuminate the wet pavement. Darcy's tulips glitter from the raindrops dripping down their petals, and the entire yard and house are splashed in a multitude of golden hues.

I hang up on Lola and groan. He'll see right through us.

I wait an excruciating fifteen minutes before allowing myself to exit the car and walk to Darcy's door. He has a pristine porch swing that looks like it's never been used, and his welcome mat sports zero cute inscriptions. Not even the word *Welcome*. Just a black rubber mat.

I ring the altogether-too-cheerful-sounding doorbell. Nerves flutter through me, and I remember my mother telling me what I lack is nerve. Clearly, I don't lack nerve at all, for I have multitudes of nerves twisting and tingling in every part of my body. Before I have time to squash them down, the door opens, and there's Darcy, up close and painfully cute in his little Mr. Rogers sweater vest. It becomes apparent, as he looks me up and down with disdain, that he does not want to be my neighbor, much less my soulmate.

"Kiches," he says. "What are you doing here?"

I widen my eyes and raise my brows in an expression I hope conveys pure, genuine shock. "Darcy?" I gasp, all theatrical-like. But I might've taken it a bit too far because my quick inhale created the urge to dissolve into a coughing fit. As I resist, pressure mounts behind my eyeballs, threatening to pop them free of my head. "What are *you* doing here?" I ask, my voice strangled.

His eye twitches. "This is my home, Iza."

I flutter my hand over my heart and immediately regret it when his eyes lock onto the movement. Maybe my acting skills are worse than Lola's. "I had no idea," I say.

Darcy's eyes narrow, his face hardening. This is far from the lovestruck stares Colin Firth had in the movie. My Darcy looks strained and pissy.

I straighten, trying to regain some of my composure. "I got a call," I say brusquely. "My roommate, Lola, she had some car troubles?"

Darcy's attention moves beyond me to the street. "Where's *your* car, Iza?"

I lift my chin. "I walked."

His lips part. "You *walked*?"

I nod and lean back against a porch post in what I hope is a vaguely seductive manner. Except the post is sort of far away. I grope behind myself blindly before stumbling and finally falling into it. *Shit.*

"So you came without a car to rescue your friend, who is now also without a car?"

When he puts it that way, my nonexistent walking hobby seems less sexy and more stupid. I push off the post and shuffle back to stand in front of him. "I parked around the block," I say, trying to salvage the situation. "When the sun came out, I couldn't resist enjoying the nice weather."

"While your friend sat sick and alone in a stranger's house?"

My stomach plummets. This flighty, ditzy image I must be conveying is not how I wanted to come across to Mr. Darcy. "I like books," I blurt. Oh god. This is going downhill fast.

Darcy crosses his arms.

When Lola pops up over Darcy's shoulder, I can practically hear angels singing. "Hey, Iza," she says, letting out a weak cough into her fist. "You came. I'm forever indebted to you. I fear I have taken ill. The weather, you see."

If possible, the sun shines brighter.

When Darcy turns his head to look at Lola, I chop my hand in front of my neck in frantic *Cut! Cut!* motions. She catches on and snaps her mouth shut.

"Let's go home, Lola." I step forward, reaching around Darcy to grab her hand. Time to abort the mission. "We don't want to inconvenience Darcy any more."

"You know him?" she asks, feigning confusion as I pull her out onto the porch. "What a strange coincidence. Almost like you two were meant to meet up."

"Coworker," I say, smiling tightly as I pull her along. "Thanks so much, Darcy. I'll see you Monday." As I reach for the porch railing, a scribble of writing peeks out from my sleeve.

I have one more point to hit.

I pause. "Terribly sorry for all this. I know your good opinion once lost is lost forever."

He gives me a weird look. "What on earth are you talking about?"

A Lincoln glides to a stop out in the street, and I freeze. Beside me, Lola's breath catches. "Is that . . ." she begins.

The darkly-tinted window rolls down, exposing my mother's face. "Eliza?" she calls, waving out her window, rows of heavy gold jewelry clanking around her wrist. "Is that you, darling?"

I shield my face as Lola says, "Hi, Lauren."

I glare at her, and she cringes in apology.

"Did you plan a family reunion in my yard and neglect to mention it to me?" Darcy leans against the doorframe.

"What are you doing in this neighborhood?" Mom can't let it go.

"What are *you* doing here?" I counter weakly. (This response hasn't worked well for me lately.)

"I was dropping some products off to a client who lives on this street and saw your car." She points at my Honda.

I wince, heat flooding my body. As I face Darcy, my insides shrivel.

His gaze shifts slowly between the three of us. "I thought you parked around the block. What's going on?"

"Is this another one of your gentleman colleagues?" Mom bellows, oblivious to the awkward moment. "I must say, I'm so glad you're exploring workplace options, Eliza. Practical to keep relations in-house. I'd love to meet him. Perhaps we should plan another outing?"

If only Jane Austen had written in her book that, after visiting Jane at Bingley's house, the earth opened up and swallowed Elizabeth. Then perhaps I could be spared this misery.

CHAPTER TWELVE

This is not how I pictured introducing my mother to Darcy. I wanted to do it after we'd already been dating for several months. We'd make dinner and invite her over, and I'd say, *"This is Mr. Darcy."* And she'd say, *"Like the book?"* And I'd say, *"In every way."* Then, as the night went on, she'd say, *"Wow, he really is like Mr. Darcy from the book. You were right! You can have love without it destroying your life! I'm so proud of you, Eliza!"* Then, she'd probably fall to her knees, begging for my forgiveness.

"I was pondering our earlier conversations, and I think you have daddy issues," Mom's voice announces, inches from my ear.

"Gah!" I jump and whirl around. She's right behind me as though, in the space of a blink, she bent over backward and scuttled across the lawn like some kind of horror movie monster.

"I listened to a podcast the other day," Mom goes on, "and it enlightened me to the trauma associated with an absent father." Blaming everything on the father I don't have is Mom's go-to move. "I think you subconsciously seek out destructive relationships because you're trying to fill a void by replicating the only male relationship you've ever known—right down to its slow, agonizing demise. So what's the verdict? Are you attracted to this man because you think your relationship will end as catastrophically as a buggy crash?"

Oh. My. God. I want to melt. "I'm not in a relationship with Darcy," I say through gritted teeth. "And my father wasn't absent. He didn't exist at all. A sperm donor is not a father. The fertility clinic had more to do with my conception than he did. Learning about the crash was just . . . information. There's no relationship to replicate."

Lola inches away. Darcy's repulsion has redoubled. He looks around as though trying to find the camera crews because we've obviously decided to film an episode of *Dr. Phil* right here on his porch.

I sigh. If this is how Mom meets Darcy, I might as well make the best of it. "Darcy, this is my mother, Lauren. Mom, this is Mr. Darcy," and then because I'm somehow holding onto a shred of hope that I can salvage this, I add, "like the book."

"What book?" Mom asks, adding insult to injury.

"Come on, Mom," I say miserably. "Don't pretend you don't remember it. Not today. You know—*Pride and Prejudice*. We watched the movie adaptation. It's our favorite book."

She shakes her head, and that's worse than everything else.

A lump rises in my throat. "We watched it together, and we laughed. I bought like a hundred copies, and you pretended not to see them, but I know you did. I know you saw them."

Mom looks dazed. "I don't know a book with that title."

Her words stab me in the heart. Of everything she's ever done, she's never gaslit me. I turn to Darcy. "You've heard of it, haven't you? Everyone has. People probably gave you a hard time about it your whole life, since your name is *Mr. Darcy*."

"I beg your pardon?" Darcy crosses his arms. "I've never heard of a book with a character whose name I share."

"Jane Austen?" Lola offers.

"Never heard of her," he says, and Mom shakes her head in agreement.

Every nerve in my body goes numb.

Impending doom sinks in. What if—what if something went wrong with the wish?

But no. There has to be a reasonable explanation for this. It's not that odd Darcy doesn't know who Jane Austen is. Maybe he's not much of a reader. Maybe he's never seen a book. He could be allergic to paper . . . or something.

Okay maybe not. But maybe he's lived a secluded life and hasn't heard of her. A very secluded life. To have never heard of Jane Austen, he probably grew up in a cave and was raised by woodland creatures . . . or something.

I whip out my phone, fingers fumbling as I frantically type *Jane Austen* into the search bar.

Nothing comes up. Well, there's a LinkedIn profile for a sales executive who happens to be named Jane Austen, but otherwise, there are no Wikipedia articles, no book covers, no movie adaptations, nothing.

Oh shit.

Pride and Prejudice doesn't exist. Neither does Jane Austen.

Everyone else thinks Darcy's been at work for three months. It's almost like I'm the newcomer in this strange reality.

The first time I met Beckett and asked about world peace, he said he'd have to send me to a universe where world peace exists to make my wish come true. Maybe that's what happened. I could have been shipped to a parallel universe—one where Darcy is real, and Jane Austen never existed to make him fictional.

But I have my copy of the book. This detail sends hope springing into my chest; I can't have the book if it doesn't exist in this world.

Or maybe I can.

A fuzzy memory resurfaces of me clutching the book to my chest as I made my wish. Maybe I brought it with me, and now it's the only copy in existence.

But if we are in a parallel universe, what happened to the other *me*? Someone must have been here in my stead before I came along and replaced her.

Heart bumping in my ears as loud as a bassline from one of Beckett's parties, I search my memories from the night I made the wish. They're as deep as Atlantis in the sea of alcohol that drowned them out. Had I verified my wish wouldn't land me away from my world? Had it even come up?

My stomach bottoms out. No. I hadn't asked. It hadn't come up. And Beckett certainly hadn't volunteered the information. In a hasty burst of resolve, I'd gone and wished myself away from my home universe. *Way to go, Iza.*

My mom isn't my mom.

My house isn't my home.

This *world* isn't my world.

Beckett is the same person; that's a given. What about Lola? She was part of the wish and knows Darcy being here is weird. Surely she's the real Lola, and she got dragged here too.

Something around my heart constricts. What about Waffles? Is he part of the wish, or is he a stranger?

At least it's a small relief to know Mom didn't lie when she said she couldn't remember watching *Pride and Prejudice.* That moment never happened in this reality because the book doesn't exist here.

I let out a shuddering breath. It's okay. Everything will be okay. I can ask Beckett if what I fear is true. If it is, I can always wish myself back, then swear off wishing forever like I meant to from the beginning.

Lola's phone rings. She whips it out, shoulders relaxing as she lets out a sigh. "Thank God you called," she says not so subtly. "Analise needs assistance giving birth? Good. Oh, not good for Analise. No. I mean, just good you called. So good. So, so good." Grimacing, she darkens her phone. "Sorry, antelope giving birth at work."

"I thought your phone was dead," Darcy says.

"That's my cue," I say, backing away. "Looks like we have an emergency antelope situation. We'd best be off."

"How about Applebee's?" Mom asks. "I can make a reservation."

"Sorry, Mom. We've got to go." I pull her and Lola off the porch, calling over my shoulder, "Thank you again, Darcy, for your help with Lola."

Lola hurries ahead to my car as Mom climbs back into her Lincoln. I try to move past, but Mom hangs out of the window to whisper loudly, "So what do your Spidey senses think about this one?"

"Are you stalking me?" I hiss, beginning to walk.

"I was merely curious." She widens her eyes as she shifts into drive to creep down the street alongside us. "After how well we worked together on the last one, I thought it might be advantageous to—what is it the kids say?—*tag team* this one as well?"

I might actually cry. "How did you find me?"

She looks away.

"How?" I grit my teeth.

Her brakes squeal, and she comes to a stop. "I've had a tracking app downloaded on your phone for years."

"Oh my *god*, Mom." When I risk a glance over my shoulder, Darcy's foot slips inside his house as the door swings shut.

I turn back to Mom. "You're ruining everything. This guy might be my last chance for love, and you had to show up here and make me look more desperate than I already did."

"Yes. You're twenty-six. Practically an old maid." She shoots a wry look to the side as though making eye contact with an invisible camera, to share a joke with a nonexistent audience at my expense.

"It's not about running out of time. I'm buckling down to figure out, once and for all, if I can have love or not. If the answer is no, then I can get on with my life instead of prolonging a futile endeavor."

"Iza, all this speed-dating is going to do is exacerbate your suffering. Giving up is the smart move. If you would only listen, you'd see that I'm helping you—"

I shake my head and stalk the rest of the way to my car. Diving inside, I slam the door over the noise of my mother, who's still rambling on, pretending to be supportive as she sabotages me.

Lola slips into the passenger seat.

"Do you need a ride to the zoo?" I ask.

"I'm getting an Uber," she says, tapping on her phone.

I let out a long breath. "Lola, we're in a parallel universe."

Lola watches me as though suspecting I'm a bit unhinged. "Are you sure? I feel like me, not a parallel-universe me."

"I think you're the original you. I think you got dragged along with the wish too, since you were a part of creating it."

She falls back into her seat, chewing her lip. "Should I let the warthogs know they'll be dining on Beckett tonight? Oh gosh, I hope the warthogs still like me in this universe. I've made such progress earning Sir Oinksalot's trust."

"How are you so casual about this?" I glance out the window, searching for her Uber. It's nearly dark now, made darker by the reforming rain clouds.

"Because I know you'll fix it." There's no passive aggressiveness in her tone. She says it like it's a fact.

If only I had her confidence. "I'm sorry. I'll get us back. I owe you one. I owe you a lot of ones between the Darcy thing and the parallel-universe fiasco. Is there any way I can make it up to you? Do you want a wish?"

"I think I'll stick to living a catastrophic mistake-filled life vicariously through you, thanks." Her Uber pulls up beside us, and she opens her door. "But stealing a person from their home universe does warrant some sort of compensation, starting with two months of bathroom cleaning duty."

With a cackle, she slams the door and ducks into the Uber. As the car whooshes away, the skies open up, and a downpour cascades from the heavens. I flip on my windshield wipers, and the rubber blades squeak rhythmically against the glass. Turning on a country radio station, I pull back out onto the road and point my car toward home.

Starting a relationship with someone who's objectively one of the greatest men in romantic literature shouldn't have gone so poorly. I'm going to be alone forever. I should adopt more cats.

I'm maybe five minutes away from the apartments when a violent vibration in my steering wheel makes me choke over the lyrics I've been mumbling. I slow down, the brake pedal pulsating against my foot. My car knowledge is limited, to say the least, but even I know something is seriously wrong. Before I can pull over and stop, there's a loud *bang* and then a jolting *wup wup wup.*

I barely manage to turn off the road as the car coasts to a stop. With shaking fingers, I roll down the window. Rain pelts my face, plastering wispy hairs to my brow. I blink moisture away and crane my neck. My rear tire is squashed uselessly against the pavement. Great. I shouldn't have ignored the guy at the shop where I got my oil changed. He'd told me I needed new tires, but I'd thought he was trying to get one over on me.

Pulling my head back into the car, I go to call for help, but my phone screen won't light up. I try again, holding the "On" button, but nothing.

"No." I let out a soft puff of air, jabbing the button again. "No, no, no."

Freaking karma.

CHAPTER THIRTEEN

Without Google, I have no life skills. I have no idea how to change a tire. Naturally, I took the phone charger out of my car a few days ago to replace the one at the office. This means, of course, the only solution is to walk.

A steady stream of curses pours from my mouth as I exit my car and begin trudging along the road ditch. I'm in a rough part of the city. Buildings sag; metal bars are bolted over windows; and where the shoulders of the street have eroded, the sidewalks are buried or washed away. My flats quickly turn sopping wet, and my toes squelch inside. The long grass drenches my jeans to my knees. Rain takes care of soaking the rest of me.

"Stupid car," I mutter before stubbing my toe against a rock. I curse and nearly trip. The cold water chilling my feet intensifies the throbbing pain.

Luckily, there should be a gas station within the next block or two. Maybe they'll let me use their phone.

The ditch levels off, and I hop over a puddle to an intact section of sidewalk. The squares of concrete lie unevenly, and I have to watch to keep from tripping again. I keep a wary eye on the abandoned businesses and run-down warehouses on either side of me. A prickle runs up my spine, but I can't tell if it's because of the cold or because there's an ax murderer in the shadows.

Headlights bounce behind me, glaring off building fronts and surrounding me in flat, white light. I squint and hurry my pace. The purr of an engine fills my ears. As the light grows nearer, the engine hum is accompanied by the whooshing, crunching noise of tires cruising over wet pavement.

I walk even faster, my flats going *splat splat splat* over the rough sidewalk. Though I long to hunch my shoulders against the rain, I keep my back rigid, hoping to show an air of confidence to deter would-be murderers.

A dark, reddish blur looms in my blind spot as the headlights move from my back to follow along beside me. Drawing a deep breath, I clutch the pepper spray inside my purse and whirl to face the street. A car rumbles to a stop beside me. It's familiar, vintage, and burgundy in color. I let the air release from my lips. The engine rattles to a stop, and the passenger window rolls down.

"There are easier ways to make money that don't involve walking the streets," Beckett says, leaning across the seat to peer up at me. "Especially when you have two wishes left."

"I had some car trouble, and my phone died." For a second, my relief over not getting murdered overshadows everything else. Then I remember I'm in a parallel universe, and Beckett didn't warn me before I made the wish that got me here.

Beckett stretches across the car and unlatches the passenger door with a click. As it swings open, I take in the black leather and shining chrome.

"Why should I trust you?" I fold my arms around my torso, shivering.

He gives me a withering look. "What am I going to do? Grant you everything you've ever wished for?" He clutches his chest. "Oh god, you're right. Run for your life."

"Or maybe you'll send me to another parallel universe," I try to snap, but my voice wobbles.

He yawns lazily and waves a hand over the empty passenger seat. "Get in."

I shiver again. He blinks ever so slowly. The childish urge to stomp my foot almost overcomes me. When he helped me with my plant, I started to think we could be friends. I trusted him, but he betrayed me.

I flip him off with both hands. "Fuck you!" I turn on my heel and march on.

"Damn it," I hear him say, followed by the slam of a car door and the engine roaring to life. Then, the headlights bob until he's cruising alongside me again, the passenger window rolled down. "What do you want from me?" he calls over the rumble of the engine. "You wished for a fictional character not just to come to life but also to feasibly exist in your own century, with a family lineage traceable to the beginning of time. You thought you hadn't gone to a different universe?"

I spin and face him. "You were supposed to warn me."

Brakes squeal as Beckett stops the car. "I did try to warn you. I believe your exact words were 'You be quiet, Becky.'" His eyes flash, and his tone sharpens with each word. "I also told you when we first met to wish for something that actually exists. Magic can't create something from nothing; that's why I can't raise the dead or take someone's free will. All magic can do is transport things through time and space. If you wish for money, it's coming from somewhere, even if that somewhere is a different dimension. You wanted Darcy to have his own time line integrated into the world, so I brought you to him." By the time Beckett's done, he's practically yelling.

I fucked up, not Beckett. All I feel is shame. So much shame. In my mind's eye, I see the server from Olive Garden and Beckett and everyone else I've hurt by prejudging them.

"I'm sorry." It feels weak, apologizing over and over again. It's like hurting people is in my genes, and no matter how hard I try to overcome it, I keep slipping up.

Beckett's face softens. "Get in the car, Iza. I promise not to ruin your life for at least five minutes."

To hide the tremor in my lips, I purse them together. "But I'll ruin your seats." I gesture at my sodden clothes.

"I don't care. You not dying is sort of a priority of mine."

I hesitate.

"I literally have unlimited wishes at my disposal. I can fix it." His voice is even and calm.

After one final shiver, I scurry in, slamming the door behind me. Immediately, it's as if I'm transported to another world. The rain muffles to a soothing patter. He has the radio on, and soft fifties music crackles through the speakers. It's muffled, and the throaty bravados, tinkling piano keys, and raspy saxophones create an eerily beautiful lullaby that soothes my frayed nerves.

Heat wafts from the vents, and I hold my fingers up to warm them. The bench seat squishes beneath me, more like a plush couch than the structural, hard-backed modern seats I'm used to. The car smells of leather and something musty but pleasant that only comes with age.

Wordlessly, Beckett performs an unsafe and very slow three-point turn in the middle of the street. The *tick tick tick* when he flips his blinker on creates a hypnotic, soothing rhythm. He places his arm on the seatback behind me as he looks over his shoulder, and I catch a whiff of cinnamon off his skin. His knuckles are knobby and dusted with fine, dark hairs. I peel my attention away, unsure why I'm enraptured by knuckles. Perhaps my brain is waterlogged. What's the brain equivalent of putting a phone in rice after it gets wet, to make it work again?

Beckett removes his hand, and my brain remembers how to be a brain. He shifts into drive, now pointed in the direction I walked from.

It's sort of strange he happened to be driving by at just the right time. It doesn't look like he came from one of his parties. It looks more like he came from his couch. Or his bed. He wears a white T-shirt and gray sweatpants; his hair is messy and curling at his neck; and every time he blinks, there's a heavy, sleepy quality to the action.

"No party tonight?" I ask, mostly to fill the silence. To my shock, my voice wavers, unsure.

"Didn't feel up to it." His lips quirk, but it doesn't meet his eyes. "How'd it go with the dreamboat?"

A silence stretches where the only noise is the whooshing of the tires on wet asphalt and the music coming through the radio.

"Awful," I say at last, drawing a pattern in the condensation forming on the window.

He side-eyes me, a bit of sparkle returning. "You're a mess."

"It's been a day." I attempt to smooth my hair, which is drying in a frizzy halo around my head. "I can wish us back, right?"

He watches the road. "You could, yeah."

"What happened to the versions of Lola and me that existed here before us?"

Beckett shrugs. "I imagine you swapped places. If you wish yourself back, you'll swap again."

I think about some version of myself in my old world, confused about what happened to the hot senior architect at work. She'll really be confused when I undo the wish and she finds herself back in a world where Darcy exists again.

But if I wish Lola and myself back, I will have wasted two wishes and gotten nowhere.

An idea hits me. Instead of giving up, I can stay in this universe and see how things progress with Darcy. If I can make Darcy fall for me as hard as he fell for Elizabeth, I can explain the situation and convince him to let me wish him home with us.

Hope sparks in my chest. I'll be able to properly introduce him to my real mom, and she'll see he's just like the Darcy from literature. My dream life will come to fruition.

Beckett slows the car and pulls onto the shoulder. "Ah, there it is," he says.

"Why'd you bring me back to my car?" I ask, wiping fog from the window to look out. "Are you going to magically fix my tire?" I hate that I need help. Today is the day feminism dies. Maybe I'll bury my dignity along with it. "All you're missing is your shining armor."

"Damn it. I should have known I was forgetting something when I dressed this morning." Beckett shuts the engine off and leans back. "Nah. *You're* going to change your tire."

I sputter, forgetting my earlier chill as heat flushes my skin. "As my spiritual guide or whatever, I think you should know that changing the tire will cause me a lot of emotional stress."

He gives me a flat look. "Iza. You can admit you don't know how."

I try to swallow my pride, but there's an edge to my voice. "Okay, fine, you're right. I don't know how to do it because nobody taught me. It's not like I had a dad. Mom gave me a ten-pound textbook about the internal combustion engine, and the only thing I remember from it is 'squeeze, suck, bang, blow.'" I'm hot and itchy all over. I cannot believe I just said that.

Beckett's eyes widen, and he bites his lip like he's holding himself back from commenting. "Don't worry. I'll talk you through it. Changing the tire, I mean. Not the other thing."

My heart softens. He's helping me help myself because he knows that accepting help makes me uncomfortable.

Still, I don't love the thought of failing in front of him either. "You're really not going to use magic? You're going to make me stand out in the rain, cold and alone?" I'm practically begging. It's pathetic.

He fishes under his seat until he finds an umbrella. "I'm not going to sit in here and laugh at you. I'm going to hold the umbrella."

Changing tactics, I fiddle with a seam of the leather seat cover and make my tone solemn. "You said you want to live a life of your own, so I really think I should let you change the tire. I mean, I'm sure you miss the trials and tribulations of real life."

The corner of his mouth twitches. "Nice try. Unfortunately for you, I have a lot of experience dealing with difficult people. You might as well give up." He leans in and whispers, "You know what determines who I'll be sent to help next?"

I shake my head.

"Every person I've ever been sent to torments me in one way or another. Part of the eternal punishment, I guess. It's not true selflessness if it's easy."

Unexpectedly, his words sting. Although his tone is teasing, he said he can't lie to me. If that's true, he truly sees me as a torment. And why wouldn't he? I've been skeptical of him since he got here. He must be annoyed.

I push off the hurt and pretend to play along. "You say being around me is a punishment." I hold out my hand. "I'll show you punishment. Give me your umbrella."

"What?"

"Give it to me so I can beat you with it."

Beckett laughs and moves to open his door. "Don't threaten me with a good time." He hoists the would-be assault weapon. "Come on. I'm not going to be here forever. I need to impart a small piece of my vast wisdom to you."

The reality of those words hit me. Not the part about his supposed wisdom, but the part about him not being here forever. After I use all my wishes, he'll get trapped inside another vessel, who knows where, until the next person summons him.

Beckett slips out into the rain. Before I can follow, he rounds the front of the car and opens my door, holding the umbrella so I don't get wet. I duck out of the car and huddle beside him, my arm brushing his ribs. Even the momentary contact sends the heat from his skin rushing into me.

"What's it like?" I ask. "In vessels, I mean."

Shrugging, he ushers me around the car to the trunk. "It's pure nothing. One minute, I'm alive, then it's like I don't even exist. I don't breathe or think or feel. When I wake up after being summoned again, I don't remember anything about being trapped."

My heart hurts. "You're jerked from place to place, skipping months or years at a time, living your life serving people who torment you? That's—horrible."

Beckett's side presses into my back as he opens the trunk and leans past me to retrieve the scissor jack. "There are upsides." He forces a strained smile. "It slows aging, in a way, and I get to see more of the world than most."

I open my mouth, but he cuts me off.

"Don't try to get to know me, Iza. Don't try to help. You'll only make everything worse."

His meaning is loud and clear: *You'll try too hard, ruin everything, and make my life even more miserable.* My eyes grow fuzzy. Water must've gotten past the umbrella. I blink away the extra moisture.

It's hard to focus as Beckett shows me how to use the car jack. He seems preoccupied too, fumbling a few times. He's probably busy trying to figure out how he can get out of this as soon as possible so he can get away from me and my destructive tendencies.

I sniff as he leans over my shoulder and shows me where to place the jack under the car. After it's situated, he hands me the tire iron. I fiddle with the steel a moment before placing the hexagonal end over one of the nuts. With a grunt, I heave, but nothing happens.

"Righty tighty, lefty loosey." Beckett's breath tickles my ear.

"I know that," I mumble, even as I scoot to the other side to pull on the bar in the opposite direction.

After a moment of watching me struggle, Beckett chuckles and says helpfully, "Lift with your back; save your knees."

I grunt. "Very funny." With one mighty heave, the muscles in my shoulders burn, and there's a squeak. The nut turns. In my excitement, I drop the tire iron, and it clatters to the pavement. I spin, beaming. "Did you see—" The words die on my lips.

I knew Beckett was close behind me, but I didn't realize how close until we're face-to-face. With my back against the cold, wet car and his chest radiating heat inches from mine, our proximity becomes very apparent.

"Super," he says, voice somewhat choked, eyes flitting over my face. "Only four left to go."

"To go?" the words leave my mouth, barely a breath over my lips. *Lips.* I look at Beckett's. They lift into a sort of barely there smile, soft, inviting, and—*What the actual fuck?* Why am I looking at Beckett's lips? Mr. Darcy's lips are what I should be focused on. Any rational woman wouldn't be able to think of another set of lips. Any rational woman would forget she has her own set of lips.

I should be focused on a good, solid man who didn't tell me minutes ago that my mere presence is torture. If I let myself fall for Beckett, all he'll do is break my heart before vanishing from my life entirely.

"Nuts," Beckett says.

"Huh?" I ask intelligently.

"Lug nuts. You've got four left." He pushes wet hair from my cheeks. Instinctively, I lean into his touch, and his hand burns against my damp, chilled skin. His fingers hesitate right at the place where my ear meets my jaw.

Some hidden, half-wild part of me, the part that still cries over cheesy movies, loves sparkly nail polish, tries to catch falling autumn leaves, and eats cookie dough despite the very real threat of salmonella—that part of me wants him to plunge his fingers into my hair, grab a fistful, and pin me against my car. The moment is frozen in time—his dark gold eyes glinting in the darkness, the scent of him amplifying as rain spits past the umbrella to dampen his skin, the *tap tap tapping* from the vinyl umbrella above our heads.

If he kissed me, I'd grab his shirt and warm the chill from his mouth, drink the rain off his skin. I'd slide my tongue past his lips and coax him to show me the parts of his heart that still hide behind his deteriorating veil of indifference.

But I torment him, so of course he won't kiss me.

Beckett returns his hand to his side, leaving the place on my jaw cold. The moment splinters. There are no signs of emotion on his face, not even a shadow of a smirk or a grin. He bends down, retrieves the discarded tire iron, and hands it to me. It feels like rejection.

I clutch the freezing metal. "Right."

A few minutes later, I manage to loosen the remaining lug nuts, jack the car up, and pull the wheel loose.

Beckett clears his throat behind me, resting a forearm against the car. "So, you like him, then? Darcy? He's everything you're looking for?"

Now winded for a multitude of reasons, I lean the ruined tire against the car and straighten. It doesn't matter if Beckett dislikes me. Not when I have Mr. Freaking Darcy. "He's absolutely what I'm looking for."

"Even though he's unlikeable?"

"Of course he's unlikeable. Nobody ever accused Mr. Darcy of being likable. He was pretty much an asshole to Elizabeth in the beginning. But if I stand by him, he'll change, just like in the book." The words sound rather problematic leaving my mouth.

"You ever think maybe Darcy hasn't aged well?" Beckett asks like he's read my mind.

"Darcy is timeless." Beckett's accurate assessment struck a nerve, and my defenses start flying up. "He takes himself seriously, values integrity, he's proud—"

"And you think pride is a virtue, not a vice?" Beckett's eyes pierce into me, commanding me to look at him.

I do, my chest tightening. "Since when are you a philosopher? I'm just saying those are attractive qualities."

"So, someone without a sense of humor, who doesn't party all the time?" Beckett reaches into the trunk and hauls out the spare with one hand, keeping the umbrella over me with the other. Rain quickly turns his white shirt semitransparent over his shoulder and bicep. A surprisingly muscular bicep. "Someone *scrupulous*."

"Beckett—"

He shoves the tire into my hands, forcing me to take it. "Maybe that's the problem with real men. They have personalities and flaws and . . . feelings."

I'm tired of Beckett goading me about Darcy. He's being spiteful for no reason. It's not like Beckett's offered to fill the position. Quite the opposite. I spin away, crouching to position the spare onto the car. "The problem with real men is they're prone to betraying my trust."

"I never told you I'd babysit you through making an intelligent wish."

I thread the nuts onto the studs and let the jack down like I've been wrenching my whole life. "I didn't realize we were talking about you."

"Maybe we are." His tone is soft but filled with so much tension, it's more powerful than a shout.

As I tighten the nuts, my arms burn nearly as much as my throat, my eyes. First, he tells me my very existence is a punishment. Now he's comparing himself to my dream man like he's hurt. "What do you want from me?"

"Iza"—Beckett's voice breaks—"that's not fair." He takes a step back, and cold rain drips into my hair, trickling down my neck and between my shoulder blades.

He's right. It's not fair to ask a question like that when he has no choice but to answer. But what's asked is asked. I move to the next nut, my shoulders protesting as I turn it as tightly as I can.

"I want you to let me be your friend," he says helplessly.

"You *do*?"

"Yes. This thing between you and me doesn't have to be difficult." Beckett takes the tire iron from my hands and replaces it with the umbrella. He tosses the jack and tire iron back into the car before slamming the trunk, his movements weighed down by the same visceral misery affecting both of us.

When he turns to take back the umbrella, his hair drips into his eyes, and his shirt is plastered to his skin. I don't let go, and his hand closes over my fist, his fingers cold from rain and chilled steel. "We can be on the same team."

"We can?" I whisper. I haven't had someone on my team in a long time.

His eyes meet mine, glassy and bloodshot. With each passing second, his palm over my knuckles heats warmer and warmer. He blinks water out of his lashes but doesn't look away. Thank god the electricity I feel crackling between us is in my head because, in this wet environment, we could fry the entire city of St. Louis.

"Yeah. You can stop picking a fight with me every time we talk, because I promise I'll give you your wishes without altering them. You'll get your perfect life, and we'll go our separate ways."

"Oh." I feel stupid. He's cooperating, not caring. He wants to help me on my way as quickly as possible. I suspect he only sees friendship as a transaction, not as a thing built on affection.

I let go of the umbrella, wriggling my hand out from under his. He's being civil—nice, even.

That should be enough.

* * *

Beckett instructs me to keep it under fifty miles per hour and follows me home.

Although we agreed on a friendly arrangement, the air between us buzzes with awkward tension as we clomp up the apartment stairwell to our floor.

Beckett pauses in front of his door. "What's on your arm?"

"Huh?"

"I noticed it earlier. When you pushed your sleeve up to do the tire, I saw writing on your arm."

"Oh." I lift my sleeve and show him the smudged letters, as though displaying how agreeable I can be. As though proving I'm as happy as he is to be friends, even though *friends* suddenly feels like the most disagreeable word ever uttered. "It was guidelines for how today was supposed to go."

Beckett leans over my arm, his damp hair falling over his brow. "You like to walk?"

I shift my weight. "Well, no."

The third line is partially hidden under my shirt, and he gently pushes my sleeve back. I shiver. "What's this last one mean?"

"It's his greatest fault," I say, fighting to keep my tone conversational. "Elizabeth tells Darcy she's trying to find something to tease him about, but she says she can't tease him about his fault."

Beckett steps away and blinks. "Why not?"

"You can't tease Mr. Darcy."

He tilts his head. "Why?"

"Well, the pride thing."

Beckett snorts and leans in. "For the record, I happen to like a tease."

My heart stumbles while confusion floods my head like molasses, slowing the neurons in my brain. "I'm not sure you understand the meaning of friendship. It doesn't involve flirting."

"I'm simply stating a fact." A smile plays on Beckett's lips. "Friends tell friends facts about themselves."

My face heats. Obviously he's not flirting with me. He's put me firmly in the friend zone.

"What's Darcy's greatest fault, then?" he asks.

I try not to notice how Beckett's sweatpants are soaked from the rain, weighed down and hanging low on his hips, exposing a sliver of skin. "His good opinion once lost is lost forever," I manage.

Beckett side-eyes me. "Is that his greatest fault or yours?"

I invented a whole dating plan that involved judging people from first impressions, casting aside and condemning anyone who didn't immediately measure up.

"It's *Darcy's* greatest fault," I say firmly.

"Ah, of course. Obviously, your greatest fault is undressing people with your eyes."

Shit, he caught me. I tear my eyes off the thin shirt stuck to Beckett's defined chest. He's muscular, but not in a body builder kind of way. More in the quietly defined way of someone who has muscles because they use them.

And—oh my god. Judging by what I think I see under the wet, transparent material of his shirt, his left nipple is pierced. Of course it is.

"I'm not staring," I say. "I'm a friend looking at a friend in a friendly way."

Beckett steps closer. "That was really . . . not convincing. Good job." He presses something cold and metal into my hand. With wide eyes, I look up at him. He snorts. "Relax, killer. If you give me yours, I'll take your car to the shop Monday for tires."

I glance at my hand, which is clenched so hard around his car keys, the metal gouges into my palm. He let me off the hook. Majorly. He could've given me so much more shit than he did. Kalyan wouldn't have let that opportunity pass by.

Wordlessly, I hand him my keys.

Nodding, Beckett says, "Keep her under a hundred and twenty. I'm going back to bed."

He shuts the door in my face.

Back to bed? He randomly woke up, decided to go on an evening cruise, and happened upon me? Had he somehow known I was in trouble? There's more meaning behind that statement, but I don't know what.

CHAPTER FOURTEEN

I have to admit I feel like a badass rolling into work in Beckett's flashy car. Since Beckett accused me of sharing Darcy's fault, I decide to prove him wrong by happily being his friend. The amount that I enjoyed driving his car is really just a sign of how strong that friendship is.

My day gets better when I step out of the elevator and am not immediately fired for stalking and harassment. In fact, Darcy gives me a nod. Considering, in the book, Darcy doesn't portray outward signs of being in love with Elizabeth for a long time, things are looking up.

My morning consists of working on the rooms Darcy actually lets me design, mostly bathrooms and closets—and the cesspool to collect the building's waste.

In terms of what's next in the winning-Darcy-over mission, a quick reference to the book indicates we're to the point Darcy should be falling for me (doubtful), and I should be hating him (not so much). There really ought to be a ball or two thrown in there too, but there's a sorry lack of balls in the twenty-first century.

I glance around the male-dominated office. Okay. There are plenty of balls in my life.

The elevator dings.

As Julia Felmont sweeps in, the bustling office goes quiet. Everyone stands frozen in shock until Chester drops a massive stack of papers, and they go soaring and fluttering before gravity scatters them across the floor.

"Ms. Felmont." Chester shuffles over, straightening his glasses. "We weren't expecting you."

She ignores his extended hand and strides further inside, flanked by her bodyguards. One holds a teacup poodle in his arms. She places her fluttering fingers to her collarbone. "Is my palace done?"

Chester shoots a frantic, pleading look my way.

I stand, smoothing my blazer. "We're working overtime to finish the designs. We plan to send them to the contractor as soon as possible, pending your approval, of course."

Chester gets a hold of himself. "Yes—what she said. I planned on calling you in for a meeting soon. Very soon."

Darcy descends the staircase like a princess in a teenybop movie making her grand entrance into a ballroom. He adjusts his shirt cuffs, and the pretty ballgowns dancing in front of my eyes poof out of existence. Now, if I squint, I can almost imagine him on a grand cement stair, trotting down a veranda in the Pemberley estate.

"What's wrong with your face?" Julia asks.

I stop squinting. "Nothing."

"Did I hear you want to see some of what we've drawn up?" Darcy nears with rolls of paper tucked under his arm.

"All of it, yes," Julia says.

Darcy walks to my desk and pushes aside my succulents and the many, many photographs of Kalyan's face. For a wild moment, I picture him shoving aside the clutter, grabbing my waist, and flinging me onto the desk—

The image shatters thanks to a loud sniff from Chester. He's so stressed, he's probably on the verge of a nervous breakdown. My imagination is overactive this morning. I shouldn't have let the barista put that third shot of espresso in my coffee. Or maybe I shouldn't have stayed up late imagining all the different ways last night could have played out.

"Iza, pull up some of the virtual 3-D models we have," Darcy says as he unfurls his papers.

I jolt forward. "Of course." Turning to Julia, I say, "These should give you a much clearer idea what the final product will look like."

Julia scrutinizes the drawings and digital images for about thirty seconds before declaring, "I hate them."

Chester tugs on his collar, teetering. "What about them don't you like? We have to make sections of the structure modular, so they can be assembled before we lower them into the ground and fit them together. This limits the scale and how creative we can get with the layout. Perhaps, though, with some minor tweaking—"

Julia holds up a hand. "No amount of tweaking can fix this. It's not only the dimensions and layout; it's the overall *feeling*."

"The feeling?" Darcy echoes, like feelings are a foreign concept.

On top of the 3-D image of the entryway I pulled up, I place some experimental finishes—marble and mahogany. The picture is rough and basic, but the grandeur of the room is easy to imagine.

Julia wrinkles her nose. "It looks so cold."

"Yes, well, marble has that effect," Darcy says.

With a few clicks, I change the marble to burgundy carpet.

In response, Julia shudders. "No. No, this won't do. Overhaul it. Start over."

"Maybe if we scaled it back, it would feel more . . . cozy." Darcy grimaces like he wants to hurl over the word *cozy*.

Julia gasps. "Scale it back? It's small enough already. I can't have my friends describing it as . . . as . . ." She leans in and whispers, "Quaint."

"How do you suggest we proceed, then?" Darcy asks, a knot forming in his jaw.

A little thrill goes through my stomach at the word *we*. He acknowledged a *we*, as in *him and me*. In terms of seducing Darcy, I'm kicking Elizabeth Bennet's ass.

Julia takes her dog from her bodyguard and strokes it obsessively like she's Gollum clutching the One Ring. "I don't know. You're the *paid* professionals. Do it again, but better."

Chester quickly steps in. "Of course. We won't disappoint." He reaches to pet the dog, but it lets out a whiny, pathetic growl that nonetheless makes him flinch.

* * *

An hour later, I'm torn away from my computer by a stack of papers slamming onto my desk. Darcy looms over me, a lock of his usually combed-back hair falling over his brow. "I've received some distressing news from home. I'm going to be out of the office for a while."

Panic constricts my heart. "I'm sorry. What?"

He nods curtly. "I've told Chester I think it's best for him and this project if I take a step back. I'm too distracted to do the job to the best of my abilities."

Pressure closes in, threatening to pop my heart altogether. I plaster on a confident smile and squeak, "Sure. No problem. I can handle it."

"I've suggested Kalyan should join the team."

That's an annoying inconvenience, but I nod. "Sure."

Darcy eyes me warily. "This is important."

"Of course." The fact Darcy's leaving it in my hands must mean he thinks I'm capable. This is promising. Still, his leaving sort of crushes our blossoming romance.

Darcy nods, turns, then walks away toward his office without another word.

I should have expected this, since Darcy makes a hasty departure from Netherfield in my handy-dandy field guide, *Pride and Prejudice*. To follow the book, all I have to do now is show up to his relative's house, and—oh god. What kind of monster will his Aunt Catherine be in this century?

I take a deep breath. It will all fall into place. When Elizabeth visited Rosings Park, Darcy proposed. Still, even if our strange relationship somehow does lead to a proposal, to stick with the story, I'll have to turn Darcy down the first time he asks. This realization doesn't fill me with disappointment, but . . . relief?

Keys jangle near my ear. I whirl around.

"Car's taken care of," Beckett says, handing me the keys. He wears cargo shorts, a fitted T-shirt, and a guarded expression.

I take the keys. "Thank you." My gaze drops to his chest, my memory overlaying wet-T-shirt details I can't unsee—from dripping, transparent fabric and a nipple piercing to gray sweatpants, darkened by the rain, nearly sliding off his body.

My overactive imagination goes wild, and I squirm in my chair. He's a distraction I can't afford—a pretty distraction, but still a distraction. Despite everything, I can't let go of my initial reservations about him. He told me how he treated another one of his "friends."

Does he define a friend as someone who won't be an annoyance, as someone he can push aside and forget about unless it's on his terms? Did he give me that title in hopes I'd stop disrupting his life? Or has he learned and now defines a friend as someone he wants to help for their gain, not his?

He lingers on the other side of the desk.

"What?" I ask.

Beckett blinks slowly. "I need my keys." His eyes drop to look at my pocket. "Unless you'd like me to get them myself."

"They're in my purse, you weirdo." Fumbling, I dig the keys out and hand them to him.

"Were you aware you were, like, six thousand miles overdue for an oil change?"

"You call it neglect. I call it frugality. I'm conserving Mother Earth's natural resources."

Beckett waves a hand. "Don't worry about it. Got it taken care of."

"What do I owe you?" I reach for my wallet.

He leans against my desk. "Don't worry about that either."

I shove a wad of bills into his hand, and he sighs and takes it.

"Last night you said something I can't stop thinking about," I say.

"Samesies. I keep thinking about how you said, 'Suck, squeeze, bang, blow.'"

I make an exaggerated sound of disgust. "Grow up, Beckett. Those are the strokes of the internal combustion engine."

"They're the strokes of something."

My traitorous mouth forms a smile. Maybe being friends with Beckett could be kind of nice. "I was thinking of how you said you were going back to bed, like you'd gotten up specifically to find me."

"I did. I woke up with a feeling like you were in danger. It's yet another perk of the wish-granting gig. My whole purpose is to help you, so if you're in danger, it's like a magnet pulls me toward you. If I resist, it will pull harder until I lose control of my body altogether, and I'm forced to do all I can to save you."

He has to help people, even if they don't deserve it. Even if they hurt him. The image of Beckett wrapping his broken ribs makes me wince. Being forced into true selflessness—I'm not sure if the star was teaching him a lesson or simply punishing him. "If the only reason I was alive was to serve others, I think I'd grow to resent it."

"I do resent it." He picks up a picture frame off my desk and turns it over in his hands. "But I found saving your life to be . . . not the most unpleasant thing I've ever done."

"That's the nicest thing you've ever said to me," I joke.

"Who's this?" Beckett holds up the frame, showing me the picture of Kalyan.

I resist the urge to let my head fall into my hands. "That's Kalyan. We have a sort of prank war going on. He started messing with me a few weeks after I started working here, and it's never stopped."

Beckett breaks into a grin, crinkles and all. "That's the greatest thing I've ever heard."

Darcy sweeps by, briefcase in hand. When he notices Beckett, he gives him a long, inscrutable stare. In response, Beckett scrunches his face, giving him a look that clearly says, *What?* But his thumb scrapes absently on the side of the picture frame he still holds, betraying his unease. After a moment, Darcy spins on his heel and stalks into the elevator.

When the doors shut, I ask, "What was that all about?"

Gingerly, Beckett sets the frame back on my desk. "I have no idea."

"Do you two know each other?"

He gives me a withering look. "No, how would we know each other?"

"Well, you sort of created him."

Beckett throws his head back and laughs, causing several of my coworkers to stare. "He's not like a son to me, Iza." It takes him another second to compose himself. "I didn't create him. I simply took you to him. Can I ask you something?"

"I think it's fair, considering I can ask you anything."

"I was thinking about last night too—beyond your filthy mouth, I mean. Why do you make excuses for Darcy and not for anyone else?"

I click aimlessly at my computer, my smile fading. Sure, maybe Darcy and I got off to a rocky start, but in the end, he'll be everything I need. With him, I'll earn the right to use those three sacred words reserved for life's most precious moments: *Told you so.* I envision Mom's dumbstruck face as she tries and fails to find a flaw in Mr. Fitzwilliam Freaking Darcy.

"There are no risks with giving Darcy a second chance because I know he won't let me down," I say.

"So you admit your first impressions of other people may not be correct, but you're too scared to find out."

I stutter, trying to collect my thoughts. "Darcy's different. The book proves he's more than he seems."

"What if I prove I can be more than I seem?" Holding eye contact, Beckett digs the money I gave him out of his pocket and tosses it onto my desk. "Try to control yourself. I know how hot you are for redemption arcs, and I don't want you trying to marry me."

I don't want you trying to marry me. From anyone else, I could tell myself it's sarcasm. It actually stings from a man who can't lie.

I scrunch my entire face into the biggest, brightest fake smile I can muster, then let it fall slack. "Funny." I turn back to my computer.

Beckett chuckles like he thinks he won.

When I next risk a peek over my shoulder, he's gone. Good. He is a distraction.

Hard plastic wheels rumble across the floor. Kalyan crashes into my desk, knocking over the picture Beckett so carefully positioned. "Lunch plans?" he asks.

"I don't have time for this today."

He breaks into an open-mouthed smile. "Ah, you heard, then? We're partners." He slugs me on the shoulder, and I wince. "So, what do you say, partner? Lunch?"

I give him my full attention. "Why?"

"It was such fun last time."

"Look." I cross my arms. "I don't know what kind of game you've been playing all this time with your pranks and your ceaseless pestering and now this lunch thing, but I'm not interested."

"You mean you didn't think the pictures were funny?"

"Funny?" I stare him down. "When will I have time to change them back? Especially now with the increased workload with Darcy gone. What if people see them? What if people think we're . . . we're . . ."

His face falls. "You mean you don't feel as I do? Tell me you are in jest! Can you not feel the sexual tension underneath all our witty banter?"

My eyes bulge, straining in their sockets. "No. Keep it down."

He clutches his chest. "Even your mother thinks I'm perfect. Does her opinion mean nothing to you?"

Yes. "No!"

Then he lets his arms drop, and he laughs. "That's what you're afraid of? That people will think we're dating?" He snorts as he watches me struggle to follow his abrupt mood shift.

"Fine, yes," I say, lowering my voice to a vicious snarl, looking both ways to make sure nobody's watching. "With this ridiculous prank war you started, I'm pretty sure they already suspect that's the case. And why shouldn't they? What's your end goal here? What are you getting out of this?"

"Not everyone wants to get in your pants, you know." To my amazement, he's still smiling easily. "All this time I haven't been trying to hook up with you. I've been trying to be your friend."

My mouth opens and closes like it knows I should have something clever to say, but my brain has failed me.

"You're wound so tight, we've started a betting pool on how long it'll take you to finally snap." He scrunches his lips. "After you began working here, I thought you might chill out over time, but when you didn't, I started messing with you, hoping you'd open up. All those invitations to the bar on Fridays and lunches . . ."

I can practically hear the wires buzzing in my brain as they short-circuit. "Oh."

"Everyone thinks you look down on the rest of us like you think you're better or something." He shrugs. "And maybe you are, but you have to play the game and pretend you're not because it's not earning you any friends or respect."

I've been so scared everyone thinks I'm inferior, I've worked extra hard for years to prove myself. The whole time, they've been thinking I believe I'm above *them*?

I blink, dumbfounded. "Oh."

"Yeah, 'Oh,' you nut. I'm going to lunch. I'll bring you back a sandwich."

He leaves, and my only thought is: Kalyan isn't so bad.

My gut instinct was wrong.

CHAPTER FIFTEEN

Doubts creep in over the next week and a half of red-eyed overtime. If I was wrong about Kalyan, I might be wrong about others.

Maybe it's a fluke. Perhaps, the day I met Kalyan, I ate some questionable cheese, and it threw off the whole reading. My gut has been right so many times before. I sensed Tyler was a sneak on our first date, but chalked his wandering eye up to nerves. I was suspicious of Beckett before he told me I had every right to be.

But then he asked, *"What if I prove I can be more than I seem?"*

I need to run an experiment to test my instincts. If Beckett wants to try and prove he's changed, I'll let him. I'll place him before the Judge Judy of Karens: my mother. I need a fresh impression because mine has grown too muddled. If his old faults still remain, Mom will sniff them out.

I'm not sure what I want to come from this. If this meeting somehow goes well and Beckett proves to be a true, genuine friend, will that change everything? Could it mean my dream man could still be out there, and Darcy isn't my last and only option? Should I stop fixating and start giving more people a chance?

I knock on Beckett's door, and he answers, blinking blearily in the light of the hall.

"Hi, new friend." I beam.

"Should I be happy or suspicious?" he asks, but he smiles.

I almost feel bad as I say, "My mom asked if I'd come over and help her move some stuff."

"Using a wish to move shit is honestly the best use of magic I've heard of."

"I'm not here for a wish," I say. "I'm here for . . . help."

Beckett groans, but that smile hasn't budged. He's smiling like he can't quite believe he has the right to be happy.

"Friends help friends move," I say cheerily.

* * *

"I'm going to use magic as soon as she turns her back," Beckett threatens, heaving a cardboard box filled with disassembled pieces of my childhood nightstand.

We're at Mom's house in my old room, helping her empty it so she can repaint and put up shelves for inventory. When she saw Beckett, I could tell she wanted to say something, but since he's here to work, she's holding her tongue. For now.

Mom turns in a circle, surveying our progress. All the childhood magic has left the space. So many daydreams were imagined here. Now, all that's left are dingy yellow walls and a bed frame.

"Good," Mom says. "Run that last box to the attic, and I can take care of the rest."

She walks out of the room. I turn to Beckett. "Don't you dare—"

Beckett snaps his fingers, but the box doesn't vanish as I expect. Instead, with a twirl of his wrist, a perfect yellow rose appears in his hand. "I can't lie." He gives the flower to me, balancing the box with one arm.

The rose is huge and flawless, with a few drops of dew rolling over its petals. I lift it to my nose and smell its perfume, feeling Beckett's gaze on me as I do. "It's beautiful. Where'd you get it from?"

His smile looks a little sad now. "More like when. It came from our universe from about 1970."

I look down at the flower. Moments ago, it saw the world how it was over fifty years ago. "Isn't dragging stuff through time dangerous? Like, won't it cause a butterfly effect and risk ending the world or something? What if someone noticed this flower vanish, and it altered the course of the universe?"

Beckett readjusts the box and walks out of the room. Out in the hall, we've pulled down the ladder into the attic, and he carefully begins climbing. "Someone did notice." His voice grows muffled as he pokes his head into the attic. "Later that night, he did something very stupid that did alter the course of the universe."

My head spins. Beckett disappears into the hole in the ceiling. I scramble up after him, crawling onto the sheets of plywood laid out over the rafters where Mom stores things she doesn't want to look at all the time, like Christmas decorations and her daughter's childhood memorabilia.

"*Beckett.* You shouldn't go around changing the universe all willy-nilly-like." I shove the flower at him. "Undo it. Put it back."

Beckett doesn't take the flower, just slides his box so it sits next to the others we spent the evening lugging up here. He sits against the boxes to catch his breath. "No. I don't think I will."

If the flower altered the universe in 1970, I've already seen the result. Maybe I don't want Beckett to undo it. Who knows what the world would be like without that one small change. A feeling of discomfort settles over me. "How do you know what happened to some guy with a missing flower in 1970?"

"Because I was there."

A chill crawls down my spine. Just how long has Beckett been around, granting wishes? Or maybe he's time-traveled. "If you can drag things through time and space, can you move people through time and space too?"

"Probably, but if I get too far away from my charge, I'm teleported back. That eliminates most travel, period, not to mention time travel."

Yet another way he can't have a life of his own. "But you'd go if your charge wanted to," I say. "Have any of them wished to go back in time?"

"Not yet. I try not to tell people it's an option. I'm lucky enough that each time I'm summoned, I end up back in my own universe, forward in time. Frequently jumping around to different universes and time periods would disrupt what little order my life has."

I shake my head as if to clear it. "How can you be so calm about this? It makes my head hurt to think about it."

Beckett plucks the flower from my fingers and begins pinching off its thorns. "That's the difference between you and me. I don't think about it. What's the point?" His fingers are deft, like he's done this a hundred times.

"How old are you?" I ask, not quite realizing how badly I want—need—to know the answer, until I voice the question.

Beckett nearly drops the flower. Setting it aside, he slides forward to sit crisscross applesauce in front of me. At once, he seems approachable. Nice. Someone I can take at face value—his current face value, not the value I estimated when I appraised his face the night we met. "I was born in 1952—"

The 1950s. Something inside me sinks. "But that would make you—"

"—like, twenty-seven? Twenty-eight-ish by my calculations?"

I swallow hard. "I think your calculations are a bit off. You're old enough to be my grandfather."

"Oh my god." He gently flicks my knee. "I might puke if you ever say that again. I don't count the days when I'm bottled up. I was cursed when I was eighteen. So, if I add up all the days I've actually been out and alive, I'm like twenty-seven, twenty-eight-ish. I think."

Ten years. For ten years of his life, he's been fulfilling other people's wishes, paying for a mistake he made when he was a teenager. For over fifty years, he's been *not* living his own life. "Well, I guess that explains why your slang is so dated."

"Excuse me? I'm hip. The hippest." He picks up the flower again.

"No one has unironically said the word *broski* ever, but especially not in recent years."

Beckett's eyes glitter in the near darkness as he leans forward. "But you find it charming. Why else would you want to know my age so badly?" He tucks the flower behind my ear.

Warmth spreads to my cheeks, and I duck my head. His crooked, knowing smile makes me focus exclusively on keeping my cool, which isn't a talent of mine. "If you've been granting wishes for ten years, why have I never heard of anyone talking about magic before?"

"Would you have believed someone who said magic was real before you met me?"

"I guess not." I do some quick math. "So if you were eighteen when you were cursed, and you were born in 1952, then you were cursed in 1970, which is the year you stole a flower from a few minutes ago. You weren't just there. You *were* flower-guy."

Beckett nods. "Yep."

"In 1970, you noticed a flower disappear, and you didn't understand why until about two minutes ago?"

"More or less."

My heart picks up speed. "You said that flower led to someone doing something stupid that would alter the course of the universe. You were that someone. Was that something wishing for unlimited wishes?"

"Yep."

Thoughts spin around my head as I try to piece together the story. "If a disappearing flower somehow led to you getting cursed, why did you *give me that flower?* You basically cursed yourself!"

Beckett smiles. "My family owned a flower stand. When I was working one day and saw a flower vanish, I convinced myself someone passing by had simply swiped it. It angered me that our livelihood rested on something so fragile, and I was only thinking of myself later that night when I made that wish. It wasn't until I thought about it after that I realized the flower probably vanished because of magic, and my future self had to be to blame. I couldn't understand a scenario that would compel me to seal my own fate like that. I vowed I'd never draw that flower through time, like I thought I could undo what happened. I thought I had the power to control my destiny, but then I met you, and I was powerless." He shoots me a wink.

My body responds like it's gasoline, and that wink was a spark. "You gave up your only chance to reverse what happened for a pretty party trick. You didn't think twice about it."

"It felt right."

"Why?"

"Because you knocked on my door and called me your friend. I wasn't capable of friendship fifty years ago."

"I was kissing up to you because I was about to ask for a favor," I point out, but I'm teasing, and he knows it.

"Shh. Let me have this."

We grin at each other. Something shifts between us. It starts to feel like a real friendship. It starts to feel like more. Why would Beckett sit up here, huddled in an attic crawl space with me, tucked between boxes, if he truly sees me as a torment?

If Beckett were anyone else, I wouldn't be so unsure. But he can't lie. I compare everything he's said with everything he's done. *"A girl like you . . . don't look twice at a guy like me . . ." "I don't want to accidentally seduce you . . ." "Every person I go to torments me in some way . . ." "Don't try to get to know me, Iza. Don't try to help. You'll only make everything worse . . ." "I don't want you trying to marry me."*

And yet he's been there for me over and over again.

My heart pounds in my ears. He's pushing me away verbally while his actions tell me the opposite.

My heart aches, as though, in shifting the contents of my childhood bedroom, all the dreams got stirred awake too. Now, they're alive inside my chest, ready to burst free. Beckett brought back the magic.

"Does that box say, 'Iza, Sixth Grade'?" Beckett asks with glee, spotting a box beside me.

My fight-or-flight response engages, as anyone's would when confronted by memories of middle school. *"No."* I gasp as I dive forward and shield the box with my body.

"Truly, destiny has smiled on me today." Beckett pokes my ribs, tickling me so I yelp and spring away. I try to recover, but he grabs my ankle and pulls me back, my butt sliding easily over the smooth plywood until I end up nearly in his lap. I scramble, but he reaches past me and pops the lid off the box.

Resigned, I sit back, burning with mortification as he flips through school papers on horticulture, looks over a crumbling diorama of a greenhouse, and reads a weird combination of pop and country song titles off a burned CD.

"If I could be sarcastic, I'd say this really screams 'future architect,'" he says at last.

"I'm multidimensional." My voice fades as he pulls out an envelope of pictures. "If you're a real friend, you won't look at those."

It's too late. He has them out, already grinning at a photo of me in braces. He thumbs through them. I can tell he's trying not to laugh, but his eyes are doing the crinkle thing, and his dimples are peeking around his clamped-together lips.

I scoot closer and peer over his shoulder. I start explaining the pictures as though I need to defend my eleven-year-old self's life choices—even if those life choices involve purple eyeshadow and a One Direction obsession.

Grandma appears in a few of the photos. Soon, my descriptions turn less defensive and more eager. Beckett asks questions, seeming genuinely interested to hear me share my past. Before long, my embarrassment is gone.

I don't know how long we're up there, but Beckett snaps his fingers, and LED candles pop up all over the attic, scattered over the boxes at different heights. He snaps his fingers again, and a battery-powered CD player appears beside us and starts playing my mixtape.

When I think about the family I'm trying to create, I can always see Mom and myself clearly. The third figure is usually fuzzy, a faceless man who somehow fits right in. Now, he takes shape. He looks a lot like Beckett.

I'm just not sure if he fits in yet.

Suddenly, more rides on today than merely testing whether my instincts can be trusted. I need to find out if Beckett could be an option I didn't anticipate.

I'm wheezing with laughter, telling Beckett a story about how Grandma sneaked me backstage at the One Direction concert she took me to without Mom's permission, and Beckett's snorting as he tries to stifle his own amusement. Everything I've ever imagined and more sits within my grasp. I wanted a guy who would be loyal and who would get along with my mother. I never thought it could feel like—

"Eliza? What on earth are you doing up there?" Mom's voice cuts through our impromptu party.

"Shit," Beckett hisses. A split second later, the attic goes dark and silent. No more candles, no more music.

Mom pokes her head through the trapdoor. "Did I hear music up here?" she asks, giving Beckett the evil eye.

It's like I've been caught with a boy in my room. Her words make me feel so much like an eleven-year-old again, I can almost taste the metal of my braces.

"Come down," she says. "It's time we talked."

CHAPTER SIXTEEN

Of all the silences that have haunted this kitchen, this one is the most quiet. Beckett and I sit on one side of the table, Mom on the other. Mom does not offer Beckett a refreshment, even though he spent the entire evening hauling stuff into her attic.

Nerves flutter through me. Everything rides on this. If tonight goes well, I'll ask Beckett straight up if he likes me. A shot of excitement zings through my belly at the thought.

I try to send him telepathic messages. *Behave. Be polite. Don't crack jokes.*

Oh god. This is going to be a disaster.

I'm frustrated with myself for being so critical again, but the only way I can imagine Beckett getting along with Mom is if Beckett changes everything about himself.

Maybe Beckett and I don't make sense outside of dark attics filled with other forgotten, impossible daydreams that can never come to fruition.

"Do I need to ask you what your intentions are with my daughter?" Mom asks.

"She's twenty-six, so probably not," says Beckett.

I cringe. Beckett doesn't have to answer Mom's questions, but apparently being forced to answer mine and all his other charges' has made him a bit of a smartass.

Mom gives me a disapproving look. "Come on, Eliza. You must be joking."

I bristle. This is where I could assure her that we're not dating, but I need to hear what she thinks. "I'm not joking."

She waves a hand. "Look at him. This isn't you."

For the first time in a while, I take note of what Beckett's wearing: beige plaid shorts and a linen shirt. Does it scream "successful businessman"? Maybe not, but she can't dismiss him based on the clothes he wears.

But you did.

I squirm.

Beckett looks between us. "Iza, why did you bring me here? Really."

Mom smiles. "Don't feel bad. You're not alone. You're the third one of Iza's experiments I've met this month."

My stomach churns. I can't look at Beckett. This is where I expect him to correct her, assure her that we're not an item before he walks out.

"So what?" Beckett leans across the table. "She's figuring out what she wants. Why do you look down on her for that? You think it's shallow to want love? You think it's pathetic to keep trying?"

I burn with mortification.

As though he can sense I'm about to bolt, Beckett rests a hand on my knee under the table. "She cares so damn much about everything, and maybe I don't understand it either, but I admire it. Finding someone who will care about her half as much as she cares about everything isn't something she should be embarrassed about; it's something she deserves."

I blink hard to keep from crying. Beckett could absolutely be talking out of his ass because he can lie all he wants to my mother, but if his words are lies, I'll lie to myself and believe they're truths.

Mom looks unimpressed. "She won't find someone who cares as much as she does, and that's why she should quit."

"You don't think anyone is worthy of her?"

Mom shifts uncomfortably. I'm breathless, waiting for her answer.

"Iza talks about you constantly," Beckett says in a low voice. "I have a lot I'd like to say to you, but mainly I just want to know if you're trying to protect her, or if you're trying to control her."

There's a tense silence, and then Mom lets out a bark of laughter, as though the conversation is a joke. "Are you asking me what my intentions are with my own daughter?" She stands up and walks into the kitchen, where she begins rifling through cabinets for a glass. "Iza isn't good at picking men. She has father issues, you know. She finds relationships that remind her of him." Mom fills her glass with water and comes back to the table.

"How can I remember what I never had?" I ask because I'm tired of being talked about like I'm not here. "How can I be trying to recreate a relationship that never existed?"

Mom ignores me. "Did she tell you her last boyfriend cheated on her?"

Beckett stiffens and looks at me. "No. You didn't tell me that."

Mom settles herself back into her chair. "You know you won't last either, right? Especially if you keep playing the part of her knight in shining armor."

Pulling Beckett's hand off my knee, I give it a tug. "We should go," I whisper. I want to cry again, this time for a totally different reason. If Mom sees him as a prince coming to my rescue, then it's over.

Beckett turns his hand in mine, curving his fingers over my knuckles to still me. "I've known I won't last from the beginning. If I'm a knight, then I'm the type who dies, not the type who gets the girl." His gaze doesn't waver as he stares Mom down. "I don't think love from a man is what Iza's even after."

"Beckett, don't," I whisper.

He doesn't listen. "You know she has a list of all these things she wants out of a partner? She wants to love him, and she wants you to love him, but her last priority is the man loving her in return. All she wants is to love, and if that's too much for you, then you're not enough."

Mom's expression goes hard.

My limbs tremble. I'm cold all over. Never has anyone talked to my mother like this. Part of me is doing backflips because, finally, someone is on my side, saying things I've only secretly dreamed about in a guilt-ridden corner of my brain. The other part of me is sick because the person who is on my side is also the one destroying the relationship I value most.

I stand. "I'm sorry, Mom. We'll go."

Beckett doesn't move. "Maybe you're right, Lauren. Maybe Iza is mirroring the only parental relationship she's ever known, and that's why she finds men who don't give a shit about her."

Mom jolts to her feet. "Don't insinuate that I don't love my daughter!"

Beckett stands too, much calmer. "Then tell her you love her."

"Get out of my house. Both of you."

The room swims before my eyes. I can't breathe. My whole world is crumbling around me. I try to tell myself that it's fine, that this isn't really my world, and when I wish myself back, my real mother won't hate me. It doesn't help.

I'm barely cognizant of myself running from the house. Nearly tripping over a crack in the driveway. Fumbling for my keys. Then I'm behind the wheel. My door slams. The world goes quiet. The passenger side door opens and closes.

I turn the key in the ignition. Tears blur my vision. "She hates me," I whisper. "She hates me, she hates me, she hates me."

"She doesn't hate you," says Beckett. "She hates me."

"She thinks we're together. She thinks that I think what you think." I barely know what I'm saying. "She's a good mom, you know. She does care. She chose to have me, and she worked so hard to give me a good life." I put the car in reverse and pull out of the driveway.

"Iza, pull over," he says. "You can't drive like this."

"I'm fine," I say, even though I've never been less fine.

"I'm sorry," he says. "That was out of line. I know it wasn't my place to speak for you."

"You're right." My foot presses harder on the accelerator. "She thinks a man would either hold me back or try to overshadow me, and you proved her right by talking for me."

"Is that why you brought me here? Iza, I said I wanted to be your friend, not your boyfriend."

Mortification joins the pity party of emotions in my head. It dances right between guilt, anger, and devastation. "Then be my friend and don't do what you think is best, when you know it's the opposite of what I want. You know I hate being rescued. It doesn't make me feel safe; it makes me feel helpless."

"I couldn't stand by and do nothing. I've done that before."

I come to a jerky stop at the end of Mom's subdivision. "You're making the same mistake all over again! The core problem isn't that you stood by. It's that you didn't think of the other person's needs and feelings. Are you trying to make up for how you treated your last friend like you're settling a deal with karma, or do you actually care about me, specifically? Because if you actually feel something, then how could you ruin my life?" My voice breaks.

"I don't know! I don't know how to be selfless, but you make me want to try. I screwed up. I'm still learning how to do this . . . how to care. But *I'm* a screw-up, and I'm honestly terrified I can't be more."

I pull onto the highway. "She was all I had left, Beckett." Road noise whooshes in my ears. "It's not like I have a bunch of siblings to go to."

"Iza, slow down."

"We're not going to have a good laugh about how difficult Mom is. I'm not going to go to a grandparent who will then go to my mother and tell her how tough she's being."

"Iza!"

"I don't have some assurance that next Thanksgiving, with the whole family around and a few glasses of wine, all our dysfunctions will become something endearing we bond over."

A car horn blares. Beckett dives over the center console, reaching for the wheel.

A loud crack makes my eardrums throb.

Silence. A silence more silent than the ones found around Mom's dinner table.

I blink. My vision clears. A few wisps of purple smoke curl across my vision. The call of a bird soothes my ears.

Beckett and I are still in the car, which softly purrs. There's no fire and no airbags and no destruction. The car sits in a vast, endless field of wildflowers. I roll down my window, and the sweet scent of grass and pollen meets my nose and eases the tension behind my eyes.

"Where are we?" I swallow down the lump in my throat.

"A world peace universe." After the chaos, Beckett's soft voice in this place feels like warm tea on an autumn day. "Though the peace may be ruined now." Reaching over, he brushes a few tears off my cheek.

"Are there any other people here?"

He shakes his head.

I look out the window at the endless sea of grass dotted with pinks, yellows, purples, and blues. It reminds me of my apartment. Full of life and utterly empty.

I begin to cry. "I am so alone."

"You're not." Beckett unbuckles his seatbelt and fights his way past the center console to wrap me in his arms. "You're not alone."

"She couldn't say she loves me." Voicing it makes it so much worse. Sobs wrack my body.

Beckett fumbles with my seatbelt. It clicks open, and then he's hauling me over the center console into his lap. My legs are thrown over his and wedged against the door, but I don't care. I tuck my face into his shoulder and let him stroke my back and whisper sweet nonsense to me as I cry. I notice his hands are shaking too and realize he isn't as calm as I thought. Standing up to Mom, the near-crash—it wasn't as easy on him as he made it seem.

"I'm sorry," I say when my eyes are dry, with nothing left to give, and my chest is hollow. "I didn't listen to you either and decided to drive. And I yelled. And I ruined your shirt."

"No, I'm sorry. I fucked up. I finally had your trust, and I broke it." He shakes his head, visibly angry with himself.

Beckett is trying. It's more than I would have given him credit for when we first met. He cares, even if he only cares because he's trying to be a better person in general. I don't know if he can ever grow to have the capacity to care for me more, selflessly and unconditionally, or if he even wants that.

He said he'd be my friend, and he's trying to be that. I shouldn't have put hopes on him when he didn't want them. I see no way Beckett could ever fit into my life in the way I want. He is more than I thought but less than I'd hoped.

I climb back over to my side of the car, sighing as I fall into the driver's seat. "Why is everything so messy?"

"People are messy. Messier when you factor in magic. If you want to go home, I can take you and Lola back. You don't even have to use a wish."

I did test my instincts today, and they were wrong. I don't know how to read people, not from a first impression or a second—maybe not at all.

It's not comforting. People could be better than I think, but they could also be a whole lot worse. I don't know how to know who is good and who isn't. All I know is I can't choose anyone over Mom, not when this hurts worse than any breakup I've ever experienced.

If my first impressions are wrong, maybe there's still a real man out there who can fit into my life, but why spend years on another failure when I have a sure thing right now?

Fictional Darcy is the only man Mom's ever said a nice thing about.

I know his story right up until the end. I have a first and last impression of him, and the latter is a good one. Sure, there may be small trials and tribulations after the last page of *Pride and Prejudice*, but it ends with a happily ever after.

"Not yet," I say.

That daydream floats behind my eyes, the one where Mom and I and a fuzzy third person are sitting around a dining table, only it's not silent. We're laughing. Now, that fuzzy third person takes shape again, and I see Darcy.

I take the rose out of my hair and set it in the car's cup holder before facing Beckett. "Take me back to the Darcy universe, please."

He does it, and he doesn't even ask for a wish in return.

CHAPTER SEVENTEEN

Mom's not answering my calls. Even though I know this is temporary, her disapproval hangs like an anvil over my life because I know my real mom from my universe would have reacted the same way. It bothers me. At the very least, she should be able to see that Beckett's outburst, however out of line, displayed that he cares. I would think she'd place value on that.

I have to get out of this universe and get back to my real mom, the one who doesn't hate me, as soon as possible. So, I figure out where Darcy went. It doesn't take too much nagging for the frazzled Chester to relinquish his whereabouts.

Darcy took time off for his aunt's funeral in a little country town called Tightwad. I try not to feel too happy that, thanks to her recent death, Catherine is a nonissue.

According to Google, Tightwad is over three hours away and is technically classified as a village with a population of only sixty.

Well, now fifty-nine.

Also, there's a bank in the village, and the knowledge that a Tightwad Bank exists is a fact that my sleep-deprived brain finds humorous for far longer than is strictly warranted.

When I learn the funeral is Saturday, I book a room at a seedy motel in a nearby town (lodging is not an amenity Tightwad offers) and arrive late Friday night.

As I unpack my appropriately dismal gray dress for the morning, I decide *sketchy* is a fitting adjective for this place with its dated decor, rickety furniture, and questionable stains on the upholstery.

After eyeing the yellowed shower and deciding I'll feel cleaner not using it, I change and tuck myself into bed, carefully avoiding the comforter. I'm so tired, I can almost imagine the springs jabbing into my back are the equivalent of a spa's deep-tissue massage.

* * *

I hoped the funeral would be better attended. The people clustered in the rows of metal chairs serving as pews are few and far between. Not that the late aunt will mind, but a crowd would make it easier to blend in. As it is, as soon as I enter the worship center, Darcy's eyes lock onto me. I squirm in my snug dress. My "deep-tissue massage" from the night before did more harm than good, and my heels only worsen the situation.

The church is plain but nice, with gray carpet and white walls. There is a raised stage area with a podium and an altar. This is where the coffin is positioned and where Darcy stands, a small crowd of mourners surrounding him. It's been two weeks since I've seen him, and a little thrill of nerves zings through my stomach.

He spots me, and I let my gaze slide over him, as though I hadn't been staring. I turn in a circle, pretending to be fascinated by the angles of the ceiling and the recessed lighting.

"Iza."

I snap my attention from the ceiling to the broad chest planted in front of me.

"What are you doing here?" Darcy asks.

I try to contort my features into one of those quietly serene yet sad expressions people resort to at funerals. "Catherine was a marvelous woman. Knew her from my Girl Scout days. I had no idea she was your aunt until I read the obituary." Truthfully, I *haven't* read the obituary.

"My aunt despised children."

I shuffle my feet, wincing as my shoes pinch my toes. "Then her contributions to the troop are all the more admirable."

He lets out a long breath and runs a hand down his face. He needs a shave, and his eyes are strained. "This is getting a bit odd, Iza, to tell the truth."

He's right. Unless we're in a questionable teen movie, true love doesn't come from one person stalking another. It's time to come clean. Well, clean-ish. Due to the crusty shower and the fact that I can't disclose that Darcy only exists in my life thanks to a wish, I can't come *clean* clean.

I draw myself up. "Okay. I was worried about you. For some reason, I care if you're upset." I think fast. If only I had Austen's reference material with me to flip through. On that note, if only all men came with reference material. "I heard what happened with your aunt and decided to come by. I know you aren't blessed with . . . happy manners, and talking to people is hard for you. I want to let you know I'm here if you need me."

His face hardens. "Talking to people is a requirement for my job. I hadn't realized I was such a failure." He sticks his hands into the pockets of his dress pants as though the act will remove this confrontation from his sight as well.

"Of course, you can talk with *clients* fine," I say quickly. "I'm talking about opening up. Talking about your feelings." I should have my own self-help daytime TV show.

"I have other things to worry about right now besides my feelings." Darcy nods at his aunt's open casket.

"I think funerals are *the* time to worry about your feelings."

His withering gaze shoots poison into my insides, turning them into a shriveled, polluted wasteland.

"You know what? This is stupid. I shouldn't have come. It's totally unprofessional." Parallel universe or not, shooting my shot with Mr. Darcy at his aunt's funeral is taking things a bit too far.

"Wait." His voice is so quiet I barely hear it.

I pause.

"My sister, Georgiana, couldn't make it. My parents died many years ago. You're right." He shrugs. "I'm alone."

Now we're getting somewhere. "I'm sorry," I say. "I had no idea." Well, I do have an idea, thanks to my little Darcy instruction manual, but no need to freak him out further.

The corner of his mouth tugs up, as though if it weren't for the weight of his circumstances dragging his features down, he'd smile. "It's not like my dismal past is water-cooler conversation. Speaking of which, how are things back at the office? I regret that I've had to leave you with all the responsibilities there these last few weeks."

"Julia shoots down every new idea we come up with." I shake my head. "It's like what she wants is different from what she thinks she wants." My tongue sticks to the roof of my mouth. Something about that last part resonates with me.

I look Darcy up and down. I think about Beckett.

I stop thinking altogether when I realize my blank stare has drifted to the vicinity of Darcy's crotch region. Judging by the look he's giving me, he's noticed.

I avert my attention elsewhere, face heating. "What a nice funeral and what lovely . . . plants."

An array of droopy floral arrangements are arranged around the coffin—wilted roses, white lilies, and sprigs of lavender. What an odd tradition to have so much life at an event centered around death.

Life.

Death.

Plants.

"Oh my god." A few haggard funeral-goers send disapproving looks my way. I lower my voice and sidle closer to Darcy. I place a hand on his arm. A millisecond later, I chicken out and remove it. "I think I have a concept Julia will love."

I take his typical silence to mean *"Oh my gosh! Tell me more!"*

I lower my voice more, as though Tightwad's populace might come together and plagiarize my idea, should they overhear. "Plants." I nod, widening my eyes, hoping he'll catch on.

He doesn't. "Plants?"

"Yes." I clamber up the stage as best I can in my heels and pick up a heart-shaped rose arrangement from the casket. "In a barren wasteland, the last thing you'd want to look at all day is cold marble and dead trees made into flooring."

A few attendees of the funeral gather closer, sitting in the chairs before the coffin. They look up at me with rapt attention as though they think my outburst is the opening lines to a eulogy. However, the only face I focus on is Darcy's, which is unjustly skeptical.

"That seems like more of an interior design feature than anything to do with architecture," Darcy says.

I grin. "Julia would say you're not thinking grand enough. We need walls made of material that's durable, but also porous enough for vines to climb, to create living walls. We need irrigation systems running through the floors and integrated grow lights for the plants. We need a sublayer of soil for the oak tree in the entryway, ceilings high enough to account for it, and room dimensions large enough to accommodate it all."

More people press in. Some start sniffing and wiping their eyes.

"An oak tree? In the entryway?" Darcy's eyes gaze from the congregating people to me.

"And a separate heating system for each room to mimic the different climates for each region of fauna every room will represent. Rainforests and desert oases, a flowering garden to put the Botanical Gardens to shame." I clasp my hands together. "A waterfall off the grand stair."

"A waterfall? Iza, you've lost your mind."

"Each room won't even feel like a room, but like you're outdoors, and the world hasn't ended. Imagine a shoe closet with a floor of faux moss, decorated with toadstools, with faux decaying logs for shelves." Excitement threatens to burst my chest wide open and land me in the same boat (er, wooden box) the unfortunate late Catherine is in. "Sure, maybe some are interior design features," I say more calmly, "but if we can sell Julia on the idea, she won't care so much about the rest. For the same reason people bring flowers to a funeral, a bunker of teeming vegetation would be desirable at the world's end." I gesture to Catherine's cold face. "Death is easier to look at through a filter of life."

The gathering bursts into applause. They seem to have taken my business proposal as an elaborate metaphor of some sort because there isn't a dry eye in the house. Old men clap each other on the back, saying things like, "She was a fine woman," or simply, "Plants," before bursting into wracking sobs. The women pass around tissues while murmuring, "A beautiful service," over and over again, like they're trying to summon something, maybe Catherine herself.

Darcy is unreadable.

I replace the flower arrangement, steadying it on the coffin before offering Catherine an apologetic smile.

I dismount the stage. A guy in a white collar closes a bible and tucks it under his elbow, nodding in acceptance, knowing he has no chance of following my apparently moving performance. He salutes me as I pass.

I stop in front of Darcy. "I should go, right?" An old man with a walker creaks my way, an obituary grasped in his gnarled hands and a gleam in his eye that alerts me he's about to ask for my autograph.

Darcy nods tersely. "Yeah, you should go."

* * *

If that girl from *The Princess and the Pea* could feel a pea through twenty mattresses and twenty feather beds, the mattress in this motel would rupture every disk in her spine.

I should've driven home after the funeral, but I couldn't face my empty apartment. Lola went away with her sister, for the weekend, to some expensive spa. Splurging is very unlike Lola, but she was unconcerned, saying that nothing she did here mattered anyway, so why not live a little before we went home? She didn't sound bitter about it, which was also weird. She's treating this whole thing like a vacation and not the catastrophe it is. Her confidence that I'll get us back to our universe redoubles the pressure hanging over me.

I could have knocked on Beckett's door, but that doesn't feel right. He's made it clear he thinks Darcy is a mistake, and I can't take advantage of his friendship by using him for comfort.

On my nightstand, my phone lights up and buzzes. The screen shows an incoming call from Chester.

Sitting up, I answer. "Hey, Chester."

His shallow breaths rasp in my ear. "Good. You're still up. Darcy called me with the most brilliant idea. You have to hear it."

I nearly choke. "Oh, really?"

Chester lets out a puff of air, and the speaker crackles. "Yes. Plants. Lots and lots of plants. Think giant oak and waterfall staircase. It's brilliant. An oasis in a nuclear wasteland."

The room tilts and grows fuzzy as my gut drops. "This was *his* idea?" I feign nonchalance.

"I know. So out of the box for him. Anyway, I couldn't contain myself, so I thought I'd ring everyone from the office. I'll give you and Kalyan more deets on Monday, and you guys can get cracking on the new sketches." He lets out a little squeal that would make a schoolgirl cringe. "I think this will work, Iza. Leave it to Darcy to save the day, working even while on vacation."

I hang up the phone before Chester can, and hurl it across the room—onto the other bed (I don't want to *break* it).

I thought Darcy was classic and timeless—as though being timeless is a good thing. It's not. Chivalry is dead, but assholes are immortal. He's a classic, timeless jerk—one of the really horrible ones that can be found all throughout history, like Napoleon, Edison, and whoever the fuck invented alarm clocks. He's like the founding father of douchebaggery.

Once again, my first impression was wrong. I'm barely surprised.

A knock on my door causes me to put my rage on a brief hiatus. When I answer, I'm met with Darcy, his hair tousled, his tie loose, jacket undone.

The threat of an assault charge keeps my fists pinned to my sides. "What are you doing here?"

His eyes shift away, and he scratches the back of his neck. I wait for him to explain *something*, whether it be his presence on my doorstep or why he stole my idea. I didn't know it was possible to burn with anger and suffer from painful awkwardness simultaneously, yet here we are.

At last, he breaks the uncomfortable silence. "I'm glad you're still here." He shifts his weight before adding, "This is the only accommodation nearby, which is how I found you." As though he needs to provide an explanation to the person who stalked him twice.

"Of course." I stand aside. "Come in." This motel looks like something right out of a crime show. Fitting, since it's about to become a murder scene.

He enters, scanning the seventies wood paneling, floral wallpaper, and puke-green carpet. Perching myself on the edge of the bed, I debate whether to let him talk or go ahead and lay into him.

Darcy wanders from the dresser to the wicker chair, to the TV. He fiddles with the remote, turning it over in his hands as though it's the most interesting object he's ever seen. If he were the nineteenth-century Darcy, it probably would be. He sets the remote down and directs his full attention . . . to the floor under my foot, which I tap impatiently.

"I know this is wildly inappropriate to tell you now of all times"—Darcy addresses the floor—"but I have to get it off my chest. Especially after what you said today at the funeral."

Oh god. This isn't going where I think it is, is it?

Darcy stares at the floor harder. "You should know I admire you"—briefly, I wonder if the floor is flattered by this declaration, before Darcy adds—"most ardently." His face pinches into a frown, and his eyes finally dart up to mine. "Shit. Who says 'ardently'? That was a bit far, wasn't it?"

His confession is so far opposite my feelings toward him, I'm at a loss for what to say.

"I don't know why," Darcy says, "because I normally wouldn't get involved in an office drama. Then there's the matter of you. At work, you're composed. Outside work, your behavior borders irrationality. You're smart but unreasonably spontaneous, professional sometimes and flighty others. These behaviors should repel me, but you're a paradox I can't tear myself away from. So I have to tell you . . ." He focuses on the empty air beside my ear. "I'd like to go on a date. With you."

I barely manage to keep my composure. "You're asking me out after saying my personality repels you?"

He blinks rapidly. "*Should* repel me."

"And what about the Julia project?" I rise. "Are you going to claim stealing my idea and pitching it to Chester behind my back is also a sign of how deep your affection runs?"

He leans against the dresser languidly. "No. I won't claim that. My actions regarding that had to do with what's best for Chester and the project. If you'd pitched that idea, it would've never taken off."

I march up to him. "Why? You think my abilities are so far beneath your own?" I'm not quite sure why I'm talking like someone from Regency England. Maybe my subconscious is channeling his source material in my time of distress.

Darcy scoffs. "Please. A mossy shoe closet? That idea coming from a woman? I'm sorry, Iza, but it's a fact; everyone would've laughed at you. I did what was best, and I'm glad I did."

A hysterical laugh flies from my lips. "You have the nerve to insult my personality, patronize my entire sex, steal my idea, and then *ask me out?*"

He throws up his hands and stalks to the other side of the room. "Yes. Silly me. I didn't follow the normal dating rituals. I should've given you flowers and chocolates before asking."

"Women like it when a man shows a shred of human decency before asking them out, yeah," I snap.

"It's that guy from the other day, isn't it? The one who dropped off your car?" Darcy snorts. "You're dating him?"

"And why would that be any of your business?" *What the hell? Why didn't I squash that idea down?*

Darcy's lips twist, and he strides over until he's mere inches away, looming over me. "I know little about him, but it's enough to deduce he's scum of the earth."

My hands shake. "All the chocolate and flowers in the world wouldn't have solicited a different response from me. Fuck off, Darcy."

His mouth tightens, and he nods. "You've shown my feelings to be as misplaced as I suspected. Thank you for the clarity."

I flinch when the door slams behind him.

I take a few steadying breaths. It's okay. This fits with the plan. Darcy will prove himself in the end.

But there's something that's not fine at all. Between the tense look at the office between Darcy and Beckett, and Beckett coming up again in tonight's argument, it seems like Beckett might be Mr. Wickham.

CHAPTER EIGHTEEN

I hunch over the kitchen table and stab a fork into my container of leftover takeout. It's the Thursday after the funeral. Darcy hasn't returned, stating he's still managing his aunt's affairs. This leaves Kalyan and me with the task of drawing up his new plans. Knowing there's no way anyone would believe the idea is mine, I keep my head down and go with the flow. The added pressure of Darcy's absence means Kalyan and I work more hours than ever.

It's nearly midnight. Lola's already asleep, so I'm alone. The bite of cold hibachi feels like a three-hundred-pound weight my tongue is trying to bench-press. I swallow, and the unchewed bite scrapes ever so slowly down my aching throat. I try to console myself with the knowledge that if my plan works out, I'll never be alone again.

Last week at the motel was Darcy's and my rock bottom. Our story will follow the book, and it only goes up from here. I expect a long, beautifully written letter to arrive any day, in which Darcy will explain why his opinion of Beckett is so low. While I struggle to imagine Beckett doing anything truly terrible, considering Wickham tried to get with Darcy's underage sister, to swindle her out of her dowry, I've been avoiding Beckett until I see what's in that letter.

A soft but deliberate knock sounds at the front door, and I jump.

"Iza?" Beckett's voice on the other side of the door whisper-shouts.

Because midnight-me apparently suffers from bad judgment, I slide off my chair and let him in. The sight of him stirs something inside me.

"What are you doing here?"

"I missed you." Beckett closes the door with his foot. "Magic sucks when there's no one around to be impressed by it. Up for some fun?"

"I think I've had enough fun for a lifetime."

"Correction. You've had no fun in your lifetime. Come on, Iza—I'm trying to grovel here."

"Wait, what?"

"I'm trying to apologize for not listening to you the other day when I said that stuff to your mom."

"I think groveling involves you on your knees."

"You'd like that too much." His eyes glitter. "I was going to do a whole grand gesture thing and talk to your mom, tell her we had a big fight and you brutally dumped me, so she'd know the other night was all on me. Then I realized I'd be doing more stuff you didn't ask for, so instead, I'm giving you me. Tonight, whatever we do is your decision."

I feel myself blush. *I'm giving you me.*

"Easy, Iza." He smirks. "Your freak flag's showing. I mean my magic is yours until tomorrow. Tell me what you want, and I'll wish it for you. You don't have to use any of your own wishes. Let's have an adventure."

The gravity of what he's trusting me with slams into my chest. He can't lie, so he has to keep his promise. I have complete power over him for a night. He's being incredibly vulnerable, especially considering how some of his other charges have treated him.

I want to forgive him completely, but I hesitate. If it weren't for what Darcy said, I wouldn't be wary. We're not in a *Pride and Prejudice* novel; Beckett might not be Wickham. But I can't imagine a reality where Darcy is mistaken about this.

I can't trust my instincts anymore, so I lean on other peoples' impressions. Nearly the whole world loves Mr. Darcy, including my mother. He can't be the bad guy in this scenario.

"You don't have to do this," I say.

Beckett smiles. "Does this mean you forgive me? Your good opinion once lost isn't lost forever?"

"I do forgive you," I say carefully, "for Mom's house."

"Prove it." Beckett raises an eyebrow mischievously. "Let me make it up to you."

"Well, there's no point in you talking to my mother, since I'll hopefully be leaving this universe soon. But if you happen to see her, tell her I called you a lemming. I told her men are the lemmings of human society once, and I think it was her proudest parenting moment."

"Noted. Is there anything you do want? We could fly on the back of a pterodactyl. We could go to the moon. We could—"

"I'm kind of hungry. Can we get pizza?"

Beckett laughs. "Yes, we can get pizza. What else?"

Waffles rubs against my ankles. I scoop him up and scratch his ears. Beckett is offering me a chance at something. He is chaos, and I could embrace him.

Not literally, of course.

While I'm waiting around on Darcy to get his shit together, I can turn a moment of uncertainty into certainty. For one night, I can intentionally choose to enjoy not being in control. I can be the girl who has fun. I don't have to trust Beckett completely, but I also don't have to write him off without proof. Being friends with Beckett can have benefits—the benefit in this scenario being one tiny, safe adventure. No pterodactyls.

I set Waffles down. "Does prank war revenge sound fun?"

When I say the word *fun*, Beckett presses his lips together and holds back a smile, like I've just said my first curse word and he finds it adorable. "It sounds very fun. You're going to see magic can be useful when it's not being totally awful. For instance, you can travel anywhere in an instant." He extends a hand. "Ready?"

A zing shoots through my stomach as I lay my fingers over Beckett's. "Let's have an adventure."

* * *

A loud crack smacks into my eardrums. Then I blink and find myself and Beckett standing next to my desk at work, purple fog dwindling in the air around us.

"You didn't actually have to hold my hand." Beckett smirks. "But I'm flattered."

Immediately, I release his hand. Turning in a slow circle, I take in the office at night.

The shadows the moonlight casts across the floor turn the office into something eerie and otherworldly. Without tapping keyboards, humming conversation, or Chester's hysterical yelling, the dead quiet adds another layer of weirdness. Outside, the twinkling lights of the city merge into the sky, like the city is a lake reflecting the stars above.

"That's his desk, right?" Beckett points.

"Kalyan's? Yeah." I wander over. Stacks of paper coat every surface. Unbeknownst to him, I've been adding ten to fifteen extra sheets of blank pages under the disaster every day for the last week. He has yet to notice. "We need plastic shot glasses and glitter," I say, getting down to business.

With a snap of Beckett's fingers, a few packages of small, red disposable cups and a couple of bags of glitter appear on Kalyan's desk. "What's the idea here?" he asks.

"We'll fill every cup to the brim with glitter and place them all over his desk, chair, and the floor surrounding his desk. It'll be impossible to clean them up without disaster. He'll be finding glitter for the next decade." I read the label of one of the bags of glitter. "Biodegradable, huh?"

Beckett shrugs. "Can't let the baby seals suffer because of our juvenile games."

I trample the mushy *Aww* rising in my chest. Clearing my throat, I nod. "Cool. This will either go down as the greatest office prank of all time, or I'll get fired."

He smiles. "Why not both? Go out with a bang."

Carefully, I open the bag of glitter and begin filling cups. As I finish each one, I hand them to Beckett, and he arranges them on Kalyan's desk so close together they touch. I dust glitter off my hands, but it's futile. Despite my best efforts, this prank might affect me more than Kalyan. When I come in tomorrow still covered in glitter, there will be no doubt who did this.

We work in silence for a while. When Beckett concentrates, the tip of his tongue barely sticks out of the corner of his mouth. How have I not noticed that before? *Why* am I noticing it now?

Before I know what I'm doing, I take one of the miniature cups and flick it through the air. It bounces off the side of his head. He turns slowly. "Oh really?"

Giddy excitement bubbles inside of me, as though I'm a schoolgirl who has finally managed to catch her crush's attention. "I don't know what you're talking about."

There's a gleam in Beckett's eye, like he's a cat and I'm the mouse he thought was dead, but I've just twitched. He crosses the distance between us. "Are you flirting with me?"

"That would be ridiculous," I say breathlessly, the back of my thighs digging into the desk behind me.

"Ridiculous." he agrees, leaning forward so he presses against me. "You have glitter on your nose."

I flick my fingers at him, sending specks of glitter dusting onto his face in a spattering of ethereal, moonlit freckles. "So do you."

"That was very rude." His voice is low, portraying a gravity his words don't. Diving forward, he snatches the bag of glitter. I let out a horrified yelp as he plunges his hand in and draws out a sparkling handful.

"Don't you dare!" I try to scoot away.

He grabs me behind the knees and hoists me onto the desk. Instinctively, I lock my legs around his hips to steady myself. Before I can become suitably embarrassed, a glitter explosion erupts in my face. Spluttering, I leap off the desk, shoving Beckett away as I swat glitter out of my vision. "You could've blinded me!"

"No," he says, laughing. "I wished for it to stay out of your eyes."

"You'd better wish for it to stay out of yours too." I dive for him, prying the bag out of his hands and pelting him in the chest with a fistful of glitter.

His open-mouthed shock quickly turns into a hard smile. "Don't start what you can't finish."

I scuttle backward, clutching the bag of glitter protectively. "Pretty sure you started this."

"You threw a cup at my face." He follows me, and the image of him stalking toward me across the dim office does strange things to my head.

Beckett rushes forward. I try to run backward, holding the bag behind me. His body slams into mine, his arms wrapping around me as he reaches for the glitter. A giggle escapes my lips. I try to twist away. He plants his foot behind mine, and my knees buckle. I let out a squeak as he gently tackles me onto a rug. His hands behind my back and head provide a surprisingly gentle landing to his linebacker-quality tackle.

Flat on my back, I blink up at him. He slips his arms out from under me and stretches to grab the bag of glitter. An evil grin spreads across his face as he holds two handfuls up. I barely have time to try to wriggle away before he falls onto me, laughing and digging his hands into my hair. His fingers rake over my scalp, sending shivers down my spine.

I freeze, too enraptured by his exuberant face inches from mine to care that I'll have glittery hair for the rest of my life. He pauses, smile fading as his eyes drop to mine. His fingers are still wound in my hair. The heavy weight of him on top of me warms me from head to toe.

I pant. So does he. *He. Is. Wickham.*

"We shouldn't." My voice is husky and foreign in my ears. Maybe I inhaled some glitter. I'll have to google if that will cause permanent vocal cord damage.

Beckett lays a gentle finger over my lips, barely touching me, but the brush of his skin across my mouth sends tingles coursing into my body. "We definitely shouldn't." His lips barely move, and he stares at me like he's stuck in a trance.

I've literally embraced chaos now, and I'm scared by how good it feels. Almost without knowing what I'm doing, I trace my finger over his shoulder. "What if we did?"

"I told you I wouldn't." His voice lowers, "But now, I've got you under me, looking like the sexiest goddamn stripper fairy I've ever seen, and—"

"Stripper fairy?" I wrinkle my nose. *Stop, Iza. End this now.* But I don't want to end this.

"Yeah." He looks away, and for a moment, I think that's all he's going to say. But then he dips his head until his nose nearly brushes mine. "Because you're beautiful like a fairy, but you're covered in glitter like a stripper."

"You're such a dork." Heat floods my body, but I try not to show it as I flick glitter up at him. "Have you seen many stripper fairies?"

Beckett cracks a smile. "Not many promiscuous ones."

I dissolve into giggles. "Did you just say 'promiscuous'?"

"Yeah, I could've used another word, but I figured you'd get your panties in a wad."

"Spend a lot of time thinking about my panties, do you?"

His eyes darken and fall to my mouth. "Fuck, yes."

I stop laughing. He stops smiling.

I forget how to breathe, so I swallow the air instead. Beckett has his serious expression on. Not sarcastic-serious or mocking-serious, just serious.

"I can't." He releases my hair and pushes himself off me, and I'm more confused than ever.

Maybe I really do torment him, and he can't stand the thought of kissing me.

I tell myself he's Wickham, so I'm better off, but I don't believe it.

Fighting down my hurt and disappointment, I focus my attention elsewhere. Glitter covers every square inch of the office in a fifty-foot radius. It ingrains itself into every fiber of the rug and coats many an important document.

I stand up. "If we don't clean this up, I'm fired."

Rising to his feet, Beckett manages a smile and snaps his fingers. "Forget about my super impressive magical abilities already?"

Glitter rises into the air, working its way out of every crevice—slipping off of every strand of our hair and every fold of our clothing. It swirls into a churning vortex above our heads while the packages pop open and stacks of cups spring out like coiled slinkies. The cups separate and fly through the air to settle themselves all over and around Kalyan's desk. The plastic clicks as each cup falls deliberately into place. Then, the glitter cloud descends, raining down to fill the cups to their brims without spilling a speck. When everything settles, Kalyan's desk is covered in glitter-filled cups, but the rest of the office shines immaculately.

Beckett looks over at me. "Why'd you ever stop being glitter girl?"

"I grew up."

"Fuck that. Age is a ridiculous reason to avoid things that make you happy. There's this quote by C. S. Lewis. He said when he became a man, he put away childish things, including the fear of childishness and the desire to be very grown up."

Like that, Beckett made everything I'm working for feel like one giant, silly insecurity. "*Get over yourself,*" his words say.

My gaze catches on the large windows behind him. The Gateway Arch is lit up in the distance. A wild, very childish idea takes hold of me. Before I can overthink it, I point. "I want to go there."

CHAPTER NINETEEN

Beckett sits me on a chair and tells me to close my eyes. The next thing I know, I feel cool night air against my skin. I open my eyes to find us sitting high in the air on top of the Gateway Arch, our feet hanging over the edge. A breathtaking cityscape sprawls before us. If I squint, I can't tell where the stars stop and the city lights begin.

A box of pizza materializes in my lap. We eat in silence for a while. When we're done, another snap of Beckett's fingers makes the box disappear.

I pretend to take in the view, but I'm hyperaware of him sitting beside me, mere inches away.

"This is what made me want to be an architect," I say finally. That and Mom handing me a list of acceptable careers to choose from. "It felt . . . magical. Creating something."

"You grow steel because you couldn't grow plants?" His eyes pierce me.

I look away, swallowing hard. "I like both. If only they weren't mutually exclusive."

"Do they have to be?"

I don't answer. I'm not afraid of heights, but with my legs hanging over nothingness and the Arch swaying ever so slightly in the wind, vertigo makes my vision swim. We're high over the tops of skyscrapers, but my head's stuck back at an office building.

I'd be lying if I said I hadn't wanted to kiss Beckett earlier. Not that it's worth thinking about because he didn't want to. Still. I *do* think about it. I'm wildly curious what his lips feel like, whether he tastes like cinnamon, whether he kisses like the wild party boy he pretends to be or has a tender, attentive side—

"You can't fall, you know." Beckett lays his hand over mine, covering my trembling fingers in warmth. "I can't let you, not while you're my charge. I'd wish you right back up here."

I tear my gaze off the ground below. The wind off the river behind us is cold, and I shiver.

Beckett stretches to pull his hoodie over his head. The edge of his shirt lifts, exposing a nicely defined hip bone.

He hands me the hoodie, and I pull it over my head. It's soft, warm, and smells like French toast. "Why didn't you kiss me?" I ask before I can think better of it. "I thought you were Mr. Live-in-the-Moment."

He stares off into the distance. "Not giving a damn about consequences used to be easy because nothing matters when you're a phantom—slipping in and out of reality, helping people impact the world, but never leaving anything of yourself behind to show you were there too . . . to show you even existed at all. Who gives a damn about the fallout when you won't be around to witness it?"

I close my eyes and listen. His tone is different, soft and low. A spoken lullaby. One of those creepy ones that talks about roses and death.

He's been used and hurt and gets nothing in return. It's an endless cycle. *An eternal punishment.* It's no wonder his guard is up. It's no wonder he rebels, finding freedom through little acts of defiance—a party here, a nice car there, a manipulated wish, a stolen kiss.

"Is that the real reason you brought me here tonight? For a good time?" I've always known Beckett is not the forever type.

Brows knitting, he turns to face me. "I brought you here to apologize, but I almost did something I would have regretted forever."

For a moment, I think I might have slipped over the edge because of the way my stomach plummets. "Oh."

"Shit," he says under his breath. "That's not what I mean. If it would've been anyone else, sure, maybe—"

"You would have kissed anyone else, but not me? You would have regretted kissing me forever?"

His fingers wrap around the edge of the Arch, knuckles pale. "Yes, but listen to me. You're more than collateral damage. You make me want to be careful. That's why I didn't kiss you."

A rush of goose bumps washes over my skin. "Not because you can't bear the thought of kissing me?" My voice comes out small, and I blush, feeling ridiculous for needing his affirmation.

"I promise I can bear the thought of kissing you." His tone is firm but gentle.

"I don't understand how you can say that when you also said that I'm your punishment."

"What are you talking about?" He sounds aghast, but that can't be right.

I tuck my hands into the too-big sleeves of his hoodie and shrug like it doesn't matter. "You said you're sent to people who torment you."

A short, breathless laugh flies from his lips. *"What?"* The way he says that one word, filled with so much disbelief and affection, sends warm shivers through my body. "There are a lot of different ways to torment someone. The way you torment me is my favorite."

Now it's my turn to go breathless. My turn to ask, "What are you talking about?"

He thinks a minute. "Tell me what you find inside the pocket of that jacket you're wearing."

I slip a hand into his hoodie pocket. My fingers come into contact with cool glass. I close my hand around the object, pulling it out to discover a bottle of sparkly purple nail polish.

Gently, he takes the bottle from my hand. "When we first met, I figured you were just another difficult person in a long line of difficult people."

"A torment." I swallow hard.

"Yeah." He laughs softly. "That night I asked what kind of vessel I came from started the real torment. You looked so sad when you said you weren't the glitter type anymore. It didn't make sense. It seemed like an easy fix, so I drove across town and bought a damn bottle of nail polish. I thought if I could give it to you, it might make you happy, and then I could stop thinking about it."

I just stare. For once, my brain shuts up. It doesn't overanalyze. It just takes in his words.

"Give me your hand," he says, opening the nail polish.

"Huh?"

"I need something to do while I tell you this, or I'll chicken out. Or if you're too cool for purple nail polish, I'll paint my own."

I give him my hand. He's painfully gentle as he curls my first finger over his knuckle and supports it with his thumb. Bowing his head over my hand, he begins. The polish is cold, but his hand is warm enough I barely notice.

"Anyway, after I bought it, giving it to you seemed like a pathetic thing to do, so I've just been carrying it around. Keeping my distance seemed like the safer option and the option you preferred. So I watched you make your wish, and it tormented me. I put you to bed that night, and you talked to me like we were friends, and it *tormented me* because I knew in the morning, we wouldn't be."

"Oh my god, Beckett." I don't know what else to say.

His hand, under mine, twitches. He's reached the third finger now. "It torments me that I keep hurting you."

As he finishes with the first hand and reaches for the other, his fingers shake. So do mine, but when we join them together, they steady.

"It torments me when you ask me questions like I'm a person instead of a party trick, because I want to tell you everything you want to know, but in the end, opening up will mean nothing."

Turning my hand, he paints my thumbnail. "It torments me to watch you try so hard." His voice drops. "Especially when it involves Darcy."

"Beckett, I—"

The brush pauses over the nail of my pinky. "Hold on." He finishes the rest of my fingers in silence, then screws the cap back on the bottle and meets my eye, still holding my hand. "It torments me how much I like it when you're smiling instead of frowning."

As if he coaxed it into being, a smile tugs at my lips.

"Even your hair torments me." A slow smile forms across his own mouth. "It pisses me off. Why is it everywhere all the time? I find it on my clothes, in my car, my apartment, in my bed—where the rest of you can never be." His smile fades. "Sorry."

Fire races up my arm from his touch. "Don't be," I breathe.

His grin is back. "You like hearing how I'm in agony because of you?"

"Maybe. Tell me more."

He moves closer. "Like what, Iza? What do you want to hear? That those short shorts you're wearing live up to their name and have been driving me wild all night?" Propping a hand beside my hip, he leans in. "Does that make you happy?"

My gaze drops to his lips. It would take so little to close this distance. "Ever since that night in the rain, I thought I annoyed you."

He touches the back of his hand to my cheek. "No. I don't dislike you at all, and that's the worst part. Under everything you think you want, all you really want is love, and it kills me that I can't help you with that."

I recoil. All the warmth inside me crystalizes and shatters. "Why would you tell me all that just to say you can't be with me?"

"So you can finally understand I'd never do anything to hurt you."

I don't know what to do. All my plans and everything I thought I knew are upturned. The world feels as strange and dangerous as it did the night Beckett appeared. My eyes prick with tears, but I refuse to break now. Not in front of him. I'm stronger than that.

Grandma told me if I held my breath while running barefoot over her yard, the bees wouldn't sting me. In this situation, though I try, no amount of holding my breath takes the sting of his words away. Of course, if I asphyxiate and die, that might help, but that's slightly extreme.

"Please say something." There's an edge of urgent desperation to Beckett's voice I've never heard before.

"I think you might be Wickham," I say quietly, both for his benefit and mine. Resolutely, I stare straight ahead. "It's better this way."

"I don't even know what that means."

"You've never read the book? Or watched the movie?"

A bitter laugh escapes his lips. "I had better things to do than watch movies about boring rich guys."

"Darcy isn't—"

"Right for you," Beckett finishes. "I saw the memo about Darcy's new idea. I saw the drawings on Kalyan's desk. Anyone with eyes should be able to tell you're the plant girl, and that idea could never be his."

"But you're not right for me either?" I hold my breath, waiting for the sting.

He turns the nail polish bottle over in his hands. "Maybe I could be if I weren't what I am."

And there it is. He's temporary. We both know it. "I never meant to hurt you," I say.

"I know."

If I wrap my arms around myself, I can almost pretend like his hoodie is the touch I want from him. In a different universe, maybe it could be something more than emptiness and impossibility. If I talk, I'll cry. So I don't.

After a long while, he sighs. "It's late. We should head back."

When I get home, I scrub the polish off my nails until my fingers are as raw and red as my eyes.

CHAPTER TWENTY

I can't bring myself to call in. Though I catch only a couple hours of rest, the thought of all the work left to do at the office forces me out of bed.

"You look like a raccoon." Lola leans against the counter, sipping a cup of coffee. She's perfectly put together, with her glossy braid and crisp khakis.

"Late night. Beckett stopped by." I yawn. "We went on an adventure."

Lola widens her eyes. "Is that a euphemism for something?"

"Please." I force a joking tone. "He lives in a bottle of nail polish. Mom would disapprove. And I don't think we could survive the long-distance thing."

Her eyes sparkle as she bites into a plain bagel. "Why are you lying to yourself?"

"It's just not possible, Lola. Darcy is for me." If I keep my tone confident, maybe I'll feel confident too.

Beckett's fun, but Darcy is forever. It may not seem like it, but Darcy's good inside. I have the spoilers. Everything he does, he's doing because he believes it's the right thing to do.

"Why isn't it possible?" Lola wipes her fingers on a dishcloth. "Wish him free. One wish to go home, one wish to free him. You're overcomplicating it."

"If it were that simple, wouldn't he have told me?"

She chews thoughtfully. "Maybe not. Men can be dumbasses."

I can't let go of the suspicion that's been in the back of my mind ever since the night Darcy asked me out. Beckett might be Wickham. There might be something about him I don't know yet. "If his curse were the only thing holding him back, then why has he also said so many things that make it sound like he, specifically, is the problem? He told me to stay away from 'someone like him.'"

"Maybe he feels like he doesn't deserve you? You're overthinking this."

My heart speeds up. Could it be that simple?

Maybe there's a simple solution to the curse Beckett didn't think to mention. Even if wishing him free won't work for some reason, there has to be another loophole. I could just never make my last two wishes, and he'd never have to leave. We shouldn't give up. He even demonstrated that he's willing to work things out with my mother. We could really be something.

"Well," Lola says, "I've gotta go. I'm meeting my sister before work. She's trying to set me up on a blind date."

"And you're letting her?"

Lola shrugs. "I figured why not take a page out of your book and test-drive a few men?"

"I'm not test-driving," I splutter. She makes it sound so terrible. "I'm on the search for true love."

Sweeping her bag and keys off the counter, Lola gives me a look. "Uh-huh. I expect a full report tonight." With a little wave, she whisks out of the apartment.

Collecting my own things, I think about what she said. *"You're overcomplicating it. Wish him free."* I rush across the hall and pound on Beckett's door, but he doesn't answer. I check my phone and realize I'm running late, so I send him a text.

Me: Can we meet up after work? Need to talk about last night.

* * *

"Touché," is Kalyan's first word to me when he sees his glitter-covered desk. Then he makes an intern clean it up.

It's the slowest workday of my life. Every minute is agony. Beckett texts about an hour later.

Beckett: Definitely free to talk later.

His enthusiasm makes a goofy grin spread across my face. He's turned me into one of those people who smile at their phones.

But around three, I receive another notification. A thrill goes through me because, at first, I think it's Beckett again, but no. It's an email. From Darcy.

After I read it, the day passes slowly for an entirely different reason. Not because I'm excited to meet Beckett, but because I need to confront him.

Dear Iza,

Don't worry. I'm not sending this in hopes you'll reconsider the date. You brought up two particular things I feel I need to set straight. One is the matter of the Julia project. If you had let me explain further, I would have told you that, after the idea is approved by Julia, I intend on giving you full credit. I simply believed the project needed to be backed by me, the senior architect, for it to have legs.

Now, for the bigger reason for this email. With regard to your affiliation with Beckett, I write only because I think you deserve the truth. I must admit, I don't know him personally, and everything I tell you, I have learned secondhand. But my source is a good one. My sister, Georgiana, relayed the information I am about to disclose.

She is not entirely blameless in the following, but I think you'll find his faults far exceed her own. I will preface this by telling you my sister is only sixteen years of age.

She and her friends heard of Beckett's notorious parties and decided to try to get in. Their fake IDs were challenged at the door.

It was then Georgiana made the acquaintance of Beckett, who I'm sure waited by design to introduce himself until the moment he could swoop in like some sort of hero. He let them all inside, singling out Georgiana, serving her alcohol, and offering her drugs. As she grew more and more inebriated, Beckett grew more friendly. Luckily, my sister, at last, came to her senses. I shudder to think what could have happened to her if she hadn't.

Realizing she needed to leave, Georgiana gathered her friends, and they made their exit. With the drugs and alcohol in her system, she collapsed only a few blocks away. By the time her friends had the presence of mind to call for help, Georgiana's life hung in the balance.

She had her stomach pumped and remained in the hospital for several days. She was too weak to even attend our aunt's funeral. I only wish I could gather enough evidence to press charges. Somehow, there seem to be no witnesses. Likely, Beckett has something over them. Perhaps he's paid them off. Considering she nearly died, he could be convicted of a felony if only I had substantial proof.

I should reiterate that Georgiana's word is good. She wouldn't lie about something like this. I hope this has provided you some clarity regarding our prior disagreements.

—Darcy

Although it isn't a beautifully crafted letter, it's by far the most disturbing email I've ever received. By the end of it, I'm so nauseous, I almost ask Chester if I can go home. If I go home, though, I might run into Beckett. I need time to collect myself.

When I first met him, I thought Beckett had the potential to be dangerous. But now . . . the guy who worries about baby seals choking on glitter can't be so disgustingly void of basic morals.

I think of party-loving Beckett and how his entire philosophy of life revolves around living in the moment and never giving much thought to consequences. Maybe he let Georgiana and her friends in under some delusion that everyone should have a good time.

While I know many good things about Beckett, I've barely scratched the surface of who he is, and only recently became something resembling friends. There's so much about him I *don't* know.

My Darcy should have all the same morals as the Darcy from literature. He surely wouldn't lie. And I have no doubt sweet little Georgiana wouldn't make false claims. Which means Beckett truly might be Wickham. Which means the rest might be true too.

By five, I've finally gathered myself enough that I'm ready to call it a day. The drive home is a blur, and by the time I park next to Beckett's shiny car, my hands shake, and bile rises in my throat. Through my fogged mind, it registers that Lola's car is missing. Her sister must've kept her late.

After barely managing to fit my key in the door, I step inside my apartment. The fairy lights in the living room are on, twinkling in the darkness, and faint music meets my ears.

Beyond the chair, the same one Beckett appeared in, the TV is on, credits scrolling up the screen.

"Lola?" I ask.

Someone sniffs wetly. Lola, historically, is not a sniffer.

Slowly, I set my purse down and inch around the chair. Beckett sits curled in it, tucked into a fuzzy blanket. Waffles purrs on his lap, and an empty bottle of chardonnay sits on the end table beside him.

"Why are you in my apartment?" As hard as I fight to keep it steady, raw emotion makes my voice waver.

He looks up at me with glassy eyes. "You wanted to talk tonight. I figured I'd conjure up a copy of *Pride and Prejudice* to watch while I waited. I wanted to see what all the hype is about, and—you were right. He's not boring." Beckett hiccups. "He's perfect for you."

A grumpy Waffles jumps off his lap.

Beckett leans forward, resting his head in his hands, as though hoping to steady the world. "And you think I'm Wickham." He spits the name, his tone somewhere between disgust and disbelief.

I cross to the TV and turn it off. "I got an email from Darcy today. It's just like the letter in the movie. Please, please explain what you did."

He lifts his head. "What I did?"

I pull up the email and shove the phone into his hands. "Maybe this will refresh your memory."

His eyes flit slowly over the screen. As he scrolls down, his body grows more and more tense. By the end, he's resting his mouth in his palm, his eyes wide. Darkening the screen, he lets out a long, shuddering sigh. "And you believe I did this?"

"It's *the* letter, Beckett," I say helplessly.

"Despite what you know about me yourself, you think I'm some kind of sick predator? You think I nearly got a girl killed?"

"I don't know what I know about you at this point." I rub my eyes. "Beckett, you talk about twisting wishes. Maybe you manipulate people too."

He stands, swaying. "I never manipulated a wish to hurt anyone. Usually, if I was fast enough, I tried to keep people from hurting themselves. You think hurting people would be fun for me?"

"I don't know; you talk about everything like it's funny!" I explode.

Beckett's eyes flash. "If I don't joke about the things that make me uncomfortable, I won't have much left to joke about."

That shuts me down. My voice is small as I ask, "If it's true you twist people's wishes for the greater good, why not just tell me that?"

He throws up his hands. "I've been doing this a while, Iza. When people spend time second-guessing and thinking about their wishes because they think I find joy in messing with them, they're less likely to waste them."

"And Georgiana?" My heart pounds.

Beckett flinches. "It's fucked up you have to ask. No. I didn't let a minor in, much less serve one. I didn't"—he makes a strangled noise in the back of his throat, looking close to being sick himself—"push myself on Mr. Darcy's sister."

"So Darcy's lying?"

"If Darcy's little sister sneaked into my party, I was unaware. How's it my fault if she drank enough to need her stomach pumped?"

My insides twist into knots so complex they'd leave an Eagle Scout baffled. "I can't believe you'd say it's her own fault. That's messed up."

Beckett runs a hand through his shaggy hair. "More messed up than you falsely accusing me of—what? Harassment? Involuntary manslaughter? I can't lie to you, Iza, and you're still questioning me. Do you know how messed up *that* is?" His voice breaks. "I hadn't realized I seemed capable of . . . of . . ." He sinks back down into the chair. "I've never met her, and I've certainly never . . ." He trails off and shakes his head.

Guilt and shame pour into me. Beckett didn't deserve my accusations. I'm the first person he's opened up to in who knows how long. He showed me his vulnerabilities, and then I told him I believe he's capable of all kinds of horrible things.

Now he believes I'm disgusted by the real him he finally showed me. But that's not true. I latched onto Darcy's email because it fed the prejudgments I cast on Beckett from the beginning.

I just don't understand how *Mr. Darcy* can be so wrong.

"If that's true, why—"

"If that's true? Iza, are you testing me? You even think my truthfulness is a lie?"

I stand, unable to stay still, and pace the small living room. "I don't know. What should I think?"

"I don't know!" His voice rises. "You know I even have to answer your rhetorical questions, right? I know you think I don't have scruples, but believe it or not, I do have at least a scruple or two."

"Why are you so fixated on that word?"

"Because you called me unscrupulous a month ago, and I hate it!"

"Why?"

"Because I don't want to be unscrupulous anymore!"

I stop in front of him. I need all the answers right now. I need to know there's nothing but a curse between us. I can deal with that. I can't deal with secrets. "Almost the whole time I've known you, you've told me to stay away from you. Is that because of your curse or is there anything else I should know?"

"Stop it, Iza," he rasps. "Enough with the questions. The more you ask, the more they burn in my head, demanding answers."

I can't stop. "How can I trust you? If you can't lie, tell me the curse is the only reason I shouldn't want you. What are you holding back? Why are you keeping me suspicious of you unless there's something for me to be suspicious about?"

Beckett shoots up and grabs my elbows, face inches from mine, his hot breath, sweet and heavy with wine, tickling my cheek. "Because I think I love you, damn it."

It's like an explosion goes off, but I don't hear the big *kaboom.* My eardrums close over, and the death tone rings in my head. I've gotten the truth, but it's tainted and twisted, and no longer the thing it could've been.

Beckett releases me. "And I don't want you falling in love with *me*."

I hide my hands under my armpits to hide their shaking.

He steps aside. "Happy now?"

Lola's words echo in my head. *"You're overcomplicating it. One wish to get home. One wish to free him."* My ears clear, and I become hyperaware of Beckett's ragged breaths, my shallow ones, and Waffles's wheezing ones from behind the chair. Turning, I brush his knuckles with my own. "Beckett . . ."

His Adam's apple bobs, and he shies away. "There's more." His voice is so low, I barely hear it. "Since you asked what I'm holding back, now you get to hear it all." He blinks hard, eyes bloodshot. "The star told me I can't use my power to change my punishment, but someone else could. When I met you, you asked about world peace and love. I asked you what you'd do for love, and you said anything. So at first, I wanted you to fall for me because I thought if you loved me, you might make the mistake of wishing me free."

"Mistake?"

He shrugs helplessly. "The star told me I can only be freed by an act of complete selflessness. Someone giving up a wish for me would be selfless, but not *completely* selfless, not when they'd still have two others to obtain anything they want. Complete selflessness is giving up everything for another person. That's why, if anyone wishes me free, they have to take my place."

I back away until my legs hit the couch, and I fall onto it. Pulling my feet up, I wedge myself into the corner. "You wanted to trick me into setting you free? That's why you were so nice to me?" My throat tightens, and a massive weight crushes my chest.

"It *was* the plan." Beckett steps closer, but when I shrink farther into the cushions, he flinches back. "You asked if my whole game was to get my charges to fall for me. It was my game, but not for all my charges—just you. For a long time, I told myself I'd never ask anyone to take my place, but years went by, and I'm tired. I'm so fucking tired of this life that isn't a life. And then I met you. You said you'd do anything for love, and I was desperate. The temptation was too great. So that first morning when you came to my apartment and told me my party was too loud, I was nice to you because I wanted you to fall for me."

"You are Wickham," I say, every muscle in my body quivering. Betrayal settles in my gut, heavy and rotten. "You're just like him, using people for your own gain."

"Listen," he whispers. "Please listen. As soon as I started the plan, I knew I couldn't see it through. That evening, I asked you what object I came from. Remember how I said the vessels I come from are emotionally significant to my charges? I don't know what I was hoping you'd say—that I came from a candlestick that you used to kill Mr. Plum in the billiard room? All I knew is I needed to feel less guilty. I wanted you to have some horrible story that would show you deserved my punishment, anything to help me justify what I'd almost done to you. And then you said sparkly nail polish, the most innocent and unexpected thing I could have imagined. That's why I told you not to look twice at someone like me. To ease my conscience, I decided to help you as much as I could. I'd be your friend, but nothing more."

"I never wanted your pity or your guilt." My voice trembles. "I wanted you to care."

"I do care. The more I watched you, the more I realized your determined drive to love someone, no matter what, is something I've never had. Getting you to take my place might free me, but I'd be the same as always—selfish and cold. So I started trying to be a better person. I let you wonder about my intentions so you'd never be tempted to wish me free. I tried to keep my distance, even when being friends with you stopped feeling like it was enough. It's the hardest fucking thing I've ever done, and I'm pretty shitty at it, to be honest. Last night, for example, was another selfish mistake I couldn't resist."

For someone who can't lie, he'd managed to do it better than anyone I'd ever known. My fractured heart hardens into a thousand tiny spikes. "So I'm supposed to look past the fact that, a few weeks ago, you planned to trap me, because—what? You think you're a changed person now?"

"I don't know what you should look past, Iza. You generally don't look past much."

My anger flares, and I stand. "You made me doubt myself, but I was right about all along."

"You know something?" he snaps. "For someone so good at pointing out others' flaws, you're blind to your own. You want to know the real reason you're alone? You're insecure. You're worried about other people's opinions and can't let go of this fantasy you have about perfection. You're suspicious of everyone who tries to care for you because you don't believe there's a person alive who could love you unconditionally, not when your own mother can't."

His words chill my insides. It feels like cold fingers have reached into my very soul to rifle through all my vulnerabilities. He has no right to comment on my life, not after he tried to take it away from me. "Yeah, well." I splutter incoherently for a moment. "At least I'm not a selfish player."

"No, you're a judgmental—" He snaps his mouth shut.

I narrow my eyes. "Go ahead. Finish that."

Closing his eyes, he takes a deep breath through his nose. Then, he shakes his head.

I fight back hot tears. "If you were planning to manipulate me into imprisoning myself, you're also more than capable of the things Darcy accused you of. I don't trust you. I don't trust that you can't lie to me, and I certainly don't trust that you won't still try to trick me to save yourself."

I draw myself up, shoulders thrown back. I was right to be wary of him. He'd proved that tonight.

With his revelation, a bridge burned; the ashes polluted my veins; and a section of my heart died as a result. Half of it still pumps with life, with hope, and it's that half I need to focus my efforts on. Beckett's wrong; perfection isn't a fantasy, not when I have the perfect man here waiting for me.

"I'm ready to make my second wish."

I don't know how Beckett will manage this wish, given what he's told me about the rules of magic, but I don't care. He'll have to figure it out.

I lift my chin. "I'm going out with Mr. Darcy, and I wish for it to be the best date you can imagine."

He tilts his head to the side and sighs. Then wearily snaps his fingers.

CHAPTER TWENTY-ONE

"I adore it." Julia bursts into tears over the digital rendering we've made up with the help of the design team. They've embellished our 3-D depictions of the rooms, hanging chandeliers from the oak tree and photoshopping Prada into the fairy garden master closet.

Chester wipes at his eyes, close to tears himself.

"Thank god," Kalyan says under his breath, sighing and leaning back in his chair beside me.

Their overwhelming joy hits my foul mood like the buggy hit my father: hard, crushing, and life ending. *Whoa, Iza. Dark.*

My eyes shift to the empty chair on my other side. Darcy still hasn't returned. I've been too freaked out, unsure, and panicked to text him back after Friday. Sure, the date will be the most epic one of all time, but I have to get him to agree to *go* on one first. After how we left things, he might not still want to. Going on a date doesn't technically fit Austen's guide to Darcy's heart, but I don't care at this point. It's time to go all in.

With one wish left, I can still wish Darcy, Lola, and myself home if things work out. (I doubt Beckett's offer to take us home for free still stands.) If things don't work out with Darcy, I'll wish Lola and me home, no better off than I was at the start of all this.

"Iza?" Kalyan asks.

I jump, the papers in front of me sliding to the floor. The meeting room is empty aside from Kalyan and me. Something inside of my already slouching, exhausted body manages to slump even more. "Darcy didn't call, did he?" I rub my temples. He said he'd give me credit for the project when Julia approved it. Where is he?

Kalyan waves his hand in front of my face. "Nope. Did you fall asleep with your eyes open?"

I let out a noncommittal grunt. The events of Friday produced a restless weekend where sleep was dissatisfying at best.

Kalyan stands, tucking his own stack of papers under his arm. "At our firm, we'll have mandatory afternoon siestas."

"Our firm?" I ask, suddenly alert.

He stops in the doorway, leaning against the frame. "Sure. When we branch off together to do our own thing."

"You mean become independent architects? Together?" I search his face. It's dead serious. Even his eyebrows are drawn up with sincerity. "Don't mess with me when I'm sleep deprived. The ice is thin, Kalyan."

He makes an exaggerated *sheesh* face. "Yikes. Someone's extra grouchy today. Just think about it. If you ever get tired of killing yourself to make other people look good, let me know."

"How do you know about—"

He shakes his head. "Plants? Come on. That's not Darcy's idea." He raps his knuckles against the doorframe. "I ran some numbers, and I think we could do it."

"Numbers?"

He tilts his head. "Sure. I can show you."

Dumbly, I follow him out of the meeting room to his desk. "Think about it before you immediately shut down the idea," Kalyan says, leaning forward to grab his mouse, his stripy tie brushing his desk. He pulls up a spreadsheet with what looks like start-up costs laid out on it. He pulls up another depicting monthly overhead, and another with a projected profit and expense overview.

I take in the numbers. *"If only they didn't have to be mutually exclusive."* That's what I'd told Beckett on top of the Arch. Maybe my two dreams *don't* have to be mutually exclusive.

I meet Kalyan's eyes. "You really worked hard on this. Are you sure this isn't some elaborate prank to get me to turn in my two weeks' notice right before you say, 'Never mind. Gotcha'?"

His eyes light up. "Are you saying if I'm serious, you're considering doing this?"

I shift my weight. "Maybe? Yes? No? I mean, your numbers look good."

He runs a hand through his hair and leans back against his desk with a flirty smile. "Yeah, they do."

"I'm reconsidering."

"Lighten up."

"Maybe we should hire Cindy from HR to keep the peace."

He laughs. "I knew there was a human in there somewhere. We'll stay on here until after the Julia project. I think it would be wise since your underground greenhouse mansion is sure to make a splash."

"Wait a minute. You're not just using me as a stepping stone to make a name for yourself, are you?"

His mouth forms a wry line, and he blinks. "Really?" he asks mildly. "I started working on this before you ever had your mansion idea. It was my evil plan all along. Befriend you, then propose . . . a business deal."

I roll my eyes at his joke. He is a good architect. It wouldn't be completely stupid to have him as a partner.

I can practically hear Mom's outraged voice when I tell her. *You quit your job? Have I taught you nothing?*

And then I hear Beckett's voice, telling me it's my own insecurities holding me back from things I want.

Resting my hand on Kalyan's desk, I steady myself. "I'll—I'll have to think about it."

* * *

Because I think I love you, damn it.

I shoot upright in bed, chest heaving, a cold sweat over my skin. I swing my legs over the side of the bed and slide on my slippers. In the kitchen, as I pour myself a glass of water, noises from the hall catch my ears—shuffling and a few whispers.

Horror-movie curiosity takes hold of me, and I tiptoe to the door. Breath hitching, I crack it open. My hand clenches around the knob. A long line of club-goers stretches down the hall. I tug my oversized sleep shirt farther down my thighs.

Beckett's door swings open, and he steps out. He wears all black, from his dress pants to his button-up. His face is gaunt, dark circles under his eyes, hair wild, and he needs a shave. Tilting his head to the bouncer, he says, "All right. Let's get this damn thing started." When his eyes catch on me standing across the hall, his dark gaze trails from my toes to my face.

My skin burns with anger, but my insides burn with something much different. *No. No, your insides don't burn with anything other than pure rage.*

"'Sup, dude?" Beckett lifts his chin. "Darcy in there? You guys have your date?"

Dude? It takes me back to the moment he called me *bro* in that thirty seconds he existed before he knew me at all. For some reason, this stings almost worse than anything he's ever done.

"No," I grit out.

He hums and shrugs.

I slam the door, march back to my room, whip my phone off my nightstand, and text Darcy.

Me: *U up?*

* * *

The lion lies before me, motionless save for the steady rise and fall of its chest. Swallowing hard, I inch back.

On the other side of the operating table, Lola peels off her latex gloves. She's just finished telling me about the complicated and somewhat gross-sounding procedure she and her colleagues performed. She's alone, cleaning up the equipment, because her colleagues had to rush off to attend to yet another birthing antelope. Sounds like a made-up excuse to me, but then again, working with Kalyan has probably scarred me, making me eternally suspicious of coworkers.

The small, sterile white room doesn't seem big enough for the two of us and an oversized, man-eating feline. I wistfully think of Waffles, appreciative his mouth isn't big enough to bite my head off.

"Relax," Lola says. "He'll be out for another half hour at least. I'm about to radio for some help to wheel him out."

"What did you need me for that was so urgent it couldn't wait until you got home?" I have more important things to do than expose myself to murderous lions, like sequester myself at work and pretend my text hasn't been completely ignored. It's Saturday, and it's been several weeks since I texted Darcy. Several weeks since he *didn't* respond.

I check my phone, just to be sure. It's becoming habitual, this perpetual need to check my texts. No new messages. I set the phone face down on the counter, as though I can hide the mortification of being left on read.

Chester says Darcy's been absent so long because of unexpected family matters, but I know the truth. By texting him, I've prematurely accepted what's basically his marriage proposal. I've disrupted the flow of the story and screwed the whole thing up. Now, the rest of the story will never play out chronologically like it's supposed to. I'll never get my magical, perfect date, and I'll be alone forever.

Magical date.

Beckett.

I don't know why my wish hasn't come true yet. Maybe it was impossible. Beckett said magic can't create something from nothing. I haven't even seen Beckett since the other night, the only evidence of his existence being the line of partygoers stretching down the hall. I wouldn't know what to say to him even if we did run into each other. After thinking about our argument, part of me wonders if making a wish was impulsive. Despite everything, I'm starting to doubt Beckett would do the things Darcy accused him of in his email. Not that Georgiana was lying about her story, but maybe Darcy misunderstood Beckett's involvement in it. Even though Beckett told me he'd planned on tricking me into a life of eternal servitude, he also told me he'd decided not to.

He also told me he loves me.

"I'm cashing in that favor you owe me since I helped you invade Darcy's home," Lola says, interrupting my depressing thoughts.

"My sister set me up on a blind date, and I need you here to make sure he's not a creep. I'm here to test-drive, not get hit by a bus."

I fiddle with a cotton swab big enough for a giant to clean his ears with. "How am I supposed to help with this?"

The metal surgical instruments clatter together as Lola puts them away and slides the drawer closed with her hip. "Easy. You stick around until I give you the signal."

"What signal? Will I know it when I see it?"

Lola flicks her braid over her shoulder. "I hope so, considering the signal is 'Hey, Iza, this guy isn't a creep, so you can go now.'"

"Ha ha. What if he is a creep?"

"Then you distract him while I make my escape. Or even better, try to scare the guy away. You're good at that, aren't you?"

I wave the cotton swab at her like a rapier. "That's low, Lola."

She swats the nonthreatening weapon out of her way as she breezes by. "The truth hurts—" The words die on her lips as conversation from down the hall meets our ears.

"Lola's right through that hall in the room at the end," someone outside says, and a male's voice thanks her—a strangely familiar male's voice.

Lola goes pale. "He shouldn't be back here. I specifically told my sister to tell him to wait for me outside." She straightens her khaki shirt and lifts her chin like she's preparing for battle. I say a silent prayer for her victim—I mean, her date. "Okay," she says to me, "you're on."

The door creaks open a crack, and the face that peeks through makes me bark out a laugh of surprise. It's Kalyan.

"Kalyan!" I can't hide the bubbling mirth in my voice.

"Kalyan?" Lola echoes. "*The* Kalyan? Asshole-prank-guy from your work Kalyan?"

"*The* Kalyan," Kalyan says. "I like that."

"Fuck off, Kalyan," Lola says.

"We like Kalyan now," I say softly, laying a hand on Lola's arm.

"Sorry, Kalyan," Lola says in the same sharp tone she'd used to tell him to fuck off.

Kalyan gives me a weird look, stepping into the room. "Why are you here? Were you so upset you didn't score a date with me that you decided to show up and share Lola's?" Then, seeing the lion sprawled across the table behind us, he grimaces and steps back, using the door as a shield.

Lola crosses her arms. "I don't know if you've figured this out yet, but Iza and I are friends. Roommates. I don't even know you aside from what she's told me, which aren't good things, I might add."

"I see why you're skeptical." Kalyan offers a thin smile oozing with venom. "Our Iza is known for her generous opinions of others."

That one stings a little. I swallow my pride. "He's right, Lola. Give him a chance."

The look Lola gives me is one of complete bewilderment.

"I promise he's not a *total* creep," I say.

"Well, all right, then," says Lola, gesturing to the door. "Let's do this."

I follow them out of the room, lingering a few steps behind to make it look like I'm giving them privacy while I eavesdrop.

"How did this happen?" Kalyan is saying.

Lola laughs. "My sister said she ran out of doctors and lawyers to set me up with. I can only assume when she was scraping the bottom of the barrel, she came across you."

He laughs along good-naturedly, and something about their teasing, gentle banter creates a hollow ache within me. It's easy for them. They know neither intends any harm. They're on the same side, both setting out to achieve the same goal: being together.

I reach for my phone, just to make sure my own soulmate hasn't texted me back. My back pocket is empty. Realizing I left my phone back in the operating room, I say, "I'll be right back," but Lola is too wrapped up flirting with Kalyan to hear.

This will only take a second, and Lola said the lion would be asleep for another half hour.

I slip back into the room and immediately spot my phone on the counter. I cross the room, pick it up, and check my messages. I stare at Darcy's name at the top of my screen, willing a response to buzz in. I glare at my last text, *U up?*, and immediately hate myself.

Shame twists my stomach. This is truly sad. He clearly isn't interested. I should stop trying and go home. Sure, constantly bumping into him worked for Elizabeth, but I can't even manage to bump into him in all the right places.

Okay. That sounds dirty.

Locations?

No. Still doesn't sound right.

I frown.

A low growl reverberates around the room, and my phone slips from my hands. I whip around, horrified to find a huge, Iza-eating lion awake on the table between me and the door.

Its eyes are open and trained on me. Apparently, Lola was wrong, and the lion decided to wake up early.

The lion's giant paw twitches. I clench my hands into fists until my knuckles turn white, trying to steady myself. I should dive for the drawer where Lola stashed the medical tools. Maybe there's a scalpel in there I can use to defend myself. But then the nation will have another Harambe situation on its hands, and universal hate isn't something I need to add to the list of stressful things in my life right now.

My head goes dizzy. I've forgotten to breathe.

This is it. Oh my god, I really am going to die this time.

Except Beckett said the other day that he could feel when I'm in danger, and it's his duty to protect me.

My panic bleeds away. "Great." I sigh, cross my shaking arms, and address the lion. "Please eat me quickly before *he* decides to show up."

The lion seems to find this request agreeable because he heaves himself off his side and rolls to a crouched position, his amber eyes fixed on me.

My heart clenches. "I didn't mean it." I hold my hands up as if I could hope to stop a lunging, fierce, terrifying, humongous—

His tail flicks side to side as he lowers farther, shifting his weight onto his front paws. I freeze. So does he. From my experience with Waffles's antics, to move now will mean a quick death. The lion is a giant cat. That's all. No big deal.

My clothing choice for the day includes a blouse with a tie-up front, and the strings dangle, tantalizing to any feline, big or small. A pretty ribbon wrapped around a nice snack.

The lion executes a booty wiggle, the signature move of a cat about to pounce. It's a far larger, more fear-inducing booty wiggle than any chubby little Waffles could ever pull off.

The lion lurches forward. The table shoots out from under its paws to crash against the door. With a squeak that probably sounds like a mouse's and thus multiplies my snack appeal, I squeeze my eyes shut.

A thundering crack splits the air, and my eardrums hiss and throb in protest. A strong arm wraps around my waist, jerking me to the side. I stumble and fall against a very broad, very naked, very *wet* chest.

My eyes fly open.

Abs. Purple smoke.

Weird first thoughts after a near-death experience, but here we are.

I jolt to my senses and push off said impressive torso, searching for the lion. It sits mere feet away in the dissipating purple smoke, a confused expression on its face. I scream, my voice muted in my still twingeing ears, and cower back into the aforementioned impressive torso.

"Dude, chill," Beckett says mildly, patting my arm with one hand and hiking up the bath towel tied around his waist with the other. His nipple piercing glitters at me, inches from my nose.

Realizing I've mashed myself up against my archenemy, I back up, but only like an inch. There's still a lion sitting on the opposite side of me. Sandwiched between the bane of my existence and a lion, I can't decide which I'd rather face.

Okay. Yes, I can. Those abs are defined enough I could use them as shelves to store cans of cat food. My eyes sink to the ridges of his lower stomach that disappear under the bath towel low on his hips, leading down to—

Beckett clears his throat. "My eyes are up here." His voice has the lazy, sleepy quality it used to have. Unperturbed. Unreadable.

Heat drenching my face, I tear my eyes off the suggestive and highly intriguing folds of the towel to find Beckett's stare firmly planted on my face. He snaps his finger, and the lion slides even farther away from us, its eyes rolling wide in shock.

Water rolls off Beckett's curls and falls into his dark lashes. "You're aware you were about to be eaten, right?" he asks.

"Yep." I manage. "Were you . . .?"

"Showering," he says brusquely, ears pink. "Hoped I'd have time to dress when I sensed you were off getting killed, but ended up teleported here instead. You're getting faster at the almost dying thing."

"Showering? It's, like, noon." My eyes travel back down the angles of his collarbone, shoulders, pecs. A wobbly, poorly done tattoo of a gnarled tree snakes up his right side. Somehow, the imperfect tattoo seems right, very *Beckett.*

He crosses his arms. "Yeah, bro-bean. It's 'like' noon. Slept in. Long night last night."

"Stop doing that," I say viciously. "Enough with the bro thing. I don't care if it's a coping mechanism—I have a name."

He bristles, drawing a sharp breath. "Okay, Eliza." Arms still crossed, he steps away from me until he backs into the counter. Something about the way he says my full name, somewhere between a purr and a sneer, sends a shiver down my spine.

"Don't call me Eliza."

In my peripheral vision, the lion cocks its head. Keeping an eye on it, I inch sideways, shrinking closer to Beckett. I don't notice I stand between Beckett's bare feet until my shoulder bumps his chest and my hand brushes the towel. The towel starts to slip, but he catches it, adjusting it back around his hips.

"Fucking hell, Iza." His warm breath ripples against the side of my neck.

"Sorry." I cringe, pressing my palm against his tight stomach to balance myself. His muscles quiver under my touch.

Catching my hand in his, Beckett pushes off the counter and turns me until we swap places. Now it's my ass pressing into the counter and him standing between my feet.

His eyes pierce into me, and now they're not guarded; they're a churning storm of misery, frustration, and yearning. My heart constricts. Despite everything—what he's been accused of, what he almost did, the freaking lion sitting behind him—I want to wrap my arms around his neck and ask him to kiss me until I forget it all. For a few minutes, I could ignore my better judgment and this whole disaster I've gotten myself into.

Bracing myself against his chest, I lift my face until millimeters separate us. The moisture clinging to his body is slick under my palms. He burns, still hot from the shower. His nose brushes my cheek. Our mouths are one tremble away from touching. He smells like soap and spearmint and sadness.

I can't. It's cruel. Cruel to him, cruel to me.

I pull away.

Beckett reaches for me, and for one wild moment, I think he's going to crush me to him and make the decision easy, but he doesn't.

He only lifts the strings of my shirt, which have come untied in all the action. As he ties them, his movements are slow, like their weight is unbearable. His knuckles brush the tops of my breasts, and his throat lurches roughly. "Let's get out of here before anyone comes in." Finished tying, he lets his hands drop to his sides.

Slowly, I nod and step aside.

Beckett snaps his fingers, and the vast expanse of bare skin before me vanishes under a loose Hawaiian shirt and cargo shorts. Not a revealing towel in sight. As he brushes by, his sleeve grazes my shoulder, leaving the smell of cedar and cinnamon in his wake.

I retrieve my phone from where I dropped it. Still no text from Darcy. Opening the door, Beckett lets me slip under his arm, then shuts it securely.

Lola and Kalyan still stand in the hallway. They fall silent as they notice us.

Beckett runs a hand through his hair, slinging freezing water drops over my neck. "Lola, just so you know, you have a very awake, pissed-off lion in there."

"You went back in?" Lola's face pales. "Oh no. Iza, did it eat you?" She rushes over and examines me, probably to make sure there aren't any chunks missing.

"No." I tip my head at Beckett. I've clued Lola into all Beckett's various duties, and she nods, catching on quickly.

However, Kalyan is looking around, as though trying to figure out where Beckett came from. "Did he save your life?" Kalyan asks with a delighted smile. "I think that means you're forever indebted to him."

"No," I say quickly. "No, no."

I usher Beckett away before Kalyan can ask more questions.

"Sorry I interrupted your shower by almost getting eaten," I say, focusing on the floor. Without a life-threatening lion around, the awkwardness between us is heavy.

Beckett touches my elbow, and I draw up short. "You really think I can't be bothered in the middle of a shower to *save your life*?"

I shrug. "You seemed kind of agitated. I thought you were annoyed."

He grimaces. "I was embarrassed."

My eyes fly up to meet his. "You get embarrassed?"

"Well, yeah. I would have preferred to do a few push-ups or something before you saw me mostly naked."

I laugh, then clap a hand over my mouth. "I'm not laughing at you, I promise. You have nothing to worry about."

He smiles. "And you should know, magic or not, if you need rescuing, I'm there."

"Thanks," I say simply, and we walk on.

We emerge by the lion enclosure—a giant pit in the ground surrounded by a moat. Above, the sky is pure, robin's-egg blue, the sun shining brightly. In the pit below, a lioness paces back and forward, head swinging, tail twitching.

"She looks sort of pissed, doesn't she?" Beckett leans against the fence and clasps his hands together.

I contemplate the lioness for a few silent moments.

"She feels trapped," I say quietly. "She doesn't understand what she did to get herself here, and she doesn't know how to get out. She's confused—angry, yes, but also afraid and ashamed." I swallow past the sudden tightness in my throat. "She doesn't know what to do or who to trust."

In the sunlight, Beckett's eyes turn pure gold. "So she lashes out at everyone to hide how deeply unsettled she is? Scared she might be wrong about her choices, might have been mistaken about her previous ideas, she resists growth, instead stubbornly pacing and thrashing and pushing back at the world"—his voice drops—"and those who care about her the most."

Shaking my head, I lift my hair off my neck, sighing as fresh air hits my hot skin. "I think you're reading too deeply into the inner workings of a lioness."

The corner of Beckett's mouth twitches as he faces me, leaning his hip into the rail. "Who wouldn't want to understand something as wildly complex and terrifyingly beautiful as a lioness? To unravel the secrets of such a creature"—he breaks into a full-on smirk—"the reward would be great indeed."

Just like that, the rest of the tension between us dissolves. Snorting, I turn away and watch the lion. "Did you just say 'indeed'?"

"Indeed."

I remember him covered in glitter, carefree and laughing, eyes all crinkled. Suddenly hot, I pull the hair elastic off my wrist and twist my hair into a bun. "Are we still talking about lions?"

When I face him again, his eyes are wide and innocent. "Indeed." His voice is tender, barely audible.

Beckett's hand brushes mine, and I recoil, flexing my fingers. His gaze snaps to the movement. "What was that?"

"What was what?" I shrug.

"You Darcy-hand-flexed me."

The damn humidity is making my face sweat. "I don't know what you're talking about."

He grins. "You did. You did the Darcy hand flex."

"I literally don't know what you're talking about."

The grin spreads wider across his face, and his dimples look cheekier than normal. "Don't act like you don't know it—the 2005 adaptation of *Pride and Prejudice*. Darcy helps Elizabeth into her carriage, then he flexes his hand."

I shake my head. "Nope. You've lost me."

"Iza." He draws out my name.

I turn my face away. "I literally don't speak English and therefore cannot possibly know what you're talking about."

"Uh-huh."

Rolling my eyes, I shove my hand into his chest, and he breaks into laughter.

I don't withdraw my hand. Only the thin material of his shirt keeps our skin apart, and his chest burns through the fabric.

Beckett looks at my hand. Under my palm, his heart pounds. My hand trembles, and my insides bunch, somewhere between nausea and . . . butterflies. Yes. Fucking butterflies. How can I be drawn to someone so utterly wrong?

He chews his bottom lip, and I'm transfixed. Voice vibrating against my palm, he asks, "Did you enjoy your date?"

"My date?" I nearly choke.

"With Darcy."

"Haven't gone yet."

"Oh."

I should ask him why that is—why my wish didn't come true.

"Do you want to do the zoo with me?" Beckett asks out of nowhere.

"I've done the zoo a lot. Because . . . Lola." Do my words even make sense? Do his?

"You've never done the zoo with me, though. We could teleport. Swim with the sea lions. See the elephants up close."

"Get kicked out," I tack on. Still, I remember how good it felt the other night to let loose for once, and I want to agree—but then my eye catches on something, *someone* just beyond his head.

Darcy, deliciously dressed down in jeans and a white T-shirt, walks through the crowd, toward us. In front of him, a giant mist machine kicks on, sending a fine veil of water swirling in his path. Rainbows of light arc in the air, wavering as he passes through. The moisture clings to his shirt and glitters on his skin. I can practically hear cheesy, romantic music filling my ears, a stringed quartet building to a crescendo—

"Hello, Iza," Darcy says, now standing before us in all his damp, white T-shirt glory.

I jerk my hand from Beckett's chest because, of course, it's still planted there. I'm such a freaking weirdo. "We were just . . . I mean, we're not doing it." *Fuck.* "We're not doing the *zoo*, I mean, not *it*. Not together, that is." *Fuck.*

Beckett shakes his head, turns on his heel, and walks away.

CHAPTER TWENTY-TWO

Not only did I screw up the story by accepting Darcy far too early, but now he's caught me feeling up the embodiment of Mr. Wickham.

"I didn't expect to see you here," I say, then immediately regret it because it makes me sound guilty.

"I came here to clear my head." Darcy clasps his hands behind his back, and his shirt stretches across his chest. A perfectly adequate, normal chest. No nipple piercing. No dark outline of a tattoo beneath the transparent white shirt. Perfectly adequate.

I tear my gaze off his perfectly adequate chest. "You wanted to clear your head, and you came to a *zoo*?" I ask, then bite my tongue. I should be nicer to my future husband.

Darcy ignores the question. "Sorry I haven't been around. I had to extend my leave. Something came up with Georgiana." He looks away.

Thoughts of chests, adequate or otherwise, vanish from my mind. "Is she okay?"

"Of course." A tight smile forms on his face. "It's a positive development, actually. With any luck, it'll be resolved soon, and justice will be served."

My heart skips. "You mean you have evidence?"

He nods, and my skipping heart face-plants. "Yes."

I look over my shoulder, but Beckett's long gone.

Darcy found the proof, and Beckett will be convicted. If that's the case, wouldn't Darcy have had some sort of reaction to seeing Beckett here, even if it's just to gloat? After their first cold meeting and the history between them, Beckett's presence should have Darcy seething, especially since I had my hand on Beckett's chest and Darcy is *supposed* to be my soulmate.

"I got your text."

Between the temperature of the day, the number of chests thrown my way, and my now boiling mortification, I'm going to have heatstroke. I push back the frizzy hair sticking to my forehead. "Oh yeah. That. I shouldn't have bothered you. Delete that. And maybe burn your phone. And bleach your brain so you forget the text ever existed."

Darcy shakes his head, his usually slicked-back hair falling across his brow. "Iza, Iza, no. I only brought it up to apologize. I was otherwise engaged when I received it, and I meant to respond later. I got so caught up in other responsibilities that by the time I had a moment's peace, I fell asleep. The next day it slipped my mind."

"I don't think any of that made me feel better," I remark.

Chuckling, he steps forward and takes my hand in his large ones. I pray my hand isn't clammy, but it definitely is. "Then maybe this will," he says. "If I've misread the text and misinterpreted your meaning, please let me know, and we'll never speak of it again. But if I haven't . . ." He smiles crookedly. "Then I'll pick you up at five thirty next Friday."

* * *

"A date?" Mom's voice booms so loudly, I fear my phone speakers might burst. "With that Beckett man?"

It's the night of the date, and I finally caved and broke the radio silence between us with a call because I was feeling triumphant. However, Mom is not acting the part of a contrite woman who's been proved wrong. "Not Beckett," I say.

"Kalyan?" she asks.

"No, Mom." I sigh, flipping through my closet. "I'm going out with Darcy. I fear Kalyan is betrothed to another."

On my bed, Lola doubles over, making gagging noises. Kalyan has been beside himself all week, entranced in a lovestruck haze. It's provided me with endless ammunition I've been using to mercilessly tease the usually untouchable Lola.

"Betrothed?" Mom's voice could be an audio track recorded to demonstrate the word *disgust*.

"To Lola." I wiggle my eyebrows at her.

Mom scoffs. "Doubtful. Dear Lola isn't like you. She knows what's important."

"Ouch, Mom." I feign sarcasm to hide the sting of her words.

All I have to do to keep bees from stinging is hold my breath. Mom demands much more. "Oh, please, Eliza. You're taking it all wrong," Mom says. "I simply meant Lola knows better than to subject herself often to the self-abuse of the dating world."

I can practically hear the buzz of pissed-off bees circling overhead. "There's the confidence boost I need for tonight."

Mom lets out an exasperated huff, and the bees close in. They're coming from all sides now, crawling across the grass, surrounding me. "Oh, Eliza. You're so sensitive sometimes." The bees creep over my skin, their humming wings vibrating as they crawl between my toes, up my legs, worming under my armpits, into my hair.

I hang up before they can burrow into my flesh, cluster around my heart, and inject it full of venom. For a shining moment, things felt like they were turning around, but one conversation with Mom, and I still feel like a loser.

At this point, I'm not sure she'll ever admit she was wrong. No matter what I throw in her face—a wedding, my first child, *Mr. Darcy*—it will never be proof enough. She'll always have her reservations, biting her tongue until she can say, *"I told you so."*

"You should go with the white one," Lola says, smacking her gum.

"What?" I ask, clenching and unclenching my fists to calm myself.

Leaping up, Lola points at the white off-the-shoulder dress in my closet. "For your date. That one."

I chew the inside of my cheek. "I don't know, Lola. I don't even know where he's taking me. And a white dress on a first date screams desperate, doesn't it?"

Lola rolls her eyes as she blows a bubble. It snaps over her nose, and she peels it off. "You showed up at his house, his aunt's funeral, and texted him, 'U up?' We passed desperate a long time ago. You know you want him. Now's not the time to hold back."

A loud buzz sounds, and for a wild moment, I think I've imagined the swarm of bees into existence, but then Lola says, "I'll let him in while you finish getting ready."

I change as quickly as I can, before smoothing down my hair one last time. I look in the mirror. Not bad. "*Dude* and *bud* and *bro*, my ass," I mutter. I've seen no sign of Beckett since he rescued me from the lion. Even his parties stopped. I consider both those things to be blessings. After applying lip gloss, I hurry out into the living room.

Some sort of standoff is going down between Darcy and Waffles. Darcy stands in the doorway, hands in the pockets of his slacks. Waffles crouches, all puffed up in the middle of the floor as he growls low in his throat. Standing on the sidelines, Lola holds back a smirk.

"Ready to go?" I ask breezily, hoping to ease the tension. "Don't mind Waffles. He doesn't like most strangers." I would say *any* strangers, but Beckett disproved that statement when he showed up and Waffles basically imprinted on him.

With a nod, Darcy says, "Absolutely. I have the car running outside with the AC on, so it should be nice and cool for us."

Perfect date starting with zero swampy, nervous sweats? Check. "Perfect," I say, striding forward and swiping my purse from the entryway table before following him out.

"You look beautiful," he tells me in the hall, right on cue.

"You look nice too." I smile. It's true. He's rolled up the sleeves of his blue button-up, and his forearms are everything a man's forearms should be: muscular, but not grotesquely so. Perfect.

His Mercedes idles in the parking lot. Slate gray in color, it could haul a family of four comfortably. *Family of four? Too soon, Iza. Calm down.* Just because it's guaranteed to be the best date in the history of the world doesn't mean I won't still find a way to mess it up.

"So, where are we going?" I ask once I'm buckled into the car, which is ice cold as promised. The leather seat chills my skin, and my nose fills with a crisp *new car* smell. It's nice, but no safe haven of warmth and oldies and cinnamon. *Stop thinking about him.*

"It's a surprise." Carefully, Darcy backs out of the parking spot.

I'm disappointed when he doesn't rest his hand on the back of my seat to look over his shoulder. If only he wasn't so reserved. Sure, I sort of know him from *Pride and Prejudice*, but I've never really gotten to know him on a personal level here, in the flesh. Hopefully, tonight will change all that.

Darcy turns on the radio, and one of my favorite Tim McGraw songs starts playing. "I love Tim McGraw." Beaming, I sit up straighter. "You like him too?" Finally, a connection.

"I listen to jazz." With a sharp flick of his wrist, he turns his blinker on and pulls out into traffic. "But I know you like it."

"Oh." Smile slipping, I sit back. "How'd you know that?"

A crease forms between his brows. "Must've picked it up somewhere along the line."

"Must have."

Silence stretches between us.

Some perfect date. Doubts creep in. He said he was going to come clean about the Julia project, but he never did. He let it play out, seeming to think, as long as everything works out okay for Chester and the project in the end, then it's all good. Never mind *me*. Never mind *my* feelings.

Maybe he's another failure in a long line of failures. I've placed large expectations on men before. I thought others were perfect for me right before they let me down.

Maybe I'm wrong again.

I push the thought away, finally asking, "How's Georgiana," to break the silence of the car and silence my thoughts.

Darcy brightens. "Much better. Especially now everything's resolving. It's good to have closure."

Will Beckett be arrested? I twist my fingers together. How would law enforcement go about throwing him in jail, anyway? Beckett could wish himself right out.

"Did a witness come forward or something?" I ask.

Darcy watches the road ahead as he shifts in his seat and purses his lips. "Something like that."

There's something he's not telling me. "When do I get to meet Georgiana?" If Darcy won't tell me the truth, maybe I need to hear the story straight from the source.

"Maybe another time."

Something about Darcy's avoidance of my questions isn't right. Maybe I was too hasty condemning Beckett.

No. That's the aftershock from seeing nice abs talking. This is Mr. Freaking Darcy. I'm being stupid. Darcy probably has abs too. Or, at the very least, a respectable dad bod. I can work with a dad bod. It isn't like I've been hitting a gym lately. Or ever.

Outside, the buildings grow shorter and farther apart. Instead of heading deeper into downtown as I supposed we would, we're heading away, leaving the city. "Where are we going?" I ask again, pressing my nose against the window and then instantly regretting it when I smudge the glass.

"It's a surprise. How are things at work?"

Trying to be inconspicuous, I rub at the glass, only succeeding in smearing it worse. *Beckett wouldn't care if I smudged his window.* Oh. My. God. Darcy probably doesn't care either. "Great. Julia approved the sketches, but Chester said he told you that." I rub harder.

Darcy runs a hand over his jaw and nods. "Good. Glad to hear it."

Letting my hand drop from the window, I swing my knees around to face him, pinning him with a stare. "Don't you remember what you promised?"

Darcy has the decency to grimace. "Of course. I plan on doing it as soon as I can get back to the office. Doing it over the phone felt like a cop-out."

The pressure around my ribs releases. Breathing comes easier, whether from relief or because the air blowing through the vents grows fresher, more *alive* by the second.

We make small talk for a long while until we turn off the highway onto a winding back road.

"Wait a minute." With a jolt, I shoot up straight. "I know this road." I abandon all pretense of being cool and mash my face against the window like an eager child.

Trees on either side of the road grow larger the farther we go. They press in on both sides, covering the road in a twisted canopy of limbs and leaves. As the sun sinks lower, the sky burns gold. The hue brings images of Beckett's eyes flickering up in my mind, but I push them away as I crane my head to look up. The leaves above mesh together, filtering the sunlight. Dappled splotches of brilliant green light speckle the road. Through the trees, I catch glimpses of fields dotted with horses and cows.

A burning, overwhelming sense of nostalgia settles over me. Homesickness twists my gut. It's the ache of witnessing a magnificent sunset. It's a beautiful pain that makes you want to cry because it will only last a minute before it's gone forever, never to be duplicated, and no photograph can ever bring back its true essence.

I crack the window and lift my nose like I'm a magical bloodhound who can sniff out memories. Mixed with the scent of freshly turned dirt and the sharp smell of hay baking in the fields, I catch a whiff of my mother's perfume. I smell the mud on my child-sized purple rain boots and Grandma's fresh, homemade bread. I feel dirt caked under my nails and a sunburn chafing under my shirt and a blister on my heel.

Blinking against the prickling in my eyes, I turn from the window and look into Darcy's face. He's simultaneously watching the road and stealing little looks at me, his eyes gentle, a soft smile playing about his mouth.

"How'd you know?" My voice is rough as I force it from my swollen throat.

Again, the little crease forms between his brows. "You must've mentioned it in passing."

I don't have much time to puzzle over that because a minute later, Darcy takes the next left exactly where I knew he would. The world opens up before us as we swerve into a cobblestone drive. The clearing is so small, the trees encircling it nearly touch overhead, leaving only a little circle for sunbeams to arc through. The ethereal rays wash the clearing in gold.

Without waiting for Darcy, I stumble out of the car. Dust we've stirred drifts upward, blurring the sun's rays in a haze. I trip in my haste and grab onto the post of the white picket fence.

I give myself a moment to take in the reality before me.

The stone cottage, with the peeling turquoise shutters and the crooked chimney. The leaning chicken coop. The clothesline. The little red goat barn that only ever housed the stray cats Grandma could never turn away. The whispering pine tree with the rotting swing. The garden, now grown into a wild, unkempt tangle. My chest constricts as I imagine Grandma's face if she were to see it so uncared for.

A warm hand presses into my back, and a breath tickles my ear. "I thought you might like to see it." Darcy rubs slow circles on my skin.

An eddy of cool air swirls across my face, making me aware of the dampness on my cheeks.

"I'm sorry," Darcy says, turning me around to brush the tears away with his thumbs. "This was a mistake."

I shake my head and fling myself into his arms, squeezing him tight and burying my face into his chest. No more doubts. I was right. “I haven’t seen it since she died. Bringing me here—” I shake my head. No words exist to explain how deeply his actions affect me. “It’s perfect.”

CHAPTER TWENTY-THREE

I hold my shoes in my hand, running to the middle of the lawn, the soft grass tickling between my toes. I've just started explaining the breath-holding-bee theory to Darcy when a car door slams. The words die on my lips as I read the letters on the side of the SUV parked next to Darcy's car: "Meryton Realty."

Chuckling, Darcy takes my free hand. "I thought you might like to see the whole thing."

Only then do I notice the "For Sale" sign by the fence.

"Hello." The realtor, a massively pregnant woman in her late twenties, waddles across the yard. "Lydia Hansted." She holds out her hand.

There's a bit of awkwardness as I fumble between my shoes and Darcy's hand, which I'd rather not relinquish from my clutches because he's literally the epitome of perfection. But I look like an idiot, so I drop the shoes, slip my feet in, and step forward to shake the woman's hand, like a normal human. "Eliza Kiches," I say.

Lydia beams a practiced, toothy smile. "Ready to look inside?" Her smile fades, and she grimaces, touching her stomach.

"Are you okay?" I ask, eyeing her.

Her smile reconstructs itself. "Of course. Your fiancé told me on the phone you're really getting serious about house hunting as your wedding date approaches? That's exciting." She prattles on about the details of the house, but I tune it out.

"Fiancé?" I mouth to Darcy as we fall back to trail behind her.

He shakes his head. "Just go with it," he says under his breath. "Wanted to seem seriously interested so she'd take her time giving us a thorough walk-through."

I almost open my mouth to say, *Wait, I* shouldn't *be serious about buying this house?* because in the moment it seems like the next logical thing to do.

I close my mouth. Of course, it's not the logical next step at all.

Without Grandma's furniture, family photos, and my crummy crayon drawings filling every room, the house is empty. Soon, my imagination fills in the blanks. I see the chicken-patterned curtains in the kitchen, the sprinkling of flour over the countertops, the potatoes sprouting in the windowsill. Echoes of her laughter, her teasing tone as she tells Mom to lighten up before turning to share a knowing, mischievous look with me. The *clack clack clack* of her old pedal sewing machine.

Somewhere along the line, Darcy's hand again finds mine. Every so often, the realtor's speech falters, and she touches her stomach. I try to catch Darcy's eye, but he seems oblivious. Maybe I'm imagining things.

The tour passes in a glorious blur. No matter how much I strive to latch onto every moment, to drag out every second, there are only so many questions I can ask about outlet locations and insulation grade. In passing, I inquire what the asking price is, then nod when I think it might be doable. Darcy shoots me a weird look.

We exit the back door into the yard, and I itch to trim the rose bushes growing up the lattice leaning against the house. My fingers twitch, yearning to weed the garden, to restore it to its proper state, with its neat little rows and hand-drawn signs: "Tomatoes." "Corn." "Beans."

I see the little orange marigolds planted around the perimeter to keep the bugs away. I see the fence, freshly white, and Darcy crossing the yard, his hands splattered with paint. He reaches forward, a glint in his eyes as he grasps my face in his messy hands and kisses me. I hear children laughing.

Chill out, Iza. Geez.

"Oh my god!" Our realtor, Lydia, drops her clipboard, hands flying to her stomach. "I think my water broke."

Darcy releases my hand, and I'm sure his panic-stricken expression mirrors the horror on my own face.

Lydia goes from professional to not-okay real quick. She falls to her knees, bellows at the sky, and for a moment, I think she's going to hike up her pencil skirt, spread her legs, and give birth right there. Sure, the resulting fluids would benefit the soil for my future garden, but while kids are a nice thought for the future, I'm neither prepared nor equipped to aid Lydia's birthing process right here and now.

"Oh my gosh." I spin in a circle, as though I expect to find a pair of stirrups or a birthing ball among the weeds. "If you were in labor, why did you come here?"

"My career," she manages to say between gasps.

I stare at her on the ground. I thought I was extreme. This woman came to show us the house because she thought saying no would mean she'd sacrificed her career. I blink, gawking at her, speechless. The realization I would've done the same thing in her position hits me. I would have wanted to prove to my mother that I could have a baby and a career, but this isn't balance . . . this is unhealthy. Lydia can have both, but she needs to know it's okay to take time for personal matters. It's okay to ask for help.

When Lydia's furious eyes meet mine, I realize I've been staring far too long. I address Darcy. "You're a man of many talents. Do you possess any midwifery skills?"

"Midwifery skills?" he blusters. "I'd think that would be more your department, seeing as you're the one who wants to be a housewife so badly."

Even the wailing Lydia goes quiet at that.

Darcy holds up his hands, palms out, like he's taming a wild horse. "That came out wrong. You asked about the price, and—"

Lydia moans.

Lifting his voice, Darcy finishes, "And I worried you were considering quitting your career to live out here."

I plant my hands on my hips. "And why couldn't I have both?"

He throws his hands up. "The commute would be impossible. By the time you add driving time to the hours we work, you might as well live at the office."

"I want both." I resist the urge to stomp my foot. "Why can't you people understand what I want is *both*?"

"I never questioned you," Lydia manages between shallow pants.

I pat her head. "Thank you, Lydia. You're doing great, by the way."

Eye twitching as he looks between us, Darcy steps forward. "It's not possible to find time to do both. I'm not saying there's anything wrong with quitting to be a homemaker. I don't think less of you for it. In fact, I admire that. I only think holding onto your unrealistic expectations is holding you back from either path and setting you up for disappointment and failure."

I lift my chin. "I'll prove you wrong." Looking down at Lydia, who's counting under her breath, I ask, "What's your email, so I can make an offer on this place?"

Lydia finishes counting and hands me her card.

"Thank you, Lydia. You've helped me more than you know." *Take that, Beckett. How's that for not overthinking? How's that for living in the moment?* Granted, he was probably referring to partying like there's no tomorrow, not impulse-buying a house. But whatever.

I eye Lydia. "I think we ought to get you to a hospital."

"You think?" Lydia snaps.

* * *

Darcy pulls to a stop in front of my apartment. By the time we half carried Lydia into the hospital, then waited around for her boyfriend to show up, it was quite late. Both too tired to continue the date, we swung by a McDonald's on the way home. Some perfect date. I can't help but think, if I can't make a things work with Mr. Darcy, then maybe I'm hopeless at relationships.

Darcy walks me to the apartment door. How did such a promising start lead to this? He runs a hand down his face. Fluorescent lights hanging on the side of the building emphasize the heavy bags under his eyes. "I'm sorry for how things went," he says.

"You didn't know the realtor would go into labor," I say, not meeting his eyes. "It was nice of you to help Lydia out."

"I mean about what I said—the housewife thing. I didn't mean to insult you. I had a whole night planned. After the house, we were supposed to get gyros from this little street vendor I know of, then take an evening walk around the Botanical Gardens."

"I love gyros," I say softly. A tickling sensation crawls up my spine. "How do you know all this about me?"

Darcy rubs the back of his neck. "I guess I've been subconsciously paying attention."

"Oh."

The next thing I know, he's leaning in, a question in his eyes. What else can I do? He's Mr. Darcy, and we've been on what, in theory anyway, should've been the best date of my life. So, I close the distance between us. He angles his head at the last minute, and his lips brush my cheek.

In terms of the perfect end to a perfect date, it sucks. No cheek kiss has ever been described as perfection. As he pulls away, my face burns. He's the one who insulted me. I should've been the one turning my head to the side, not him. It's a great injustice, and I'm pissed—the kind of pissed that only comes from being snubbed by someone who should've been on the receiving end of a snub.

"Goodnight, Darcy," I say, giving him a stiff, Austen-esque nod before turning on my heel and ducking inside.

It's late, and I don't expect to run into anyone. Then, as I'm walking down the hall, fishing for my keys in my purse, I quite literally bump into someone. There's a masculine "Oof," and I bounce off a hard shoulder, nearly falling on my butt. My nose fills with woodsy cinnamon, and I close my eyes and count to ten.

When I open them again, Beckett's waiting patiently. His usual "frattire" is gone. He's clean-shaven and wearing a somewhat rumpled black suit—the jacket unbuttoned and the tie loosened. His eyes linger on my form-fitting dress.

"So you aren't in jail yet." I shake my hair off my bare shoulders.

His eyes lock onto the exposed skin as he spreads his arms wide. "You could arrest me, Officer, if you think I've been such a bad boy."

"You promised me," I hiss. "You said you wouldn't mess with my wishes."

He lets his hands fall to his sides. "You went on the date." At last, lifting his eyes, he searches my face. "How was it?"

"It should have been amazing."

For the briefest moment, he lights up. But then, he looks past me, down the hall, expression souring. "Darcy's parking the car, then?"

"The date was a disaster!" I'm unable to contain it anymore, and my voice bursts free.

Beckett steps back, lips twitching. "You got what you wished for. Sorry it fell flat."

I lower my voice to a reasonable level, but the rage behind it makes it dangerous. "This isn't funny. You promised the date would be perfect, but it wasn't. How'd you lie?"

"I didn't." Face setting into a stony expression, Beckett steps forward. "You still think I can lie to you? Why the hell would I confess I briefly entertained the idea of switching places with you?" He jabs a finger at me. "Why wouldn't I, like everyone else who thinks a hundred terrible things a day, take my secret thoughts to the grave?" His voice drops. "Why the fuck would I tell you I love you when it means nothing and never *can* mean anything?"

His words turn my thoughts sideways. As they scramble around, clicking together like an upside-down game of Connect Four, they arrange themselves into a new pattern. Things line up that never did before, sending me reeling.

The Tim McGraw music. I wore my Tim McGraw T-shirt the day after Beckett showed up.

The gyros. Beckett brought me gyros the night I made my first wish.

Grandma's house. I hadn't told Beckett about it, but maybe Lola did. He knew how much I cared about Grandma from our time in the attic.

My wish echoes in my mind.

I wish for it to be the best date you *can imagine.*

You.

Beckett.

It's Beckett's date from beginning to end. The music and road trip to visit Grandma's house, the gyro at his favorite street vendor, the walk in the gardens. The kiss at the end?

"I wasted it," I choke out. "I freaking wasted it."

"Iza." His voice is painfully tender as he backs away. "I would've changed it if I could have, but I promised not to mess with your wishes. You think I'd want him going on my date with you?"

"No," I allow. "How'd you manage it? You said magic can't take anyone's free will, so how'd you get Darcy to take me everywhere you would've?"

Leaning against the wall opposite me, he runs a hand through his wild hair. "I sent him an anonymous text with some helpful tips."

"How is that magical?"

"I'm physically forced to try to fulfill your wish, even if I have to do it by hand. Plus, I don't know his number, so magic was useful there."

I imagine Beckett sitting in his apartment, drafting a text with everything he knows about me in it. He would have had to convince Darcy his advice was pure, tell him he was genuinely trying to help because he wants Darcy and me to be together. I imagine Beckett thinking about what kind of date he'd take me on if he could. I imagine Beckett giving his ideas, his daydreams, to Darcy and allowing Darcy to be the one to live them.

"You didn't enjoy any of it?" Beckett asks, a raw vulnerability to the question that makes my heart clench.

I didn't enjoy it, but not because it was bad, not even because it was cut short. It was the person I'd been with. The perfect man and the perfect date, but I still wanted the imperfect man. The imperfect man would've seen the turn our evening took as an adventure. He would've made tired jokes in the car on the way home. He would've made getting McDonald's something cozy and intimate in its simplicity.

But I can't say any of that because the imperfect man is just that: imperfect. And not an imperfect that's forgivable. "How'd you know about my grandma's house?" is all I ask.

With a shake of his head, Beckett says, "You *told* me—don't you remember? You told me how upset you were that your mom sold the house. I was curious and looked up the address, which you *also* told me, and that's how I saw it was for sale again. Anyway, were the Gardens nice?"

I don't remember telling him any of that. It must've been that night he tucked me in, and I was too drunk to remember. "Our realtor started giving birth, and the date got cut off," I say absently, still trying to sort through my memories.

Becketts sticks his hands in his pockets and jingles his keys. "I'd like to say sorry, but I can't lie."

I roll my eyes and head for my door.

"How was the kiss?" His tone is unreadable, so I turn, but his face is unreadable too.

"I guess you planned that too?" I rub my eyes, but they're dry and gritty. I'm too tired for emotion.

"I told Darcy if he got the chance and you wanted him, he shouldn't let it go. Because he'd regret it."

I chew my lip, debating. A spiteful part of me wants to tell him Darcy and I banged it out in the alleyway. But I don't. "He kissed my cheek—stop looking so happy about it."

Although he tries to hold it back, a moment later, Beckett's head is thrown back, and he's laughing. "I thought this guy was supposed to be some super-suave ladies' man."

"Well, how would you have done it?" I shoot back before I consider my words. Embarrassment and anger take turns playing with the heat levels of my face.

Before I quite understand what's happening, Beckett's crossed from his side of the hall to mine. The now very familiar scent of him cocoons me as he plants his hands on the wall above my head. Although he's nearly pressed against me, he doesn't touch me.

"That depends," he says, his sleeve brushing my cheek. "Pretend we're in a different universe, one where I was in Darcy's perfect shoes. Now, I'll ask you again—did you enjoy the date?"

In a flash of reckless abandon, I throw away my misgivings, worries, logic, and reason, and lift my chin to look him square in the face. "It made me cry."

For a second, he looks taken aback. "Oh, shit."

"Sunset tears."

And although he can't possibly understand a term originating from my internal ramblings, the skin around his eyes softens like he does. His throat lurches as he swallows. "Then, passionately."

"That could mean anything." My voice is strangely composed despite the fact that my insides are a fireworks display. I never understood what people mean when they say they see fireworks. Now maybe I do. Except some hooligan kids got a hold of my fireworks before the certified pyrotechnicians could arrive, and they lit the whole damn display at once. Now, thousands of dollars' worth of explosives are going off inside me. It burns and crackles. It's a cacophony of bursting color, and the splintering booms reverberate inside my chest and shake me from my head to my toes. It hurts, but it's beautiful—an explosion of chaotic beauty.

Beckett tilts his head to the side, eyes glinting like he can see through me to the raging light show inside. Or maybe the fire inside of me is bright enough that the whole world can see it, and that's why it looks like the sparks of my heart reflect off his irises. God, I hope not. If I show up to work as luminescent as a snapped glow stick, it'll make for an awkward Monday.

He's so close, his hair tickles my brow as he dips his head. "I'm Wickham, right?" His soft breath dances across my lips. "How do you suppose the rakish, devilish Wickham would kiss the woman who looked past his bullshit, softened his heart, and finally, truly won him over?" He pushes off the wall, widening the space between us, and I'm suddenly cold all over. "That's how I'd kiss you."

Fishing his keys out of his pocket, Beckett turns to unlock his door like we're two neighbors who've exchanged nothing more than pleasantries in the hall.

"Wait," I say, breathless. "Why are you dressed like that? Where have you been?"

His shoulders stiffen. He doesn't turn around when he says, "Court," before jerking open the door and disappearing into his apartment.

And there it is. The very real reminder of all the reasons he's Wickham, of why being Wickham isn't a good thing, no matter how tempting his words are. I let my head fall against the wall.

CHAPTER TWENTY-FOUR

Monday morning, Darcy slaps a paper on my desk. He looks down at me, a small, secretive smile on his face, before turning and heading up to his office. I read the form.

Form 223: Workplace Relationship Disclosure.

In other words, Darcy's second proposal. The one I'm supposed to accept. I have no emotional reaction to it.

With a frown, I lean back in my chair. He isn't going to acknowledge how we left things Friday night. It's like he thinks everything's fine, and I'm not upset by what he said.

I thought wishing for a twenty-first-century Darcy would rid him of his old-fashioned ideas, but apparently, that's too deeply ingrained into his psyche, and no amount of time can change it. While he didn't say I *am* a housewife necessarily, he did say I can't run a home and a career simultaneously, which somehow feels worse, especially because he was the one who was supposed to make that possible.

I gnaw on my lip and tap my pen against the paper Darcy left. Darcy takes life seriously. Even though I chose him because I thought Mom would like him, he is also the type of man I thought would complement me. Equally dedicated to his goals, and therefore understanding of mine. Or he should have been.

Something catches my eye. Half tucked behind my monitor, a twist of paper peeks out. My stomach does weird, tingly things as I pull it out.

The sandpaper rose.

Unconsciously, I pull out my phone, bringing up my text conversation with Beckett. His last text is from that same day he sent the rose. It was after I'd told him I wasn't going to waste my second wish on a bouquet of sandpaper flowers.

He'd sent back: ☹ ☹ ☹

And those three little frowny faces stab me in the heart. I remember how his smile used to be—the crinkles around his eyes, the dimples around his mouth. Now, his smiles are sans crinkles, his eyes dull and lacking their customary sparkle. I did that. I took his joy.

No. It's his own fault. He's only sad because he's guilty, since he got caught.

I pivot in my chair, turning between Form 223 and my phone. Back and forth. Back and forth.

Plastic wheels rumble across the floor. Someone clears their throat like they're legitimately trying to hack up their big toe.

"Hi, Kalyan," I say, not looking up.

"So, Darcy's back," Kalyan says. "And he still hasn't confessed."

"He said he would." I click my pen. "He said he needed to get the ball rolling, then he'd give me credit."

"I'd say the ball is rolling." Kalyan rises from his chair to sit on my desk, his butt squishing Form 223. "Why'd it have to be his idea, anyway? Because he's a man? What is this, the nineteenth century?"

I choke.

Kalyan smiles smugly. Taking one of my highlighters, he throws it in the air and promptly fails to catch it. It rolls under my desk. "I heard you two went out. If you ask me, you two would make the worst couple."

"No one asked you."

"I mean, just look at Lola and me," Kalyan goes on, like going on a handful of dates makes him a relationship expert. "We were made each other. At first, she was unsure, but I've grown on her like mold on cheese."

"Hot."

Kalyan takes another highlighter from its holder and taps it against my forehead. "The point is she makes me feel alive. We make each other happy. She also scares me a bit. You'll understand when you're older."

"Shut up, Kalyan." Gripping the edges of Form 223, which is still mostly wedged under his butt, I try to tug it free. "Get your ass off my marriage license."

He leaps up like my desk burned him. "Marriage license?"

After giving the page a slow, careful smoothing out, I clutch it to my chest and lift my nose. "Well, *basically* a marriage license. It's too complicated for you to understand. Maybe when you're older."

With his middle finger raised in a gesture suspiciously close to flipping me off, Kalyan scratches his ear.

"Oh my god!" Faking a gasp, I find the nearest notepad on my desk and knock it to the floor for dramatic effect. "Is that Cindy from HR?"

Kalyan drops into his office chair and launches himself across the floor back to his desk. After approximately two and a half seconds of pretending to scribble furiously at a sketch, he looks both ways. Then, seeing Cindy from HR is not in fact lurking nearby, he shoots me the bird for real. Maturely, I stick my tongue out at him.

For the second time today, someone clears their throat. But this throat clearing is rather subtle, dignified. Grimacing, I peek up. “Hey, Darcy.”

His gaze drops to the now crumpled Form 223. “If you’re finished, I’ll take it down to HR.”

“Oh.” Hands clammy, I rub the back of my neck. Now my neck is sweaty too. Great. “Not quite done with it. Do you have lunch plans? I thought maybe we could pick up where we left off Friday night. I feel like we haven’t gotten a chance to get to know each other.”

By the time I’ve finished talking, he’s already been shaking his head for several moments. He’s radiating his disappointed professor vibe, hard. Only now, it feels less sexy and more patronizing. “Sorry, Iza. If you haven’t noticed, we’re behind schedule on the Julia project. Maybe another time.”

He pronounces *schedule* like he’s British: “shej-ool.” It feels excessive, pompous.

“Well,” I say, “I was thinking more about the house and how I might be able to make the commute work, and—” But he’s gone.

We’re half a date in, and already, work is getting in the way of us seeing each other. Maybe we’re too similar—two serious, duty-bound souls who can’t or won’t sacrifice our time or our work for anything.

Across the room, Kalyan isn’t even pretending not to watch. He’s miming playing a tiny violin, his lower lip set in a mocking pout.

I let my head fall into my hands. My elbow jostles my phone, illuminating the screen. Those three frowny faces stare up at me, inches from my nose. At once, I want nothing more than for Beckett's last text to me to be frownless. Although Kalyan is the last person I should take advice from, something he said resonates with me. Lola makes him happy—*alive.*

The times I let go of my suspicion, when Beckett and I live in the moment, truly alive, truly happy . . .

Before I can think about it more, I snatch my phone up and text Beckett.

Me: What's up? ☺

I add a smiley face for good measure.

Letting out a breath, I set the phone down far away, like I'm scared it'll sting me.

A few minutes later, my phone buzzes, and I almost Ctrl+A+Delete Julia's entire mansion. Kalyan looks up, and I rest my chin in my hand and stare at my computer, acting as though I haven't just knocked over every picture frame on my desk. When Kalyan shakes his head and turns away, I slide my phone over.

Beckett: Not sure it matters. You've probably already decided I'm out doing Wickham shit: ripping bodices, stealing dowries, plotting world domination.

At the mention of *Wickham shit*, my face heats. I'd like to pretend like I haven't spent a fair amount of brainpower contemplating how an in-love Mr. Wickham would kiss. Truthfully, *Wickham shit* might be contributing to my lack of focus today. I read his text again. And again. There's not a telltale emoji in sight. How am I supposed to judge his deepest, truest, internal emotions without the help of an emoji?

At once, it's become my goal in life to get him to send a smiley face. Eradicating the frowny faces isn't good enough anymore.

Instead of a frown, his last text will be a smiley face, and balance will be restored to the earth. Once he does that, I'll end the conversation there, and that will be that.

At first, the texts start out short. Simple.

Me: Want to hear a joke?

Beckett: Oh god. Please no. Your jokes make me feel secondhand embarrassment on your behalf.

Me: Fine.

Me: Kalyan started whistling Christmas carols at his desk. He keeps looking over. I'm sure he's doing it to get the song stuck in my head. What should my retaliation be?

Beckett: When he's not around, plug a wireless mouse into his computer. Then, every once and a while, bump the mouse from your desk and watch as he spirals into madness.

There are long delays between his texts, like he's busy doing something. In an attempt to look cool and not desperate, I have to wait an equally long time before sending responses. Therefore, by now, most of the morning's gone. I'm starting to sweat from the lack of emoji life in his texts. If I hadn't seen him use them before, I'd think being born in the fifties made him incapable. What will it take to crack this guy?

Me: I've been thinking about Friday night.

Shit. Shit. Shit. Abort. Delete. That's not the answer. But the text's already been sent into the void. His response takes forever.

Beckett: I don't want to hear more about your date with Mr. Delightful.

Me: Not Darcy. Thinking of a different character.

I shouldn't be flirting with him. But it's harmless, right? All I want is a smiley face.

Okay. So it is a little messed up. Why the hell do I feel the need to reawaken old wounds?

Beckett: Yes. Your mother is quite the Mrs. Bennet. I could see why you'd spend time thinking about her. ☺

There it is—the smiley. I can be done. One polite little smile. *"It's okay. You're off the hook,"* that smile says. He's giving me an out if I want it. I can send an LOL, and we can pretend it never happened.

I don't ever want to pretend it never happened.

Me: Slow and sensual or devouring desperation?

As soon as I send it, I cringe. Hard.

I nearly throw my phone in the garbage. I ought to throw myself in there as well.

"I'm off to lunch." Kalyan slaps the side of my desk, and I jump, tucking my shaking fingers under my armpits to conceal their tremor. "Tell Beckett 'Hi.'" He smirks.

"Tell Lola that divulging secrets is grounds for . . . for . . ."

One of Kalyan's eyebrows goes up. "Uh-huh. That's what I thought."

I stand, gathering my things to preoccupy myself. Maybe lunch will make me behave like a normal human being again.

My phone buzzes, and I execute an NFL-worthy dive to grab it.

Beckett: Fuck, Iza.

And that's all it says.

He must think I'm messing with him. And aren't I? This isn't going anywhere. It *can't*, and we both know it. He's no good, and he'll be gone soon.

By the time I'm in a diner, biting into a cheeseburger, I'm texting him again.

Me: What kinds of things did you like to do before you were cursed?

Beckett: You'll laugh at me.

Me: Won't. Girl Scout's honor.

Beckett: This is going to make me sound about a thousand years old. I spent a lot of time outside. We played baseball, went cruising, listened to music, went to drive-in movies.

Me: Walked barefoot in the snow to school uphill both ways? (P.S. I was never a Scout.)

Beckett: You're an asshole.

I'm snickering and ignoring the stares from everyone around me. It doesn't feel like I'm messing with him. It feels . . . real.

Me: Do you have a family?

I ask it as the realization hits me; if he was born in the fifties, his siblings might still be alive.

Beckett: Not anymore

Drumming my fingers on the table, I debate how best to respond. It looks like he might be shutting down. Trying for more information might be a mistake.

Then, my phone buzzes again.

Beckett: I was able to visit my parents a few times when I was summoned by charges in the area. Eventually though, my abnormal lack of aging raised suspicion. After that, every time I was summoned, I'd write to them. I invented a whole life. A job six states away. A girl I moved abroad to marry. Two kids. Then, one day I was summoned, and my parents had been dead for three years.

I swallow hard, my unladylike bite of cheeseburger grating past the lump in my throat.

The more I learn about the baby-seal-loving, flower-stand-working, broken, lonely, goofy man, the less it seems plausible he'd be capable of the things Darcy accused him of.

Beckett was right to ask if I shared Darcy's flaws, because maybe I do. We're both stubborn and stick to our beliefs no matter what. Even if they're wrong.

It kills me to call on any of Kalyan's advice, but I think about what he said about Lola making him happy. What they have is so simple and so good, and what Darcy and I have has never been that.

Whether Darcy was right about Beckett or not, there are too many other reasons why Darcy and I will never be right for each other.

I need to find out the truth, but most of all, I can't fill out that damn form.

* * *

I stumble into the office after lunch. "Chester." I gasp for breath, jogging to where he stands by the printer. "I'm taking the afternoon off. Not feeling well."

He pales and licks his lips. "But you can't. The project."

"I haven't used a sick day since I started here," I say. My swollen throat makes it hard to choke out words. "You'll survive."

"What's going on?" a deep voice behind me asks.

I spin. It's Darcy. "Not feeling well. Going to go home."

He frowns.

"We're—we're counting on you." Chester twists the corner of his paisley cardigan. "Darcy's project is counting on you."

Kalyan's walking by with a coffee, but when he hears that, he turns on his heel to stick his nose into our group. "I'm sorry? Darcy's project?" He gives me a significant look.

I'm done. I'm so done. This man, Fitzwilliam Darcy—my supposed soulmate—he's tried to make me small in his shadow.

Maybe a perfect on paper isn't perfect for me.

I'm going to stop getting in my own way. I'm going after what I truly want. I don't care if it's messy and imperfect, and I don't care what anyone thinks.

Resolve settles in my stomach. "It's actually *my* plan." My voice comes out barely a squeak. So much for resolve.

"What?" Chester pushes his glasses up his nose.

I clear my throat and say louder, "It's actually *my* plan." Okay, maybe a little too loud. Now everyone's staring.

Darcy's face is stony. Chester looks up at him. "What's she talking about?"

"She's right," Darcy says, sounding bored, as if it doesn't matter at all. "I thought I should back it so it would be taken seriously, given how unorthodox it is."

Kalyan lets out a dramatic gasp, hands flying to his cheeks. "Oh my god, I am shaken to my core and definitely have not known this all along." His mouth forms a perfect "O."

By now, the herd of curious onlookers has drifted slowly closer. They're under the pretense of doing something else—going to the printer, getting coffee, consulting with someone across the office—but they're fooling nobody.

Chester fidgets with the hem of his cardigan and chews his chapped lips. He looks about as nervous and unsure as someone trying to order their correct bra size off the internet. "Well, I—in this company—equal opportunities—don't discriminate."

Chester is precious, but he's a wet noodle of a boss who lets Darcy dictate everything. Enough is enough. If Chester won't grow a spine, I will. "You know what?" I draw myself up. "Forget the afternoon."

As his shoulders relax, Chester lets out a long breath.

"This is my two weeks' notice," I say.

Subtly, Kalyan executes a little fist pump behind Chester's head.

It's as if I've been breathing oxygen-deprived air for years, and I've just gone outside. If Kalyan's serious, I can freelance and work from home. And that home is a small cottage in the country.

"You can't quit," Darcy says as though it's a fact.

Chester is well on his way to hyperventilation. His glasses fog over. "We can talk monetary compensation."

"Um, so, I quit too," Kalyan says. He makes a big show of crossing his arms and lifting his chin. "This has been a great injustice." He goes so far as to wag his finger in Darcy's face. "How dare you? In this day and age? You should be embarrassed."

Darcy looks down his nose at Kalyan's finger like he might dart forward, strike like a cobra, and bite it off. Losing a bit of his bravado, Kalyan backs away.

"What about us?" Darcy asks me.

This man really thinks half of one date puts us in a serious, exclusive relationship? I don't know how Elizabeth ever forgave him if what he did to her sister Jane felt anything like how I feel after what he did to my career. I don't care if he thought it was a worthy and noble thing to do or not. My good opinion of him, once lost, is lost forever.

I dig the crumpled Form 223 out of my pocket and slap it against Darcy's chest. "There is no *us*."

CHAPTER TWENTY-FIVE

My plan was to find out the truth about Beckett. Instead, almost against my will, I find myself driving in the opposite direction. It's muscle memory. The organ in my chest drags me here every time it gets hurt.

I knock on Mom's door, self-loathing rising inside me. Here I am again, crawling back after another failed relationship, seeking comfort from a viper. I don't know why I do this to myself.

The last time I stood here, it was after Tyler. *Fuck Tyler.* I'd felt so close to success. He was a doctor, someone who understood work commitments, dedication, and responsibilities. But although he hadn't tried to make me small, he'd hurt me. I never knocked on Mom's door. I didn't want to give her a new reason to be smug.

Instead, I walked away and developed a plan to sort through as many dating profiles as I had to until I found the best of both worlds—a successful man who also had good morals, someone who would make both Mom and me happy. It was supposed to be a foolproof way to weed out unsuitable men before our roots grew too intermeshed to separate without damage.

But I am a fool, the plan was not foolproof, and again I'm hurt.

Mom opens the door. She doesn't even look surprised to see me, as though she knew this would happen. "Why aren't you at work?"

"Darcy—" I stop talking when she rolls her eyes. "Actually, work is part of the reason I wanted to come over. I wanted to tell you about something." I bite my lip.

Mom's eyes light up. "You were offered a promotion?" She clasps her hands together. "Why, you accept, of course. It may mean more hours, more responsibility, but this is what we've been waiting for."

"No." It's seventh grade again, and I'm telling her I have a date. I'm nine, asking her if I can have the pretty skirt at the department store. I'm eighteen, asking her not to throw out Grandma's quaint knickknacks, the ones she found too domestic. Like every time before, my stomach twists, and the words lodge in my throat. "Not a promotion. A coworker and I are thinking of branching off and doing our own thing."

"You mean"—Mom's eye twitches—"*freelancing*?"

"Sure." Shrugging, I stare at the ground. "Isn't that basically what you do?"

"No, Iza. No, no. This is a mistake. You'd be throwing away years of hard work. You have a concrete path in front of you. Why venture off into the woods? What's gotten into you lately? I knew no good could come from online dating."

"You act like dating is a gateway drug." My face heats, but not with shame. With anger. She's the one who's supposed to have my back, no matter what. Without Grandma, I have to have my own back. "I already quit."

Mom gasps. "What about your future?"

The ball of frustration in my gut bursts. My whole body shakes. "I have more than one dream!"

Mom jumps.

Tremors of emotion wash over me. "I'm a person. I'm allowed to be multidimensional. You think the things I place value in are unimportant or frivolous because you have this twisted idea that feminism means being a career woman and nothing else. Feminism is simply being able to choose what future you want. I can wear sparkly nail polish and be professional. I'm allowed to want a career and a husband and two kids—and damn it, I'm allowed to try for it all without sacrificing anything."

I know now I don't need Mom's approval or love, because I've never had it anyway.

I straighten my shoulders. "I've been stuck in this never-ending rut, and it's time to change something. Darcy and Tyler and all the others couldn't mesh into my life, but that doesn't mean someone else can't. I don't *need* a perfect man. I just *want* a good man. I'm not giving up. Never."

Something in Mom's expression splinters. "This is about a man."

My body stills. I'm spent and quiet. "This is about you and me. My father's love isn't the love I'm trying to replace. Beckett was right. It's yours. I was cheated on, and Tyler—"

"Fuck Tyler," Mom says under her breath.

"Yeah, fuck Tyler, but also fuck you because his lack of loyalty didn't hurt me half as much as yours. He cheated on me, and all I could think about was how you'd see it as more proof that I should give up, like it was my own fault I chose him." My voice strengthens with each word.

It's not men or even a prince that isn't enough; it's my mom who isn't enough. My whole life, I thought I needed a reason for her to love me, whether it be our sharing a favorite book, or

Grandma loving both of us, or an "acceptable" man asking me to marry him. I never thought she could love me for me.

"I chose men who were bad for me because I was choosing ones I thought you'd like, but your standards didn't look out for my best interests. All you should have cared about was whether the guy loved me. I was never after romantic love—not really. I just needed you to care about me."

"Of course I care—"

"I'm done letting you control me. I want love, and I no longer care if it comes from you. It's my choice. I'm not giving up my career. In fact, quitting my job to do my own thing means I'm taking on even more work; you just can't stand that it doesn't look like your version of success. If that means you win, then fine. If your idea of success involves me becoming an empty shell like you, then fine. So, you win for now, but in the end, maybe I'll be the one saying, 'I told you so.'"

She's stunned into silence. Her eyes are glassy, but that's impossible. Mom doesn't cry.

I turn and walk off the porch. A nasty feeling settles in the pit of my stomach—regret, loss, guilt? Whatever it is, it's the same one I get every time Beckett looks at me with hurt in his eyes. The same one the server at the restaurant had. The same one I see every time I misjudge someone.

I shake my head. I don't have time to dwell on what the feeling means. I think of Beckett, the one person who always seems to have my best interest in mind.

Wickham needs the chance to explain himself that he's never had. It's time to figure out the truth, starting with the source herself—Georgiana.

* * *

I call my bank on the way to Darcy's house. My loan officer tells me it should be no problem to obtain preapproval for my offer amount and promises to fax over the documentation to Lydia as soon as the paperwork clears.

Darcy's house looks as disgustingly quaint as it did the first time around. There's a lime-green Ford Fiesta parked in the driveway, which I take as a good indication Georgiana's home. I'm sweating by the time I climb the porch steps.

When I press the doorbell, chimes echo into the house. Soon they fade away, and complete silence looms behind the door. I ring a few more times, then step back and peel off my blazer. My thin camisole exposes my skin to the air, cooling it.

The door flies open, revealing a teenage girl. She's wearing ripped fishnets, a ratty crop top, and a mini skirt. Her hair looks like an oil slick, dyed in murky blue, green, purple, and black.

She looks me up and down with heavily lined eyes as she bites into an apple. It's a Granny Smith. What kind of monster willingly chooses to eat a Granny Smith? I shudder. Of all the varieties of apples that exist—

"What do you want?" Her voice is odd, too high and sweet to be emanating from such a hard exterior.

"Are you Georgiana?"

Her belly-button piercing flashes in the sunlight. "I prefer Gigi."

"Hi, Gigi. I'm Iza Kiches, and I was wondering—"

"Ah. Darcy's bitch." She takes another loud, smacking bite of the world's blandest fruit.

"I'm nobody's anything."

She sucks juice off her teeth, her mouth nearing something close to a smile. "Good." Standing in the doorway, she continues chomping away at the apple, her slate-gray eyes never leaving me.

I scratch my arm and shuffle my feet. "I don't know how else to begin—"

"At the very beginning," she says through a mouthful, cocking a brow. "It's a very good place to start."

"Are you quoting *The Sound of Music*?"

"Damn," she says, wiping her chin with the heel of her hand. "Was hoping you wouldn't recognize it and would think me profoundly wise." She gnashes her teeth into the core of the apple, and I swallow uncomfortably. People who eat apple cores unsettle me; what else could they be capable of?

"I'm sorry," I say, stepping forward, "*you're* Georgiana?"

"Gigi." She spits a seed to the side, and it bounces over the wooden porch to skitter to a stop by my foot.

"Satisfy my curiosity. Is your playlist exclusively full of songs written by people who are mad at their dads?" I shouldn't goad a teenager, but I can't help it.

She blinks slowly. "My father is dead."

"Oh, shit. Of course. I'm so sorry."

Just as slowly, a smile spreads across her face, and she tosses the remaining bit of apple off the porch. "It's okay. You're right about the playlist. Though I don't limit myself to artists who are mad at their parents. I'm accepting of artists who are mad at everyone else too." She jerks her chin. "Come on in."

Georgiana sits me at an oval dining room table before crossing the kitchen to put a teakettle, of all things, on the stove. I suspect she's playing the part of the perfect hostess in order to be ironic rather than hospitable. In fact, the glass-topped stove set into the dark granite countertop looks like it's never been used. The rest of the kitchen is the same way. There isn't a chicken-patterned curtain in sight.

The table's mahogany finish is glossy—not one scuff to indicate anyone's ever shared a meal here. Grandma's kitchen floors have deep gouges worn into the wood from chairs sliding around the table day after day. If I kept pursuing Darcy, my floors would've ended up looking like this.

"Tell your friend thank you for what he's done," Georgiana says abruptly.

"I'm sorry, what?"

With a grunt, she heaves herself onto the counter. "Beckett's your friend, right? Tell him I say thanks." She swings her feet like a little kid.

I realize I'm scratching my thumbnail into the edge of the table, and I clench my fist. "Are you being sarcastic right now? Because that's not funny."

Her eyes go wide. The teapot screeches, and she bounds off the counter to remove it from the burner. "Oh my god. He didn't tell you. Darcy didn't tell you either?"

Unable to sit quietly, I stand. "Tell me what?"

Closing one eye, Georgiana squints down into the belly of the teapot. "How do you make tea, anyway?"

Fiddling with a button on my blazer, which I'm still holding, I step forward. "You need a teabag."

"You're a teabag," she shoots back in a grumble, turning to reach into a cabinet and pull out a mug.

"What didn't Darcy tell me?" I steady my tone, forcing patience.

Face scrunching in concentration, she pours steaming water into the mug. Then, she hands it to me, her expression solemn.

I look into the mug of hot water. "Golly. You shouldn't have."

"Beckett isn't the guy," she says, her bitter snark gone. "I really thought he was."

"Beckett's innocent?"

She nods. "It was dark, and there were so many people, and the flashing lights . . . the guy *looked* like Beckett. Then, he was shoving a drink into my hand and . . ." Her voice wavers, and the teakettle clatters in her shaking hand. "He was all over me, whispering shit into my ear and . . ." She shudders and sets the kettle down like it's burned her. "I thought it was him. I'm sorry." She hugs herself. "I'm so sorry."

By the end, she's transformed from the vibrant, tough girl with the iron will and the in-your-face personality to this broken creature, and I know, even without her words, there's no way Beckett could ever do this to another person. Beckett is not unscrupulous. Beckett is human, and he has flaws, but he is so scrupulous it makes my heart ache.

In a moment of weakness, he may have thought about getting me to switch places with him, but he never went through with it. If everyone were condemned for their thoughts, we'd all be damned. After all, I used to have frequent daydreams about stabbing Kalyan. Most of us keep our thoughts inside, but I forced Beckett's out.

If I were in Beckett's position for ten years, I'd be driven to desperate measures too, frantic to escape. He's proven his remorse, and it's time for me to forgive him.

"Do you want a hug?" I ask Georgiana, opening my arms.

"Hell no."

Biting my lip, I nod. "I hope they find out who did it and catch him."

Her head snaps up. "That's right. You don't know. They did find the right guy. And that's what I wanted you to thank Beckett for. He threw a party every night until he found several giant sleazeballs who resemble him. Once he narrowed down the pool, he talked to other guests until he found enough people who'd witnessed the *actual* guy that night, and he was able to build a strong enough case to have the guy convicted. He was sentenced today, actually." She smiles wryly. "They say it's over now."

"It doesn't feel over for you, though, does it?" I ask.

She shakes her head.

This time when I open my arms, she steps into them.

* * *

"What the hell is wrong with you?" I yell into my cell phone, swerving to avoid hitting a parked car.

"You turned in your resignation and walked out," is Darcy's calm reply. "Direct that question to yourself."

"I talked to Gigi."

"Oh."

"Yeah, *oh*. Want to explain?"

"There's nothing to explain. I didn't think it mattered if you knew or not. It didn't affect our relationship."

"Your accusing Beckett very much affected our relationship." But I'm not talking about the relationship between Darcy and me.

He's smart enough to know it. "So I was a second choice." His voice sharpens. "The next best thing."

"No," I say coldly. "You were my first choice, but I make bad choices. People think you're so dreamy, but you're a cold, calculating man. Where's your warmth? Do you even know how to laugh? Have your eyes ever *thought* about crinkling?"

"What are you talking about?"

I'm too far gone to care if he's still following. "Just because you take a break from being indifferent every so often to show a shred of normal human decency, that doesn't make you some sort of gold standard for men. If you add up your net worth—all the shittiness along with all the mediocrity—you come out somewhere below average. I can't believe Austen got it wrong. Has Wickham, not you, been the one who's been misunderstood the whole time?"

"I have no idea what you're talking about."

My tone is savage as I mash the brakes at a stop sign. "You saw Beckett and me together. You knew we were close, and you capitalized on your sister's misfortunes to make yourself look good."

As I jolt forward from the stop sign, my fingers turn white around the wheel.

He starts to say something, but there's someone else I'm so very far from angry with who holds my total attention. This conversation with Darcy isn't worth it.

I cut him off. "I'm sick of this stoic, tortured act of yours. You're not the misunderstood good guy. Being at the right place at the right time to perform a few moderately kind tasks doesn't make up for all your bullshit. You can't just neg women for months on end so you'll look like a hero when you finally decide to do the bare minimum. This isn't the nineteenth century."

I hang up the phone.

A second later, it buzzes with a text. I'm about to turn my phone off when I see Lydia's name lit up on the screen. At the stoplight, I read it.

Lydia: So sorry. Heard from your bank. Everything is okay there, but unfortunately, the owners just accepted another offer this morning. But I have some other listings—

A horn honks, interrupting my reading, which is fine by me. I don't need to see the rest.

My phone buzzes again. This one's from Beckett. I wait until I park in front of my apartment to read it.

Beckett: Sorry. I know that's heavy. Didn't mean to bring you down.

My stomach bottoms out when I read his last text that I never responded to, the one where he told me his parents died. I'm the shittiest person ever. I'm right up there with people who run over turtles and put tags in underwear. I've beaten him down time and time again, and he's still worried that his opening up to me made *me* feel down.

Exiting the car, I run up the sidewalk as fast as my heels allow. Inside, I abandon the shoes completely, leaving them at the bottom of the stairwell as I thunder my way up. At Beckett's door, I pound my fist into the wood until my hand numbs.

"Beckett?" My voice shakes. I try the knob. It's unlocked, and because I'm apparently okay with inviting myself into people's homes, I let myself in.

I don't know what I thought I'd see. A disheveled apartment, a dirty kitchen, unwashed laundry—all the signs of a distraught man? There aren't any of those things because Beckett's not a distraught man. He has a clear conscience because he's made up for his mistakes.

From somewhere deep in the apartment, oldies are playing. It's some crackly tune with a tinkling piano. Some guy with a husky voice sings about love.

The furniture in the living room is arranged in a normal configuration instead of being pushed aside for a party. In the kitchen, there's a plate and a fork in the dish rack and an open book face down on the table. It's *Pride and Prejudice*, and the pages are dog-eared, like he's been scouring it for information, clues.

"Beckett?" I drift farther in, carpet squishing under my bare feet as I make my way down the hall and nudge his bedroom door open. The bed's made, the dark comforter plush and smooth. There are stacks of folded laundry on top of his dresser.

The scent of him is everywhere, drifting around me in a subtle wave combined with laundry detergent, leather, and . . . paper? My eye catches on the giant beanbag chair in the corner. Littering the floor around it are hundreds, maybe thousands, of sandpaper roses. They're scattered across half the floor and range from crudely done to perfect. On top of the beanbag chair, half-hidden under a pile of roses, is an origami book.

Behind me, the door creaks.

CHAPTER TWENTY-SIX

I whirl. Beckett stands in the doorway in much the same dress as last Friday. His suit is crisp, tie done, jacket buttoned, and hair combed back. I have the unquenchable desire to mess it all up.

"Why are you doing this to me, Iza?" His eyes are full of wounded tension.

"Texting you all day or breaking into your apartment?" I toe the carpet.

"Texting. No, both." He lets out a huff. "No, caring. Or acting like you do."

"Beckett." I take a cautious step forward. "I do care. I went to see Georgiana today."

Letting out a long breath, he runs a hand down his face, looking away. "Yeah. I know you did. She texted me."

"And?"

He shrugs and smiles tightly. "And what?"

I fight to see through my stinging eyes. My stomach churns with a mix of nerves, guilt, and self-loathing. If only I could go back in time and shake myself for letting us get to this point.

I take a few more steps until I stand before him, toe to toe. "I messed up. Everything can be different. Stop distancing yourself. Let me in again. I shouldn't have asked you if you did those things. I should've known. I should've—"

His face hardens.

"What can I do to make it better, to apologize, to make it all okay again?" I touch his arm, but he shakes his head, pushing me away.

"Nothing's changed. It doesn't matter what you think of me, what you—" He lets out a ragged breath. "What you feel for me."

"Beckett, are you okay?" My voice comes out small,

"Of course I'm not okay!" he explodes, eyes flashing with wild hysteria. "You think I've been okay this whole time? You think after you believed—without question, without concrete evidence—the word of the man competing for your attention, we'd be *okay*?" He jabs a finger. "How many times would I have had to tell you I can't lie to you before you would've believed me?"

My eyes burn. My throat burns. Everything burns. It's not the fire of sparkling explosions from the other night. It's real, searing, deep pain. "You watched the movie. You read the book. Can't you see why I thought knowing he's Mr. Darcy *was* the proof? Why would I assume Austen had no idea what was going on beyond her own pages?"

Beckett brushes past me, walking farther into the room. Running an agitated hand through his hair, he faces me again. "This isn't a story. This is real. *I'm* real."

I walk up to him, resisting the urge to reach out and touch him. "I know that. I'm sorry."

He shakes his head. An overwhelming sense of dread settles over me. "You need to leave," he says.

"You—you're pushing me away? When you asked me to do the zoo with you, when you told me how you'd kiss me, when we were texting—I don't understand. Why do all that to push me away now?"

His eyes are clear and bright. The guard he's had up has, at last, shattered completely. As his nostrils flare, his warm breath grazes my cheek, tender as the brush of a cracking whip. "Because I'm a selfish prick who can't leave well enough alone."

"No you're not. What do you mean?" Emotions hang suspended in my body. I imagine a rainstorm of every label I ever used to stereotype him, the letters of words like *player, selfish, untrustworthy* crumbling apart and cascading around my body until I'm buried alive in past sins and regrets.

Corded tendons strain under the skin of his neck. "I want my life to be meaningful again so badly, I played pretend with you, knowing what could happen if you—" Something in his expression cracks.

"I don't care about long term," I say. "I want you now for as long as I can have you."

"I can't," he chokes out.

"You could at the zoo and in the hall. Why then and not now?"

"Because," he snaps. "I was hurt, but it didn't matter because all I wanted to do was make as many memories as I could with you before I come back one day and you're married or a grandmother or dead." The last word, *dead*, leaves his lips like a thundercrack. He's so close I can see his pupils changing shapes as he scans my face.

When he next speaks, his voice has softened to the cadence of rolling thunder far out on the horizon. "My goddamn feelings weren't the most important thing because being sad wasn't worth losing a spark of happiness with you."

"And now?" Drawn forward by his soft tone, I reach out and place my fingertips to his chest. Even under his jacket, I can feel the tremors in his body from anger or fear or simply a mess of pure, raw emotion.

"And now"—he presses his hand over mine, his fingers steady despite the evidence the rest of him is on the verge of coming undone—"it's not pretend. Now, it's real. Now, one moment, one shard of happiness, isn't worth *your* sadness."

"It won't have to end," I say in a rush, hope flooding back into my veins. "You won't ever have to leave. You can take Lola, yourself, and me home to our universe. We can build a life together there. I'll just never say I wi—" I catch myself. "Anything about wishing."

Beckett smiles ruefully, his expression borderline pitying, and I can hardly bear it. "It will happen. Maybe not now. Maybe not for years. But it'll happen. You'll see a falling star or blow out a birthday candle or slip up in conversation. It's easier to end it before it begins, before it's been fifteen years and we have two kids and a mortgage and enough love between us that we could really, truly make it."

"We won't have a mortgage because the house already sold," I say, like that even makes a difference. "But maybe we could fix that. You can still make wishes. You could wish us back in time so we can do things differently. You could wish that I never used my wishes."

He laughs the sad, tired laugh of someone who's laughing because if they don't, they'll cry. "I'm not able to use my magic to undo your wishes. Being able to take away the things I'm forced to give wouldn't exactly teach me how to be selfless. I can't wish us back in time to undo things. I can't wish away your wishes. I could wish you, Lola, and myself back to our universe, though. I could even wish you the house. But then what? You waste your life building a future with me that can't last?"

Clenching my fist into the lapel of his jacket, I give it a little tug. "Hey." I search his face. "I used to think if I ever had something like this and lost it, it would break me. Now I know having a chance at something like this and never taking it would be worse." I can't keep eye contact anymore. "We have issues. We've both hurt each other. But if you say it's only a matter of time before I accidentally make a wish, then let's live in the moment and enjoy every second together until that happens. I don't care if I get hurt. Let's be selfish. Let's ignore our problems. Let's be irresponsible, irrational fools together."

Beckett's lips part as he watches me talk.

"Nobody has ever made me want to stop thinking," I say. "I overthink everything, but you make me quiet inside." I touch his face, my fingers brushing the angle of his cheekbone. The stubble under my skin reminds me of the sandpaper roses. "We have fun. You make me want those moments—those fleeting, impossible moments—the ones where we feel alive. You like doing things that make you feel alive." I spread my arms and grin. "Do me."

Now he laughs for real—eyes crinkling and dimples creasing. "Who taught you that sick pickup line?"

I tug him closer. "Kiss me. Kiss me like Wickham so I don't have to live my whole life wondering what it would've been like."

Beckett goes still, absolutely still. In the dim light of his bedroom, his eyes darken to the color of a well-worn penny, a coppery glint reflecting through a haze of brown. For a moment, I think he's going to ask me to leave again. Then, he brushes a stray curl out of my face, his fingers barely a whisper against my skin. He runs his knuckles down my jaw, his head slightly tilted, eyes following the movement like it's the most fascinating thing he's ever witnessed and he can't look away.

A delicious shiver runs down my spine, and I lean into Beckett's touch. With both hands, he tilts my face up, his thumbs under my chin, his fingers splayed across my neck. His hands are steady. He's no longer torn apart inside, no longer unsure or angry or hurt, and neither am I, because it doesn't matter. For this one moment, we can let it all go.

Heat from his skin warms me from my outside to my inside and back again in an endless cycle. I wind my fingers into his suit jacket, probably wrinkling it horribly, but that doesn't matter either. Nothing matters anymore.

Beckett's throat bobs as his breath catches. "I think I've hyped this up too much." He breaks into his dimpled smile, the one where he bites his bottom lip, and his eyes shine. "Not sure it'll live up to expectations, and it's kind of a lot of pressure."

"Oh my god, Beckett." I tug on his jacket. "Just kiss me already."

He's still smiling when he presses his lips to mine, and I can't help but do the same, which creates some initial awkwardness of lips and teeth and breathless laughter. Then, he winds his hands into my hair, and I'm wrapping mine around his neck, and neither of us is smiling anymore.

His mouth is soft but purposeful as it slides across mine. I catch his bottom lip, and he makes a barely audible noise in the back of his throat. The next thing I know, he's pushing me backward, his hands finding my waist, pulling me into him. I let out a girly yelp as we crash into the dresser, which makes him chuckle against my mouth. I decide his laugh is the sexiest damn thing I've ever heard.

Whatever he's got on top of his dresser topples over, clattering and crashing to the ground. A stack of laundry flops over my shoulder before tumbling to the floor, and a sharp knickknack bounces off his head, earning a preoccupied, mumbled, "Shit."

Now I'm the one snorting with laughter. And he's kissing me again, even though I'm still fighting this irrational, giddy mirth welling up inside of me and threatening to burst free. I stomp it down because dissolving into a full-on laughing fit in the middle of making out with him would look rather deranged.

His mouth coaxes mine open, and I tug at the hair curling at the nape of his neck, fulfilling my desire to destroy his put-together appearance. I push against him, and we stumble sideways, his elbow knocking over a lamp and my arm brushing into a picture on the wall, causing the whole thing to tip over on top of us. Beckett shoves it off, kissing me the entire time.

Then, we're trampling sandpaper roses, the roughness biting into the soft arches of my feet. The paper slides over the floor, and we lose our balance. He falls back, dragging me along with him. We topple onto the massive bean bag chair, me landing hard on his chest, my elbows crashing into his stomach.

The wind's knocked out of him, and a stream of curses flows from his mouth, but he's still smiling, so I don't think he's terribly upset.

Beckett watches as I pull off his jacket and loosen his tie. His chest is still heaving as he tries to catch his breath when I start on the buttons of his shirt. My fingers fumble, but finally the last buttons release, and his shirt slides open. I trail a finger down the tattoo crawling across his skin. His breath grows ragged as I trace the design.

As my fingers graze his hip, he catches my hand and rolls until I'm half under him. Something abrasive digs into my back. I wriggle my hand behind me until my grip closes around a handful of scratchy sandpaper roses. I pull them out. "I thought you used magic to make those. I had no idea you were into origami."

He cringes, dark lashes sinking over his cheekbones as his gaze drops to my mouth. "It turned into a hobby, I guess. It's kind of therapeutic. Meditative and all that. Helps me think."

"You need all the help with that you can get, don't you?" Snickering, I toss the roses at him.

He bats them away easily. "Maybe."

"This isn't a hobby, Beckett." I give him my best stern expression, failing miserably because my mouth has been rendered incapable of anything except smiling and kissing. "This is borderline obsessive."

"Oh yeah?" He pins my arms down, lacing his fingers with mine. "I know a girl who wished for Mr. Darcy and spent weeks stalking him because she thought that would win him over. That's . . . a"—he's speaking between kisses now—"little . . . obsessive." He nips playfully at my jaw, and I tuck my chin, fighting the shivers running down my spine.

Releasing my hands, he presses closer, resting his forearm beside my head. This kiss is slow, annoyingly so. I glide my hands up his chest and over his shoulders, pulling him down. He lets out a soft groan, something encompassing lust and ecstasy and despair. He kisses me like he never will again. He kisses me like we're the first two people ever to say, "Hey, let's try mashing our mouths together," and we've just discovered how wondrous it is. He kisses me like he never plans to stop.

His warm hands slip under my shirt, spreading fire through my limbs. Cinnamon and cedar fill my nostrils, the scent of him all around me, all over me. With him clumsily trying to figure out my bra, like a teenager, and me awkwardly fighting back giggles as I try not to laugh at him, I could live in this moment forever.

He mumbles some excuse about how difficult it is to keep up with underwear trends for seventy years as he sits back, pulling me with him until we both kneel on the floor. Instead of lifting my shirt over my head, as I assumed he would, he cups my face and kisses me so deeply, so tenderly, my throat tightens.

Beckett is sunset tears. He's a massively out-of-control fireworks display threatening to burn down an entire city. He's a borer bee, sometimes bumbling and annoying at times, but incapable of stinging anyone. He tastes like honey, he smells like Saturday morning French toast, and he feels like a serene cottage in the middle of the woods. He's a cool spring breeze through chicken-patterned curtains. He's fragments of dandelion wishes floating in the summer heat, and autumn leaves in my hair, and snowflakes on my tongue.

At last, Beckett pulls away. When he looks into my eyes, I jolt because, instead of the reflected joy and yearning and peace I expect, I see . . . something else.

"Iza?" He brushes a thumb across my cheek and swallows hard before continuing. "What would you do right now if you had a choice? If you could choose between me and your old life, what would your decision be?"

I recoil, and his hands fall from my face. "I want you, of course."

"Wouldn't it be nice if could have made different wishes than the ones that landed you here? You wouldn't have had to come to this universe at all. You could have wished for your house, your own firm, and something to help mend the relationship with your mother. Without me in the way, you could be free right now to build something real with someone else."

I run my fingers down to his waistband, but he doesn't move. "I want you. There's no point in thinking about it. My wishes can't be undone."

He catches my wrists. "Say it were possible for the past to change. If you had a do-over, what would you do?"

Beckett seems intent on hearing my answer, so I give the question a few moments of thought. It's easy to say I'd choose him when he's in front of me, but my answer would be different if I had been given an objective choice at the beginning, before feelings got in the way, before I got to know Beckett. If someone had asked me a few months ago if I'd be willing to spend a portion of my life on a relationship that was good but couldn't last, I would have said no.

Beckett sees my answer in my eyes. I expect him to look wounded, but he only smiles. "Imagine what could be different," he says gently.

I blink back tears. The real kind this time, not the sunset kind. I don't want to imagine a future without him in it.

Frustration pushes words past my lips before I can stop them. "If only I could have seen things clearly from the beginning. If only I knew then what I know now. I could have found a way to avoid my mistakes and hold onto you. I wish I could go back and talk some sense into myself so you, Lola, and I could be happy and home right now."

We go still. *I wish.* An off-handed comment. A daydream that has turned my life into a nightmare. Sickness weighs down every nerve in my body as the horror of what I've done settles around me. "I didn't mean to say it like that. I take it back. I—"

I meet Beckett's eyes. Instead of widening into shock, they soften. A small smile plays over his lips. Lightly, he kisses me on the nose before releasing my wrists.

"You said you can't use your magic to undo my wishes," I say, scrambling to find a scrap of hope.

"But you can," he says softly.

I suck in a sharp breath. "You were *trying* to get me to say that? You knew what would happen. Why'd you make me do it?"

He shakes his head, and I know this is it. I made my last wish, and he doesn't have to answer my questions anymore.

"Why the hell did you do that?" My voice breaks. I lunge for him, open palms slamming weakly into his chest. Becket holds onto my elbows as I thrash against him. I don't know if I'm trying to hold on to him or get away.

Beckett draws himself to his feet, dragging my flailing body with him. His fingers wrap around the base of my skull as he gives me a little shake and forces me to look at him. His hazel eyes are rimmed in red. His body is coiled, taut, fighting off whatever inner force compels him to fulfill the wish. "You never wanted this life," he rasps. "Redo everything. You shouldn't give up the chance to build an amazing future for a short, doomed relationship with me."

"I can't rewrite the past." I frantically shake my head. "I'll erase our memories together. You already have so little control over your life; I can't take away another piece of it."

"When you see me again, that part of my life will already be gone."

He's right. When I meet his past self, his memories of our time together won't exist yet. There will technically be nothing to lose by changing things . . . nothing to lose except the tiny future we had together, that is.

I told him once he wasn't a good friend because he didn't think about other people. Now he does. He still thinks I'm better off without him.

Beckett could have told me his plan, but he knew I wouldn't have made the wish, not when it meant I'd hurt him. He saw the truth behind my assurances and is sacrificing his memories willingly.

The choice for what I do with my life is wholly mine. He took himself out of the equation.

I'm left shaking as the fight leaves my body. "I could have been happy here with you."

Beckett nods. He knows. He fucking knows.

I could have been happy here, but it wouldn't have been my first choice. He's finally listening to what someone else wants, putting my feelings and desires above his own.

"If I redo my past, I'll lose the memories of our time together too," I say, a lump lodging in my throat.

"It will be less painful to forget than it would be to hold on." A slick sheen of sweat covers his skin now, and his arms tremble with fatigue.

I remember what Beckett said that night in the rain when he changed my tire, when he asked to be my friend. *"You'll get your perfect life, and we'll go our separate ways."*

A sob escapes my throat, and I wrap my arms around his chest and bury my face in his neck. He holds onto me just as tightly, his breath rattling in his chest. And then I pull back because I don't want to miss my last glimpse of him, and I don't want his last glimpse of me to be filled with fury and tears.

I wipe my eyes and touch his cheek, mustering up a smile.

Beckett doesn't smile back.

He dips his head and kisses me. And he doesn't taste like honey. He tastes like salt, the tears of a thousand dead sunsets. Ghosts of fireworks haunt this kiss—milky cobwebs of smoke across an inky night sky—all promise of fire and beautiful chaos dissolving in the wind.

His lips glide from my mouth, brushing across my cheekbone to my ear.

"You made it all worth it," he whispers.

CHAPTER TWENTY-SEVEN

There is no loud noise, no purple smoke, nothing. One minute, I'm in Beckett's arms, and the next, I'm standing cold and alone in my kitchen.

Squeezing my eyes shut, I imagine myself away from this reality, transporting my soul to another universe. In this universe, I'm cocooned in the warm, dark safety of Beckett's car. Rain patters on the roof, and oldies crackle through a vintage radio. He slides me across the seat, bending to whisper in my ear, to nuzzle my jaw, his smile against my neck.

I blink away both my fantasies and my tears. I used my last wish. He's gone forever.

When I was little, I used to listen to "Call Me Maybe" on repeat. Carly's lyrics say before she met the guy in the song, she missed him. Mom said that was ridiculous. You can't miss something you've never had.

Now, I've had it. I've experienced someone coming into my life in the way that makes you want to trade your soul for a wish. Just one more wish. One more fucking wish.

I choke on a sob, then choke again when my eyes lock onto a figure seated across the room.

There's someone sitting on my couch.

A woman who looks identical to me is sitting on the couch. She hasn't seen me yet, since she's preoccupied poking through a small cardboard box. I steady myself against the counter, recognizing the box as the exact one Mom gave me after the infamous Olive Garden excursion.

My hands tremble against the cold countertop.

"I wish I could go back and talk some sense into myself."

I'm looking at me from the past.

I swallow hard and try to keep my breathing even. I've gone back to the *before time*, the time before Beckett appeared, before my world turned upside down. But she's here too, the before-time me. And I'm here—the post-time, new, improved, better-in-every-way me.

Across the room, my double twirls my high school boyfriend's class ring around her thumb, and I know what she's thinking: *"Call Me Maybe." Souls and wishes. Will Mom ever accept me?* Dark circles lie under her eyes. Her shoulders are tense, her face hard and unforgiving. It seems so long ago that I was that person.

She picks up the bottle of nail polish and turns it over in her hands.

My breathing grows shallow. Maybe Beckett isn't gone forever. Although I lost the version of him I fell for, a past version of him is here. I can't do what Beckett asked and give him up.

My first instinct is to launch across the room and warn my past self. I can tell her about the house, tell her to stop caring about what Mom thinks, tell her to live her own life. Tell her to hold onto Beckett. Maybe I could rewrite our love story and make it longer. I need to tell her she should never make a wish.

But as soon as she makes a choice that's different from the one I did the first time around, my past will change. If she doesn't make wishes and go on the same journey, she won't end up where I am. I might cancel out everything I did, and I—this future version of me—might cease to exist, and then I couldn't be here to warn myself at all.

I need to be careful. I need time to figure out what to do next.

Before my past self can see me, I dart across the kitchen and slip into the pantry. From here, I can see into the living room, through the cracked door. I'm just in time.

Past-me shakes the bottle of nail polish.

A loud crack splits the air.

Someone coughs.

From my hiding place, I can't see the chair where Beckett sits, but I know he's there. My heart clenches, and it takes all my willpower not to burst from the pantry. But this past version of him has no idea who I am.

"'Sup, girl?" His muffled voice reaches me, and I press a hand against my mouth to hold back a sob.

My past self gapes at him from her spot on the couch. She looks the way I imagine a drowned fish would if fish could drown.

I told Mom what I need is a good man. Beckett didn't demand my time. He was grateful for what moments we had. In the end, he sacrificed his happiness for mine. Beckett is a good man.

I listen to my past self accuse him of being a serial killer. I listen to her call him a liar, call him by the wrong name, and call the police. It's hard to watch me like this. I know now how much I misjudged everything.

My past self enters the kitchen, searching for a skillet to use as a weapon. My breath catches as she draws near. She pauses, wrinkling her nose as Beckett gives her the rundown on wishes behind her. I didn't even know my face could make that expression. She looks like she smelled something terrible.

A minute later, a muffled voice from her phone asks, "Nine-one-one, what's your emergency?" and she backs into the living room to take the call.

Through it all, Beckett's light, carefree voice makes me want to bawl because I know he's *not* carefree. Underneath it all, he's probably worried—scared about what I'll make him do, wondering what year it is, hoping he'll have at least a few good days to live his own life.

The whole time, he hovers out of my line of sight. All I can see during the exchange is my own stupid self. The universe is laughing at me, torturing me by making me watch myself repeat my mistakes.

After a while, I close my eyes and tune out my own voice, listening to Beckett's instead. If I don't think too hard, I can pretend he's sitting beside me, maybe simply retelling the story of how we met instead of reliving it.

The police come and go. My past self demands that Beckett show her he's real, and he complies, filling the apartment with chaos. It goes on and on. It's agony, having my own life mere feet away, begging to be reclaimed, but being unable to do anything about it. I just want it to be over.

Something rustles against my pantry door.

I snap my head up, eyes flying open.

Waffles noses open the door. *No, no, no.* I can't have resisted this long only for him to blow my cover. "Shh," I whisper, pulling him inside and scratching his ears, willing him to be quiet.

Waffles lets out a meow. *Damn it.*

I shove him back out of the pantry and shrink into the darkness, hoping if either my past self or Beckett comes to investigate, they'll somehow miss me.

But they don't come to investigate.

Instead, I hear Beckett making little "Pss, pss," noises, calling for Waffles.

Inching forward, I peek through the crack.

A jolt goes through my body. Beckett kneels in the living room, looking directly at me.

It takes a wild, panicked second to realize he's not looking at *me* exactly. He's looking at Waffles, who's still hovering in front of the pantry. My heart slows back down.

Beckett holds out a hand and wiggles his fingers, and it takes everything in me not to throw open the door, cross the kitchen, and climb into his arms right behind Waffles.

I almost do it. My muscles coil, and I even reach for the pantry door. Then I remember his last words to me: *"You made it all worth it."*

Beckett gave me a flower that sealed his fate because he valued how much he grew with me. We learned how to be kinder people together. He learned how to love, and I can't take that from him, even if that means I can't be the one he will love anymore. If I try to save him, I'll condemn him.

Beckett turns away, and I can't help but wonder if that was the last time I'll look into his eyes.

As their conversation continues, Beckett talks about wasting wishes on love and how he gave up on real . . . I have to cover my entire face in my hands and turn away from the crack. I curl my knees to my chest and let my tears silently fall.

And then, at last, he leaves, my past self trailing out after him. Britney Spears thunders to life a few seconds later.

Not long after that, my past self comes back. It takes her a few minutes to collect herself before she finally heads to her bedroom, her brows so furrowed, I'm not sure they'll ever unknot.

Still, I wait, staying put for what feels like hours, to make sure she falls asleep, before emerging from my hiding place.

I rummage around the kitchen as quietly as I can, grabbing a snack that I don't think she'll miss and a drink of water. If I remember right, tonight is Friday. Lola won't be back until Sunday night, so I can hide out in her room until then.

A scuffling sound from the living room causes me to snap my head around. Waffles's butt pokes out from under the couch. He wiggles as he swats at something, and there's a faint *tink tink tink*.

The nail polish bottle. I move Waffles out of the way and dig under the couch until my fingers touch cool glass. I pull out the bottle. Inside is a churning puddle of liquid space, a thousand galaxies. Even though I know nothing will happen, I give it a shake. The marble inside clacks into the glass against my palm. It's empty, as empty as my heart.

I close my eyes against the pain but only see more of it against the backdrop of my eyelids as memories assault my senses. Good memories. Memories I can't risk by screwing this up. They were real, even if they didn't last. Even if it all ended in pain, it's better than if it hadn't happened at all.

My eyes fly open. Earlier today, when I rushed to Beckett's apartment to find him, he hadn't been inside. But his car had been in the parking lot, his apartment door unlocked, and he'd had music on. What if he'd been in *my* apartment?

Maybe he'd used magic to somehow send a clue back in time to help me.

I turn in circles, searching the room.

I rush to the counter and flip through the stack of mail. Nothing.

I dart over to the calendar and look through the pages. *Nothing.*

My eye catches on the cardboard box Mom gave me. I stride across the room and snatch it up. It's full of birthday cards. Most are generic, with a hastily scrawled signature of a distant aunt or forgotten childhood friend. As I flip through, my eyes catch on familiar looping cursive. The front of the card has a black and white picture of a rose. I flip it open to the writing on the inside and read.

Thank you for showing me how to try. —XO

Beckett didn't leave me a clue for how to fix this and save him. He sent a card back in time, to say goodbye. He suspected my feelings had changed as we'd texted throughout the day, and his plan had always been to get me to wish myself back home. He kissed me until I fell for him enough to be filled with yearning, to wish for things to be different. He left me, thinking it was for the best. It's infuriating and unfair. I hate him for it, but I hate myself more for not realizing what was in front of me for so long.

It's like the last firework has twinkled out into nothingness, the last sunset has been snuffed, the final page turned. The end. Game over. Except my life has to keep on going even though the story died.

I lift the card to my chest. Under it is an old birthday card full of Grandma's bold, blocky handwriting. Heart drumming so hard it aches, I read it.

Iza, Happy Birthday. I'm proud of the woman you've become. You never doubt yourself, but see the world the way it is, not the way people tell you it is. Don't ever let that change. Don't ever let outside forces sway what you know to be true. Lots of love, Grandma.

Too little. Too fucking late.

If I'd looked at this card before any of this happened, things might have been different. I might have tried to do better sooner.

Guilt consumes me. Guilt I failed Grandma, guilt I failed Beckett, guilt I failed myself. And grief because I lost it all.

And then I sink to the floor and burst into tears, muffling the sounds behind a couch pillow. Somewhere along the line, I lost the person Grandma talked about, the person who would've never let Beckett go, who would've been smart enough not to doubt, assume, and judge. I've barely started to find that person again, and now it's too late.

Telling my past self what to do won't truly help. I need to allow her to learn from her own decisions. Because, if this past version of me doesn't make my mistakes, she also might not experience the good that came from those mistakes. She might never face her own words reflected in the hurt in Beckett's eyes and finally understand the damage they cause. She might never stand up to her mother or end up in Beckett's arms. She'll still believe she can judge a person by their shoes, without needing to walk around in them for a day.

For once, I don't want to change my life. I accept what happened. I'll let my past self mess up because otherwise she won't learn that imperfection is human and she doesn't need anyone's validation.

Finally, I understand how Beckett was able to seal his own fate by handing me that yellow rose. Without my past, I wouldn't be who I am.

And not just me, but Beckett too. He learned how to be a friend. He learned to hope. He learned to try, and I can't take away those memories he fought so hard to make by undoing our time together.

I have to make sure everything plays out exactly as it did the first time around.

CHAPTER TWENTY-EIGHT

If I don't want to screw this up, I have to avoid running into my past self.

Luckily, I happen to know myself very well and remember with decent clarity what I did that weekend, like how I slept in on Saturday after Beckett's party kept me up all night.

While my past self tosses and turns in her room, spewing muttered curses and threats, I sit with my back against the front door and listen to Beckett's party raging across the hall. A soft smile plays on my lips. I entertain a fantasy about dressing in a disguise and heading over to the party, but think better of it.

I'll have to content myself with catching glimpses of Beckett and overhearing scraps of conversation before Sunday night comes. Once my past self wishes for Darcy, they'll all go to the parallel universe, and I'll be left here, hiding from the parallel-universe versions of Lola and me who come here to take our places. Three versions of me. It's a lot to think about. Then again, if I consider the infinite number of parallel universes that must be out there, there are probably also an infinite number of Izas, which is even more baffling.

When morning comes, I hide in Lola's room while my past self marches across the hall to give Beckett a firm talking-to. After she comes back a little while later, all in a huff and grumbling something like "I don't need him," and "I fulfill my own desires," I lock Lola's door and settle in for a nap.

* * *

"Oh my god. You're cheating on me." Beckett's distant voice snaps me awake.

I tiptoe out of Lola's room toward the voices in the hall. My past self must be on her way to the date with the prince. I shake my head, remembering how sure of myself I'd been.

I press my ear to the front door and listen to the end of their conversation.

"I'd better go," she says. "I'm going to be late."

"Good luck," Beckett calls after her, but her retreating footsteps are her only response.

I can hear his sigh, then the click of his door.

I step back. I should find something to eat and hide again before past-me gets back from her date. But I have one more day until I lose Beckett all over again.

My feet shift this way and that, my conflicting thoughts and feelings providing them with no clear direction. I shouldn't give in to the temptation. But he's right across the hall. And now I understand how Beckett felt when he wanted to be selfish just one time. It's the wrong thing to do, but I can't stop myself.

* * *

I knock on Beckett's door a minute later, brown take-out bags clutched in my fist.

Adrenaline races into my limbs as his footsteps approach. My heart thuds in my ears. I half expect to vanish at any second, considering I'm messing with the past when I shouldn't be, but I don't. At least, not yet.

His door opens, and everything stills. The adrenaline bleeds away. My heart seems to stop. My racing thoughts slow to a leisurely stroll.

Beckett's beautiful eyes widen when he realizes it's me outside his door. Although he stands mere feet away, the distance seems insurmountable. Any distance between us feels like a tragedy. But even I'm not stupid enough to cross that boundary. This Beckett hardly knows me.

"What are you doing here?" he asks. Although it's only been a day, it feels like forever since I heard his voice without the barriers of doors and walls.

"Making good memories." I smile and hold up the bags. "If you're hungry, I got gyros from that vendor down the street."

He steps aside, giving me a weird look. "You didn't have to do that."

I shrug. "I didn't have to. I wanted to."

"Thanks?" Still looking at me sideways, he steps aside and waves me in. "Make yourself at home."

His living room furniture is still pushed to the sides of the room, so I head to the kitchen, set the bags on the small circular table, and take a seat. Beckett follows after me, settling himself on the opposite chair. "Short date, huh?"

"We had to reschedule." I send his take-out bag sliding across the table, and he catches it right before it falls off the edge.

"You didn't have anyone else you wanted to make memories with?"

I fiddle with the edge of my take-out bag. I have to be careful about what I say. If he knows something is up, everything will be ruined. I'm pushing my luck as it is.

"Sometimes you don't appreciate things before they're gone," I say slowly. "Then, when it's too late, you hold onto everything you can, no matter how small."

"What do you mean?" he asks, unpacking his gyro.

"It's like after I lost my grandma. After she was gone, it wasn't the big things I remembered. It was the little ones. The exact expression on her face that one time Mom and I stopped in to surprise her on a random Tuesday. The way that ring she wore on her right pointer finger was always crooked. Her phone number. Her address. I still remember that." I rattle off the address and shake my head. "Weird how it sticks with you."

"Mellowlight Lane?" Beckett asks. "It doesn't even sound real."

"Check it out sometime. It doesn't look real either." I bite my lip as silence stretches. "I don't know," I say at last. "I guess what I'm trying to say is something made me want to come over here and make one of those small memories with you."

Beckett leans across the table and steadies my fidgeting hand with his. His palm is warm, his fingers sure. I hyper-fixate on his hand, wondering if his knobby knuckles will become one of those random things I remember long after he's gone. "You good?" he asks. "You seem weird. Weirder than normal."

My hand twitches as I fight to keep from flipping it over to lace my fingers with his. He misinterprets the movement and pulls away. "I'm okay," I say, drawing my hands into my lap and twisting my fingers together. "I found a birthday card Grandma left me. It made me think about things."

"She meant a lot to you."

"Yeah. I liked how it felt, thinking someone was great and having them think I was great in return. Having someone on my team. She showed my mom how to care for me—" I bite my tongue before I say too much. The words hover in the air for us both to look at, and I feel exposed.

Now that they're out there, I can view them from a new angle. They make it so obvious that this whole time, it truly wasn't a boyfriend or a husband I was after. I was trying to replace something that I lost, something to make my life feel whole again.

Beckett is smart. I shouldn't have given him so much insight. The person he knows me as is not the person I currently am. If I want to preserve how events unfolded, I can't change his opinion of me too much. It's amazing I've gotten this far without erasing my own past.

"I think you're pretty great, Iza." My gaze snaps to his. After a second, he blinks, tearing his eyes away. "Deep down. Like, really deep down. If I hired a well-driller or something, maybe they could find the great in you. Maybe."

"You're such an asshole."

"Yeah." He chuckles.

I stand, my chair scraping across the floor. "I should go. It's late. I didn't mean to bother you. You probably have things you'd rather be doing—partying or whatever."

Shrugging, he follows after me as I make my way to the door. "Nah. I was having kind of a weird night and didn't feel up to doing much anyway."

I stop at the door and face him. "I'm sorry to hear that."

He smiles but it doesn't reach his eyes. "Nothing like some soul-searching to ruin an evening."

I blink. "Wow, I didn't know you had one of those."

"Huh?"

"A soul."

"Unreal." His dimples split his cheeks. "Is that a sense of humor?"

I press my lips together and look away. It is a sense of humor. *His* sense of humor that rubbed off on me. "I'm sorry your evening is ruined," I say, to divert his attention.

Beckett looks me up and down. "It doesn't have to be."

My breath catches.

He steps closer. I stare at our toes, inches apart. Cinnamon and cedar settle around me as familiar as a favorite song. Letting out a shaky breath, I tilt my chin to look into his face. His eyes drop to my mouth, and he smiles.

I jolt back—directly into the door. "Ouch." I yelp.

Beckett jerks away. "I'm sorry."

"We can't—" I stutter over words, trying to come up with a sentence that won't give anything away.

He grimaces. "You're right. I'm sorry. I don't know what I was thinking."

My hand closes around the doorknob. "I'd better go."

"Yes—yeah." He runs a hand through his hair. "Thanks for the food."

"Of course." I hesitate. "Goodbye, Beckett."

He doesn't even meet my eye when he says. "Yep. See you later, Iza."

When I get myself safely back into the apartment, I rush to Lola's room, bury my face under her pillow, and silently scream.

I severely fucked up.

I told Beckett way too much. What if he acts all nice next time he sees past-me? What if he talks about birthday cards or soul searching, and she has no idea what he's referring to? It could derail everything.

But I haven't vanished off the face of the planet yet. I can still fix this. With past-me, Beckett, and Lola leaving for the parallel universe tomorrow night, I don't have much time. And I won't be able to follow them. I need help.

* * *

The next evening, I hide out in the janitor's closet in the hall until I hear Beckett go into my apartment. Then I hang out in the stairwell as darkness falls. I start to worry I somehow missed Lola, but then I hear footsteps echoing up the stairs.

"Lola," I whisper-yell as she rounds the corner.

She lets out a curse and almost drops the bottles of wine she carries. "Iza, what are you doing?"

"This is going to sound weird, but hear me out." I pause and spread my hands. "I'm from the future."

Lola squints. "I'm not sure humor is your strong suit."

"No, really." I let my hands fall. "When you go into the apartment, you're going to see me again. That's my past self. And I might have screwed up my entire time line last night, so I need your help to make sure she makes the same choices I did."

Sighing, Lola rubs her brow. "Oh my gosh, Iza. It's been a long day. Can we do this later?"

She tries to move past, but I block her path. "Listen to me." I lower my voice. "The me in there is going to introduce you to a guy called Beckett. I'm going to tell you he can grant wishes. Play along, and you'll see it's real." I shove a piece of paper into her hands. "If you still don't believe me after that, you can throw this list away."

Tucking the bottles of wine under her arm, Lola unfolds the paper, squinting in the dim light of the stairwell. "I'm supposed to suggest you wish for a fictional character?" Her eyes dart as she scans the list. "You wish for *Mr. Darcy*?" She looks over her shoulder. "Okay. Where's the candid camera?"

"Yes. I wish for Mr. Darcy, which will send us to a parallel universe." I let out a frustrated growl. "I shouldn't have told you about that, actually. You'll have to pretend to be surprised when it happens."

She refolds the paper. "If we go to a parallel universe, I'm not sure I'll have to pretend."

"Trust me on this. I'll hear Darcy insulting me behind my back. When I accuse Beckett, of giving me the wrong Darcy, you have to interrupt and tell me the insult was just like when Elizabeth heard Darcy insult her. Then I'll come up with a plan to reenact *Pride and Prejudice*. We'll go to Darcy's house, and you need to do a terrible job acting like your car broke down so he doesn't actually fall for me."

Lola holds up a hand. "Wait. This makes no sense. You want me to help you by sabotaging you?"

"Yes. I'm supposed to fall for Beckett, not Darcy."

"Couldn't I just tell you that?" Lola asks. "Hey, Iza, don't fall for Darcy. See? Easy."

"No," I practically yell the word, and it reverberates around the stairwell. I lower my voice. "Sorry. I need to figure it out by myself." I take a deep breath.

Lola cranes her neck, trying to see past me. "Come on, Iza. Give it up. Am I supposed to fall for some story you clearly pulled out of your ass?"

"Please listen." I tap a finger against the paper she still holds clenched in her fist. "Your sister is going to set you up on a blind date. You need to ask me to be there to make sure the guy isn't a creep because I have to almost get eaten by a lion. After that, I'll go out with Darcy, but you can't say anything about how it's a mistake."

"I'm starting to think coming home was a mistake," Lola grumbles.

"Lola, this is important. It all ends when I make my third wish. I tell Beckett I want to talk to my past self, but I also say I want to end up with him and you here, back home. Because of that last part, we should all end up back in this universe after the wish—I just go back farther. I'll be here waiting for your time line to catch up to mine."

She gives me a long look. "So I may or may not end up stuck in a parallel universe. Super cool, Iza. This really makes me want to help you out."

"I'm, like, pretty sure," I insist. "It was a vague wish, and I know Beckett would've used that to make sure you ended up back home too."

Closing her eyes, Lola lets out a long breath. "Fine. But I'm warning you, if I go into our apartment and find out you're messing with me, I'll make your little office war with Kalyan look like child's play."

"I'm not messing with you," I say quickly. "You'll have to wait and see. I don't know how else to prove it to you."

She shakes her head. "All right. I can't believe I'm saying this, but all right."

"Thank you." I throw my arms around her. "You're the best."

After Lola leaves, I walk to Beckett's door. I hear voices across the hall from my own apartment and consider listening in, but it would hurt too much. Instead, I try the knob on Beckett's door. It turns, and I slip inside.

I'm too tired for tears, so I make my way to Beckett's bedroom, tuck myself into his bed, and close my eyes with the scent of him surrounding me. If I pull the blankets tight, I can imagine his arms are around me instead of empty sheets.

My world shattered, but Beckett gave me the pieces. Now, it's up to me to put them back together. I see now how misguided I was. A relationship was never going to magically fix my life. It was never going to fill the emptiness that came from Grandma's death, Mom's distance, and my own discontentedness with myself.

It's time to fix the things that make me unhappy head-on. I'll take control of the plant mansion idea without Darcy interfering. I'll make an offer on the house before it's sold out from under me. I'll try to fix things with Mom. With this new chance at life, I'll become the person *I* want to be, not what others want me to be.

CHAPTER TWENTY-NINE

I continue living in Beckett's apartment. Once my past self and Lola left, they would have switched places with their parallel-universe selves, and I'd rather avoid bumping into them.

As the days go by and I don't suddenly vanish off the face of the earth, I can only assume Lola's doing her job to ensure my past self is on the right track. It finally makes sense why she was so chill with being in a parallel universe; she knew it would happen.

I remember Beckett's rose, the one he summoned through time. He fulfilled his own destiny. I wonder if all time travel is self-fulfilling, and I couldn't have changed the past even if I tried.

Once we reach the day when past-me makes her last wish, parallel-universe Iza will return to her own world. Not only that, but the time loop will close. My past self will stay in the past as nothing more than a memory while my time line continues.

The moment in time right after she makes her last wish is when the unknown starts. The wish will finally be fulfilled. Lola and Beckett will return to this universe. Beckett, however, will immediately be sucked into a new vessel.

All I know about how the wish works is that he'll go to someone difficult to help. The likelihood of me finding him is very, very small. He would have a better chance of seeking me out if he's lucky enough to be summoned by someone nearby. Not that he would seek me out. He wouldn't want to reunite with me just for us to have to break up again.

So I focus on fixing what I can. I make an offer on Grandma's house. I meet up with Kalyan and apologize for pushing away his friendship, and we make plans to talk about our future business ventures. Although I could keep my job since Darcy isn't here to steal my idea, I don't want to. Maybe everything else was a disaster in the parallel universe, but I liked how that one thing turned out. Replicating it will allow me to take full control of my future.

I save my dying plant from root rot, only barely managing not to cry as memories of Beckett meticulously sorting the bad roots from the good replay in my head. I set my jaw and push through. While it was so nice having someone on my team again, I know now I'll be okay on my own.

Then, when I can put it off no longer, I decide it's time to face her—the real thing that's been wrong with my life all along.

I paint my nails with the sparkly nail polish from the bottle Beckett came from, like I'm donning armor. If her respect for me is swayed by the color of my fingernails, then that's on her, not me.

I knock on Mom's door as I've done after every heartbreak. I vow this meeting will go better than the last. I won't ruin our relationship this time. I'll fix it. Somehow. I'm not sure how this will go. All I have is a vague plan to hash shit out. So here I am—hashing shit.

Mom answers the door, a paintbrush in her hand and a bandana holding back her hair.

"Hi, Mom."

She breaks into a smile. "I knew you'd come to your senses."

In this reality, the last time we spoke was at Olive Garden. "This isn't about my dating plan. Well, kind of. It was a stupid plan. You can't know anything about a person at first glance, maybe not even after years." Now I'm talking, I can't stop. "For instance, I have no idea what the hell's going on in *your* brain." *Way to dive right into hashing shit, Iza.*

Mom steps aside, giving me a look like she doesn't know if she should be pleased or offended. "Come in. I'm repainting your room. You can help."

She leads me through the house to my old bedroom. She already has everything taped off—plastic covering the floor, and newspapers spread out under a paint tray. Thrusting a paint roller into my hands, she says, "Preoccupation is the best way to thwart heartache."

A knot forms in my throat. She thinks she knows me. She thinks she knows what happened, that it's the same story all over, that I'm crawling back because, yet again, she was right. But this relationship didn't end because the man fell short of expectations. It ended because he exceeded them.

Focusing on the task at hand, I try not to think about the last time I was here with Beckett and that moment we had in the attic. "I never took you as the pink type," I say, squishing my paint roller into a tray filled with pungent pink goop.

"It's *mauve*." Mom enunciates the word deliberately from her perch on the stepladder, her mouth stretching almost grotesquely around the vowels.

"Mauve is pink." I turn to the wall and paint a pink stripe over the pale yellow of my childhood bedroom. The foam roller makes sticky squelching noises as I lean into it, and specks of paint mist my arms.

"I thought, with some black shelving and the silver and gold packaging of the products, it might come together nicely. Sort of a pink chic." She smiles to herself, clearly pleased with the term she's coined.

I shake my head. With the paint on the roller drying, I have to press down harder.

"It'll be a big hit at the next meeting I host," she says brusquely, as though simply admitting she thinks pink is pretty would be like pleading guilty to a crime.

I roll the dry sponge back into the tray. Again and again, I roll it—the action somehow hypnotic and soothing. The pink slop churns and slaps wetly against the sides until some of it sloshes out, glopping onto the newspapers. The puddle spreads, a strange, whimsical pool of pink blood consuming the black-and-white words beneath it.

The sponge is saturated to the point it's dripping, but I place it against the wall anyway. It smears downward, painting a thick, streaky mess over the dark shadow where my headboard used to sit against the wall.

As I work, the trance the pink paint put over me fades. My muscles ache, and with them, so does my heart. With this monotonous task in front of me, my mind is free to roam. I think of Beckett. It's a feeling of great loss, a feeling like I'll never be understood again. It reminds me of the weeks after Grandma died.

After the shock had worn off and the funeral was over, life kept on going on, like it hadn't realized my world ended. An empty pit opened in my heart that I was sure could never be filled again. I was able to move on, but now there's another pit in my heart, and it hurts all over again, even though I now know I can eventually get past it too.

"Eliza." Mom's sharp voice interrupts my thoughts. "Watch what you're doing." She points at the thick paint dripping down the wall. When I say nothing, she wrenches the roller from my hands and attacks the wall, zipping the roller this way and that, working the heavy paint until it thins out. The roller clatters and hums louder and louder. It sounds a bit like a swarm of angry bees.

My insides a twisting mess, I return to the paint tray and start picking up the newspapers I sloshed paint onto before pink can bleed through to the carpet.

I'm laying out fresh sheets when something catches my eye—a familiar address in the classified section under realty. It's been circled with a yellow highlighter and then crossed over with a black "X." My eyes skim the words. Cottage. Country living. Quaint. Five acres. Garden plot.

Judging by the circle and the "X," Mom's clearly seen it. And now she's using it as masking.

With shaking hands, I hold up the paper. "Were you not going to tell me about this?"

To her credit, she looks guilty. "Well, I was." The roller drifts down to her side, and she chews her lip. "But obviously I couldn't buy it, and I knew you couldn't either—and then Friday you started in on another one of your daydreams, and I suppose I didn't want to fuel it."

I jolt. "You didn't want to fuel my *dreams*?"

"Oh, Eliza." She tosses the roller onto a newspaper and brushes her already perfectly clean hands off. "Don't be dramatic. Of course, I care about your dreams. That's why I didn't tell you. I know how important your career is to you, and I didn't want to tell you anything to distract you or, heaven forbid, derail you."

Words stick in my throat.

"You can't turn into your grandmother." Mom's brows furrow as her eyes scan the room, like she's trapped, looking for a way out. "A single mom alone, scraping by on canned vegetables, altering clothes for pennies, leaving nothing behind after you're gone."

My stomach untwists. Words aren't stuck anymore. They're soaring. "She left you! She left me! How the hell is that unsuccessful in your eyes? You, of all people, should admire a single mother getting by without help."

Mom scoffs. "She could have done so much more. Instead of adopting twenty cats, maybe she could have used that goat barn. Goat's milk could've been quite lucrative. She could have—"

"She never did anything for the money, Mom," I snarl. "That wasn't the point. Her material value wasn't a reflection of her actual value. She didn't leave behind an empire, but kings couldn't live a life as full as hers."

I sink onto the arm of a plastic-covered divan. Grandma had had everything she wanted. I never once thought she'd sacrificed something to raise Mom, garden, and live in the country. She was content. "Why did you make me think wanting what she had was a projection of my grief? Are you happy? With your life, are you *happy*?"

She blinks, the splattered pink dots of paint on her false eyelashes giving her a cartoonish quality. "Of course."

"But not as happy as you could be, right?"

Resting the roller on the edge of the tray, she straightens stiffly. "What's this about?"

In an attempt to steady my hands, I twist my fingers together. "It's about your obsession with trying to turn me into you. Why discourage me from pursuing my own dreams? Why—" My voice cracks. "Why would you want that for me when it's your job to want me to be happy, and you're clearly not happy at all?"

Tendons constrict in Mom's throat as she swallows. For a long moment, I don't think she's going to say anything. Or if she does, I expect her to tell me to leave.

"I don't want you to get hurt." She's so quiet, her voice so strained, I can barely hear her. "It wasn't about your grandmother at all. I don't want you to become me."

To become her? But that's all she ever wanted.

Mom lets out a long breath and wipes her brow with the back of her hand. "When I decided to have you, I told myself what I was doing was strong—empowering. For most women, that's true. For me, it was a sign of my weakness."

I push myself off the couch. "What are you talking about?"

"I gave up, Iza." Her voice gains power. It's hard, blunt, like if it isn't that, it will dissolve to nothing at all. "I decided to have you by myself because I gave up on my dream of having you with someone else. I couldn't make myself vulnerable again—not like you can. I was weak, and you're strong. Your strength stems from your vulnerability, and my weakness stems from my inability to be vulnerable." Her voice had started as unwavering, but now it's broken, rough, and jagged—an ancient wall finally crumbling.

Quiet understanding settles around me. "Mom," I choke out, "that's so sad."

She lets out a noise halfway between a laugh and a sob. "It is. And while I cower from myself, my biggest fear is you'll become me."

"But all you've done is try to turn me into you." Frustration causes my voice to come out sharper than I intended, and she flinches.

Her hands shake. "I've tried to make you strong so you wouldn't get hurt like me. I didn't want you to be like I am on the inside. I never want you to feel what I felt, what I feel every day."

My shoulders soften, and when I next speak, I'm gentle. "If you know these things about yourself, why don't you do something?" I walk closer to her. "Why not work on them? Why not try for some happiness?"

"That's what I want you to understand." She meets me in the middle and grips my arms. "Striving for happiness only buries you deeper into a pit of darkness until you're so far in that not only can you not get out, but you've lost the will to try."

I realize Mom has her own empty pits in her heart. Instead of moving past them, she has stared into them so hard, she's fallen in.

I search her wide eyes, the glassy surfaces turning her irises vivid green. "What happened to you, Mom?" I ask quietly.

Letting out a long, shuddering breath, she releases me and turns away. "I once shared your dream," she finally says. "I wanted it all—the adoring husband, the kids, the house. I finally met someone. And he was wonderful." Even from the side, I can see her eyes grow haunted. "Until he wasn't," she finishes. Now, her eyes are distant, and I wonder if she knows I'm even here. "I simultaneously wanted never to see him again and to fling myself into his arms and beg for him to take me back, because then maybe everything would be okay again. Your grandmother kept me from that regret. While logically I knew she was right, I resented her for denying me the one ridiculously simple act that would stop the pain in my heart.

"Everyone said time would heal me. Things did get better, but I wasn't healed. I was numb. I knew I couldn't subject myself to something with the capability to hurt me like that again. I needed guaranteed love. So, I had you." At last she faces me, and my stomach constricts because there's a tear running over her nose. Touching my cheek, she smiles. "And I wasn't so numb anymore.

I grew less afraid for myself and more afraid for you. Then, when I found out that not only was your father run over by an Amish man, but he himself was also an *ex*-Amish man . . ." Her expression spells doom.

"What the hell, Mom?" I pull my face away from her hand.

Her voice wavers. "The domestic lifestyle runs through your veins, Eliza, and I had to protect you from that!"

"Oh my god, Mom." So that's what her investigation into my dad's past had been. She hadn't been afraid I carried some gene that would compel me to step in front of buggies. She was afraid I carried genes that would make me want a family. I begin to laugh. "Why couldn't you tell me the reason you didn't want me to date was because you were afraid I'd get hurt, not because you thought I'd destroy my career?"

She won't meet my eyes. "How irrational would that be? It would be like telling you not to drive because some people get hurt in car accidents."

The realization that she guarded herself even from me causes my eyes to become wet. "You had me chasing Mr. Darcy because your standards were so unachievably high."

Mom makes a face. "Mr. Darcy?"

"Well, someone a lot like him. He was the only man I'd ever heard you say a good word about, so I thought you might approve of someone like him."

"I loathe Mr. Darcy," she says with venom. "I *used* to like him before my frontal lobe developed, and I realized what a self-righteous prick he is."

I almost laugh. It's so ridiculous. This whole time, we've been totally out of touch with each other. I take her hand and squeeze it. "Love isn't rational. I'm not going to end up like you. I don't want *you* to be like you. How you're living, it's not really living."

Shaking her head, she tries to pull her hand away, but I hold on.

"Let me in." My throat clenches, and I push past the pain. "I'm your guaranteed love, remember? Let me in, and trust I'm wise enough to pursue my dreams without losing myself."

Nodding, she blinks, more tears rolling down her cheeks. Hesitantly, I step forward and pull her into my arms. For once, her amber perfume is warm, comforting.

She lets out a long, shuddering sigh and squeezes me tightly. "You must allow me to tell you," she whispers, "how ardently I admire and love you."

A painful lump lodges in my throat, but it's a good kind of pain. I think, maybe, that night we watched *Pride and Prejudice* meant a lot to her too. "I love you too, Mom," I whisper into her hair. I hug her tighter. "Even if you do run a pyramid scheme."

She dissolves into jittery giggles. *Mom* is giggling. And so am I.

CHAPTER THIRTY

I get a phone call as I'm pulling into the parking lot at home after visiting Mom. A jolt goes through me when I see Lola's name on my screen, then another jolt when I see the date. Time got away from me. Today marks the day when I made my last wish. If my theory was correct, and Beckett was able to manipulate my wish enough that he and Lola got sent back to this universe, *my* Lola could be on the other end of the line right now.

"Hello?" I answer breathlessly.

"Iza?" Lola asks, her voice uncharacteristically nervous. "Is that you? Are you home?"

"I'm outside." I half-fall out of my car and race for the door.

Lola bursts from the building before I reach it.

"Lola?" I clap my hands over my mouth. "Is that you? The real you?"

She waves a wrinkled sheet of notebook paper in the air. "It's me."

I charge across the lawn, and she meets me halfway like we're a couple in a cheesy movie reuniting on a sunset-lit beach. We smash together in a bone-crushing hug and nearly fall to the grass.

"This feels really dramatic considering I just saw you this morning," she whispers.

"It's felt like years for me," I say, squeezing her tighter. "You did it, Lola."

"You wrote down the time when you made your last wish on my list," words tumble from her mouth in an excited jumble, "but then ten minutes passed, and I didn't feel different, so I started to get worried I was stuck in the Darcy universe. But I called you, and here you are."

I pull back. "I can't believe everything happened just like it did the first time, right down to the exact minute I made my last wish."

"Maybe there was no way it couldn't work out." Lola frowns. "Maybe it's impossible to change the past."

"That's what I think too!"

This mind-fuck sends us into a long debate over time lines and free will and predestination and if there was ever a different version of my past, or if my future self was always in the background, manipulating everything from the sidelines.

I think about my wish again: *I wish I could go back and talk some sense into myself so I could be home with you and Lola right now.* In a way, it came true. I'm in my home universe with Beckett and Lola right now instead of back in the parallel one with my life crumbling around my ears. The only problem is, Beckett isn't *here* here. He's stuck in a new vessel who-knows-where, awaiting his next charge to summon him out.

Lola and I both go silent. I look up at the apartment building as though I can see through the walls into Beckett's room where, just minutes ago in a parallel universe, he talked me into making a wish to separate us forever.

"Come on." Lola links her arm through mine. "I don't know about you, but after the time-travel conversation, I need some ice cream to soothe my melted brain."

I tear my eyes from the building. I have to let go.

* * *

That evening, I'm not ready to go back home yet. The silence across the hall will be too much to bear. I drive by myself for a while, not sure where I'm going until I end up at Art Hill. I park and walk out onto the grass. The St. Louis Art Museum stands at the top of the hill, its white pillars lit golden in fading sunlight. Manicured lawn stretches down the huge slope to the lake at the base where people float around in paddle boats. It's a beautiful day, and the hill is occupied with people stretched out on picnic blankets, exercising, or flying kites. Their conversations are snatched away in the light breeze, making me feel strangely set apart from the scene. Alone, but not lonely.

I settle into the soft grass, pulling my knees to my chest. Contentment is something I haven't felt in so long, I almost don't recognize it when it blooms behind my ribs. Closing my eyes, I breathe in the clean air and the scent of freshly cut grass. I'm going to be okay. I'll let myself heal, and one day, I'll try again.

The sound of footsteps brushes my consciousness. I think nothing of it until it grows closer. Grass rustles, and I'm aware of someone settling next to me on my left. I open my eyes and look over.

My heart lodges in my throat. Beckett is here. *My* Beckett, sitting next to me, his eyes blazing in the sunset. He's exactly as I left him after I made my last wish, his hair a mess, His white shirt wrinkled, his suit jacket missing.

The corner of his mouth tugs upward into a smile. "'Sup, girl?" he says softly.

With a broken noise catching in my throat, I throw myself into his arms. He nearly topples over but braces a hand behind him at the last moment. His laughter reverberates softly against my cheek, and I feel it against my skin more than I hear it, the silent joy meant just for me. He's warm, solid, and most importantly, he's real.

Burying my face into his chest, I burst into tears. Beckett whispers my name over and over, cradling my head, pressing his lips into my hair. I grab his wrists and lift my mouth to his. His breath is ragged against my cheek, his lips achingly tender in the way they tremble against mine. After a long, lingering moment, Beckett pulls away, cupping my face in his hands, brushing away my stray tears with his thumbs.

"Sunset tears?" he asks, even though there is still no way he can know what that means.

I bite my lip and nod, scanning his face. "But how are you here?"

He shakes his head. "I should be asking you that. This shouldn't be possible. I was trying to get you to wish that you could go back and undo everything. I asked what you'd do if you had a choice, and I gave you that choice. How am I here with all my memories?"

"I could never undo us," I say. "Even if I wanted to, I don't think I could have."

"What?"

"I turned out to be my own yellow rose. Going back only sealed our fate." I smile. "I'll tell you everything later, let's just say that last wish wasn't quite the fresh start you were hoping it would be. Sorry."

Finally, his shoulders ease, and he winks. "You should be sorry. I'm deeply enraged to be sitting here kissing you in front of a fucking sunset." And he does. He kisses me in front of the fucking sunset, his lips hot and urgent.

"Making out in public?" I murmur against his mouth. "Scandalous. You're a reformed man now. What about your scruples?"

"Fuck my scruples."

Giddy joy crackles within me as we fall back against the hill, our feet twining together, hands winding into fabric, lips caressing lips.

At last, I pull away. "But the curse? Did you get summoned again?"

He sits up, face clouding over. "No. Nothing happened. You made your wish and vanished from the room, and I was left standing there. I walked into my living room where all my furniture was pushed aside from one of the parties I threw before we left for the parallel universe, so I knew I was back in our world. I didn't know what to do until Lola came home. I asked her where you were, so she called your mom who has apparently been tracking your phone, and now I'm here."

I think hard. A moment ago, Beckett said, *I'm deeply enraged.* He clearly isn't enraged, but he shouldn't be able to lie even if he's being sarcastic. It shouldn't be possible, and yet Beckett lied to me.

"Beckett." I swallow. "I think the curse is broken."

His eyes widen, but his brows draw together as though trying to cage in his hope. "It's not possible. The star said someone had to take my place. She said only a true act of selflessness would save me."

"Try to use magic."

He snaps his fingers. Nothing happens. He does it again. Still nothing. "I wish for a rose." Nothing. "I wish for a drink."

Nothing. "I wish for a car." Nothing. "You try," he says, voice wavering. "Maybe I can only use my magic for others now or something."

"I wish for a rose," I say, even though it feels so wrong to say those words, *I wish.* Still, nothing happens. I grin. "I wish you'd stop being in denial."

Maybe there is some magic behind my words because a hesitant smile flits across his face.

"I wish you'd let yourself be happy."

Now the smile is more than a phantom.

"I wish for you."

Beckett leans over me, cupping the back of my neck. He kisses me like he hasn't yet, long and slow, like we have all the time in the world.

"How is this possible," he whispers, pulling away.

I think of all we've been through and how much we grew to get to this point. We both learned how to be kind. We learned how to love and be loved. I stopped needing someone else to approve of my life and started valuing it myself. Beckett did the opposite and let go of the importance he placed on his life and started valuing others' instead.

It hits me. "Beckett. The true act of selflessness. What you did, your motivations were pure. You didn't care about saving yourself. You knew you could never ask me to give up everything for you. You let me go purely and completely out of selflessness. *You* broke the curse."

Beckett licks his lips. "What does that mean?"

"It means your future is real."

Beckett covers his face in his hands as the enormity of what this means hits him. I scramble to kneel next to him and hold him as his shoulders silently shake with raw, painful relief. Tears flow down my cheeks as he clenches his fists into my shirt as though he fears, if he lets go, it will all slip away.

We cling to each other until our emotions are spent, and then we stretch out in the grass, our fingers woven loosely together as we watch the evening fading away.

"What does this mean?" Beckett asks again, softly, lifting our entwined hands.

Actual possibility weighs down the air between us. Before, we could live in the moment. Now, we could have unlimited moments. Or we could have none. Or we could have a few.

Against my will, old fears threaten to surface. Can Beckett actually fit into my life? Beckett has displayed massive amounts of effort, but for how long? Will he go back to his old, selfish ways? Can I truly, honestly, trust him forever?

Before the thoughts can overwhelm me, I remember the birthday card from Grandma: *"You see the world the way it is, not the way people tell you it is. Don't ever let outside forces sway what you know to be true."*

I won't fail myself, Grandma, or Beckett again. I won't doubt what I've seen with my own eyes. I've seen over and over how Beckett fits into my life, and it's not always perfect. It's messy because he's real, and real is what I want.

With new resolve, I stomp the sprouts of doubt with a pair of purple rain boots conjured up from a memory of a girl who saw the world as it was. The girl Grandma wrote about. The girl who was so full of optimism, nothing could stand in the way of her happiness. I'm done doubting.

Lightly, I clear my throat. Beckett gazes into my eyes, a muscle in his jaw jumping as he waits to hear what I'll say.

"It means *our* future is real."

CHAPTER THIRTY-ONE

After I tell Beckett everything I did after going back in time, we decide to spend a night away together before fully returning to reality. There's tension between us as we check into a hotel for the night. Beckett hasn't said much, but he keeps finding excuses to touch me, his hand on my back as we check in, lacing his fingers with mine as we walk to the elevator, brushing a kiss across my temple as we wait for the door.

The elevator lets out a muted ding, and the doors slide open. Nodding to the handful of people inside, Beckett presses the button to our floor as we squeeze ourselves into a corner. As we go up, he traces his thumb in slow circles along the inside of my wrist. Sparks crackle in my stomach, and I smile, leaning into him, his body solid and warm against mine.

"So wait," he whispers. "You're telling me that at one point I was in the same world with two of you at once? The past version of you and the future version? And I *survived* that?"

I laugh. "You only met the future me that one time in your apartment. I really thought I messed everything up by coming to see you."

"No." He kisses my temple again. "You visiting me that night made me realize there was more to you than I first thought. I don't think everything would have happened like it did if you hadn't come over."

I smile.

"It is a shame, though," he says.

"What?"

"The missed opportunities." Beckett bites back a smile. "Is it still considered a threesome if—"

"Don't you dare finish that sentence."

"I'm kidding," he says, low against my ear. "You're the only Iza for me."

The elevator dings again, and we walk down the hall to our room.

Our room.

The sparks morph into twingeing nerves.

He must notice a change in my expression because he turns me to face him. "Just because I'm free, I don't expect us to pick up where we left off," he says gently. "We can take it as slow as you want." With a knuckle under my chin, he angles my head until my eyes meet his. "Tell me what you want."

My breaths become shallow. "What do *you* want?"

As he steps closer, he curves his fingers around the nape of my neck, pushing aside my hair. The stubble of his jaw is rough against my cheek as he whispers in my ear. "Anything you give me. If that's you calling me some random-ass name starting with 'B' as you tell me to go fuck myself, I'll take it. If it's you moaning my actual name while you beg me to fuck *you*, I'll take it. If it's one last kiss goodbye before you tell me to fuck off forever, I'll take it."

My heart pounds in my ears, and I haven't taken a breath in so long, I'm dizzy. "Option D," I say. "We'll wing it as we go. No plans."

Pulling back, he laughs, long and hard, in that way he has that makes me feel like the funniest girl alive. "I think I can manage option D." His shoulders are still shaking with mirth as he unlocks the door with a swipe of our keycard.

I stand in the entryway, suddenly awkward and unsure what to do next.

He follows me inside. "That's how I knew you didn't hate me as much as you let on, you know."

"Huh?"

"You may have intentionally messed up my name over and over again, but you never called me Beck. I told you I didn't like it, so you didn't. Not once."

"Oh," I say, unable to say anything else.

He smiles wryly. "It's the only thing that kept me from losing my shit." Setting the room key aside, he gestures to the two queen-size beds. "Which do you want?"

I hesitate only a moment. "Whichever one you're in." I'm surprised by how easy the words slip out. "But not *now*. I'm gross because I was painting earlier with Mom, so I have pink in my hair, and I was outside, so I'm sweaty, and—"

"So take a shower," Beckett says, like it's obvious. "I'm not going anywhere."

"Yes, you are," I blurt out. Him leaving my sight again so soon—even for a few minutes in an adjacent room—feels wrong after everything we had to go through to be together. "If I'm taking a shower, you're coming with me." I hold out my hand.

Beckett arches an eyebrow, and his lips twitch like he doesn't believe me, but he takes my hand and follows me.

The hotel bathroom is cramped, with only a few feet of space between the sink and the tiny shower. We do a bit of an awkward dance as we shuffle around, trying to figure out who should stand where. My elbow jabs his ribs, and he winces.

"Sorry." I cringe, shrinking back toward the door. "Maybe this was a bad idea."

Grabbing me by the waist, he hoists me onto the countertop. He stands between my legs, his body heating my thighs. "Would you relax?"

My gaze slides from his. "I'm trying."

"Iza"—he takes my hand and starts massaging my fingers—"stop trying."

After a moment, I nod. As his thumbs knead my palm, the tension drains from my body.

He kisses my fingertips. "Good?"

"Very," I breathe as he releases my fingers.

Slowly, he slides his hand to the back of my knee and down my calf, stepping back as he extends my foot to untie my shoe. "Iza," he says softly, "do you think we'll make it? I know I'm not what you thought you wanted. This isn't going to be easy. I'm not out of a storybook. I don't fit into some perfect glass shoe. It's not like I can force myself into one, and we'll live happily ever after. Maybe I can't be your Cinderella."

I start to giggle. It's an exhausted giggle, delirious from both emotional and physical fatigue.

"What?" He slips the shoe off, a smile quirking his down-turned face.

Embarrassingly, I snort. "Is it true what they say about big feet?"

"Oh my god, Iza." Beckett groans as he tosses the second shoe to the side and comes to stand between my knees again.

My laughter redoubles, and he smiles, his eyes flitting over my face as he watches me dissolve into hysteria.

"We can't ignore our problems forever," he says softly.

Sobering up, I loosen my hold on him and lean back, resting my palms on the cool marble. "Relationships aren't made of two people who never have problems. It's not about finding someone who fits into a perfect glass slipper. It's about two flawed people choosing and promising to be the best versions of themselves they can be for each other."

Beckett's hands grip my thighs as he pulls me closer again. "Who are you, and what have you done with Iza?" There's a new light in his eyes. Reaching around his back, where my feet are linked together, he pulls off my socks.

"It's only complicated if we make it complicated." I unbutton his shirt.

"So forgive and forget?" With gentle fingers, he lifts my own shirt over my head.

"Not forget. Learn." I tug his shirt off his shoulders until it slides down his arms and hits the floor.

"I like that." His eyes are hazy as they trail down my body, and I wonder if he even knows what he's saying 'I like that' about anymore.

The air in the hotel is chilly, and I shiver a little. He notices and turns, stretching to reach into the shower and flip the water on. I let my eyes travel up his torso, admiring the planes of skin and muscle.

His words from a few minutes before echo in my head. *"I can't be your Cinderella."* My mind travels back to a memory of when I was six in Grandma's living room.

"Men don't like being the princess."

"I'll find a good one who won't care."

"Wait," I say, my voice laced with excitement, "you'd be my princess?"

Beckett gives me a weird look, touching his fingers to his chest. His voice is flat as he asks, "OMG. Are you asking?"

He doesn't care. Mom was wrong. He's not lesser in any way. *Take that.* I slide off the counter. "Never mind."

Shaking his head, he cups my jaw, leaning in to kiss me long and deep. With his other hand, he reaches around and unclasps my bra.

I feign a gasp and pull back. "Oh my gosh. You did it."

He chuckles. "I was off my game before. Had other things on my mind, like how to get you to wish yourself away from me, et cetera."

"And now?"

"Now," he says, lips inches from mine, "you're not leaving this room for a very long time."

I wrinkle my nose. "The bathroom?"

He grabs my butt and presses me firmly against him. "The hotel room, smartass."

An ache begins low in my belly. Steam coils out of the shower, turning the room hot. Or maybe the steam has nothing to do with the temperature at all. The room clouds up, enveloping me in sticky heat and the scent of him: soft, woody cinnamon.

Reaching between us, Beckett unbuttons my pants, his fingers warm and sure. I wriggle out of them, a little embarrassed because there really is no seductive way to get out of skinny jeans.

His eyes smolder like coals as he watches me, like my wiggling and hopping is as sensual as a pole dance. Under his gaze, my body pinches and tingles.

As soon as I kick the last pant leg over my foot, he grabs my hips, spinning me to push me against the wall. *Kiss* seems too tame of a word for what he does to me. There's a feverish desperation between us, two people kept apart time and time again, two people who have literally traveled across universes to be reunited.

Beckett finds my wrists and pins them over my head as he grinds against me. Desire knots in my stomach, and my body responds in kind, moving against his. Against my sensitive skin, every seam of clothing left between us feels like a knife's edge.

When he relinquishes my wrists, I grab him by the belt loops and pull him against me even tighter. His hands ignite fire over my skin as they explore. He brushes my nipple with his thumb, trails knuckles down my navel, slips a warm hand between my legs.

His tongue grazes my bottom lip as his fingers explore the hem of my panties. I let out a little whimper when he touches me in a way that sends a tremor up my whole body. Smiling against my mouth, he continues to stroke me, teasing me until my back arches, and I'm gasping. Before he can push me completely over the edge, I straighten, biting his lip and fumbling for the button for his pants. As he steps out of them, he slides my panties over my hips until the silky material falls to my ankles.

He opens the shower door and pushes me inside with a strange kind of gentle forcefulness, smacking my butt as I slide past him. I yelp, and he laughs, closing the door as he follows me in.

With his dark hair dripping into his eyes and water rolling off his shoulders, all I can do is stare. Sorting through the tiny hotel soaps, he finds the shampoo and squirts an obscene amount into his palm.

"Close your eyes," he says.

"What?" Why does he care about soap right now when all I want is his skin against mine?

Beckett gives me a look. "You asked me to take a shower with you. What did you think we'd be doing?"

"Well . . ." I direct my gaze downward, then slide it back up. I smirk ever so slowly. "I think we had the same thing in mind."

"Shower sex ends in ER visits nine out of ten times. Now close your eyes because I want you in bed as quickly as I can get you there."

I do as he says right before he runs his soapy hands through my hair.

In contrast with the kiss moments before, he takes his time now, working the suds through my hair. He's probably tangled it beyond belief, but that's okay; his hands feel incredible.

His hands pause in my hair, and a moment later, the soft touch of his lips presses against my mouth. Under the stream of water, squeezing my eyes hard to keep the soap out, I kiss him back slowly, running my hands over his slick chest.

We savor every second. Every one of my senses is heightened, his touch against my skin, the soothing stream of the showerhead, the slightly soapy taste of his lips.

Pulling away, I wipe water from my eyes as he pushes hair away from my face. Grabbing the soap, I give him the same treatment. His hair between my fingers is silky, and he leans into my touch with a little groan that sends a twinge deep into my stomach.

He's heartachingly chaste and sweet when he finds a washcloth and begins scrubbing flecks of pink paint from my arms. We're mostly quiet, aside from a shared smile or a teasing look when one of us catches the other staring.

The mood begins to shift again. Hands linger and breaths grow uneven. Soapy rivulets trail down my body, and I notice his gaze darkening as it traces their paths. "You feel un-gross yet?" he chokes out.

Under his eyes, I feel like a goddess, so I nod.

He tosses the washcloth aside, a gleam in his eye. "Rinse." There's an edge to his voice, a promise of what's to come, and my heart skips a beat. The rest of my body responds with a surge of tingling anticipation.

I do as he says. Tightening the distance between us, Beckett trails a knuckle up my sternum, between my breasts, past my collarbone. His fingers curve around my neck, but I feel oddly safe. Protected. His pupils are blown so wide, his eyes look black. Holding my eyes, he runs a thumb roughly across my throat. "I know you thought I was messing with you every time I complimented you before, but *damn, girl*."

"That's the most eloquent compliment I've ever received." I run my palms down his chest—slick with water and soap. His body feels good beneath my fingers, solid, hot, velvety. Biting my lip, I smile teasingly at him, rolling his nipple piercing under my thumb. He makes a low noise in his throat and grips my butt with his free hand.

Beckett's next kiss is fueled with urgency. He slides his fingers behind my neck and his thumbs under my jaw, tilting my face to claim my mouth with his. When that isn't enough, he twines his fingers into my hair for better leverage. When that, too, isn't enough, he tears himself away and says, "Shower's over," his voice low and husky.

Using an elbow, he shuts off the water before hooking his hands behind my thighs and hoisting me off my feet. Our bodies fit together perfectly. His heart drums against mine, and it's strange to think each loud beat is because of me. I can't believe we're here, at last, and he still wants me after everything.

I cling to his shoulders, kissing his neck as he carries me out of the bathroom. The cool air hits my wet skin, and I tighten my grip, drawing warmth from his body.

My world swoops sideways as he tosses me onto the bed before crawling up after me, his body dripping water over mine.

His breathing is heavy when he bends down and kisses my shoulder. As I run my fingers through his wet hair, he trails kisses up my neck before playfully nipping my jaw. He nudges my legs apart, settling between them. Instinctively, I arch against him, and I feel the breathy warmth of his smile against my neck.

"This is real, isn't it?" His voice rasps in my ear.

Tingles run down my spine. "It's real. It means something."

"No." He traces my lips with a knuckle. "It means everything."

I bite at his finger, and he smirks. He brushes the back of his other hand down my side so lightly, I shiver.

I take a deep breath. "Wait." I touch his face. "There's one more thing."

He lets out a fake frustrated growl and lets his head fall to my chest.

"I think I love you too," I say casually, twirling my finger in his hair.

He freezes. A second later, his muffled voice issues from my chest. "You just put so much pressure on the next twenty minutes." But when he lifts his head, he's smiling, eyes crinkling, cheeks dimpling—the works.

EPILOGUE

Chester was all too eager to comply when Kalyan and I told him we'd stay on until the end of the Julia project, but only if he threw a 1950s-style party in the mansion upon completion. Considering it was wildly extravagant and company-funded, Julia was all for it too.

We went over our deadline for the project. Way over it. Luckily, the world decided not to end in that time, so Julia found it in her heart to forgive us.

The ballroom turned out to look spectacular. Morning glory vines climb up the walls in full bloom, like living wallpaper. The marble floor is a deep earthy brown shot through with veins of moss green. The double staircases at the far end of the room curve around two identical pink magnolia trees. A waterfall tumbles down the middle. Overhead, lights encapsulated in crystals are splashed across the ceiling, twinkling like the Milky Way.

The room is packed with the firm's employees and their families, as well as Julia's own guests. A live band plays on stage between the staircases, singing oldies.

Someone comes up behind me and wraps an arm around my waist. My stomach flips like it does every time he touches me. Smiling, I turn in Beckett's embrace and look up into his face.

"You know I don't really remember the fifties, so I feel like I'm dressing up as my father," he says, smirking. He's wearing a boxy suit and a Cordova hat.

I raise an eyebrow. "So that means I remind you of your mother?" I'm wearing a black cocktail dress with a netted bodice and a flared skirt.

He places a warm finger against my lips and hushes me. "No, no. Stop talking. You're ruining it." His eyes travel down my body in a way that assures me I don't remind him of his mother. He pulls me close, and we sway to the music.

Chester shuffles by, stopping when his eye catches on me. "Great work," he says. "I do wish you'd reconsider . . ."

But I'm already shaking my head—Kalyan's counting on me, and Beckett and I are already planning on moving into the house next weekend. Everything's coming together. The perfect balance.

Beckett's been there for weeks, working on the greenhouse I designed. It sits beside the house, a cozy glass enclosure ready to foster life. At first, Beckett thought I was joking when I suggested he get back into his family's business. The more we talked about it, looked into the market, and ran the numbers, the less outlandish it sounded.

Across the room, Mom catches my eye and waves cheerily. Even without a nearly empty glass of champagne in her hand, her mood has been significantly improved. Although she was skeptical about Beckett, he soon won her over by pretending her snide remarks go over his head, simultaneously winning *me* over by replying to those snide remarks with remarks of his own that are so sarcastic, she thinks he's sincere.

I grin up at Beckett, and he brushes a kiss across my temple. Closing my eyes, I imagine the new life before us.

I see the clearing in the woods. The stone cottage is power washed, the shutters freshly painted turquoise. The garden is freshly weeded, and the smell of wet dirt and freshly mowed grass fills the air.

I'll round the house and step inside the greenhouse, breathing in the stuffy air. Sunlight shines through the hazy glass, lighting everything in refracted light.

Beckett looks up from pruning a rosebush, his skin gleaming and slick with sweat, his dimples creasing. Pulling off his gloves, he'll walk forward, cupping my face with rough, earthy hands to kiss me, even though I'm still in my work clothes.

"Beckett," I say softly, bringing myself back to the present.

"Hmm?" he asks, his voice vibrating against my ear.

We pause in the middle of the ballroom, the music and other couples swirling around us like river water around a boulder. I pull away from his chest and look up. The twinkling lights overhead glitter off his bright, honey eyes. "You're going to marry me one day, aren't you?"

His eyebrows shoot up. "Wait. No. You're not supposed to do that."

"What? Do you have some hang-up about gender roles?"

"No. I just—no!"

"No?" I pretend to pout, crossing my arms and turning away.

"No, not *no*." He grabs my elbow and turns me back around. "You're not supposed to spring it on me out of the blue like that." He gives me a stern look. "And where are my diamonds, anyway? Aren't you supposed to have a ring before you go asking me to marry you? Frankly, I'm insulted."

"I'm not proposing," I say, giving in and abandoning my pout. "I just mean *someday*. Do you think you would?"

Thoughtfully, he pulls me back into his arms. Silent, we sway to the music again. I rest my head on his chest, closing my eyes.

His feet slow, then stop. Against my ear, his voice rumbles in his chest. "What if I asked you right now?"

I stumble, bracing my palms on his chest as I gaze up at him. "You mean it?"

"Sure." There's a glint in his eyes.

"*Sure?* I'm really feeling the commitment, Beckett."

He slides his hand over mine, lacing our fingers together awkwardly. "What are you—?" When he withdraws his hand, there's a ring on my finger.

It's yellow gold with intricate rose vines scrolled into the band. Small diamonds nestled within the twisting patterns twinkle up at me. In the center rests a sparkling oval diamond. My heart pounds so hard in my chest, it almost hurts.

I snap my head up, but Beckett's looking casually around the ballroom like he's oblivious to what happened.

It takes me a minute to find my voice. "Yes."

He frowns and leans in, pulling on his ear. "Sorry, what was that? The music's a bit loud."

"I said yes," I say louder.

He wrinkles his nose. "What? Speak up, woman."

"I *said*"—his eyes are crinkling up, his dimples twitching to life—"you're an asshole."

He snorts with laughter, pulling me roughly against him. "I take that as a yes." I make sure to step on his toe, and then his mouth is on mine.

I push away. "What kind of proposal was that?"

His eyes are dark as he kisses me again, his tongue skimming over mine. "At least *I* was prepared," he mumbles against my mouth. Pulling me into him, he deepens the kiss. It tastes like forever. Trusting him to care for me has been the best decision of my life.

I imagine the greenhouse again, years from now, blooming with flowers and full of life. There will be a soft evening rain, and water will flow off the glass building in rippling sheets. We'll be sipping wine, watching the world go by.

Maybe a small pair of muddy, purple rain boots will lie discarded under our chairs, and a little girl with golden hair and eyes will be asleep on Beckett's shoulder. I imagine the life—the possibilities. Maybe, with that little girl, Mom will find a second chance to be vulnerable. Beckett will have meaning and plenty to leave behind to prove he existed.

I'll have it all. The loving family I always wanted, the partner by my side, the support of Mom. I'll have my career, home, and a thousand adventures.

Beckett pulls away, looking around to search the room. "Didn't you say something about a fairy garden closet?" He grins, his eyes glinting. "I'll find some glitter, and we can reenact the stripper fairy thing. Again."

I reach out to swat him, but he grabs my hand, pulling me across the ballroom. I let him because overthinking it or being scared of what might happen if we're caught will ruin it. As soon as we're out of the ballroom, our hands and lips are all over each other. I shove him against the wall, laughing, kissing him, tossing his hat to the side.

Letting out a growl, he grabs my waist and pushes me backward down the hall. Nearly tripping over my feet, I unbutton his shirt as we go, stealing kisses between each one. We don't make it long before we pinball against the other wall, laughing, kissing, shedding clothes.

Someone clears their throat as obnoxiously as they possibly can.

I peel away from Beckett's heaving chest to find Kalyan wedged in a doorway behind us, dunking a giant shrimp into cocktail sauce. Lola stands beside him. "Keeping it classy, I see," he says.

Beckett lets out a breathless laugh, and I giggle.

"None of these shenanigans during work hours, Iza," Kalyan says mildly as he bites into the shrimp. But then he rolls his eyes, shaking his head. "You crazy kids."

"Talk to you Monday," I say, taking Beckett's hand and tugging him after me.

I live in the present now, not the past or the hypothetical future. I value living every moment as the passionate, messy, complicated human I am. If that involves sex with Beckett in the closet of a multimillion dollar underground mansion belonging to my ex-boss's client, so be it.

ACKNOWLEDGMENTS

First, I would like to thank my incredible agent, Lucienne Diver. I feel so lucky to have found someone else who thinks Mr. Darcy is a little bit of a jerk. On a serious note, thank you for picking my wacky story out of your slush pile and finding it a home. Your expertise and endless patience when answering my frantic, debut-author questions were invaluable. You are truly a role model in this industry, and I'm grateful to have you championing my stories.

Second, I would like to thank my editor, Holly Ingraham, for seeing something special in my story and helping me mold it into what it is today. Your enthusiasm, kindness, and passion made editing this book a delight.

A thank-you to everyone else on the Alcove team: Melissa Rechter, Jess Verdi, Hannah Pierdolla, Thai Fantauzzi, Madeine Rathle, Dulce Botello, Doug White, Matthew Martz, and all the others behind the scenes. Special thanks to Ana Hard for the beautiful cover.

A huge thank-you to the beta readers who suffered through my early drafts, especially Gabriella Gamez, Phil Gross, Adrianna Schuh, and Rosslyn Shields.

A thanks to Anthony LeFauci because explaining time travel to me earns you a place in my acknowledgments, even if you are my arch-nemesis.

To Beka Westrup, for being not only a great critique partner but also an incredible friend. I am inspired by your kindness, talent, and the class you display when dealing with internet trolls. Thank you for always being willing to listen to my latest story ideas, plot problems, or real-life conundrums.

Thanks to Kirsten Bohling for being an incredible critique partner and introducing me to the em dash. Swapping manuscripts with you was a privilege. The comments you left in my document always brightened my day.

My thanks, too, for the rest of #teamsinkpickle, who helped me brainstorm and provided encouragement along the way: Dina S., for your fiercely loyal friendship and your eagerness to become enraged on my behalf whenever I vent about the slightest of inconveniences; producer Sean, for your confused but earnest support; Daniel Quigley, for your uplifting golden retriever energy and typo-riddled pep talks; Rance, for being Rance and for helping me write a killer query letter.

Thank you to my parents, who gave me the unearned confidence I needed to pursue traditional publishing. I hope neither of you read this book.

A thank-you to my two cats, who did nothing but who are very cute.

Of course, thank you to my amazing husband, Shawn. Some people say book boyfriends set unrealistic standards for real-life men. You set unrealistic standards for book boyfriends. You are my friend-to-lover, the sunshine to my grump, and you have the biggest heart of anyone I've ever met (but don't worry; I won't tell anyone and ruin your tough-guy reputation). You graciously encourage me to disappear into my office for hours on end, interrupting only to remind me to eat occasionally. You never fail to call out my sudden urges to remodel our entire home as procrastination ploys. You're always excited to talk through plot points and ask the important "But why don't they just" questions. I never would be able to keep writing without your optimism and support.

And last, thank you to anyone who reads this book. I am endlessly grateful you decided to hang out with my characters. I hope this story made your day a little more magical.

ABOUT EMBLA BOOKS

Embla Books is a digital-first publisher of standout commercial adult fiction. Passionate about storytelling, the team at Embla publish books that will make you 'laugh, love, look over your shoulder and lose sleep'. Launched by Bonnier Books UK in 2021, the imprint is named after the first woman from the creation myth in Norse mythology, who was carved by the gods from a tree trunk found on the seashore – an image of the kind of creative work and crafting that writers do, and a symbol of how stories shape our lives.

Find out about some of our other books and stay in touch:

Twitter, Facebook, Instagram: @emblabooks
Newsletter: https://bit.ly/emblanewsletter